THE SURF HOUSE

LUCY CLARKE was inspired to write *The Surf House* after falling in love with surfing in her thirties and visiting a wild, wave-pounded spot on the Moroccan coast. She is the million-copy-bestselling author of eight other destination thrillers, which include *Sunday Times* bestseller *The Hike*, the Richard and Judy Book Club pick, *One of the Girls*, and *The Castaways*, which was released as a major international TV series for Paramount+.

When Lucy isn't away on research trips (her favourite part of the job!), she can be found catching waves and writing from a beach hut on the south coast of England. She lives with her husband and their two children.

www.lucy-clarke.com
@lucyclarke_author
lucyclarkeauthor

Also by Lucy Clarke

The Sea Sisters
A Single Breath
No Escape (previously published as *The Blue*)
Last Seen
You Let Me In
The Castaways
One of the Girls
The Hike

THE
SURF HOUSE

Lucy Clarke

HarperCollins*Publishers*

HarperCollins*Publishers* Ltd
1 London Bridge Street,
London SE1 9GF
www.harpercollins.co.uk

HarperCollins*Publishers*
Macken House,
39/40 Mayor Street Upper,
Dublin 1
D01 C9W8
Ireland

First published by HarperCollins*Publishers* 2025
1

A catalogue record for this book is available from the British Library

ISBN: 978-0-00-863938-9 (HB)
ISBN: 978-0-00-863939-6 (TPB)

This novel is entirely a work of fiction.
The names, characters and incidents portrayed in it are
the work of the author's imagination. Any resemblance to
actual persons, living or dead, events or localities is
entirely coincidental.

Set in Sabon LT Pro by HarperCollins*Publishers* India

Printed and bound in the UK using 100% Renewable
Electricity at CPI Group (UK) Ltd

MIX
Paper | Supporting
responsible forestry
FSC™ C007454

This book contains FSC™ certified paper and other controlled
sources to ensure responsible forest management.

For more information visit: www.harpercollins.co.uk/green

For the next generation of surfers in the family . . .
Cash, Theo, Maggie, Sienna, Lucia,
Benji, Noah, Tommy and Darcy.

Prologue

In the sweltering, diesel-filmed heat, we drove down the clanking ramp of the car-ferry, tyres hitting Moroccan concrete. The smell of fish and something spiced drifted in through our open windows.

We were a convoy of just two vehicles, boards strapped to our roofs. A strange family of sorts. We had no plans to pause in the hot blast of the city, so, pedal to the floor, we headed for the coast.

We'd dreamed of the waves we'd find in Morocco – built from stories and photos and tales of other surfers – but we'll all remember the first glimpse of swell rising from the horizon, ready to hit the African continent. They were storming walls of water that shouldered into the bay, feeling for reef then cracking open in perfect, peeling lines.

Overflowing with adrenalin, we were too impatient to watch and learn where the rips pulled and how the peaking tide steepened the faces. We just needed to be in that wild howl of blue.

The first waves we paddled for let us ride them. We sprang to our feet, sun in our eyes, the roar of blood in our ears, hollering and whooping each other's rides. As the tide dropped, the waves began to hollow, slamming us gracelessly into the pit. We paddled to shore that day, exhausted but laughing, salt burning our sinuses, justice served.

In those first weeks, we surfed endlessly. Morocco was blue skies, white heat, and the cold bite of the Atlantic swells. It was driving empty dirt tracks, hunting for fresh waves, plumes of dust clouding behind us. It was torn flatbreads eaten with our hands, the slide door of the van open to the ocean. It was wood-smoke and hashish stinging our eyes as we sat cross-legged around a fire.

We were happy. It was such a pure, easy happiness – just friends, waves, and sunshine. It's hard to accept it's over.

Harder still to believe what we did.

Now, we must live with the memories. The crack of gunshot in a moonlit desert. The iron-scent of blood pooling on the sand. A body rolled within a beach towel, stiffening in the deep Moroccan night.

The waves roll on, but the dream is finished.

We killed it.

1

Bea locks the bathroom door and leans her back against it. The heat feels solid, immoveable. Sweat prickles across her brow beneath the thick layer of make-up.

She focuses on her breathing, trying to deepen the shallow draw of breath – but she can take only small sips of air because of the boning of the floor-length gown she's been dressed in. God, she longs for her loose T-shirt and denim shorts, which are hanging on a wardrobe rail. She wants to pull on her own clothes and walk out into the thrust and bustle of Marrakesh.

But everyone on set is waiting – the other models, the photographer, his assistants, the art director, the lighting team, the stylist, the make-up artist. She's been in Morocco for twenty-four hours and has only travelled from airport to hotel to set. She doesn't know which way the mountains lie or the direction of the coast. She's not wandered through colourful markets, nor learned how to greet people in their own language. She is here – but not here.

In her damp palm, her phone continues beeping with notifications. She sinks down onto the closed toilet seat and unlocks the screen.

Messages from her agent flood through. There's a schedule

3

for next week's castings and fittings when she returns to London. She pictures herself zigzagging through the city, standing in lines of jittery girls waiting to be judged, or shivering in cool fitting rooms, a tape measure snaked around her hipbones. Dates and times and locations swim before her eyes. It feels like she's riding a carousel, spinning faster and faster, shrill music blasting so loudly that no one can hear she's begging to climb off.

A WhatsApp message flashes up from her mum. Bea feels the briefest lifting of her heart – a butterfly wing of hope. She's heard almost nothing in the weeks since her mum moved to Spain.

Hello from Málaga! Babe, d'you mind pinging me a grand? Just to tide me over. Things are a bit tight while we're getting set up out here. You're a peach!

Bea stares and stares at the message, tears pricking the inner corners of her eyes. She presses her teeth together, her thumb hovering over the phone as she thinks of and discards a dozen replies.

With a sigh, she deletes her mum's message and turns off her phone.

She stands. A head rush sends black dots whirling in front of her eyes, the floor wavering beneath her feet. She reaches out, a hand pressed to the stall door. She's not eaten today, and it takes several seconds for the dizzying sensation to pass.

Beyond the bathroom, she hears fast, clipped footsteps approaching. They halt outside, and there's a sharp drill of knuckles against wood, the jangle of bracelets. 'Bea? Everyone is waiting.'

She reminds herself how she needs to be: bright and pleasing and compliant.

She drags in a breath. Straightens. Then unlocks the door.

*

The photographer crouches, lens focused on Bea. 'Go!'

The two Russian models she's working with begin to walk towards the camera. Bea, a second late, starts to move. She crosses the ornate tiled floor in four-inch heels, trying to work a smile into her features. *Click*. Exaggerate the sway of her hips. *Click*. Lift her chin. *Click*. *Click*.

She sees the furrow of the photographer's forehead above his camera. 'Again!'

Bea feels the hot pinch of a blister as she returns to the start point. They are shooting in a riad in Marrakesh, and the heat is engulfing, throbbing between the high walls. Sweat slides down the backs of her knees.

The photographer squints at the monitor, then looks up. His gaze searches out Bea. 'Make it sexier.'

Heat spreads up her neck. The two models glance at her, then look away.

Sexier, she tells herself as they are given the command to walk.

The Russian models saunter. They toss their hair; they smile – all white teeth. Bea tries to do the same. She drags the corners of her mouth upwards and attempts to add a jauntiness to her movements, but she feels awkward, stiff, overly aware of her limbs. She is good at her job usually, able to mould herself into the image a photographer or client or casting agent wants to see. Not today.

The art director's gaze flicks warily to the photographer, who is now shaking his head. The two begin conferring in whispers, turning their backs to the models.

Everyone's been on set since first light, and it is now approaching midday. The heat is relentless, and they are behind schedule.

'Let's take five,' the art director says with a tight smile. 'Sacha, we need a make-up refresh on Bea.'

Sacha unfolds himself from a stool with a sigh. He gestures impatiently to the vacated seat.

Bea comes to him. Sits. Her dress tightens across her ribs, forcing her to perch pin-straight. Sacha doesn't talk as a series of brushes and powders are swept across her face.

She's not vigilant enough and catches her eye in the mirror. The make-up is heavy, deep contouring sharpening her cheekbones, a slash of red lipstick widening her mouth. She can see the protrusion of her collarbones and the sharp points of her shoulders. Her hair has been scraped from her face into a high bun that's pulling at her temples. Her thick brows have been exaggerated and combed so that she is all edges and angles.

She stares, wondering how this face can be hers when she recognises nothing of herself. She looks and looks until her features distort and bleed. 'Who are you?'

Sacha draws back the blusher brush. 'What?'

She blinks, realising she must have spoken aloud. 'Nothing.'

The hair stylist is upon her now, running clammy hands over her bun, tucking in stray stands. Bea tries not to flinch.

Beyond her, she can hear the tinkling, light sound of the water fountain at the centre of the riad. She wonders how cool the water is, how the jets would feel running down her collarbone. She peers beyond Sacha's make-up brushes, needing to glimpse it.

A tiny bird dips into the water, washing itself and sending a spray of droplets from its delicate wings. She stares at its fragile legs, its miniature beak, its perfect, black bead eyes. It looks joyful as it shakes again, then lifts off, leaving the heat and stillness of this place behind.

I need to leave, she thinks. It is a whisper of thought.

The photographer, his assistant, and the art director are now crowded around the monitor, studying Bea's enlarged image.

'Do something with the eyebrows,' the photographer tosses at the make-up artist. 'Tame them.'

The art director is pointing at the screen. 'I'm more concerned about this.'

She is indicating the waist of Bea's dress, where the fabric is bunching.

Bea knows what they'll be thinking: that she's put on weight since last week's fitting. But how can she? She's barely eaten. She had a light dinner last night – no carbs – and skipped the hotel breakfast this morning, even though her stomach rumbled at the smell of the fresh, buttery pastries.

Her fingernails dig into her palms. Sacha tells her to close her eyes, and she feels the press of eyeliner being dragged across the roots of her lashes.

The air thickens with the sweet, chemical vapour of hairspray, and Bea feels like she cannot breathe. There is not enough air. Her skin is too hot, the dress too tight. Sweat pools underarm.

She wants to pull away, run. Leave this stool. Leave this riad. Leave this shoot.

She hears her mother's voice: *We do not quit.*

She hears her agent's voice: *There are a hundred girls waiting to take your place.*

She listens for her own voice, hears the faintest whisper: *Leave . . .*

'It's her eyes,' the photographer is saying. 'There's no light in them.'

She tries to draw herself away from her body, separating herself. It is a trick she's learned over the years to make this job easier. Because then it is no longer her – Bea – whose eyes hold no light, whose brows look too masculine, whose waist is too wide, whose body isn't sexy enough. The hands all over her won't feel like an invasion, as she will be somewhere else.

But today, she cannot quite manage it. The voices and hands and gazes and heat and hunger are overwhelming.

'I need to—' She pushes off the stool.

She moves unsteadily on her heels, desperate to find somewhere cool, quiet. But there is nowhere to go – the riad crawls with people. She passes the Russian models, who smile tightly. She aims for the marble fountain, which is cloaked by colourful climbing plants.

Bea plunges her hands into the cool water. Sighs with the relief.

Somewhere behind her, she can hear the photographer calling time on the break. She doesn't move, just stays as she is, breathing slowly, her fingers swirling in the water.

She hears someone close at her shoulder saying, 'We're restarting.'

Perhaps she answers 'Okay', because the person leaves. She removes her hands from the fountain and begins unbuckling her left shoe, then the right. Freed, she stretches and wriggles her bare toes. Then she hitches her dress and steps into the fountain.

Cold water kisses her swollen, blistered feet. She can feel the faint slick of algae beneath her toes and scrunches them. She knows the bronzer that was lavishly applied to her too-pale skin this morning will be starting to run.

It feels so good, this cool, dark water around her legs, being surrounded by living, breathing plants. She needs more of it. She stretches forward, putting her face into one of the arcing jets. It pitters against her forehead, runs down the sides of her nose, into her mouth. She tips back her head and it pours into her hairline, runs down her scalp, her neck, her shoulder blades.

Then she lowers herself into the water. The fabric of her dress darkens and billows.

Distantly, she is aware of someone gasping.

Another voice shrieks, 'The dress!'

But the words wash over her, because Bea has finally succeeded in dislocating herself. Her body is lying there in the cool, still water, her skin grateful to be drenched. But she – she is floating somewhere above, in that wide, blue sky with the tiny bird and, for a moment, she smiles, light finally in her eyes.

2

'Do you know how many girls would kill to model for that client?' Madeline asks.

The phone is hot against Bea's cheek as she sits on the floor of her hotel room. She's scrubbed the make-up from her skin and washed the product from her hair. Now it hangs wet at her back, soaking into her cotton T-shirt.

'If you're having a difficult time – then you talk to me. We work it out. I explain to the client.' A pause. 'But you do not climb into a water fountain in a £9,000 couture dress.' Madeline lets the silence bleed.

Bea's never done anything like this. She turns up on time. She is polite to clients. She doesn't complain if there is nowhere private to change or if pins have been left in an outfit. She accepts the bookings she's told to. She walks the runways, smiles and juts her hips for the cameras.

Madeline continues, 'Your portfolio is building. You've been getting booked for great jobs. Your star could really start to rise' – a pause – 'but not if you ever, *ever*, pull a stunt like today again. I need to know you're taking this seriously. That you want this.' A longer pause. 'Do you? Do you really want to be a model?'

Bea pushes herself to her feet. She crosses the room, passing the hotel mirror over which she's draped a thin scarf to block her reflection.

She anchors herself at the window and looks out across the rooftops of Marrakesh. Below, tourists and locals are moving, talking, buying, selling, hustling, living.

Do you really want to be a model?

She didn't choose modelling. It chose her. It was a wet Saturday morning in a shopping centre in Reading. A scout spotted her and introduced herself to Bea and her mother, explaining about the agency and inviting her for a test shoot. Bea had searched for a group of schoolkids laughing, certain that it must be a joke. Models were meant to be beautiful – and no one had ever used that word to describe her. She was gangly, all elbows and knees. Her brows were wild and bushy. Her eyes were so spaced apart that the girls in her class called her *Space-Bea*.

After the scout had left, Bea's mother had taken her for lunch at Nando's and been so animated, her face blooming with excitement at the prospects unfolding before her daughter – world travel, designer clothes, money – that Bea mistook it for her own excitement.

Did she ever enjoy it? There were moments of camaraderie backstage where she'd laugh with the other models. There was her mother sitting in the front row of her first show, clapping. There was a buzz of being cast by a big designer. But mostly, she finds it lonely and exhausting. The daily battle to stay thin enough. The disillusionment of being told what is right and what is wrong with her appearance – and having no influence to affect those things. The guilt of earning more than nurses and teachers when she is merely a walking clothes hanger.

Yet this is a career other girls long for. There are TV shows dedicated to people realising their dream of becoming a top model. Bea is meant to be shimmering with happiness and confidence. So what is wrong with her? She is only twenty-three. This life should feel fresh and exciting and full of a whirl of emotions and experiences. Yet she feels . . .

She stares through the window, wondering what it is she feels. She tries to push it open, let the noise of the city flood into the room, but there's a safety lock. She flattens one hand against the cool glass. It is like she is swimming underwater. The rest of the world is right there, wavering out of reach.

'Bea?'

She blinks, attention returning to the phone.

Madeline waits for an answer.

All Bea knows is that if you stay underwater, eventually, you drown.

She presses the phone close to her mouth. 'I don't want this.'

Bea yanks the scarf from the mirror, loops it around her neck, then grabs her rucksack – and leaves.

She hurries through the hotel lobby, causing a woman in a jade headscarf to glance up from her paper. She skirts two tourists returning from the medina, laden with shopping bags, and heads for the reception desk.

'I'm checking out early,' she explains, handing in her key. She can't stay here with the risk of crossing paths with the team from the shoot. She'll find somewhere else for tonight and fly back to London tomorrow as planned.

Her passport is returned, and Bea slips it into her rucksack. And then she is walking outside, into the bright slap of the day as the noise of the medina floods in. A cacophony of music, voices, the shuffle and step of hundreds of feet, the cries of hawkers, calling, 'Lady, lady . . .'

Bea drifts through the throngs of people into the main square, eyes widening as she absorbs the chaos and colour pulsating around her. Tinkling music draws her attention towards a woven basket, from which a snake emerges, tongue flickering. A teenage boy appears at her side, hawking a string of embroidered bags. Two live chickens squawk as they're carried by their feet by a young girl in tan sandals.

Bea grips the straps of her rucksack, regretting its weight. Ahead, a stooped man in a djellaba pushes a juice cart decorated with Moroccan flags. She watches thirstily as the machine juggles golden oranges into a press. She's not drunk or eaten all day and feels hollowed out.

She fishes in her pocket for some dirhams and hands them to the man.

In return, he passes her a tall glass of fresh juice. '*Bisaha ou raha*,' he says with a beaming smile.

She puts the glass to her lips. Nectar. Her eyes close as she finishes the drink, wiping the juice from her mouth with the back of her hand. She thanks the seller, feeling the juice working through her like liquid sunshine.

Two young men are standing nearby, leaning against a pillar, talking. The taller one, who wears a red football shirt, pushes his sunglasses onto his head to look at her. He grins, revealing crooked front teeth. She nods, moving on, passing a row of traders who have their wares laid out on the ground, selling silver trinkets, woven hats, and carved wooden pots.

Bea lets the tide of people carry her. The air becomes richly scented as she enters the spice souk. Mounds of saffron and turmeric and cinnamon wait to be scooped into paper bags, the hot, still air punctuated with their aroma.

The medina feels impossible to navigate, a warren of narrow

alleyways, shaded tunnels, and wooden doorways leading her deeper and deeper. She weaves onwards, thoughts swirling in the heat, raking back through the day. She replays the gasps as she climbed into the fountain, every pair of eyes on her.

She imagines the icy response when her mother hears she's quit. *What now, hotshot?* she'll ask.

Bea doesn't know what comes next. There's no home to return to now that her mum has left. The few things she owns are in storage. She books cheap hotel rooms when she's in London. She doesn't own a flat. There are no family members or friends to crash with. She thinks of the remaining £2,000 in her bank account and wonders how long it'll last.

The heat intensifies, overwhelming her. Sweat gathers at her lower back, trapped between her skin and rucksack. She glances left and right. Turning, she has no idea where she is or how to exit the medina. She needs space. Cool air. Somewhere she can sit in the shade and take her bag from her shoulders. It feels like she's wandered deep into a maze, the alleyways narrowing and darkening.

She wipes at her hairline as she looks about her. The tourists have disappeared, the stalls ended. She's not been concentrating, her thoughts circling hotly, and now she realises she is completely lost.

She turns on the spot. She is alone in this crumbling, concrete space, which smells of diesel and the faint ammonia tang of urine. There is no one to ask for help.

Bea pulls at the scarf at her neck, hoping for air to reach her. She walks on, uncertain about the direction she's chosen. The alleyway has narrowed, and she feels enclosed on all sides.

A spider sense crawls slowly up her spine: she is not alone.

She keeps walking, but she can hear footsteps behind her.

She listens. Two sets. The deep walk of men.

The backs of her arms stud with goosebumps.

She catches the smell of cigarette smoke, hears something wet hitting the ground. Spit?

Then a male voice calls to her, 'Hey lady. You lost?'

'No,' she says, without stopping, without turning. She speeds up, hands gripping the straps of her pack.

The footsteps keep pace.

Her heart begins to pound, rushing high in her chest. She passes an old generator lying on its side, abandoned. The next two doorways are shuttered, and ahead there is a wall. She knows instinctively that this isn't a part of the medina she is meant to be in.

'Lady, we help you.'

She must turn. There is no choice. She has come to a dead end.

She swallows. Steels herself. She turns slowly, knuckles white.

Two dark-haired men are blocking her path. The first is shorter than her, with thin black hair cut jaggedly around his forehead. He has quick, dark eyes and a restless energy as he moves from foot to foot.

His companion is taller, face unshaven, wearing a red football shirt that is torn at the sleeve. A cigarette hangs from the corner of his mouth. He is wearing sunglasses on his head – and smiles, revealing crooked front teeth.

A cold fear creeps across her shoulder blades: she recognises these men from the square.

She's been followed.

The man in the football shirt watches her hungrily. His eyes scan her body. She feels a primal bolt of fear, age-old: she is a woman, alone. *Take my things,* she thinks, *but please, don't touch me.*

15

'Where are you going, pretty lady?' he asks, taking a step forward. If he reached out now, he could touch her.

'To meet my husband,' she says – but even to her, her voice sounds young and insincere.

His eyes go to her left hand. No ring. He smirks.

'We take you to him,' the smaller man says, jiggling on the spot. 'Maybe he give us reward for returning you?' He laughs to himself, and the sound is unnerving.

She knows immediately that this is not going to be a simple theft. Speed is the tool of the thief. Blood whooshes in her ears as a cold, deep fear seeps into her bones.

There is nowhere behind her to turn or run – and two men blocking her path ahead.

'Your bag – it look heavy,' the smaller man says. 'We help you with it.'

Her mind scrabbles frantically, working out what to do. She decides to play along. 'Thank you.' She removes the bag from her shoulders and hands it to the smaller man with the jagged haircut.

He looks pleased with himself as he sets it squarely on his shoulders. He tries to catch his friend's eye, as if saying, *I've got it. Let's go.*

But the man in the football shirt is still looking at her, his gaze trailing down her face, moving slowly over her body. She is grateful for the thin scarf covering her neck and chest.

He removes the cigarette from his mouth and flicks it to the ground. Then he reaches forward and pinches the end of her scarf. Eyes on her, he slowly unravels it from her neck. His breath reeks of smoke, and there's an unwashed earthy smell to his skin. Once the scarf is uncoiled, he lets it fall to the ground between them.

With her neck exposed, Bea instinctively moves her fingers

to cover it. They touch the gold chain her mother bought for her when she got her first modelling job, the letters of Bea's name spelled in gold italics. She remembers the box it came in, like opening an oyster shell revealing a pearl. Her mother had written, *To my daughter, the model.*

As the man's gaze lowers to her necklace, she instantly regrets touching it, drawing attention there.

'Very nice,' the man says with a smirk. Then his eyes harden. 'Take it off.'

She doesn't move. Doesn't tell him no.

He laughs. 'I do it.'

The threat is not an empty one – she can see that in his eyes.

The man with the jagged haircut glances over his shoulder, hissing something in Arabic. Although she cannot understand his words, she senses what's happening isn't in their script.

The man in the red football shirt ignores him, eyes fixed on Bea. 'Now.'

Her fingers fumble with the clasp, but her hands are clammy, fingertips damp.

He watches her struggling, enjoying himself.

The clasp opens, and she removes the necklace, feels the light touch of it leave her skin like a physical loss. She holds it out.

The man signals to his jittery friend – who scuttles forward and takes the necklace from Bea's hand. He backs away again, his shoulders rounded beneath Bea's pack.

The man in the football shirt raises a nicotine-stained finger and brings it towards Bea's neck. 'What else will I find?'

He touches the clavicle of her throat, and the sensation feels like a gun is pressed there. All she can hear is her own heartbeat, frantic, thundering blood around her body, priming her to fight or take flight.

17

His finger trails across her collarbone. He stares at her through narrowed eyes – and she sees nothing but hatred. Her stomach turns to ice.

She pulls herself physically from her body. It is no longer her. She is above the scene. Separated. Watching as his finger slides from her collarbone down over her right breast, squeezes at her nipple. He becomes rougher as both hands grab her by the hips, pushing her hard against the wall, the back of her skull smacking against it.

There is a shout. Someone is hollering, rushing into view.

Both men jerk around.

A dark-haired Western woman is yelling in commanding French, her teeth bared. She is brandishing a knife, pointing it threateningly at the men.

The man with the jagged haircut turns on his heel. Runs. The other lowers his hands from Bea's hips and faces the woman.

Bea sees now how small she is. She can be little more than five foot. She wears dark harem pants and a tan cross-body bag and is a few years older than Bea. Despite her stature, her arms are muscular, eyes narrowed dangerously.

She wonders if the man, too, notices this fierceness as he raises his palms, offering submission. He takes a step away from Bea.

The woman watches hawk-like as he moves past her, retreating. He smiles his slow, crooked smile, as if saying, *Congratulations, you have won.*

She continues to point the knife at him, holding it steady, eyes never leaving his.

He shrugs and then, in a burst of movement, his left hand shoots out. He knocks the woman's wrist and the knife flies from her grip, clanging onto concrete.

The man wraps his hand around the woman's throat, and

18

with a single step, he has her pinned against the wall. He says something close to her ear in French.

The woman's eyes bulge, but she fights – kicking out, clawing, but his grip is iron.

Bea stands there, frozen.

Both his hands are on her throat now. He is choking her!

She hears a raw, strangled sound escaping the woman's lips as she struggles for air. It reaches deep into Bea, seizing her by the shoulders, shaking her into action.

The knife! It's lying discarded on the ground. It has a wooden handle, a sharp silver blade.

The woman's face is turning bright red. Veins swell at her temples.

He is going to kill her.

No, Bea thinks. *This cannot happen.*

Bea snatches up the knife, then lunges towards the attacker. There is no thought – just motion.

She plunges the knife into the side of his neck. Feels the hard gristle of flesh and ligaments and tendons.

The man screams, a high, shocked shriek. He whirls, swatting at his neck.

His fingers meet the handle. His expression is one of horror. He looks from the knife to Bea, disbelief stretching his features.

Then he wrenches the knife out of his neck.

It clatters to the ground, the blade glistening with fresh blood.

Bea sees the man staggering backwards until he meets the alleyway wall. An awful jet of jewel-red blood pumps from the wound, arcing away from his body.

His fingers press against it, and in moments, his hand turns slick with blood.

His eyes are wide with shock. He opens his mouth as if he's

19

going to say something, but an awful gurgle comes out. He lurches, the wall catching him. Then she watches as his legs seem to give way, his body sliding down the wall, blood darkening his football shirt.

Bea stands there, frozen.

Behind her, she hears the woman's voice. 'Come on!'

It takes a moment for Bea to register that the woman is talking to her.

She stares, mute.

The dark-haired woman scrabbles for Bea's discarded scarf. She bundles the bloody knife within it and shoves it beneath her arm.

With her free hand, she grabs Bea's fingers and, together, they run.

3

Their breath comes fast and shallow, feet pounding concrete as they race through winding alleyways.

Ahead, they spot a growing crowd and slow their pace, weaving into the throng of tourists.

Bea's heart punches at her ribcage. She glances at the woman at her side, who walks fast but without appearing to rush. Red finger marks bloom around her throat.

'I . . . I stabbed him,' Bea whispers.

The woman keeps her eyes ahead.

Bea is trembling, her whole body vibrating with the shock. She put a knife in a man's neck. 'Did I . . . kill him?'

The woman's gaze flicks to her. Her eyes are pale blue, washed out but glittering, like sea glass when wet. 'He would have killed us.'

Bea glances over her shoulder. 'What now?' Her voice is thin, breathless.

'We get out of here.'

'The police. They need to know.'

'We had a weapon. There'll be an investigation. You could end up . . .' She doesn't need to finish the sentence. Bea can fill in the blanks: the Moroccan legal system, desperate phone calls to the embassy, the stale air of a prison cell. Her brain is tipping . . .

'Where are you staying?' the woman asks.

Bea looks at her blankly.

'Have you got somewhere to go?' she tries again.

'I . . . I checked out of my hotel. I was going to find somewhere for tonight . . . my flight home is tomorrow.' With a lurch, she remembers. 'My bag! The other man – he took it. My passport was in there—' She pats down her pockets and finds only her phone and the rectangular press of her debit card.

'Don't report it missing yet. You don't want it connected to that alleyway.'

Bea staggers to a halt. A man weaves around them, a rolled carpet balanced on one shoulder.

'But what do I do? Where do I go?'

The woman considers her. Her eyes are inquisitive, searching, as if she's trying to decide something.

After a long moment, the woman's gaze softens. 'I have a place.'

A dark-green camper van is parked in the shade. Bea climbs into the cab, the warm air smelling of neoprene and coconut.

The woman – who tells Bea that her name is Marnie – fires up the engine.

The van's rumbles and protests are drowned out by music that blasts from an old speaker, a deep reggae beat that Marnie doesn't adjust. She socks the gear stick into position and swings out of the parking space, sending a dreamcatcher swaying.

She looks small behind the wheel, but she commands the wide vehicle with ease, weaving into the stream of traffic, hand on the horn. The road is filled with cars, trucks, motorbikes, donkeys, and bicycles, all jostling for position.

Bea glances into the back of the van, which houses a small

sink, camping hob, wooden drawers, spice rack. Houseplants swing from string baskets, and two surfboards are strapped to the van's ceiling.

Bea places her hands beneath her thighs to stop them shaking. Tries to consciously slow her breathing.

Everything feels surreal, like she is in a waking nightmare. She pinches at the tender flesh at the inside of her thighs.

Marnie doesn't speak as they leave the chaos of the city behind. The roads widen, curling through the dry, arid landscape; red mountains tower in the distance. They pass roadside stalls selling cheap electronics and earthenware tagines.

The music rages, and Bea finds she doesn't mind. She doesn't need to think or be. There's a weightlessness of not knowing where she is going, of having no possessions. No passport. No clothes. No necklace. She feels adrift, like she is no longer anchored to anything.

Marnie snaps off the radio. 'I run a guesthouse on the coast.' Her accent is hard to define – British at its roots, but with an international flavour that speaks of a life lived elsewhere.

Bea glances at her. There's a gold-leaf stud in her nose and a flock of gold and leather bracelets on her tanned, slender wrists. Her dark hair is bobbed to her chin, a blunt fringe cut stylishly high on her forehead.

'It's small, just a few rooms overlooking the bay. Mostly surfers come for the waves. The guest rooms are full, but there's a spare bed in the room next to ours. You can have it for a few nights.'

Marnie doesn't say who *ours* refers to – and Bea doesn't ask. Instead, she nods and says, 'Thank you.'

They drive in silence for a time, listening to the thrum of tyres against tarmac, the vibration of something loose rattling in the back of the van.

She watches Marnie's hands on the wheel, small, tanned, a black tattoo of a wave on the base of her forefinger. They are trembling.

Bea's heart rate fails to settle, her body awash with adrenalin. Images dance in her mind. The two men blocking her path. The cold fear as the man in the red football shirt trailed a fingertip down her neck. The determined way Marnie barrelled into that alleyway, yelling, pulling a knife. Without her . . .

Bea turns in her seat. 'Thank you. You saved me.' The words could sound overplayed – but they both know they are not.

Marnie glances away from the road to look at her. 'You did the same for me.'

They hold one another's eye, an intensity in their shared gaze.

Marnie checks the road, then looks back at Bea. 'We did what we did to survive.'

Bea knows that is the truth. The alternative reality lurks there, like a dark hole she could have slipped down, never surfaced from.

Marnie's jaw sets. 'I don't regret what we did.'

Bea notices the *we* Marnie chooses and is grateful for it.

'Neither do I,' Bea says, matching her tone.

Their eyes are locked. Something forges in the furnace of that look. It burns the darkness of what happened to them to ashes.

Marnie nods once, then pulls her focus back to the road. They roar on.

4

Time seems to stretch and contract. They must have been driving for an hour, maybe two. Bea looks out of the open window, trying to feel the raw beauty of her surroundings – the barren red hillsides, the blue shimmer of the sea in the distance – but she can't access it. Her heart is still racing, and fragments of the attack replay without permission.

'What were you doing in Marrakesh?' Marnie asks.

'Working.' She doesn't offer any more. Doesn't use the word modelling. 'You?'

'Visiting an art supplier. Got lost. I was never meant to be on that street . . .' Her sentence trails off.

They both know how differently the day could have ended.

'A couple of miles ahead, there's a track that leads to the sea. It's quiet. Always empty. We'll get rid of the knife and scarf in the water. Okay?'

Bea glances towards Marnie's footwell, where the bloodied items are stuffed beneath her seat. 'Okay,' she agrees.

She wants them gone. Hates the idea of that man – his blood, his DNA – still here, travelling with them. Once they discard the knife and scarf, there'll be nothing attaching them to what happened.

Bea asks warily, 'How come you carry a knife?'

'I was robbed years ago when I was travelling in Europe. Kept a knife in my bag ever since. I'm five foot three and weigh fifty kilos. A knife gives me options.'

The warm breeze from the open window musses Marnie's dark hair, and she tucks a strand behind her ear, revealing an arc of delicate gold studs.

'I want you to know,' Marnie continues, 'that what happened back there – that could've happened in any city in the world. Those men – they may not even be locals. Most people I've met here are kind.'

'How long have you lived in Morocco?'

'Three years. Spent the first few months sleeping in this van with Ped, my boyfriend. He's an Aussie. We met on the road. He's away at the moment, but he'll be back soon. We found Mallah together.'

'Mallah?'

'It's a tiny fishing village. Nothing much there except cliffs and ocean – and the most incredible wave. We fell in love with it. Decided to build a place. Opened the doors just over a year ago. You'll—' Marnie stops. She leans forward in her seat, back stiffening.

Bea follows the direction of her gaze.

Up ahead, a police vehicle is parked on the brow of a hill, lights flashing.

Her skin cools. 'Is this a roadblock?'

'Just a checkpoint. It's normal. They pull over tourist vehicles. Like to tell the driver they're speeding or haven't got the right paperwork. Make a bit of money on the side.'

'What about the knife?'

'I know the local cop. Momo. He'll wave us through. His

mother bakes the bread for The Surf House. It's not the cheapest bread, but you tickle the right people.'

On the brow of the hill, a police officer in dark uniform indicates with firm arm gestures. To Bea, it doesn't look like they are being waved through – rather instructed to pull in. She glances at Marnie.

Her mouth has tightened. 'New guy.'

'What now?' Bea's fingers grip the edges of her seat.

'We're calm. We smile.'

The indicator ticks as they pull onto the roadside and kill the engine.

Marnie leans out of the van window and gives a friendly wave. '*Bonjour, ca va?*'

A straight-backed officer with an oiled moustache approaches the van. He speaks to Marnie in French, which Bea is unable to follow, other than catching that his name is Officer Karim. His dark, hooded eyes move between the two of them.

'*Bien sûr,*' Marnie says with a smile as she takes out her driver's licence. In a seamless movement, her second hand reaches into a pocket, removes some dirhams, and slips them on top of her licence, handing both to Officer Karim.

He picks up the loose notes between the tip of his thumb and forefinger, as if holding a rat by the tail. '*Il me semble que votre argent s'est mélangé à vos papiers.*'

'*Mon erreur,*' Marnie says.

Bea glances at a second cop, who stands at a distance, watching. This must be Momo. He is younger, well-built in his smart navy uniform and polished black shoes. A silver scar runs down the left side of his forehead, disappearing into his hairline.

Officer Karim instructs, '*S'il vous plaît, sortez du véhicule.*'

Bea's heart beats high in her chest as she watches Marnie

open the van door and step out onto the dusty roadside. Beneath her vacated seat lies the bloodied knife.

'*Et vous aussi*,' Officer Karim says, indicating for Bea to exit the van, making an impatient clucking noise with his tongue.

She blinks. Moves. Her fingers are damp as she fumbles with the door handle. She climbs out into the dusky heat, dirt crunching under her sandals. She anchors herself beside Marnie, who shoots her a quick, reassuring smile.

Officer Karim calls to Momo in Arabic, signalling to the van with a cutting hand gesture.

As Momo passes them, Marnie leans towards him and whispers something in French, lips barely moving. The exchange is a matter of seconds – and then Momo rejoins Officer Karim.

The two men begin their search of the van. Bea's heart is hammering. She cannot watch. She turns away.

Marnie draws a semi-circle in the dust with her sandals. Then she repeats the movement below it, and below that, until a rainbow emerges.

Beads of sweat form at Bea's temples.

Behind them, she hears raised voices, a displeased tone. She risks a glance and sees Officer Karim pressing the rear passenger side tyre.

A few moments later, he approaches Marnie. '*Dangereux. Très dangereux*,' he tells her, pointing to the tyre.

He continues to talk, and Marnie responds calmly, smiling just the right amount to appear interested in his findings. She then accompanies him to the police car, signing some paperwork.

Glancing over her shoulder, Bea sees that Momo has also left the van. Did he take the knife? Hide it? Is that what Marnie whispered to him?

When the paperwork is finished, Marnie says, 'We can get back in.'

Is it over?

They climb into the van in silence and clip their belts. Marnie indicates, checks her mirrors, and pulls out carefully.

Neither says a word until they've put distance between themselves and the police.

'The knife?' Bea asks.

'Gone.'

'Momo took it?'

Marnie nods.

A rush of relief floods Bea's body, but when she glances at Marnie, her jaw is tight. 'What's wrong?'

Marnie glances in the wing mirror, looking back towards the checkpoint. There's a furrow between her brows. 'Favours like that don't come cheap.'

5

Marnie swings the van onto a rutted dirt track. 'Wind up your window,' she calls, as clouds of dust are kicked up by the tyres.

Bea grips hard to the seat as they fly along, clearing potholes. The cooking gear in the back rattles and clangs. Low roadside shrubs are shrouded in a ghostly veil of dust.

As the track snakes downwards, Bea stares at the glimmer of blue where the Atlantic waits. A sweeping arc of golden sand is fringed by a rocky cliff line. High above sits a tiny village, little more than a cluster of buildings that cling like barnacles to the edge of the land.

'Welcome to Mallah,' Marnie says. 'Only fishermen lived out here for decades – and then surfers discovered the wave and started parking up in their vans. Gradually, a small community has built up with a few hostels and places to stay.'

They pass low, flat-roofed buildings painted in sun-faded colours. The homes are simply built, some with corrugated-iron roofs, wild bougainvillea climbing over crumbling walls. They drive past a narrow store shaded by tarpaulin, where a long-haired Westerner lifts a handful of oranges from a blue crate.

Marnie pulls in further down the track. A few camper vans

are parked up, wetsuits drying over wing mirrors, van doors open to the last of the light.

Bea climbs out and is met with the fresh hit of salt, mixed with the briny scent of fish and a touch of hashish on the breeze. The bay below is gilded by the lowering sun and peppered with surfers.

'We're up here,' Marnie says, already striding ahead.

Bea follows a track that passes a sun-yellow hostel, with a wave graffitied on the side. Its name, *Offshore*, is painted on a surfboard that has slipped from its plaque and hangs at a sorry angle.

As they draw alongside a stylish white stucco building, Marnie says, 'This is us.'

Bathed in light, The Surf House stands proud on the cliff edge. Wide white pillars lead to a solid wooden door framed by two huge cactus plants in terracotta planters.

Bea steps into a high-ceilinged space filled with evening light. Her heart rate is still elevated, thoughts wound tight around narrow alleyways and police checkpoints, yet something about the calmness of the space seems to enter her blood stream. White alcove shelves house smooth sculptures and ornate Moroccan teapots.

Underfoot, stone-washed tiles stretch across the wide expanse of the main room, adding to the neutral, pared-back feel. Low pallet seating is gathered in the far corner, facing a projector screen. A stack of surf photograph books sits atop a wooden coffee table.

A bank of folding glass doors opens to the view, making it feel as if the guesthouse is made of sea and sky. Drawn through them, Bea steps out onto a terrace studded with large planters containing olive trees, cactuses, and palms. A slim pool – its surface a mirror of the blushing sky – stretches above the sea. Floor lanterns are grouped at the centre of a cushioned seating area. A white cube-shaped outbuilding is perched on the cliff edge, its exterior softened by a spray of orange blossom. A discreet wooden sign reads *Surf Studio*.

A group of travellers are sitting on a wall, watching the waves break. They turn and greet Marnie in a chorus of foreign accents.

'How was the surf?' Marnie asks.

'Pumping,' a guy says, adjusting his cap over tight curls. 'There was a bit of wind on it earlier, but it's glassed off now.'

'You get in, Aimee?' Marnie asks a girl in a cropped yellow top, who is stretching out her right shoulder.

'Managed an hour. Great to be back in the water.'

Marnie smiles. 'Everyone, this is Bea. She's going to be staying for a while.'

The group greet her with easy smiles and raised palms.

After the horror of the day, it's a wild adjustment to land here in a space that feels safe and calm and inviting. Bea tries to return their smiles and mirror their easy expressions, but she feels self-conscious, as if what she's done is written on her body.

'Come. I'll show you where you're sleeping,' Marnie says. 'We'll raid lost property en route.'

She follows Marnie to a small office with a simple wooden desk, on which is a slim laptop. Marnie pulls out a cardboard box filled with clothes, toiletries, fins, surf wax, and leashes. 'Help yourself.'

Bea fishes out a bundle of toiletries, a spare T-shirt, an oversized hoodie, a phone charger, and a few other items, then follows Marnie upstairs.

'This is me and Ped,' Marnie says, opening a doorway onto a wide room filled with light.

Bea glimpses a large bed with a bamboo headboard, textured cushions piled against it, and pale linen sheets turned back. There are two low bedside tables, books and lamps on both. A simple wicker chair is angled to face an open window that looks out over the water.

'Your room is next door,' Marnie says, leading the way.

Bea steps into a smaller room, the sunset bursting through the window and splashing one of the walls gold. She notices a connecting door leading back into Marnie and Ped's room and wonders if they use this room as overspill. A yoga mat is laid on the wooden floor, and the only furniture is a narrow daybed covered with a woven throw and neutral cushions. It feels minimal yet inviting.

'It's beautiful,' Bea says. She perches on the edge of the bed and takes off her sandals.

Marnie rolls up the yoga mat and then sits beside Bea. Her eyes glitter with warmth and concern. 'How are you?'

'None of it feels real.'

Marnie squeezes her hand. 'It's the shock. We'll adjust.'

'The knife has my fingerprints on it,' she says, keeping her voice down. 'What if Momo hands it in?'

'He won't. There's no gain. He knows we want that knife – so there'll be a price.'

'A bribe?'

Marnie smiles. 'He'll call it a gift.'

'When will he want this *gift*?'

'We'll let him come to us. We can't afford to look eager.'

Bea nods, trying to get a handle on the dynamics.

'Whatever he asks, we pay him – and then it's done. Over.' Marnie squeezes Bea's fingers as she says, 'Then we put this behind us.'

'I keep remembering it . . .' Bea says, her voice small. 'All that blood . . . the way it arced from his neck . . . and then him slumping to the ground.' She swallows. 'He's dead, isn't he?'

Marnie takes Bea's other hand now, holding both in hers. She wears a gold hammered thumb ring, and her nails are short and clean, strong cuticles. 'If I hadn't come across you, what would that man have done to you?'

Into the silence, Bea swallows. Her palms are sweating within Marnie's, but she doesn't let go. 'Raped me.'

Marnie holds her eye. 'And when I came, when he put his hands around my throat, what would he have done to me?'

She'd seen the whites of Marnie's eyes as the man pinned her against the wall, choking her windpipe. She wears the trace of it as a faint red mark on her neck. 'Strangled you.'

Marnie's pale-blue gaze is locked on Bea's as she says, 'I said it in the van: we did what we had to. And now, it is over. We're here, safe.' She squeezes Bea's fingers hard. 'Our lives move forward.'

Bea stares at her, wanting to believe it's possible.

'Don't look back. Even for a second. Don't let it stain your life, Bea. I'm begging you: please don't give that man the power to do that. You didn't choose to be followed, robbed, attacked. The only choice you made was to survive.'

Bea holds her gaze.

'We wake up tomorrow, and it's a fresh start, okay?'

She feels the warmth of Marnie's hands held tight to hers. 'A fresh start,' Bea repeats.

6

Bea stands at the open window, looking out onto the night. There are no streetlamps in Mallah, but twinkling lights from homes and hostels illuminate the village. The air smells of salt and wood-smoke and something chalkier – mountain dust, perhaps.

Below, on the pool terrace, surfers and travellers sit on low cushions around a firepit, the embers of cigarettes glowing. The drift of their chatter and the regular bursts of laughter are comforting. Bea could join them – Marnie invited her – but she's not ready to be around other people and pretend that everything is okay.

She repeats Marnie's words like a mantra. *We're here, safe. Our lives move forward.*

Wood-smoke curls into the night, and the flames illuminate tanned, relaxed faces. A girl wearing a beanie gets to her feet and re-enacts a wipeout to great amusement. Accents merge and meld, rising and falling like music. Bea finds there's something she likes about the gathering – people dressed in jeans, T-shirts, loose-knit sweaters, the women without make-up or styled hair. They are talking, sharing stories, passing around drinks.

Marnie sits at the middle of the group, cross-legged, a bottle of beer in her hand. The gold ring on her thumb glitters in the firelight as she draws the bottle to her mouth. There's a deep stillness about her, rooted and at ease. She's wrapped a light scarf around her neck, and Bea wonders if the finger marks are still visible at her throat.

Bea catches drifts of conversation – talk of a movie night on the cliff top, a beach clean-up when the swell drops, other spots to surf if the wind swings east.

Eventually, the group disperses, and Bea moves to the narrow bed and lies beneath the cool sheet.

She wishes she could call her mum, tell her, *Something awful has happened. I need you.* But she knows – has spent years and years learning – that her mum won't fill those needs. She'd find fault with Bea for being in the medina when she should have been on set. There's no chance she'd jump on a flight and come to Morocco. She wouldn't help her navigate police reports and embassy forms. She wouldn't do any of that. Bea is on her own.

She rolls onto her side, knees tucked up to her chest. She catches the scent of Marnie on these sheets – the warming tones of coconut butter and vanilla – and breathes a little deeper.

She hears footsteps along the corridor outside her room, and Marnie's bedroom light flicks on. Bea closes her eyes and listens to the reassuring sounds of Marnie moving around her room. She hears the slide of wood as a drawer is opened. She catches the light clink of metal and imagines Marnie removing her jewellery, placing it into a waiting dish. Then there's the light scrape of a hanger moving within a wardrobe. Material drops to the floor.

A few moments later, Marnie's light goes out. Bea hears the lift of sheets, the depression of bedsprings, a deep, low sigh.

A thin wall is all that separates their beds. She imagines Marnie lying there, the ceiling fan stirring the dark, fine hair at her temples. She reaches out and presses her fingertips to the cool wall.

Listening closely, she thinks she hears breathing.

After a few moments, she realises that it is, in fact, the sea. Waves roll distantly onto shore, a rhythmic movement of inhales and exhales.

In the pitch dark, Bea struggles to place the closeness of the waves and imagines them breaking at the foot of the cliff where The Surf House is perched, loosening the sandstone, working their way into the cracks and foundations, the first dusting of sand falling from the cliff.

Her thoughts flash to the knife. To the blood that pumped from the attacker's neck. To his body on the ground. They stay there, circling, curling tighter around that image.

Bea sits bolt upright, heart racing. Places her bare feet on the tiled floor. Breathes.

No. She cannot lie in the dark, alone with her thoughts.

She pulls on the oversized hoodie and her shorts and leaves the room. She moves silently along the corridor, slipping down the stairs, through the lounge, and out into the night.

The stars blaze. A full moon hangs in the sky, the most incredible lantern, washing the landscape pale silver. Bea skirts the pool and finds her way past the Surf Studio and out onto the cliff.

The rocks are jagged and dusty beneath her bare feet, and she knows she should keep more distance from the edge than she does – but there is something temptingly vital about the darkness, the drop, the promise of ribbons of white waves below.

It's late September – autumn in Morocco – and while the days are still hot, the evenings are much cooler. Goosebumps rise on her bare thighs. She pulls up her hood.

LUCY CLARKE

She pauses on the cliff edge and looks out to sea. Waves roll
and roll, washing in towards the beach. She's spent her life inland
or travelling between cities. The coast is somewhere she's visited
on occasional holidays – trips to the promenaded beaches of
Bournemouth, or a charter flight to lie beneath a beach umbrella
in Spain while her mum worked on her tan. This kind of coast,
with its wild movement of water, feels unknown.

She catches sight of something out to sea. Odd. It can't be a
boat. Too small.

She blinks, refocusing on the shadow – but it has slipped
between the waves, disappeared. She watches, arms hugged to
her middle, wondering if she imagined it.

The moon casts a wide silver glow. The lines of swell are
indistinct in the darkness, only given shape when they break in a
flurry of whitewater, which catches the moonlight. As she studies
the ocean, she sees the dark shape again. It seems to travel with
the wave, riding along its face.

Is someone out there . . . surfing? At night?

She stares, entranced, as the figure carves up, then down, the
face of the wave in a thrilling, risky dance. For long seconds, the
night surfer rides across the bay on the back of this black, watery
beast, leaving only a ghostly wake. Finally, the wave folds in on
itself in a mass of white foam, swallowing the surfer.

She holds her breath. Waits. Keeps her focus. After several
seconds, she makes out movement again. The night surfer is
stroking back out through dark ocean.

Transfixed, Bea lowers herself down onto a seat of rock to
keep watching. At her feet, there is a sudden scuffling noise, and
she starts as a dog leaps out, tail between its legs.

'Oh!'

The dog – knee-high with a chestnut coat – keeps its distance,

38

watching her, head lowered. It looks young, brown eyes shining in the dark, tail clamped.

'It's okay,' Bea says softly. She slips her hand into her pocket and finds a biscuit she rescued from the hotel tea tray hours earlier. She snaps off a little, placing it carefully on the ground between her and the dog.

The dog considers it, as if he's waiting for permission.

'It's for you,' she says encouragingly.

The dog takes a step closer and delicately lowers the side of its mouth to the biscuit, then swallows it whole.

Bea offers the back of her hand and lets the dog sniff it. After a few moments, she slowly strokes the dog's head. 'Friends?'

She works her hand across the dog's scrawny back. His coat is dusty, like a powdered brush. There's no collar, and she guesses he's one of the many strays.

'Is this where you sleep?' she says, looking at the nook of rock where he sprung from. In answer, the dog flops down onto his side, setting his back against her legs, muzzle on his paws.

Growing up, Bea was never allowed a dog. She begged her mother for one, imagined letting herself in after school and finding a dog waiting for her, tail wagging. *Won't see me scraping dog shit off the pavement* was her mum's answer.

The dog suddenly lifts his head, sniffs. He barks once.

Bea follows his gaze. Someone is climbing the steep steps that cut into the cliff face. Her body reacts before her mind, sending a shot of adrenalin into her veins. Her back stiffens; she tips forward, ready to launch to her feet.

A man emerges onto the cliff top, bare-chested, a wetsuit peeled to his waist, a surfboard underarm.

The night surfer.

She is frozen, unmoving, willing herself to be invisible.

The dog trots forward, and the night surfer, unaware of Bea, reaches out his free hand to ruffle the dog's head. Moonlight gilds a lean, muscular body.

'See me slammed by that last wave, Salty?' His voice is low, warm, unrushed. An Irish accent?

The dog turns his back.

'Not impressed, eh?'

The dog trots towards Bea and flops down by her feet. She is braced on the rock, her hoodie pulled up.

The man starts slightly. 'Didn't see you there.'

She says nothing. Keeps her eyes pinned to him. She takes in the strong angle of his jawline and the dark, heavy brows. Wet hair spills to his chin and is jewelled with silver water droplets.

His head tilts minutely as he asks, 'Did you arrive with Marnie earlier?' His expression is easy, relaxed.

She feels her breath soften a little. 'That's right.'

'What brings you to Mallah?'

Bea hesitates. She doesn't want to lie, so chooses part of the truth. 'I was in Marrakesh. Got my bag stolen. Marnie helped me out.'

Delivering the information in short, quick pieces means she's able to share the facts without feeling them.

The man's stare is concentrated. 'I'm sorry,' he says, the words weighted with sincerity. He continues to look at her, his expression in danger of opening the thin stitches that are holding her together.

She glances down at her hands. Doesn't know what to say next, so she just shrugs.

'You're out here travelling?' he asks.

She shakes her head. 'Working.'

He waits.

She hates using the word *model,* so avoids it. 'I was on a photo shoot. It's finished.'

'Right.' That's all he says. Maybe he reads something in her expression as he doesn't fire further questions. Just lets it go.

At her feet, the dog sighs, and Bea takes the hint and resumes stroking him.

'Looks like you've found a friend,' the man says, and there's warmth in his voice.

Bea asks, 'Is he yours?'

'Salty? No, a stray. My *favourite* stray,' he says pointedly to the dog.

'Does he sleep here?'

'Yeah, or sometimes in the village if it's wet. He doesn't do too badly. Gets dinner at the hostel most night.' He explains, 'I run Offshore – next door to The Surf House.'

She glances around. The Surf House sits proud and moon-white on the cliff top, and crouched at its shoulder is the sunshine-yellow building that she remembers passing when she arrived.

'How long have you had the hostel?' she asks, turning back to face him.

'Coming up a year. I bought the land with Ped and Marnie. They built The Surf House, and I've built Offshore.' His gaze travels between the two buildings, and Bea thinks she glimpses a fleeting tightness in his features – but then it is gone.

'You were out in the sea. Surfing?'

'Yeah.'

'How can you see the waves?'

He turns, looking towards the ocean. Now she sees his back, lean but muscular, a tattoo that she can't clearly make out nestled between his shoulder blades. 'I listen.'

She sets her gaze on the dark water. At first, all she hears

41

are crashing waves. But as she continues to focus, she begins to make out subtle changes in pitch – the low suck as a wave rises, a hollowing boom as it breaks in a spill of whitewater, a fizzing energy as it surges across the sea bed towards the shore, the inhale as the water is drawn back out.

'Why do you surf at night?'

He keeps his gaze on the water. He doesn't speak for such a long time that she wonders if he's heard. Eventually, he says, 'It's just me out there.'

They fall silent for a moment, continuing to listen to the waves.

Then he asks, 'What about you? Why are you sitting on a cliff top in the dead of night?'

She shrugs. 'Couldn't sleep.'

There's a beat of a pause as he considers her. Then, 'I know the middle of the night hours.'

Bea looks up. Their gazes lock.

His eyes are dark, shaded beneath a heavy brow. He's a few years older than herself, she decides. Water drips from dark hair that spills to his chin. She wonders what keeps him from sleeping and draws him out to the sea.

He drops his gaze suddenly, saying, 'I better head back.'

She feels the low stir of disappointment.

As he goes to step away, he turns, asking, 'What's your name?'

'Bea.'

He considers her, his dark gaze examining her face.

A rush of warmth spreads through her body and rises to her cheeks, and she is grateful for the barrier of her drawn hood.

'Good to meet you, Bea.' He smiles. 'I'm Aiden.'

7

Bea wakes, adrenalin flooding her body. The sheets are damp and tangled around her legs, memories of the alleyway stabbing through her dreams.

She lurches to the window. Opening it wide, she sticks out her head, squinting into dazzling sunshine. The salt-tinged breeze cools the damp skin at her neck. She tries to anchor herself in this moment, gradually allowing herself to notice the glitter of the sea. She can hear the low, haunting song of the morning call to prayer and searches the spray of rooftops for a mosque. Unable to locate one, she listens for a while longer, trying to pick out any words, but they meld together with meditative effect.

When her breathing eventually settles, Bea pulls on yesterday's clothes, splashes water over her face, then heads downstairs, following the warming aroma of coffee.

In the dining area, a wooden sideboard is laid with a simple breakfast buffet: toasted coconut granola, bowls of dates, jewelled pomegranates, creamy yoghurt, sliced avocado, oven-roasted tomatoes, hard-boiled eggs dusted with sesame seeds.

The glass doors are thrown open to the terrace, where a group of tanned twenty-somethings are sitting at an outdoor table with glasses of freshly squeezed orange juice.

Bea hangs back, watching. They look so relaxed and happy. They have food, friendship, a day of sunshine and waves waiting. She wonders what it must feel like to be that at ease.

Yesterday I put a knife in a man's neck, she thinks.

'Morning.'

Bea jumps when Marnie emerges from the kitchen, carrying two pots of coffee, her arms tanned and muscular. She's wearing the same black harem pants as yesterday, with an apron tied at her front, hair wet from the shower or surf. She still wears a scarf at her throat.

She steps outside, and the guests thank her as she sets down the coffee. Not ready to let her go, they ask questions about the morning's conditions, and Marnie talks about the swell period, the wind swinging offshore, the tide starting to push.

Bea listens, the lexicon of the conversation alien and intoxicating to her.

When Marnie finishes chatting to the group, she tucks her empty tray beneath her arm, comes inside and catches Bea's fingers with her free hand. 'Come,' she says warmly, leading her into a galley kitchen.

The narrow space is clean and bright, lined with open shelves. Glass Kilner Jars house almonds, pistachios, couscous, rice, and an assortment of spices.

'We'll eat when the guests are finished.'

Bea likes that. She doesn't want to be treated as a guest.

Marnie bends to open an oven door; a cloud of steam scented with honey and cinnamon fills the kitchen. She pulls out an oven tray of freshly toasted granola, setting it on the hob. The oats are golden and perfect, and Bea feels her stomach rumble. She doesn't remember eating yesterday and feels hollowed out.

Marnie retrieves a chopping board, then reaches for a bowl

of kiwis and plump apricots and sets them in front of Bea. 'Chop these?' she asks, sliding a vegetable knife across the counter.

Bea stares at the knife. Her blood cools. This is just a vegetable knife with a blue plastic handle and small blade. But she can see the other one, lying on the ground, a trail of blood running from its tip. A pressure in her chest builds.

Gently, Marnie places the apricots in Bea's hands as if she's passed her a precious, sweet gift. 'Rinse them first,' she encourages, gaze warm.

Bea blinks, pushing the memory away, and moves to the sink. Cool water pours silver over their furred skin. Then she shakes them dry, picks up the knife and begins to chop. Gradually, the sharp-edged memories recede.

Marnie adds a pinch of salt to a dish of batter, then pours it into a heavy skillet. Hot oil hisses as it meets the batter. 'This is msemen,' she says, loosening the sides with a spatula. 'It's a little like flatbread but made with a mix of flour and semolina.'

After a minute or two of cooking, she turns it, revealing a crisp, browned underside.

When Bea's prepared the fruit, Marnie asks, 'Could you fetch the bread? It's left inside the front door by eight each morning.'

A minute later, Bea returns with a woven basket covered by a tea towel. When she removes the towel, she's greeted by the yeasty sweetness of freshly baked bread. The still-warm rolls are flat and golden, each pricked with three dashes.

'Momo's mother made these?' she asks, thoughts tugging back to the police checkpoint.

Marnie nods. 'She makes the dough, then bring the loaves to the communal oven in the village where they are baked. Each baker marks their bread differently so the loaves can be identified.'

Bea wonders if Marnie will say anything more about yesterday, but she doesn't. She thinks about Marnie's words: *A fresh start.* She takes a breath, then arranges the golden loaves onto a wooden tray and sets it on the sideboard with the rest of the food.

It is an hour before the guests are all fed, dishes washed, and surfaces cleaned. Marnie passes Bea a clean plate and points to the generous leftovers. 'It's all got to go.'

On shoot days, Bea skips breakfast, not wanting to be bloated – but today, she is ravenous. She loads a bowl with oven-warm granola, lavishing it with a hearty dollop of coconut yoghurt and homemade compote, and then sprinkles toasted nuts and a handful of dates on top.

Marnie fills a plate with avocado, eggs, and humus, then unties her apron and leads Bea out of the backdoor of the kitchen. It delivers them onto a private section of the terrace shaded by a lemon tree, where they sit on a cushioned pallet to eat.

Bea takes a mouthful of granola, and her tastebuds explode with pleasure. She's always loved food – both cooking it and eating it. One of the ironies of her profession was that she could rarely enjoy either.

Marnie watches her eat with a smile on her lips. 'Get any sleep last night?'

Bea shrugs. 'A little. I sat out on the cliff for a while.' She pauses for a moment, then says, 'I met the guy from Offshore – Aiden. He was surfing in the dark.'

Marnie shakes her head once. 'So, he's started again.'

'Isn't it dangerous?'

'Danger never weighs in Aiden's choices.' She dips her fork into the hummus and takes a small mouthful.

'He said he bought land here with you and Ped?'

'Yeah. We met Aiden in Portugal – travelled to Morocco together. We weren't originally planning on staying long-term, but then we stumbled across Mallah.' Light plays across Marnie's eyes as she takes in the bay. 'There's nowhere else like this. We couldn't leave. There was a plot of land for sale for next to nothing, so we bought it between us. Split the land. And now our lives are here.'

'I love that,' Bea says, admiring their bravery.

'It's been hard. We've had to make sacrifices – but when I look at this place, the community we have here – I know it's been worth it.'

'This is home now?'

'I didn't know what *home* was until Mallah.' There must be a question in Bea's expression, as Marnie explains, 'My mum's always anchored herself to a man, so we moved a lot. I grew up in France, then moved to Belgium, then on to England when I was ten. Lots of spare rooms, new schools, lost friends.' She shrugs. Then she sets her empty plate on the ground, draws one knee onto the seat, turning to face Bea. 'What about you? Where have you come from, Bea?'

'Reading.' One home. One school. But maybe just as lonely . . . 'It's just me and Mum. Or was. She's moved to Spain with her boyfriend.'

'So, where do you live?'

Bea hesitates. 'I . . . I don't live anywhere. I'm away a lot with work.'

'You're a model?' In response to Bea's surprise, Marnie adds, 'That willowy frame. A bone-structure gifted from the gods. Bit of a giveaway.' She grins.

'I quit. Yesterday.'

Marnie's brow lifts.

'I climbed into a water fountain in the middle of a shoot wearing a designer dress.'

'A girl's got to keep her skin hydrated.'

Bea manages a smile.

Marnie considers her. 'How d'you feel about quitting?'

Bea looks out over the sea. It has been months since she saw the ocean. All those long hours standing in heels. The boredom of fittings and measurements. The dozens of hands adjusting her clothes, her hair, her make-up. She's always indoors – in a studio, on a set, blazed by artificial lights.

And now she is here.

'Free,' is the word she finally chooses.

The smile that lights Marnie's face is wide and easy. 'The room here – it's yours for as long as you need it. I'd love you to stay. It'd be great to have an extra pair of hands around here, while you work out what it is you want to do.'

'Really?'

'What happened in Marrakesh needs to lead to something good. That's the only way to make sense of it. We turn it into a positive.' Marnie holds Bea's gaze. 'We make this our something good.'

That *we* again. She feels it deep in her heart.

'Know the first thing we should do?' Marnie asks. She turns towards the sea, which glitters with peeling waves. 'Get ourselves in there.'

8

Bea pauses at the water's edge, surfboard under her arm. Waves sweep into the bay, where surfers dot the water, zinc streaked across cheeks and noses, like an ocean tribe.

'Ready?' Marnie asks.

The sun beats down in a cloudless sky, and Bea's skin is clammy within her borrowed wetsuit. It's too short at the arms and legs and clings unflatteringly to her hipbones and small breasts. 'Guess so,' she says, feeling completely out of her depth. She can swim a length or two in a pool, but she's no water baby. They've practised 'popping up' on the beach – the quick press-up that launches you to your feet – but even on land, the movement felt weak and graceless.

She follows Marnie into the shallows, the cool bite of the Atlantic sealing around her bare feet.

'Let's start in the reforms,' Marnie says, pointing to the low walls of whitewater rumbling into shore.

Marnie is sleek and athletic in a wetsuit with a flash of leopard print across the arms. She slides effortlessly onto her mint-green longboard and begins to paddle in smooth, easy strokes, her back arched.

Bea follows, instantly out of breath as she paddles into the oncoming whitewater. Spray slaps her in the face, filling her mouth with the taste of the sea.

'Let's go for one of these,' Marnie says, turning her board and paddling for a small tumbling mass of whitewater. She pops to her feet and rides it playfully into shore.

Bea struggles to turn her board, and the next surge of whitewater hits her side-on. She pushes wet hair from her face and starts again, angling her huge foam board towards the shore.

Marnie returns to her side and holds the board steady as Bea climbs on. 'Start paddling.'

Bea does as she says. Marnie gives the board a push, and Bea feels the whitewater catch her, propelling her forward.

'Stand up!'

Feeling the small surge of swell take her, Bea scrambles onto her knees and attempts to stand but instead topples off sideways, arms windmilling uselessly. She yelps as she hits the water, going under in a bubbling mass of froth. She flails for a couple of seconds until she finds the sea bed beneath her and pushes back to standing.

Bea swipes wet hair from her eyes and glances around, half expecting to find people laughing. But no one's watching. She's not being judged on how she moves or what she looks like. Out in the water, she's just a girl in a badly fitting wetsuit who can't surf.

She relaxes a little. Tries again. Marnie gives her a few pointers, showing her how to select the right wave, when to paddle, where to position herself.

On her fifth attempt, Bea finally makes it to her feet. The ride lasts no more than a couple of seconds before she's tossed off, the board clunking her on the head as she surfaces, but she feels the buzz of those two precious seconds, the sheer wonder of standing on a moving wave.

Riding high on the exhilaration, Bea fails to see the next wave rolling towards her, lifting her board and sending it bucking into her face. Her nose takes the brunt of the force, and she cries out.

Blood starts trickling from her nose. She lifts her hands to feel the damage, and they come away red.

The sight of it trips a memory wire, and she's towed back to the Marrakesh alleyway . . . the arc of blood from the man's neck . . . the slump of his body . . . It feels like she's being sucked beneath the surface. No air. No light. No—

'Get back on.' Marnie's voice, firm but calm, cuts through the pull of memory.

Bea blinks. Tries to focus.

Marnie is holding Bea's board steady, gaze lasered on her. 'You take a knock, you get straight back on.'

A wave passes under them, lifting and dropping the board. Her nose is burning, heart rate skittering.

She dips her hands into the sea, washing away the blood.

'This wave,' Marnie instructs.

Bea looks over her shoulder towards the whitewater rumbling towards them. She clambers onto the board, trying to ignore the pain in her nose and the wash of blood from her nostrils.

'Paddle.'

Bea plunges her arms into the sea. The board feels heavy and slow. She keeps going, muscles burning as she digs through the water, breathing hard.

The board begins to glide as it's caught by the momentum of the wave. She picks up speed, the rush of water filling her ears.

There's no time to think. She springs to her feet – and

suddenly she is upright, riding straight towards the shore. Her nose streams with blood; wet hair trails behind her. The pain recedes, the memories disappear, and she is storming towards the beach, gaze straight ahead.

It can only be a few seconds, but it feels so much more. As the wave finally crumbles to nothing, she jumps from the board and bombs beneath the surface.

She rises, face washed clean by the salt. She touches her nose and realises she doesn't need to worry if there'll be bruising or swelling because there are no more castings. No more days posing for a camera. No more striding down a catwalk while being scrutinised. Her body is her own again.

She turns, grinning.

Marnie, backlit by the sun, has a fist raised in the air.

Bea lifts her arm and pumps it to the sky.

Bea wades into the shallows, exhausted but exhilarated. As she crouches to undo her ankle leash, Salty comes bounding towards her, tail wagging. He dances from paw to paw as seawater touches his feet.

She reaches for a piece of driftwood nearby – then tosses it across the beach. He barks but makes no move to go after the stick.

'Not into fetch?'

Salty looks at her, eyes wide, ears pricked.

Bea shrugs. When she looks up, Aiden is walking in her direction, board under his arm. The sun is in his eyes, and he squints or perhaps smiles. He is flanked by a group of surfers in fluoro Offshore rash vests. They go on ahead as Aiden pauses.

In the daylight, she takes him in. His skin holds a deep, even tan, his jawline darkened with stubble. There are shadows beneath his eyes, hinting that he hasn't slept, but they are offset by a burning energy that comes from his gaze.

'Bea.'

Heat rises through her body at the sound of her name on his lips.

'Had fun out there?'

'Loved it,' she answers – and she did. The sun on her skin, the physicality of surfing, the absorption in learning something new that kept darker memories at bay.

Salty weaves against Aiden's leg, cat-like. He bends to ruffle his head.

'You're teaching?' she asks, glancing at the group who are waiting in the shallows.

'Yeah. I give a couple of lessons most days.'

Aiden's gaze travels briefly over her shoulder. Bea follows it and sees a girl with blue hair approaching with short, fast strides. She grips a tripod in one hand and has a camera around her neck.

Aiden makes the introduction. 'This is Elin. Elin, Bea.'

Elin takes in the beginner board. 'Just been in?'

'First time.'

'How did you get on?'

'Apart from being smacked in the face by my board and also discovering how embarrassingly unfit I am, I had fun.'

'Twenty press-ups every morning. That'll sort the fitness,' Elin says matter-of-factly. 'And if you need someone to help keep your board in check, you're stood beside the best surf instructor in the bay.' She throws a grin in Aiden's direction.

'Camerawoman and PR officer,' Aiden says easily.

'You got it. I'm gonna set up by the rocks,' Elin tells him. She lifts a hand to wave at Bea, then disappears with her tripod.

Aiden and Bea remain on the shoreline. He glances at her, and Bea becomes aware of her wet hair against her cheeks, salt water caught on her lashes.

Up ahead, there's a shout from the group waiting for Aiden. He doesn't immediately turn but continues to look at Bea. 'Maybe I'll see you in the water another time.'

She smiles. Nods.

He holds her gaze for a final moment before turning and jogging to rejoin the others.

9

Bea takes one end of the sheet and Marnie the other, stretching it over the bed. She tucks the corners beneath the mattress, smoothing the sun-warm cotton, which she has plucked fresh from the line.

She's been staying at The Surf House for over a week now, and her days have fallen into a rhythm. Mornings are for the guests – rising early to help prepare and then clear breakfast. She likes the comfort of being in the kitchen with Marnie, the two of them moving around one another, a warm dance of chopping and stirring, the kitchen full of the scent of cinnamon and pressed oranges and fresh coffee.

Then the changeovers and cleaning begin. It's mostly mopping up salt water and sand or stripping beds – and she is grateful to keep busy, to fill her day with small tasks that push Marrakesh from her thoughts. There's been no follow-up from Momo and, with each day that passes, she lets herself hope there may not be.

After lunch, she usually walks into the village with Salty, through corridors of homes painted in rich blues, the sea always in the background. She buys supplies for The Surf House from the fruit and vegetable stalls: ripe vine tomatoes, fresh glossy aubergines, oranges with fragrant green leaves still attached.

Bea's favourite time of day in Mallah is late afternoon, pushing towards dusk, when she pulls on her wetsuit, takes her board from the rack, and jogs into the surf. She's not missed a day, even though her muscles burn and her ribs are bruised. She loves the physicality of it, and she can feel a tightening in her core and the first hint of tone in her arms. Her shins are stained with bruises, and the skin on her neck has chafed with wetsuit rub, but she welcomes it all – because out in the surf, her mind clears.

They finish making the bed, plumping pillows and smoothing out an ochre throw. Bea looks around the room, thinking how beautiful it is: the high, white walls, light filtering in from every corner, the cactus plants on the balcony, the simple line drawing of a wave on one wall, a pale dreamcatcher on another. She sets fresh towels on the bed, then waters the large palm that sits on the balcony, while Marnie wipes the surfaces using a homemade spray of witch hazel, lemongrass, and eucalyptus, which makes the air smell impossibly fresh.

They leave the room together, and Bea feels a sense of accomplishment.

Out in the hallway, they hear the main doors open as new guests arrive.

'That will be Driss and Farah,' Marnie says.

A Moroccan couple in their early thirties arrive with boards underarm and a case on wheels.

Marnie wraps them both in a hug. 'Driss! Farah! So good to have you back! How was the drive?'

Farah, slender and dark-haired, in a floaty dress, says, 'The normal chaos getting out of the city. But you know what it's like when you reach the coast. All that tension floats away.' Her English is perfect, spoken with a soft, almost musical accent.

'You both need to meet someone.' Marnie turns, placing a hand on Bea's lower back. 'This is Bea. She's helping us for a

56

while. You'll note the standard of the breakfast has gone up a level.'

'Great to meet you.' Farah smiles warmly, kissing her on both cheeks.

Driss, her partner, is immaculately dressed in a palm-motif printed shirt, open to the chest, and loose cotton trousers. His gaze travels the length of Bea, and then he says, with a wide smile, 'I hope you know you're working at the best guesthouse in Morocco.'

'I do.'

'The waves are waiting for you,' Marnie says. 'It's just coming up to high tide, so your timing is perfect.'

'I'll take up our bags,' Driss says.

'I just want to flop by the pool,' Farah tells him.

He presses a kiss on her shoulder. 'Of course.'

Marnie asks Bea, 'Is there any of your incredible cake left? Farah must try it.'

'I'll bring it out,' Bea says.

In the kitchen, she sets out a tray and makes a cooling jug of iced mineral water infused with mint and cucumber. Then she generously slices the orange and cardamon cake onto plates for Marnie and Farah. There's a hunk left over, and although she already had an oven-fresh slice this morning, she plates the final piece for herself.

Bea carries the tray to the poolside, where Marnie and Farah sit on loungers in the shade. Marnie moves up to make space for Bea, who sets down the tray and passes around the plates of cake.

Farah lifts a forkful to her lips and takes the first bite. Her eyes flutter closed. 'This,' she murmurs, 'is incredible.'

'I warned you.' Marnie smiles.

Bea feels a swell of pride in her chest.

'Where did you learn to bake?' Farah asks, wiping a crumb from the corner of her mouth.

She'd love to tell Farah that her mum taught her. That she would come home from school and find ingredients laid out, ready for the two of them to rub butter into flour or whisk egg whites into stiff peaks. What a nice story that would make.

'I liked watching cookery shows,' she admits.

They were her company on the cold, dark evenings when her mum was out with whichever man she was dating. Bea's favourite show was *The Great British Bake Off*; she never tired of seeing a set of ingredients transformed into something that made mouths water and eyes roll delightedly.

'Your family must love your flair in the kitchen,' Farah says.

Bea smiles in response, letting the assumption lie. She is thinking of their old flat in Reading, the faux-oak dining table buried beneath piles of post and catalogues. She remembers a winter's afternoon when she cleared the table, placing down a ceramic dish bubbling with lasagne.

'Smells good,' her mum said, watching closely as Bea served.

Bea assumed that she was admiring the deep colours of the roasted vegetables or the creaminess of the melted cheese that was still sizzling – but then her mum picked up her knife, leaned over Bea's plate, and sliced her portion of lasagne down the middle, scraping half of it back into the serving dish.

'You've got the Topshop casting on Friday.' Then she lifted her plate onto her lap, angled her chair towards the television, and reached for the remote.

Bea pushes aside the memory, then digs her fork into the hunk of cake in front of her. She lifts it to her mouth, savouring every note of sweetness and spice. As she eats, she lets the warmth of female chatter wash around her and is grateful for it.

She learns that Farah lives in Marrakesh and is studying for a PhD in chemistry, and her fiancé, Driss, is an entrepreneur.

'We've always driven down to Mallah to surf on weekends,' Farah tells her. 'That's how we met Marnie and Ped and the others. We were so happy when you bought this land,' she says to Marnie. 'Just look at what you've created.'

'I can't believe it's been more than a year since we opened.'

'Really, already?'

'Yep – and you and Driss were our first guests.'

'That's right. Then Savannah came next.' Farah takes a sip of her drink. 'Do you ever hear from her?'

Marnie shakes her head. 'Not in a long time.'

'I wonder if she made it all the way to Cape Town.'

'I've no doubt. She was thirsty for an adventure.'

They talk some more, and although the names and places mean little to Bea, she is content to let the conversation drift around her. Later, the three of them cool off in the pool, and Bea finds something lovely about talking as they swim slow lengths, a light breeze stirring the leaves of the lemon tree.

They pause at the poolside, resting their forearms on the tiles. Farah looks up at The Surf House and asks, 'Where's Ped?'

'Chasing waves,' Marnie answers. 'He hitched a ride with some French surfers.'

Farah presses her lips together, as if she expected this answer and is sorry for it.

'He needs it – the adventure,' Marnie says, loyally. 'He'll be back soon.'

Farah nods. 'And how's Aiden?'

'Started night surfing again.'

Farah's expression grows concerned.

'Better that he's surfing than drinking,' Marnie says. 'Offshore seems busy, which is something. He has a great rap with his surf students.'

'Particularly the female ones,' Farah says, with a grin. 'What about him and Ped? Are things any better?'

Marnie shakes her head. 'Aiden still won't set foot here.'

Farah turns and looks at the newly finished Surf Studio, a stylish white cube of accommodation with a glass balcony that stretches above the ocean. Then her gaze moves to Offshore, its flat, yellow roof just visible behind it. 'I suppose the studio does take a lot of his view,' Farah says carefully.

'I know,' Marnie says, turning to look, too. 'But then Ped argues Aiden shouldn't have sold the land if he was worried about it being built on.' She sighs. 'It was Ped's pet project. You know what he's like.'

'He was a man obsessed. Laid every brick himself. He told me it was a labour of love.'

Marnie's expression tightens, and Bea wonders if the building was a bone of contention in their relationship.

Farah swims towards the steps and climbs out of the pool, Marnie and Bea following. Stretching her arms overhead, Farah looks towards the bay. 'Better get a few waves in before the light goes.'

Bea considers the lines of swell, deciding that, after she's cleared up, she'll head out for a surf, too. She collects the empty glasses and plates and is making for the kitchen when she hears the clip of leather shoes across the terrace. When she turns, she finds Marnie standing stock-still.

There, on the far side of the pool, is Momo. He's dressed in his dark police uniform, shoes polished, eyes hidden behind sunglasses. The blood drains from Bea's body, the warmth and safety of the sun-bright afternoon vanishing.

She remembers Marnie's warning: *There'll be a price.*

Momo is here to collect.

10

Scalding water runs down Bea's scalp as she stands in the shower, heart racing. Marnie instructed, 'Go inside. I'll handle it.' But this – the waiting – feels worse.

She tries telling herself it's a good sign that Momo is alone. That means bribe, not investigation, right? She just wants to know what he's asking for. Then this can be over.

She jerks her face into the flow of hot water. The conditioner washes through the ends of her hair, trailing over her shoulder blades. She turns up the heat. Needs it to be hot enough to steam the mirror so that she doesn't have to look at herself when she steps out.

There's a quick knock – and then the bathroom door opens. There's no lock, and Marnie enters without waiting for an answer.

Bea is used to stripping from outfits in the wings, but she's never felt comfortable with her own nudity and is quick to cover herself, snapping off the shower and reaching for a towel. She steps onto the bathmat, water sliding from her skin, a cloud of apricot-scented steam filling the room.

Marnie sits on the toilet seat, hugging her knees to her chest. She's white-faced.

'What happened?'

There's a long pause as Marnie stares at the ground. Eventually, she lifts her gaze. Her eyes are a wide, watery blue as they fix on Bea. 'He died, Bea. The man who attacked us. He's dead.'

Dead.

The word is suspended there. Solid. Unchangeable.

The man is *dead.*

Bea put a knife in his neck – and now he is dead.

She has killed someone.

She feels droplets of water cooling on her skin.

When they left him on the ground, she knew there was every chance he was dead. They both did. But now, it is a hard fact.

She has taken a life.

Her body begins to tremble.

She takes a step back. Feels the cold ceramic sink against her lower back. Her wet fingertips cover her mouth.

'Momo's got a cousin who works for the police in Marrakesh. Momo must have made a few calls. Put together the bloodied knife and a man stabbed that same day. He knows.'

Bea's chest tightens. 'What's he going to do?' Her voice is thin, and there's a shrill ringing in her ears.

'He wants money. $10,000 in return for the knife and scarf.'

'I don't have that much!'

'It's not an obscene amount,' Marnie says. 'I thought he'd ask for more.'

'When does he need it by?'

'Tomorrow.'

'What?' Panic ignites. 'How am I going to find it?'

'You don't have any from your modelling?'

'I've got £2,000 in my account. That's everything. The rest is gone. I had to clear debt for my mum.'

Marnie bites down on her lower lip. 'Can you get any of it back?'

'Mum's broke. She's living in Spain with a boyfriend who's paying her way.'

Marnie continues to chew her lower lip, brow tight.

'If I could pick up another modelling job . . . but I'd need to go back to London. Beg my agent. Wait to be cast. It could be weeks.'

'You don't have a passport,' Marnie points out. 'Even if you try to get a replacement, there'll be a flag on your name. Momo's not going to let you leave until he's been paid.'

Bea squeezes the roots of her wet hair. 'What do I do?'

Marnie goes quiet, thinking. 'I'll check The Surf House accounts, but I know they won't look good. We took out big loans to finish the building work.' She swallows. 'There should be some petty cash – $500. Maybe more. I'll get it for you. Whatever we have, it's yours. We just . . . when Ped comes back, we can't tell him.'

'You shouldn't have to do this. It's my mess.'

Marnie crosses the bathroom and places her fingers on Bea's damp shoulders, stilling her. 'This comes back to both of us, okay?'

Bea feels tears stinging the back of her throat. She manages to nod. 'What now?'

'Do you have family or friends you can borrow from?'

There is no other family. Her dad was never in the picture – a chef from Sussex who doesn't even know Bea exists. As for friends – when you leave school at fifteen and work abroad most of the time, it's hard to make lasting friendships.

'There's no one,' she admits, a shameful sensation rising through her middle as if the admission reveals something lacking in Bea.

'Do you have an overdraft?'

'Yeah – £1,000, I think.' Bea is silently doing the maths. With her savings, a full overdraft, and the petty cash Marnie mentioned, they will have around $5,000 – half the amount they need.

In her old life, that sum of money would have been easy enough to earn. But out here – with no work, no passport, and no connections – it feels like an impossible task. 'What if we don't get the money?' She feels desperately out of her depth and suddenly very young. She looks to Marnie.

Marnie meets her eye. 'We have to.'

11

'I can't help,' Bea's mum says. 'I'm earning a few hundred quid a month waxing bikini lines in a scuzzy hotel block.'

Bea has stuck as close to the truth as she can, admitting that she's quit modelling and that her rucksack was stolen in Marrakesh. She's told her mum that she's still in Morocco and needs money to tide her over.

'What about Dan?' Bea asks. 'Could he lend me something?'

'So *now* you like him?'

'It's not about—'

'Look, he could probably stretch to a flight home, but that's it. Everything's tied up in his business.'

Bea stands at the darkened window of her room. She thinks of all the money she's given her mum over the years – paying the rent on the flat when her mum couldn't cover it, bankrolling the beauty salon her mum had dreamed of setting up, clearing her debts when it failed. Bea would have saved thousands by now if her money hadn't been drained.

'Ring Madeline. Get your job back. What else are you going to do that pays like that?'

'I . . . I can't do it anymore.'

'No? All those big cheques and fancy clothes got a bit much, did they?'

There it is – the bitterness in her mum's tone. Money is her mum's altar, and she is devout in her worship. Her enthusiasm for Bea's career was always undercut with an *it's-all-right-for-some* attitude. She both boasted to her friends that her daughter was a model and resented Bea for having the career that she'd have loved.

'So you're not going to help?' Bea asks.

'Sorry, I can't. You'll figure it out.'

And that's it. The call is done.

Bea is on her own.

She leans her head against the dark window, thinking, *I always have been.* The glass is cool and solid against her forehead, her breath creating a low mist. Outside, she can hear the waves breaking.

There has been no argument or shouting. There rarely ever is. Growing up, she'd have preferred raised voices and slammed doors – at least it would have shown that her mum felt something. Instead, her mum's weaponry was withdrawal, pulling back, walking away. If she confronted her mum, she'd most often say, 'You obviously don't want me around, so I'll leave.' Then she'd walk out of their flat.

Bea doesn't hear the gentle knock on the connecting door or Marnie's footsteps crossing the room. She just feels the warmth of her hand on her lower back.

'The call didn't go well?'

'There's no money.'

'But you said you cleared her debt. Isn't she saving to repay you?'

Bea's head shakes. 'Mum sees that money as payback.'

Marnie's brow dips.

'She was twenty-two when she got pregnant with me. *A mistake.*' She actually used those words. There was no softening it to a *lovely surprise.* 'She thinks I took away the life she should have had – her youth, her beauty, her opportunities.'

Bea wonders why she even bothered making the call. She knew there'd be no help. Yet she keeps coming back for more. What is it she is waiting for? To hear the words *I'm proud of you?*

'I'm sorry, Bea. Mothers aren't always the people we need them to be.' There's something in the feeling way Marnie says this that makes Bea intuit that she has lived experience.

Marnie pulls her into a hug and Bea lets her. For a few moments, the darkness that twists in her middle recedes a little.

When Bea is ready, she takes a deep breath and steps back.

Marnie is staring right at her, their faces close. Her expression moves from empathy to steely hardness as she holds Bea's eye. 'You know what? Fuck her.'

Bea blinks.

'I mean it. Fuck her. She doesn't deserve you.'

The sharpness of those words reaches deep and cuts out some of the despair.

'Fuck her,' Bea repeats, the strength of anger like a splint to a broken bone.

Bea lies in bed, unable to sleep. Anxiety wheels through her head, breaking her thoughts into sharp, unfinished pieces. She has no money, no passport, and no way of leaving.

She curls onto her side. A wash of exhaustion crashes over her. Eventually, her mind wears itself out and allows her body to soften as she gives in to sleep.

Some time later, she must stir, because there's a prickling of her senses, an alertness behind the groggy exhaustion.

She has the unnerving sensation that she isn't alone.

She holds herself still, listening, but only catches the sound of her own heartbeat.

That prickling sensation sharpens. There's a change in the air. Since Marrakesh, she knows she's been on high alert. She tries to tell herself that she is safe in this room. Marnie is next door. Everything is fine.

Then she hears it: the sound of someone breathing.

Her eyes snap wide open. She peers into the darkness.

Standing near the door, blocking her exit, she sees a figure. The proportions are tall, broad, masculine.

She lies still, frozen with fear.

There are footsteps. The low draw of breath as the figure moves closer.

Then Bea is flying to her feet, stumbling away, shouting!

Suddenly, light sears into the room.

Bea puts a hand in front of her face, blinking.

A man stands on the far side of the room by the light switch. He has a shaved head and is bare-chested, wearing only his boxer shorts.

He holds up his palms, but he doesn't look submissive – he looks furious. 'Who the hell are you?'

The connecting door opens, and Marnie steps through, hair mussed around her face. She's wearing only a skimpy vest and thong. She scans the scene, squinting against the light. 'I see you've met.'

'You could've warned me someone was in here!' the man blasts.

'I could have – if I'd known when you were coming back.'

She smiles pointedly. Marnie slips a warm arm around Bea's waist and says, 'Sorry, babe. He's not as scary as he looks. Ped, meet Bea – our new member of staff.'

His brow furrows.

'And Bea, this is Ped, who is apparently back.'

Bea takes him in now – the broad surfer's shoulders, the thickset chest ridged with muscles. His face looks weatherworn, serious.

'Staff?' Ped says.

'We'll do full intros tomorrow,' Marnie says. She releases Bea, then crosses the room, moving towards Ped. Hands on his waist, she pushes onto tiptoes and kisses his mouth. Her vest lifts. 'Good to have you home, baby.' Then she slips her small hand into Ped's and leads him towards the connecting door.

Just before crossing the threshold, she glances back at Bea. 'Sorry about the excitement.' She blows her a kiss, and then the door closes softly behind them.

In the darkness, a spill of light shows from beneath Marnie and Ped's room. She can hear their hushed voices, the differing paces and tones.

She catches her name on Marnie's lips, the single syllable lowered. Then a rush of words from Ped, something urgent.

Then there is silence.

Bea lies still, stomach knotted, teeth pressed together. She catches the sound of breath – a sharp intake – and then there are footsteps, the creak of the bed as bodies land on it.

She hears a groan of pleasure: Ped's. Imagines Marnie's lithe, tanned limbs around him. She squeezes her eyes shut, but she cannot disappear. She is inches apart from them.

Marnie moans with abandon, the sound primal and rich.

Despite herself, Bea pictures their bodies – Ped's hands pulling aside Marnie's vest, exposing her breasts, his mouth hot against her nipples.

She hears him now, a low sound of pleasure, something whispered that she doesn't catch.

A rhythm builds in the darkness, slow at first, nothing urgent or rushed. This is a dance that they are experts in. She feels the vibration of them through the walls, making her own mattress quiver.

As she hears Marnie moan in pleasure, Bea thinks, *I've never made that noise.*

There have been boyfriends in the past, but no one that she has deeply desired, certainly no one that she's loved. When she was modelling, she learned to distance herself from her body to survive, so sex often felt like an extension of her job, something expected of her. It was as if she couldn't switch off the part of her brain that was thinking about the performance rather than the experience. She'd arch her back, push out her hips, make the right noises – but she felt so disconnected from her body that any pleasure was muted.

She hears Marnie's voice, low, full of longing, saying, 'I love you.'

Alone in the dark, Bea feels her own strangeness and loneliness like a crack that she is slipping down. She pulls the pillow over her head, gripping on.

12

Bea wakes feeling unrested and edgy. She splashes cool water over her face, then she changes into her shorts and vest, and goes downstairs to prepare the breakfast service.

She pauses by the open doors leading to the terrace, taking a moment to gather herself. It is another blue-sky day with waves fringing the bay. There's not a breath of wind. It's beautiful, the surf glassy and clean, but she can't think about the pleasure of catching waves. She needs to get the $10,000 to Momo by the end of the day – but has no idea how she'll find the money.

A sparrow dips into the still pool, wetting its wings, then shaking off the water droplets. Noticing something, she blinks. Sharpens her gaze.

There are a pair of tanned hands holding the poolside. Beneath the water, someone is standing on the bottom, head bowed. Through the refracted water, she makes out a tanned, shaven head and broad shoulders.

Ped.

She continues to watch, noting that he's now been submerged for some time. She wants to turn away, move off to the kitchen – but she needs to see the moment he breaks the surface. She shifts her weight from foot to foot, waiting. How long has he been under? A minute? Two?

Just when she cannot bear it any longer, his head emerges, water sluicing from his skull, eyes closed. She watches as he draws a long, deep breath. She can see the expansion of his lungs as his chest rises. Then he opens his eyes.

He stares right at her.

It feels like she's been caught spying. Heat blooms in her cheeks, and she spins away.

Marnie is standing in the doorway of the kitchen, a tea towel in hand. 'He's breath-hold training. He can stay under for several minutes before he needs air. Could save his life out in the surf.' Marnie flicks the tea towel over her shoulder and walks into the kitchen.

After a beat, Bea follows.

As Marnie puts on the coffee, Bea notices how tired she looks. 'Are you okay?'

'Great,' Marnie replies, but Bea catches a hint of vulnerability in her tone.

Bea sets to work, taking a large glass jar of granola from the shelf and setting it on a tray with a stack of bowls and spoons. There is no music playing this morning. No easy chat.

'Is it good to have Ped home?' Bea asks.

'Always.' Marnie smiles, but there is something about it that feels off.

They work in silence for a while. Bea slices an avocado in half, scooping out the flesh, then mashing it with a fork. She scrapes it into a ceramic bowl, adding a squeeze of lemon juice and a generous sprinkling of salt and pepper.

Setting it aside, she asks Marnie, 'What did you tell Ped about me being here?'

Marnie glances up. 'Exactly what we agreed. We ran into each other in Marrakesh. You'd had your rucksack stolen. Needed a place to stay. And here you are. You're helping out for bed and board.'

Bea nods.

They both turn as Ped strides into the kitchen. He's thrown on a black T-shirt and shorts. His feet are bare.

'How was your session?' Marnie asks.

'Good.'

'Coffee?'

'I'll do it,' Ped says, opening the fridge and removing a carton of oat milk.

He and Marnie begin talking about business, the running of the day, which guests are in, what Ped thinks of the conditions. Bea listens to the flow of the conversation, sensing this is a regular rhythm – the dynamics of the day being decided over breakfast. Ped's Australian accent gives a hard twang to his vowels, and there's little expression on his face as he speaks.

'There's an XL forecast rolling in soon,' Ped says.

'And I thought you were back to see me,' Marnie retorts lightly, although Bea wonders if there's a bite to her tone.

'If it holds, it could be the swell of the season.'

'D'you think it will?'

'There's a big low pressure building across the Atlantic, so if it stays on course, then we could see something special.' Ped moves to the far side of the kitchen, passing Bea.

Getting the sense that she's in the way, she overcompensates and presses herself back against the kitchen counter. Her elbow connects with the granola jar, which teeters. She turns to grab it – but it slips through her fingers and falls.

The jar explodes on the tiled floor, glass and oats flying across the kitchen.

'Oh! God!' Bea cries. Glass glitters across the tiled floor. 'I'm so sorry.'

Marnie's hands go to her mouth. 'Ped?'

Bea turns. An inch-long shard of glass has fired out and lodged in Ped's right ankle.

Marnie tears off a wad of kitchen roll and hands it to him. He applies pressure on either side of the wound as he examines it.

'Is it deep?' Marnie asks.

Ped doesn't reply. Maintaining pressure, he slowly removes the glass on an exhale, his expression barely altering.

Bea can see immediately that it is deep, the tissues turning bright red. 'Are you okay? What can I do?'

He ignores her.

Marnie fetches the first-aid kit, and Ped removes a gauze and some tape and patches up his ankle. When he is finished, he throws the bloodied tissues into the bin.

Bea tries to apologise again, skin flaming, but Ped is already walking away.

Bea manages to stay out of Ped's way for the rest of the day. It is almost a relief when she gets into the van with Marnie and leaves Mallah. Or at least, it would be if they weren't on their way to Momo's.

The light has faded to night, and she loses her bearings as they cut into the hillside, taking sharp turns down narrow, unlit lanes.

'D'you think Momo will return the knife?' Bea asks in the darkness as she turns the envelope of money through her hands. Her fingertips are damp, stomach jittering with nerves.

'Your guess is as good as mine,' Marnie says.

Bea's done everything she can think of to get Momo's money.

She's called models she used to work with. She's asked her ex-agent if there was anything owed in her account. She's applied for a loan, but it'll be a while before she hears whether she's passed the eligibility checks. She got a lift into town from Marnie and has withdrawn every penny from her bank account and overdraft. But they still have only $5,000 – and now they're out of time.

Crockery clangs in the back of the van as they hit a pothole, the noise shredding Bea's nerves.

Eventually, Marnie pulls up outside a clay-coloured building with a narrow doorway. A pack of stray dogs scatter. The small house is tired but in better repair than most of the surrounding homes. There is a single light on at a window.

Marnie cuts the engine, and they both sit in silence for a moment. Bea feels a heavy knot in her stomach. She wipes her palms against her thighs, then unclicks her seat belt.

'Stay with the van,' Marnie instructs. 'Keep the doors locked.'

Bea should say, *I'm coming with you. We do this together.* Only, she's terrified of knocking on Momo's door and stepping over that threshold.

As she hands Marnie the envelope of money, she catches her fingers and squeezes them.

Marnie takes a deep breath and climbs from the van. She makes her way to the house, watched by a lone cat perched on a rusted motorbike, tail swishing.

Reaching the narrow doorway, she lifts her fist to knock, but the door is opened by an older woman in a dark skirt. She does not smile or invite Marnie in – just turns and disappears within the house, leaving Marnie standing on the doorstep.

Bea has a better view now that there is light flooding from inside the house. She can see a small room, a television in the corner and a single chair, from which Momo rises.

He comes to the door dressed in shorts and a T-shirt, his feet bare. He glances towards the van, eyes alighting briefly on Bea. Through the open window, Bea hears him and Marnie conversing in rapid French. Then Marnie hands him the envelope. He doesn't look inside – simply passes it straight to his mother.

She's the one who rips it opens, peers at the money. She remains tight-lipped.

Then she lifts her gaze, stares right at Bea.

Marnie is talking now, speaking fast, her face tense as she turns and gestures at Bea. Everyone is staring at her as she sits pinned to the passenger seat, heart pounding in her ears. *Give us the knife*, she silently begs.

She watches as Momo and his mother address one another. Their faces are unsmiling. Then Momo's mother tucks the envelope into the pocket of her heavy skirt. She ushers Momo away, then closes the door, leaving Marnie standing empty-handed in the dark.

Fuck.

Bea reaches over and unlocks the van door.

Marnie climbs in, her jaw tight. She shakes her head. 'He wants full payment.'

Dread lurches in Bea's stomach.

'He's extended the deadline. We've got three weeks to clear the debt.'

It's something, Bea thinks. Yet Marnie's jaw is rigid. 'What is it?'

She swallows. 'If we don't pay up, then Momo's cop cousin in Marrakesh is going to "discover" the murder weapon. Then they'll come for us.'

13

They'll come for us.

The words twist through Bea's thoughts as she shifts restlessly in bed, searching for sleep.

Eventually, she snaps off the covers and sits up. Her heart is racing, breath high and shallow in her chest as she reaches for the lamp. Blinking into the brightness, she knows she can't stay in this room a moment longer. She pulls on her hoodie and leaves.

Moving through the darkened guesthouse, she heads outside towards the cliff top.

The air is cool, the breeze up. Returning to her usual spot, she finds Salty curled into his nook. He stands, stretches, tail wagging as she strokes him. She continues to circle a hand over his flank, and the interaction relaxes her a little.

She reassures herself that, for Momo, there's no gain in handing her over to the Marrakesh police. Money is what he's after. She just needs to find a way of getting him the remaining $5,000. She'll hear in a few days whether her loan application was successful. If it is, then they are in the clear. And if not? She'll need to rethink.

Salty resettles himself at her feet, his warm back pressed to her bare ankles. She looks out to sea, scanning the dark contours of the waves for Aiden – but is disappointed to find the sea empty. She's found herself replaying their cliff-top meeting, wondering what draws him into the sea at night.

She looks up at the sky. The stars feel alive, glittering through a blanket of black. She should learn the constellations if she's going to be spending so much time awake at this hour.

At her feet, Salty's head lifts, ears pricked.

As if she's summoned him, Aiden walks towards her, board under his arm, wetsuit peeled down, just like that first night. He must have already been wading in when she looked for him.

His eyes meet hers, and she wonders if he's pleased to find her here. 'Can't sleep?' he asks.

'No.' Her eyes flick to the dark sea, recalling Farah's concern when she heard Aiden was night surfing again. 'How was the surf?'

Aiden thinks for a moment. 'Peaceful,' he says.

She likes that word. Maybe that's what they're both searching for out here.

'You've not missed a day in the water by my count.'

The corners of her mouth lift. *Aiden's been counting.* 'I love it.'

'It's a beautiful addiction.'

He is right. Surfing *is* addictive. 'After all the paddling and waiting and wiping out, those moments when I'm on my feet feel so miraculous that I just want more.'

Aiden smiles, and it changes the shape of his face, that heavy brow lifting, light moving across his eyes.

'Have you always surfed?' Bea asks.

'Yeah, since I was a nipper. It was a way to get out the house for me and my brother. We rigged up these board racks on the

78

side of our bikes. Worked a treat, except when it was windy – which is pretty much every day in Donegal.'

She tries to picture Aiden as a child, little legs pumping at the pedals, a surfboard lashed to his bike. She envies him having a sibling, someone to anchor himself to when things weren't good at home. 'Are your family still in Ireland?'

'Just my brother. Dad died. Mum moved to America – she's got a sister there. My brother's married now with a kid. Lives in Dublin. Doesn't surf anymore. Tells me he grew out of it.'

'I'm planning on growing into it.'

Aiden grins at that. He lowers the tail of his surfboard to the ground and leans against the board as he asks, 'What about you? Get to the beach as a kid?'

'Not much,' she tells him. When she was travelling with other models, she saw the way they'd light up when they arrived in Paris or New York for the first time. They thrived on the buzz and pace of the big cities – while they left Bea depleted, not energised. 'Making up for lost time.'

Aiden smiles again, and their eyes meet. Warmth spreads through her centre. There's an intimacy about being alone together on the cliff at this hour, surrounded by the song of the waves. He watches her intently, his gaze travelling over her face.

Then, as if a door has blown open, delivering a cold blast of air, Aiden shivers, then drags his gaze away. He takes a step back, as if needing to create physical distance between them. 'I better . . .' he begins, glancing in the direction of Offshore.

She wants him to stay out here, with her. She isn't ready to go back to her room, where dark anxieties will be waiting to chase away sleep.

But all she says is, 'Night, Aiden.'

14

A week passes, and Bea thinks of little else than the money she must find for Momo. As she wipes down yoga mats on the terrace, she is so preoccupied that she doesn't notice the man approaching until he is almost upon her. She starts.

'Didn't mean to scare you,' the man says, and she catches his American accent.

He doesn't look like their normal guests, who mostly arrive in salt-faded T-shirts, lugging board bags. This man, whose eyes are hidden behind mirrored sunglasses, wears a dark shirt with the sleeves rolled up, exposing winter-pale forearms and an expensive-looking watch. At his side is a black case on wheels.

'You work here?' he asks. From the tilt of his head, she senses his gaze briefly travelling the length of her. She can't read his expression behind his sunglasses.

'Yes. Can I help?'

'I'd like a room. I did email, but no one got back to me. Is there anything available?'

'The owners aren't here today.' Marnie and Ped have an appointment in Agadir and won't be back until late, but she knows they won't want to lose a booking. 'Let me check the folder. I've got a feeling the Surf Studio is vacant.'

Bea leads the way inside, and the man follows, wheeling his case.

In the office, she goes to the desk and opens the green bookings folder. Glancing up, she sees that the American is standing in the doorway, blocking her exit. Her scalp prickles. The room becomes a narrow Marrakesh alleyway, and the smell of cigarettes fills the air. Her skin turns cold as the room recedes.

'Everything all right?' the man asks.

She blinks. Makes herself look right at him, dragging herself back to this moment, this room. He removes his sunglasses, pushing them onto his blond head, and she notices that his eyes are red-rimmed.

She wipes a hand over her brow where a cold sweat has broken out. 'Yes,' she tells him. 'Just a head rush.' She takes a steadying breath, then returns her attention to the bookings folder, scanning the calendar. 'Looks like the studio is free. How long were you hoping to stay?'

'A fortnight.'

'Is the room just for you?'

He nods.

'The Surf Studio has incredible views. You can check the waves without getting out of bed. It's 150 US dollars a night with breakfast included.'

'Fine.'

'We usually ask guests to pay the first night on arrival and the remainder when they check out. There's no ATM in Mallah.'

'I read that. I brought cash. Can I pay upfront?'

'Course.'

He removes his wallet, which is thick with fresh dollars, and counts out the full amount.

Bea takes the money and tucks it into the petty cashbox, her fingers hesitating for only a moment.

'Can I take your name and address?'

'Seth Hart,' he tells her, then reels off an address in California.

She asks for a few further details and takes a photocopy of his passport. Unhooking a set of keys, she says, 'The studio is already made up. I'll show you to it.'

He follows. An odd, shifting energy radiates from him, which she finds difficult to read. 'So, are you in Mallah for the surf?' she asks conversationally.

'No.'

It is rare to get guests turning up at The Surf House who haven't booked. Mallah isn't on the tourist route, and unless you surf, there's little to do.

'How long are you in Morocco for?'

'I don't know yet,' he responds, his clipped tone cutting the cord on any further questions.

She leads him across the terrace towards the studio. It is perched right on the cliff edge, and she opens a door onto a space flooded with light. The balcony doors are thrown open, revealing a vista of endless waves. She turns in the doorway and looks back towards Aiden's hostel, reminded of Farah's remark about this studio blocking the view. She's completely right.

Seth steps inside, barely glancing at the view, and asks, 'Is there a safe?'

'Yes.' She opens the wardrobe and indicates the metal safe.

From the front pocket of Seth's case, he removes an unsealed envelope, and she glimpses a further stack of fresh dollars. *How much money is he carrying?* She drags her gaze away, reminding herself that she's not desperate enough to start stealing from guests – yet.

Seth uncaps a bottle of mineral water, then tugs a sleeve of pills from his pocket and pops two into his mouth, washing them back. There's a sheen of sweat on his brow and a sallow look to his skin. A sense of restlessness burns from him. She's trying to decide if it's anxiety, exhaustion – or something else.

'I'll leave you to get unpacked,' she says as Seth removes his laptop from his bag, then places a black leather notebook beside it.

'This is the only place called The Surf House in the area, right?'

She turns back. 'As far as I know. How come?'

He shakes his head. 'My sister, Savannah, stayed at The Surf House when it first opened.'

'Savannah,' she repeats; the name is familiar.

Noting her expression, Seth's eyes sharpen. 'You know her?'

'No. I've only been working here a few weeks.' But remembering Farah's conversation by the pool, she says, 'Another guest mentioned her name. I think she was one of the first people to stay here.'

'That's right.' His gaze darts away, glancing towards the balcony as if he is expecting someone to be standing behind him. There's that strange energy again that she can't put her finger on. She isn't wholly sure whether she likes this man.

'Is Savannah still in Morocco?' she asks.

'I don't know where she is,' he answers. 'I'm here to find her.'

ONE YEAR EARLIER

SAVANNAH

Savannah stood on the roadside with her thumb stuck out, backpack at her feet. She sighed, hot and exhausted, flicking her blonde hair away from her shoulders.

Despite the boredom of waiting, there was also a thrill in hitching. It was the uncertainty of who'd pick her up or where they'd be headed. She liked not knowing what came next. It left space for possibility.

She was done with interrailing – hanging around on train platforms, ears pricked for announcements; the saturated taste of buffet-cart food; watching the world ride by from a carriage window. No, thanks. She wanted an adventure.

That was partly why she'd left California in the first place, right? She didn't want to climb a career ladder, leading only to longer hours and more accountability. She didn't want to accrue property, a car, or a ring on a finger. That was Seth's world, not hers.

She took out her cell and snapped a photo of her thumb sticking up in front of the empty road, the wide Spanish sky and blur of farmland in the background.

She uploaded the image to Instagram, captioning it: *Where next?*

Seth would see it. Course he would. He liked to prowl. And

she liked to provoke. Sure, there'd be a backlash. But she was on the other side of the Atlantic now. What was Seth gonna do? Come get her?

Hearing an engine approach, she slid her cell into her pocket and raised her thumb a little higher.

A beaten-up tow truck rounded the bend, its flatbed empty. A man in a cap was behind the wheel. A bony, tanned arm rested on the open window, a cigarette between fingers.

The driver's gaze slid over her body, travelling down her bare shoulders, the cropped white top, the denim shorts.

One brake light flickered as the truck slowed.

Hairs rose on the back of Savannah's neck. She lowered her thumb. Gave a small shake of her head, signalling, *No. Drive on.*

Tyres moved over hot asphalt as the truck pulled in ahead of her. The engine remained running as the man watched her in the wing mirror.

She shook her head again in case he'd missed it. She would not get in this truck.

The truck driver lifted the cigarette to his mouth and took a long draw. Smoke curled through his open lips. He flicked the butt to the ground in a shower of embers, and then clanked open the door.

Her heart kicked hard between her ribs as she scanned the empty road and deserted land beyond. No houses. No people. Just sun-scorched fields panting beneath the blaze of blue.

The man started walking towards her – work boots, torn jeans worn low, a wiry, muscular frame.

She wracked her thoughts for Spanish. How to tell him she didn't want a ride? 'No, *gracias*.'

He didn't meet her eye as he continued his path, covering the ground in unhurried strides.

She thought of her Instagram post. *Where next?* Now she wanted Seth here. Wanted him to pull up in his big, shiny car that smelled of leather and mints. Wanted to hear one of his lectures and be told how foolish she'd been. Wanted to sit in the cool safety of that vehicle and hear the doors lock.

Her muscles constricted as the man neared. She squared her shoulders, made herself take up space. But the tow-truck driver didn't stop when he reached her. He walked straight past, towards the edge of the verge.

Uncertain, she turned. He stopped and undid his flies. She heard the spray of piss against dry earth, could smell the ammonia tang of it. He let out a grunt-like sigh.

She looked away.

Half a minute later, she heard his zipper pulled. Then he was walking back to his vehicle, passing right by her as if she were invisible.

Her head throbbed with a tight fury. *What the fuck was that?*

As he placed a gnarled hand on the truck door, he hacked a thick glob of phlegm onto the roadside. Then he climbed in and gunned the engine.

15

Bea slides the granola tray from the oven, inhaling the spiced scents of cardamon and cinnamon, layered with the warmth of maple syrup.

'That smells divine,' Marnie says, entering the kitchen alongside Ped. She wears a creased playsuit, her slim, muscular thighs bare. She looks radiant, blue eyes glittering beneath her blunt, dark fringe.

'You're back,' Bea says warmly. Marnie plucks a still-warm cluster of oats from the tray and drops it into her mouth. As she chews, her eyes roll with pleasure.

'Who's in the Surf Studio?' Ped asks.

'An American guy. Here for a couple of weeks. I checked the folder, and it didn't look like there was anything in the diary. He's paid upfront.'

'Great,' Marnie says, filling a glass with water. 'We can't afford empty rooms in peak season.'

As Bea glances towards the studio, she sees Seth emerging from it. 'That's him,' she says, watching Seth cross the terrace towards the main house. 'Apparently his sister stayed here when you first opened. Savannah.'

Ped turns and fixes his gaze on Seth, who approaches a shaded table on the terrace. As he sits, he hitches up his shorts as if he is used to wearing long trousers and can't shake the practice.

'Got a call to make,' Ped says abruptly, then leaves the kitchen.

Bea looks to Marnie. 'Sorry, did I . . .'

'Ignore him. There was just a provisional booking he was holding. It's great we've got someone in. I'll go and welcome our new arrival. Will you bring him a glass of iced water?'

Bea takes a glass from the cupboard and fills it with cool, filtered water. She carries it out to the terrace, where Marnie is introducing herself to Seth. Bea sets down the water, then moves to a table nearby to clear it of empty glasses.

'You're Savannah's brother,' she hears Marnie saying. 'She was one of our first ever guests here. How is she?'

Seth pushes his mirrored sunglasses onto his head. 'You haven't heard?'

Marnie's brow dips.

'Savannah's missing.'

'What?'

'I've not heard from her in almost a year.'

Bea has paused from her glass collecting and sees Marnie nod slowly as if taking this in. Then her expression shifts subtly, an awkwardness moving into her features. 'I'm sorry . . . it's just that Savannah told us she was . . . estranged from her family. Are you sure she's not chosen to be out of contact?'

Seth stiffens. 'There was a fall-out, yes, but Savannah wouldn't go silent on us for this long. Things have happened at home that she would have wanted to be there for.'

Marnie nods gently, concern creasing her brow. 'I know she planned to travel overland to South Africa. A van trip with two Dutch girls, I think. Listen, I've got a few things that need doing right now, but why don't I find you later and we can get a coffee, talk?'

'I'd like that.'

Marnie smiles warmly and moves away. As Bea follows with her tray of used glasses, she glances up.

There, on the top floor, is Ped, standing at the open window, watching.

The following evening, guests and other surfers are crowded into The Surf House lounge. They sprawl on low sofas and lean back against the walls. Elin, with her shock of blue hair, who Bea recognises as the surf camerawoman, sits cross-legged on a rug, talking to a man with blond dreadlocks. It feels like half of Mallah are here. But – Bea notes as she scans the room – no Aiden. She stole out to the cliff top last night, hoping to catch him there. She waited an hour, then another, and eventually, eyes burning with exhaustion, sloped back to bed.

The room's collective gaze is trained on Ped. He stands beside a projector, which magnifies the surf forecast onto a white wall. He's wearing a black T-shirt, which sets off his deep tan. His feet are bare, and Bea can see the white gauze covering the wound on his ankle.

'I'll check the wave buoys again when the data refreshes,' he says, his Australian accent easy and commanding. 'The long period swell should hit around three a.m.'

Marnie is sitting on the armrest of a sofa, massaging the arch of her right foot, watching him.

Last night, Bea heard them arguing, their raised voices pounding through the walls. Her muscles tightened as the exchange grew fiery – and the crescendo of volleyed words ended in sex. Bea pulled the pillow over her head, but it was impossible to distance herself, and she lay in the dark, feeling like she was a strange part of their dynamic.

She looks around the room and can see that everyone is listening closely to Ped. Bea wonders if he likes all these surfers hanging on his every word.

'How often do you see a forecast like this?' someone asks.

'We get a wave height like this once – maybe twice – a year. But to see it landing without a storm, without the wind, is . . . well, rare. If the waves do anything like what the forecast is showing, we'll see something special tomorrow.'

There's been a feverish energy building all day as surfers have been tightening fins, rewaxing decks, gathering around laptops, discussing forecasts.

Seth walks into the lounge, scanning the crowd. He stands out in his pressed white shirt and chino shorts.

'Where should we surf?' a woman in a tie-dye surf tee asks Ped.

'It's a westerly swell, so it should wrap in and hit all the spots. I don't think Bow Point will hold the period. But Jailors will be worth a look. The bay out front will be a closeout.'

'Where will *you* surf?' Elin asks Ped, and there's something provocative in her tone.

Ped eyeballs her. 'Haven't decided yet.' Then Ped tells the group that he's signing out now, getting his shut-eye before the big day.

People mill about, not quite ready to disperse. Bea, though, is exhausted and desperate for sleep. Anxiety about Momo's debt chased her through the night, and she barely snatched more than an hour or two's sleep. Momo may have extended the repayment deadline, but she's still no idea how she'll find the money if her loan application isn't approved.

As she crosses the lounge, making for the stairs, Marnie catches her fingertips. She turns Bea towards her, looking at her enquiringly. 'Y'okay?'

'Busy head,' Bea says, giving a quick smile.

Marnie nods and squeezes her fingertips reassuringly. She considers her for a moment, then says, 'I was putting some towels in your room earlier, and I noticed you keep the mirror covered.'

Bea feels heat in her cheeks as she pictures the freestanding mirror at the foot of the bed, covered with a cotton throw. 'Yeah. I . . . I'm not keen on mirrors.'

Marnie looks at her closely. Her voice is kind as she asks, 'Is there a reason?'

Bea glances down at her hands. It started when she was modelling. From her very first test shoot, her body became something for other people to comment on and judge. All those uninvited opinions and criticisms seemed to be waiting for her the second she caught her eye in a mirror. So it became safest not to look. Not to hear that crowd of voices.

'An after-effect of my job, I guess.'

Marnie nods slowly. 'I can take out the mirror.'

'No. It's fine.' She needs to get over it. Stop being so fucking strange. 'The mirror's fine.'

Marnie nods. Then her face breaks into a warm smile as she says, 'Fancy getting out of here and doing something different tomorrow?' She leans in, mouth close to Bea's ear. 'Ped's surfing a secret spot. Wanna come?'

From what Bea's heard from other surfers, Ped is one of the best big wave riders. She knows that seeing him in conditions like those tomorrow is promising will be nothing short of a spectacle. 'Yes!'

Marnie beams. 'We're leaving at six a.m. Keep it to yourself, okay?'

Bea nods, feeling the warm glow of being on the inside.

'Now, go get your sleep,' Marnie says, pressing a kiss to Bea's forehead.

Bea is about to do exactly that when Seth approaches them, his brow tight, the spiced scent of aftershave rising from his skin.

'I need your help.' He directs this at Marnie, not pausing to greet either of them. 'While my sister was staying here, she posted a few photos on social media. Would you look through them with me? See if you recognise any of the people? I want to get in contact with anyone who knew Savannah.'

At the mention of Savannah's name, Elin's head snaps around. Her gaze lands on Seth. She stares at him intently, the colour draining from her face.

Marnie says, 'I'm free now if you want me to take a look?'

'Great,' Seth replies, and the two of them move off through the milling crowd.

A moment later, Elin is at Bea's shoulder. 'Who's the suit?' she asks.

'An American guy. Seth. He's looking for his sister, Savannah. She stayed here when The Surf House first opened its doors.' Bea watches Elin, interested to read her expression – but it remains neutral. 'D'you know her?'

Elin pushes her hands into the pockets of her wide-legged shorts, gaze on the disappearing form of Seth. 'Yeah. I know Savannah.'

ONE YEAR EARLIER

SAVANNAH

It was getting dark, and the straps of Savannah's backpack were cutting into her bare shoulders. *How far away could the next town be?*

A tired-looking RV came fast around the bend. From the German numberplates and functional exterior, she hoped to spot a retired couple sitting upfront. She stuck out her thumb.

As the vehicle slowed, she saw a girl her sort of age behind the wheel. She had bright blue hair and looked squat in the hulking vehicle. 'Where ya' goin'?' she called through the open window in a broad New Zealand accent.

Savannah said, 'Wherever you are.'

The blue-haired girl considered her for a long moment. Then shrugged. 'Get in.'

The girl introduced herself as Elin. She was twenty-five. Had been travelling solo through Europe for six months. She drove with one elbow on the armrest and a bag of potato chips between her knees.

Stuffing a handful of chips into her mouth, she cut straight to the chase: 'What's your story?'

When Savannah only shrugged, Elin glanced at her, taking in

the long blonde hair, those tiny shorts and slender, tanned legs. She ventured, 'Cheerleader on the wrong side of the tracks?'

Savannah tipped back her head and laughed. 'Got tired of life on the sidelines. Traded my pompoms for a backpack.'

Elin grinned.

'What about you?' Savannah asked. 'Why did you leave New Zealand?'

'Not much for me at home. Small town. Small minds. Needed out. My flavour isn't for everyone.'

Savannah looked at her sideways, taking in the tattoos, the spike through her nose, that bright blue hair springing from her head.

'Left New Zealand six months ago, bought the RV in Germany. I'm headed for Morocco. Run to the sun.'

That wasn't a country she often heard mentioned on the travellers' circuit. 'What's in Morocco?'

'Sunshine. Waves. Desert. Mountains.'

'Sounds good.'

'Sure does.'

They drove for a couple more hours, talking, listening to music, swapping stories about the worlds they were glad to leave behind. Savannah gave Elin the headlines on her family: a father who prioritised business above affection and an older brother who had a penchant for dragging Savannah out of parties. By her hair.

Elin whistled. 'And I thought my family were fucked up.'

It was about midnight when Elin began to yawn. She said, 'I can drop you in the nearest town, or . . .' She hesitated, her ballsy tone uncertain for the first time. '. . . You could crash in the RV. There's a spare bed overhead.' She raised a fist and knocked at the cavity above her.

Savannah didn't fancy trying to find somewhere to stay at this time of night, and Elin didn't seem much like she'd murder her while she slept. She admired her for having her shit sorted: a vehicle, a ferry ticket, an adventure waiting. 'I'll take the bed.'

They found a good pull-in off the main drag. Elin threw together some noodles, which they ate at her laminate table, pouring box wine into plastic glasses and talking about travelling and adventures and all the good things they hoped lay ahead.

The next morning, Savannah made strong coffee, and they sat on the step of the RV, early sun on their unwashed faces.

'So, Morocco,' Savannah said. 'Want company?'

Elin turned and smiled at Savannah like she'd been hoping she'd ask.

16

It's still dark when Bea wakes. She checks her watch. Five thirty a.m. The Surf House is silent. She goes to the window and opens it wide.

Odd.

She cannot hear breaking waves. She waits, listening, wondering if the forecast was wrong.

She notices that the light is on in Seth's studio and wonders what he's doing at this hour.

She is considering going back to bed when she hears a deep, distant boom. From the window, she sees the dark water turn white. The building seems to vibrate as another wave breaks and then another, a set marching to the shore.

Excitement fires in her veins. She pulls on her clothes, leaves her room, and heads to the van.

Ped is loading boards in the dark, an anticipatory energy humming from him. Marnie is already in the cab, fiddling with the radio. Seeing Bea, she slides over, patting the space beside her. Bea clambers in.

As Ped climbs in on the driver's side, he halts, noticing Bea. He looks from her to Marnie.

'Bea's coming,' Marnie tells him with a smile, but her tone makes it clear there's no room for discussion.

*

First light arrives as a blush of pink on the horizon. Ped swings the van wide to avoid a loose boulder as they follow a rough track towards the sea.

Marnie sits forward, eyes on the water. From this distance, it's impossible to tell the size or scale of the waves.

After parking up, Ped cuts the engine, and the three of them climb out.

There's no beach, just a long dark shelf of rock that falls away to the water. The sea looks bruised and churning.

They walk to the edge of the rock and stand together in silence, watching. It's minutes before the first set rolls in and, when it does, it's like an army of waves lining up on the horizon. They look thunderous and wild as they rear into solid walls.

Marnie plants her hands on her hips and whistles.

'I've never seen it breaking like this,' Ped says, and Bea can hear the awe in his voice.

'What are you thinking?' Marnie asks.

Ped focuses hard, hands tucked under his arms, lips pushed out as he considers the water. He's silent for a long time. Then he says, 'It's going to get too hollow at low. Won't hold its shape. Now's the time.'

The anticipation is infectious, and Bea's stomach churns with it.

At the van, Ped takes out his board, waxing it thoroughly, tightening the fins, checking the leash. Once he's in his wetsuit, he moves through a series of stretches, circling his arms at shoulder height, then twisting from a crouch position to standing. Each movement is focused and aligned with his breath. After that, he focuses solely on breathwork, inhaling deeply and taking long, slow exhales.

Behind them comes the roar of an engine. The three of them turn to see dust billowing as a truck comes speeding down the track: Aiden's.

Ped's shoulders tense.

Marnie places a hand gently on Ped's forearm. 'He was always going to come.'

Aiden pulls up beside the van in a blare of music. He yanks the key from the ignition and climbs out barefoot. His gaze moves from Ped to Marnie, acknowledging them with a nod. When his eyes find Bea, he holds her gaze.

She remembers that first night when they met on the cliff top, Aiden emerging from the sea, his skin wet and licked silver in the moonlight. There was a stillness about him, something grounded, as if the bay at night had settled him. As he looks at her now, she feels the heat in his gaze and a different anticipatory energy burning from him.

Aiden blinks, and his focus moves beyond her to the water. 'Teeth is on?'

'Looks like it,' Ped says. 'Sure you're up to it?'

Aiden just laughs. He slides his board from the back of his truck, checks his leash, then pulls on his wetsuit.

Ped takes a long drink of water, then hooks his board under his arm. As he's striding towards the rocky edge, Aiden, already suited, jogs past him.

Ped gives him the finger.

Marnie shakes her head. 'Children, both of them.'

Bea and Marnie climb the van ladder onto the roof for the best view. They have binoculars, a blanket, a flask of coffee, and cake.

They watch as Aiden and Ped launch from the rocks. The men time it between sets, jumping in with their boards and paddling hard to make it away from the rocks and into the safety of the channel.

Marnie edges closer to Bea and pulls the blanket over their bare legs. It's still early, dawn light tingeing the water peach.

At first, the sea appears calm, almost serene, as it swells and ebbs, no waves in sight. Then Bea notices a set rolling in. The first wave rises from the ocean like an enormous blue beast, as if the very ocean were lifting off the sea bed. Behind it, other waves march, a set of six or seven that break as they hit a submerged shelf. The men stay in the deeper water at the edge of the channel, letting the waves pass.

'Why's this spot called Teeth?' Bea asks.

'The first person to surf here got his teeth knocked out on the reef.'

Bea winces.

'Just as easy to have an accident in small conditions. Ped pulled in a surfer at Mallah on a waist-high day. Needed a dozen stitches to his face.'

'Would you go out in these conditions?'

'The rush of adrenalin that Ped and Aiden are searching for – the feeling that if they get it wrong, it's their life on the line – they need it. My rush is from a perfectly shaped wave, cutting a line on instinct, pushing my own edge. Like all the wise women have said before me, *it's not the size that matters, it's what you do with it.*'

Bea laughs.

She pictures how she must look in this moment, sitting on the roof of a van in Morocco with Marnie, skin bare of make-up, the fresh salt breeze thickening her hair into waves. It's hard to believe her previous life was hers at all.

Her thoughts flash towards the money she's yet to find – but she wrestles them back to the van's rooftop, reminding herself that right now, there is no Momo. No Marrakesh alleyway. There are waves and sunshine and banana cake and good coffee. That's where her attention needs to stay.

'Here we go,' Marnie says, straightening as Aiden paddles for the first wave of the day.

Bea watches, rapt. Aiden paddles with clean, calm strokes, then springs to his feet. Behind him, the wave keeps on growing and growing, until it is several times the size of him. He glides down its face, cutting a powerful line with his board. His stance is wide, low. The curl of the wave's lip holds tons of water as it chases him down – but Aiden keeps out in front, pulling off the back at the final moment before it explodes into a bomb of whitewater.

Bea lets out the breath she's been holding.

Eyes on the water, Marnie says, 'There's something instinctive about Aiden's surfing – an intuitiveness. You're aware you are watching something raw.'

'He looks fearless out there.'

'That's the problem. Wears his safety too lightly.'

'Does anyone else surf this spot?'

'A group of locals have been surfing it for years – but everyone keeps it quiet. No cameras. No social media. Ped and Aiden discovered it on our first winter here. They'd been studying the charts. Had a hunch there'd be a wave.'

'They used to be good friends?'

Marnie reaches for the flask. 'Like brothers.' She unscrews the lid, and the smell of strong coffee fills the dawn air. She pours the steaming liquid into two enamel mugs and hands one to Bea.

Bea brings it to her lips and takes a sip. It's warm, bitter, and strong. 'Why did they fall out? Because of the studio?'

'Partly.' Marnie keeps her gaze on the water and doesn't expand.

Bea wants to ask more, but Marnie is sitting forward, coffee set aside as she pulls the binoculars to her nose. 'Jesus. Look at this set.'

Bea stares as the biggest set of the morning bowls towards land.

'They're both going for it,' Marnie whispers.

Bea watches as the men paddle towards the point where they think the first wave's going to break. She hopes one of them will pull back; they have to. The etiquette in surfing is that the person nearest the peak or on their feet first gets priority.

Ped is closest to the peak, Aiden slightly out in front – but they both get to their feet at the same time and are dropping down the face at bullet speed. Ped is coming up fast behind Aiden.

The smooth face of the wave seems to stretch, flex, and then a bubbling section of water is revealed in front of Aiden.

'No!' Marnie cries, as Aiden hits the chop.

His board skitters out from beneath him, and he's sent cartwheeling across the surface of the wave, before being sucked up and over the falls.

Ped manages to miss the flying board but compromises his position and is hit by the lip of the wave. He's slammed into the pit, both men and boards pushing through the rolling water beneath.

As the wave surges towards the rocks, it sucks up all the water in its path, and Bea sees the black spine of the exposed reef as the water shallows sickeningly.

Binoculars trained to the water, Marnie's voice is a whisper. 'I can't see them . . .'

101

17

The sea is a blizzard of white, charging into the rocks and kicking spray high into the air, before being sucked back out in a turbulent frenzy.

Bea stands on the van's roof beside Marnie, who grips the binoculars to her face. Her lips move in a whisper of a prayer that holds only one word. *Please . . . please . . . please . . .*

Aiden and Ped crashed in the impact zone, the most dangerous and turbulent section. They need to get to the channel, where the water is deepest and the waves don't break.

The next set of waves rolls in from the horizon, an army of watery giants that will not withdraw.

Bea glimpses a flash of something white – and points to it. 'What's that?'

Marnie focuses on it with her binoculars. 'Ped's board . . .' she says, voice thinned with fear. 'Leash must have snapped.'

They're both silent as they scan the sea.

Suddenly, Marnie's hand shoots out. 'There! Ped!' He's swimming towards the channel but, behind him, the first wave of the set is approaching. She hears Marnie's intake of breath as it walls up.

Ped must see it, too, because he fills his lungs with air and then dives deep beneath the breaking wave. He is down for long seconds, and Bea just catches a glimpse of him surfacing before the next wave charges.

Again, he is lost in the froth and turbulence of whitewater. When they next catch sight of him, he has been pushed into the safety of the channel.

Marnie clambers down the van's ladder, Bea following, and they race barefoot towards the rocks. Marnie is fast and agile, the muscles in her calves pronounced as she runs. She stations herself at the point Ped and Aiden launched.

Seeing her, Ped seems to find renewed energy, and he swims hard towards the rocks.

'Where's Aiden?' Bea resets her vision, squinting hard against the glare of the sun.

'There,' Marnie says, pointing.

Bea spots Aiden lying across his board. He's not moving. He's still in the impact zone, and although there is a lull between sets, it won't last long. She watches as Aiden slides his legs off the surfboard and begins to kick.

Bea knows that you don't kick on a surfboard. You paddle.

Ped, who is almost at the rocks, turns to look for Aiden now and must see him struggling.

'Help him!' Bea cries.

Ped treads water, watching.

Aiden's progress is torturously slow, and he barely manages to improve his position against the pull of the current.

Bea's teeth press into her lower lip as she wills Aiden to hurry. But after another few kicks, he seems to give up. On the horizon, Bea spots the next set coming.

She is about to yell to Ped, but he is already moving – swimming hard in Aiden's direction.

His strokes are fast and powerful, and when he reaches Aiden, he grabs the nose of his board and begins dragging him towards the channel. Both men see the approaching set as it storms in.

Bea reaches for Marnie's hand, and their fingers twine together, squeezing hard. Neither of them speaks as they watch the men – two small dots in the ocean – stroking towards the channel.

They must get lucky and catch a rip, because their progress picks up. Moments before the first wave of the set comes hollering into the impact zone, they're washed into the safety of the channel.

As the men get closer to the rocks, Bea can see that Aiden's right arm hangs limply and a swirl of blood washes over the surface of the board. Her stomach roils.

Ped helps to swim Aiden to the rocks. Aiden reaches out with his good arm and finds a nook to hold – but a surge of whitewater roars in behind him, slamming him hard into the rockface. As the sea draws back out, the backwash sucks Aiden with it.

'No!' Bea cries, as Aiden disappears beneath the surface.

Marnie's hand grips harder to hers, clammy palms meshed. The next surge of water shoulders Aiden back onto the rocks.

Bea hears a roar of pain as his injured arm is slammed into granite.

'Grab on!' Ped yells.

With his good arm, Aiden reaches for the rocks and pins himself to them, his face a mask of pain. He clings on with a steel-like grip while the water recedes around him, and then he scrambles his way up to the plateau where Bea and Marnie wait.

Aiden collapses, his skin pale, breathing shallow. The right arm of his wetsuit has been shredded on the reef, revealing bloodied, torn skin. There's something about the slump of his body and the sight of fresh blood that sends a sharp spike of memory through Bea's thoughts, splitting her open.

Marnie begins unzipping Aiden's wetsuit to look at the severity of the injury. 'Shit!' she cries as the reduction in pressure means the wound begins to pump out blood. 'I need a tourniquet!'

Bea only stares, lips parted, barely breathing.

'Your T-shirt!' Marnie instructs.

Bea blinks. *Tourniquet. T-shirt.* She hears each word clearly, but she can't make sense of them. She's trapped in the alleyway.

But instead of seeing a bloodied knife on the ground, she sees Aiden's surfboard. The sight of it pulls her back into this moment.

Tourniquet. Aiden needs a tourniquet to stem the blood.

Suddenly, she is alert, pulling her T-shirt over her head. She crouches at Aiden's side in her bikini top and wraps the T-shirt tightly above the wound.

'Good,' Marnie says.

Ped, who has now climbed out of the sea, says, 'He needs the hospital.'

Marnie and Ped help Aiden to his feet. Ped hooks his arm around Aiden's waist and helps him stagger back to the vehicles, Bea carrying his surfboard.

When they reach the truck, Aiden attempts to open the driver's door.

'There's no way you're driving yourself,' Marnie says.

'I'll do it,' Bea says.

Marnie eyes her. 'You sure?'

She nods.

Marnie throws her a spare T-shirt, which she pulls on. Then Bea climbs into the driver's seat of Aiden's truck and adjusts the mirror. She's never driven a truck before. Never driven in a foreign country. Never driven with a man who is in danger of bleeding out in the front seat.

She takes a steely breath, then turns the key in the ignition.

18

Bea sits in the hospital waiting area. The air is warm and smells of medical supplies and sweat. A ceiling fan wafts the thick air around. Beside her, a Moroccan woman in a heavy black skirt rocks in her seat as she hums.

Bea's been here for hours and wonders when she's going to hear news.

'Hey.'

She glances up.

Aiden is standing in front of her, his right arm bandaged from above the elbow. His face looks pale, washed out. His gaze is squarely on her, unsmiling. 'You waited.'

She nods.

He continues to stare, his expression stony – and it is impossible to tell how he's feeling.

'What did the doctor say?'

'To stay on land for a while.'

She knows that'll be a blow. 'I'm sorry.'

'I don't deserve sympathy,' he says, his voice low, contrite. 'I was an idiot out there.'

She thinks of the way Ped and Aiden were squaring up to one another, something uncoiling in the surf.

'Your truck is parked outside. I'll drive you back.'

He nods, eyes down. 'Thanks.'

Bea likes being behind the wheel of the truck as the road bounces beneath them. The sun is setting, and the coast road is quiet and winding.

The dash is littered with earplugs, spare fins, a nub of surf wax, a lidless biro, and a paperback. The grooves of the seats are dusted with sand, which is irritating the backs of her thighs. An album of Aiden's plays, a rock band she doesn't know; when it finishes, the truck falls silent.

Aiden sits beside her, the gear stick between them, his window down. He keeps his gaze on the road and says nothing. She is very aware of the proximity of his body in the enclosed space. She can smell the fading scent of suncream on his skin and an antiseptic tang from the hospital, but there's something else, too – a deeper, earthy musk.

The quiet between them seems to grow, suddenly looming heavy and weighted, so that the size of it overtakes the space of the truck, and she feels compelled to speak, to say something.

'What was going on in the water between you and Ped?'

There's a pause before he answers. 'Clash of horns.'

She waits for more, but Aiden turns to look out the window. 'Marnie said you were good friends, once,' she tries.

He lifts his good arm, rubbing the back of his neck. She sees the tanned stretch of his forearm, the muscular sweep of his bicep. 'I guess.'

'I heard Ped built the Surf Studio, and it's blocked the view from Offshore.'

He blows out air through his nostrils. 'Ped takes what he wants.'

107

Again, the silence. There is so much more she wants to understand about Aiden.

They drive on in silence, dusk fading into night.

'Headlights,' he says at some point.

She finds them and flicks them on.

'The turning's coming up.'

She sees it in the semi-dark, a boulder on the side of the road reading *Mallah*. She indicates and turns onto the track. Dust flies up in ghostly clouds, and she takes the bumpy track slowly. If the jolting causes Aiden any pain, he doesn't let on.

The lights of the village come into focus. 'Where do you want me to park?'

'There's space at the back of the hostel.'

She follows his instructions, finding a quiet spot to pull in. She kills the engine, and the truck falls into darkness.

Aiden makes no move to get out.

Neither does she.

'Thank you,' he says, eventually. 'For waiting at the hospital. Driving me back.' His tone has softened, and she hears the warmth of his Irish accent.

'You know you owe me a T-shirt, right?'

He looks at her.

'The tourniquet,' she supplies.

'You used your T-shirt.' He stares at her, eyes drifting briefly over her body. Then he says slowly, 'I remember.'

She feels warmth in her cheeks.

Aiden twists around, reaching into the backseat with his good arm. He produces a T-shirt. 'As seen at New York fashion week.' The T-shirt unrolls to reveal a wave with the word *Offshore* pulling out of the barrel.

'Is it couture?' she asks, deadpan.

'That's all I design.'

She smiles and takes the T-shirt and folds it on her lap, the cotton smooth against her bare thighs.

He watches her movements carefully. After a beat he asks, 'Why d'you stop? Modelling?'

She pauses to think about his question. Bea may not have chosen modelling, but she did learn to do her job well. She understood what clients were looking for, translating it into how to behave in front of a camera. She would be peppy or sultry or vivacious or imperious – an expert in shaping herself into the image they wanted.

She distils her answer down to a single truth. 'It was making me unhappy.'

'I'm sorry.'

She is, too. 'I think you need to love it. Really, really love it. It's a competitive industry. There's always someone waiting to take your place. The money was good. I liked the travel – never minded being away from home – but . . . I just . . .' *What was it?* She knew lots of models who were passionate about the industry and who grew in confidence with each job. But Bea felt like every shoot took something from her, depleted her. 'I never felt like I belonged.'

It's a strange thing to admit. She's not sure it even makes sense. She looks at Aiden, and he's watching her closely, his expression open, interested.

She lowers her gaze and sees how close her hand is to Aiden's – just an inch between them. She studies his hand, which is wide and tanned, fingernails cut short. Veins run like darkened rivers across the back of his hand, disappearing into his forearm.

They are both silent. The air in the truck is sucked away. Then, slowly, Aiden moves his hand closer, sliding it slowly over the top of hers, until his hand covers hers.

His touch is like a wild heat. She cannot take her eyes off their hands. She turns hers, so their palms meet.

She's aware of the press of each of his fingers, feels the slide of them against her own. Slowly, he moves his thumb over her wrist, tracing the soft underside where tiny blue veins run.

He looks up then, right at her, and she meets his gaze, holding it.

'I . . .' he begins.

She waits.

He tries again. 'You . . .'

Then he gives up on words. He leans forward, presses his lips to hers.

The kiss says, *I shouldn't*. But there is also desperation, hunger, release. It feels like a thousand words.

And it feels like one word.

Want.

They both want this.

His lips are warm and soft. Every nerve ending is alive with his touch. It's like a door has opened inside her, and there is a level of pleasure that exists – a whole room of it – and she wants to live in that room. Her body responds to him on a primal, intuitive level, the way her throat stretches, her back arches, her mouth makes a low hum of desire.

And then just as suddenly, he is drawing back, lowering his gaze, eyes on their hands, which are still entwined. 'I'm sorry. I shouldn't have done that.' He removes his hand. 'I'm not in a great place . . . I should . . .'

'Oh,' is all she says, face on fire.

Aiden twists in his seat to open the door with his good arm, throwing it wide onto the night.

She climbs out, too. She glances at Aiden, but he won't meet her eye. Not knowing what else to do, she begins to walk away.

'Bea?'

She halts. Alert. Waiting . . . wanting . . .

She turns, facing him.

'My truck keys.'

Oh. The disappointment stings. She still has them in her hand and carries them back to him.

As she reaches to pass the keys, his fingers catch hers. For a moment, he holds them there, his eyes pinning her, like he is deciding something. A long moment stretches out. She feels the heat of his fingers and her own pulse in her throat.

Then Aiden blinks and releases her hand, dragging his gaze away.

Her hand swings emptily to her side.

19

Three days pass, and Bea doesn't see Aiden. She has been to the cliff top every night – but there will be no night surfing with his injured arm. She asks herself over and over how Aiden could kiss her like that – like his whole being was filled with heat and longing – and then walk away. It makes no sense to her body, which feels as if it has been electrified, as if there is a new charge in her veins, and she cannot settle to anything.

Today, there's no surf, so she walks into the village to keep herself occupied. Salty joins, trotting at her side. Occasionally, she dips her hand to his head and feels the soft velvet of his ears.

Her path takes her in a loop around the harbour, passing painted wooden boats where the fishermen are pulling in the day's catch. She takes a left down an alleyway where the narrow homes are painted in various shades of blue. Locals sit with their wares spread on blankets – ornate wooden boxes, woven hats, an array of colourful ceramics. Bea smiles and says hello to the people she recognises from her daily walks to the village.

Her phone pings in her pocket with a notification. She pulls it out and sees it's an email about her loan application.

Her stomach instantly knots. Everything hangs on this.

Bea steps out of the throng of people, anchoring herself to a wall as she opens the email and reads.

We regret to inform you that your loan application has not been approved.

No. No. No.

The loan was her lifeline.

She tips back her head, hair snagging against the brick wall. Now what? There are other loan companies, but they all do the same eligibility checks.

She has only eight days left to find $5,000. A hot, panicky feeling engulfs her. She wants to escape. Get on a plane. Fly home. But she's trapped here. She has no passport and no way of leaving the country—

'Bea?'

She swings around and finds Seth staring at her.

He pushes his sunglasses up onto his head, stepping nearer. 'What's happened?'

She glances at her phone, still open on the email. 'I was rejected for a loan,' she says, unable to think of anything but the fact.

Seth looks like he isn't sure what to do with the information. After a long pause, he says, 'Maybe you could ask for a pay rise? I had a slice of your lemon cake. Based on that, I'd say you deserve it.'

She manages a flicker of a smile.

'I'm going for a drink. Let me buy you one. Maybe I can help.'

Bea doesn't particularly want Seth's company – yet her throat is dry, and she can feel a tension headache burning behind her

113

eyes. The thought of a cold drink beats going back to her room alone, so she finds herself saying, 'Okay.'

Bea sits at a plastic table shaded by a fraying sun umbrella. Salty crawls quietly beneath her legs. He finds a forgotten crust of bread on the ground and eats it delicately.

Bea orders a Coke, which arrives a few minutes later in an ice-cold glass bottle with a red straw. She takes a long drink, the syrupy, sweet bubbles instantly refreshing her. Her head is whirring, and she is grateful for a seat, the shade, an iced drink.

Seth sips from a bottle of mineral water, watching her.

Searching for something to say, she asks, 'How are you finding Mallah?'

'Not sure I've got a handle on the place yet. It's a little rough around the edges. If you like surfing, I guess I can see the draw.'

'There's a real community here,' she defends. 'People who fell in love with the place – and stayed.'

'Those are the people I need to talk to,' he says. 'People who've been here a while and remember Savannah.'

There's an intensity about Seth that borders on desperation. She wants to offer him something, so says, 'Driss and Farah were staying at The Surf House at the same time as Savannah. They live in Marrakesh but come here regularly on weekends. I can introduce you. They're back in a couple of days.'

'That'd be helpful.' He takes a sip of mineral water and asks, 'What about the guy who owns the hostel next door?'

'Aiden?'

Seth nods. 'What's he like?'

'I barely know him,' Bea says, picking up her drink.

She can feel Seth watching her. He says, 'What do you make of Marnie and Ped?'

The question feels intrusive, as if Seth is poking, looking to find a crack. 'Marnie is great. Fun. Warm. Passionate about The Surf House.'

'And Ped?' Seth asks, his gaze holding hers.

She hesitates. 'I've not spent much time with him . . .'

'But?' he prompts.

'He . . . he can be a little reticent.'

Seth leans back in his chair, his expression thoughtful, as if there is a subtext that interests him.

Bea fixes her gaze on the waterline, where fishermen are pulling in their boats. A tractor drags each of the boats out of the water onto a narrow strip of sand where the catch is unloaded. The fishermen talk easily as they lug huge buckets of fish up to the wet market, the briny scent filling the air.

With surprising directness, Seth asks, 'What size loan were you looking for?'

Bea hesitates for a moment. '$5,000.'

'Not sure you'll pay that off working at The Surf House.'

She shrugs.

He continues to look at her. His fingers steeple together as if he's making a silent calculation. Then he leans forward, eyes suddenly bright. 'Find my sister and I'll pay you double.'

She laughs, but Seth doesn't.

He moves aside his glass of mineral water, rests his forearms on the table, palms down. 'I'm serious.'

'Why would I have any more luck finding her than you?'

'Maybe you won't,' he says. 'But you know people here. You can ask the right questions.' He pauses, linking his fingers together. 'I get the feeling some people are filtering what they say to me.'

Bea watches him steadily, wondering if his instinct might be right.

115

'I'll give you $10,000 if you find Savannah,' he confirms.

All her money worries would vanish. 'What if Savannah doesn't want to be found?'

His eyes glitter. 'Then you'll have really earned your money.'

Bea glances over her shoulder towards the cliff line, where The Surf House stands in the distance. There's a sticky feeling in her gut. Disloyalty?

'So?' he asks.

She thinks about the money she still owes Momo – and her lack of means to pay it.

'I take half upfront. The rest on delivery.'

'Nice try.' He smiles. 'I'll give you $1,000 upfront. And another $2,000 each time you bring me a solid lead. Remainder on delivery.'

She hears the businessman in him and thinks, *Here is a man used to getting his own way.*

Seth stretches his hand across the table.

Bea stares at the pale offering of his palm. With the upfront payment, all she needs is two leads and she'll have the $5,000 for Momo. It's an opportunity – her only one.

Bea feels Seth's smooth fingers seal around hers as they shake hands.

'And Bea? We keep this between ourselves.'

20

'This is my sister,' Seth says, sliding a black leather notebook in front of Bea.

They've returned to The Surf House and are now sitting in his studio. The notebook is open on a picture of Savannah, who is lifting a sunbeam-printed beach blanket high above her head. The fabric billows in the breeze, and her blonde hair trails over tanned shoulders. She wears a daisy-shaped ring on her index finger, which catches in the sunlight. Bea is struck by Savannah's bright-green eyes and her wide smile that is edging towards laughter.

She glances sideways at Seth. He and Savannah share the same blond hair and eye colour, but Seth's features are narrower, a permanent furrow between his brows. She wonders how close they were growing up and whether their relationship shifted in adulthood.

'Tell me what you know so far,' Bea asks.

Seth links his hands together, his cuticles neat and pink. Soft hands that are used to tapping a keyboard.

'When Savannah turned twenty-three, she was given access to a trust fund. She'd just left college and taken a job in the family business, and our dad figured she'd put the money towards an apartment. Instead, she quit work and bought a plane ticket to Europe.' There's a faint smile on his lips as he says, 'It didn't go down well.' Bea wonders if he secretly admires her impulsiveness.

'She sent me the odd message telling me what she was up to, but mostly I kept up with her from Instagram.'

Seth takes out his phone, scrolls for a moment, and then turns the screen towards Bea. It's Savannah's Instagram page, paused on an image of her grinning on a beach. In the background, there's a man in a djellaba leading a camel along the shoreline. The caption below says simply, *Guess where I am?!* 'That's how I found out she was in Morocco.'

Seth goes on. 'So, she arrives in Morocco in August last year – slightly over a year ago. If her Instagram is to be believed, she loved it here.' He looks out through the open balcony doors as if he's trying to understand what that magic may be. There's nothing disparaging in his attitude – it's as if he cannot quite connect with what his sister would have found here.

'Back home, Savannah was used to living in a big house in the hills – and then she comes out here and is roughing it in a van. It would have appealed to her – sticking a finger up to the rest of us.' He smiles a little. 'When our dad heard she had no plans to return home, he closed down the trust fund, thinking it'd make her come back.'

'Only it didn't,' Bea says.

'Correct. She stays – but she's pissed now. Blames me. So, we had a fight. Proper showdown. She's good at those. And then Savannah cuts me out, too.'

As Bea listens, she wonders if this is the full narrative – or whether Seth is curating their history.

'Next thing, Savannah emails Rachel – that's her best friend back home, lived next door to us growing up – telling her she's

118

going offline. Says that her family aren't good for her head.' Seth turns through the pages of his black leather notebook, showing print-outs of emails to this friend, Rachel. 'So that's what Savannah does. Gets rid of her phone. Cuts contact with everyone. It was dramatic, yes, but not out of character. Savannah thrives on the big gesture.' He sighs. 'We figured she needed to be her own person for a while. She'd work it out and come back to us.'

Seth's eyes lower for a moment. 'Only she didn't come back. And then, our dad . . . he got sick.'

There's a shift in Seth's demeanour. He closes the notebook and brings his hands closer to his body. His back stiffens, as if he's trying to fend off an unwelcome emotion.

'He wanted to see Savannah before he died – but we couldn't get in contact with her. Rachel tried. I tried. Dad tried. But there's no working email address. Her phone was disconnected. She's off socials. She's a fucking ghost. You know how difficult it is to find out where a passport has been last stamped?' He shakes his head.

'And the police?' Bea asks.

'The police in the US aren't interested because she's not on US soil. And the police over here . . .' He opens his palms. 'There's been no crime. I can't even say if she's definitely still in the country.'

'Have you tried the embassy?'

'I've got a meeting with an official tomorrow. I'm not convinced it'll turn the dial. Without firm evidence that Savannah's in Morocco, what will they do?'

'Are you sure she is still here?'

'Honestly? No. There's no border control with Western Sahara. Anyone can drive in and out. It's possible she went off with those Dutch girls Marnie mentioned.'

'So, the last anyone heard of her was when?'

'Late October last year. Marnie checked the bookings folder, and Savannah's final night here was October 26th – the same day she emailed Rachel. Marnie said there was a beach party that night everyone went to. The next day, she's picked up by these mystery Dutch girls, and then she's gone.'

'No more contact?'

'None. Her phone's disconnected.'

'What about money? Have you looked at her bank accounts?'

He nods again. 'On October 27th, her credit card is used for the last time. She withdraws all her money – $11,700 – in an oasis town in the desert called Ezril. It's consistent with the plan that she's headed for the border. But what I don't like is that she apparently gets in a van with these two girls she barely knows, withdraws all her money – and then, just like that, she disappears.' He makes a light *puff* sound, as if Savannah has disappeared like a magician's trick.

Bea has been listening closely, processing all the information. 'What are you thinking?' Seth asks.

What she hears is a story of someone who is impulsive and wild and has chosen to disconnect from family and friends, from social media, from society. 'I'm sorry, Seth, but it sounds like she doesn't want to be found.'

'That's one interpretation.' He leans forward. 'But what if there's another?'

'Is there?'

'Why hasn't she been seen since? Why hasn't she been in contact once? How has she funded her travels?'

'$11,700 could keep her going for a year if she budgeted carefully.'

'It could – but why take it out in one go?'

'So there's no trace.'

'And why wouldn't she want a trace?'

'Was she in trouble, maybe?'

He shrugs. 'Yes. No. I can't tell you. Savannah invites trouble wherever she goes. Seeks it out. But here's the other thing,' he says, a building intensity in his expression. 'The money in her account was nothing to do with the trust fund. It came from three separate deposits made during her time in Morocco. Two banks in Marrakesh and another in Essaouira. How does someone earn that much money in Morocco when they don't even have a working visa?'

He pauses, letting that settle.

Bea would like to know the answer to that question for her own reasons. She also sees that these deposits throw shadow over Savannah's disappearance. Seth is right to be asking questions. 'What's your plan?'

'I don't have much of one beyond starting at the last knot in the thread and seeing where it takes me.'

'Which means what?'

'Savannah was in Mallah. There's no question there. There are photos of her here. Plenty of people who've met her. Those two Dutch girls she disappeared with are the key, but no one seems to know who they are or how to contact them. I'm wondering, did they know about Savannah's money? Is that why they invited her on the road with them? Did they encourage her to go offline, leave no trace – because they had an end goal?'

'We should start with the van community,' Bea suggests. 'There's a group of them parked up on the cliff front at the edge of the village.'

He nods. 'I'm interested to find out more about a girl called Elin. She's the one who picked up Savannah, brought her to

Morocco. They shared an RV for a month. That's intimate, intense. They'd have talked about things, shared stuff. But then Savannah ducks out and moves into The Surf House. Why?'

'She wanted more space?'

'Or did Elin chuck her out? Apparently, Elin's still knocking around Mallah.'

'Yeah, I know her. She heard you talking about Savannah in The Surf House the other night.' Bea hesitates, wondering whether to say more. She thinks of the handshake, their agreement. 'When Elin saw you, she looked . . . kind of uncomfortable. She came over. Asked me what you were doing here.'

'Interesting,' Seth says slowly. 'Would you talk to her? Keep it casual – nothing linked to me. Find out what she knows.'

Bea feels the $1,000 upfront fee stuffed in her pocket, warm against her thigh. She's accepted Seth's money – and now she must earn it.

ONE YEAR EARLIER

SAVANNAH

Savannah made a cushion of her arms and looked up at the wide blue sky. A vapour trail hung in the corner of her vision and reminded her of those days in California when she'd stare out through her bedroom window, see a plane leaving, and think: *Take me with you.*

She had done it. Left. Here she was. Morocco.

God, it was good to be away from that world. Her father's constant disappointment and quick temper. Seth following in his footsteps, always breathing down her neck. She needed space – and this was the place to find it.

She and Elin arrived three weeks ago, driving through the arid mountains and sprawling cities – and finally washing up at the coast in a little surf village called Mallah. There was nothing much here, but Elin was hooked on the waves and Savannah liked the relaxed, easy vibe and spending her days on the beach.

She rolled onto her front, propping herself up on her elbows, scanning the surf for Elin. She'd tried surfing a few times as a teen but could never get past her fear of being rumbled underwater. Other people surfaced from wipeouts exhilarated, like it was all part of the fun, but she preferred to be able to take a breath whenever she chose.

Elin was wading in, flanked by two surfers. The man, who had broad shoulders and a closely shaven head, turned and pointed towards the cliff line at a white two-storey building that stood on the edge.

The woman he was with – dark-haired and elfin-featured – reached forward and squeezed Elin's arm as she smiled. After a few moments, the man and woman walked off together – a couple, Savannah decided, judging from the way the backs of their hands brushed as they glided up the beach, their strides in rhythm.

Elin jogged back to Savannah, blue hair pasted to her scalp, eyes sparkling.

'Who were they?' Savannah asked.

'Marnie and Ped. He's an Aussie. She's British, I think. Incredible surfers. They've just finished building a guesthouse up on the cliff. They're having an opening party tonight. Asked if we wanted to come.'

Squinting against the sun, Savannah's gaze trailed back to the couple who were now ascending the cliff steps, sleek and athletic in their wetsuits.

'What d'you reckon? Wanna go party?'

A grin spread across Savannah's face. 'Always.'

Savannah wore her only dress, enjoying the brush of fabric against her bare ankles as she swept through The Surf House.

'This place is incredible,' Savannah said.

The space was pared back and minimal, with gorgeous pops of textiles and mosaics drawing the eye. A relaxed crowd of locals and surfers milled about in flip-flops and Birkenstocks, lounging on low sofas and clinking drinks on the terrace.

'Very on-brand crowd,' Elin commented with a hint of snarkiness.

Savannah spotted Marnie and Ped on the terrace and urged Elin to make the introductions. The girls were welcomed enthusiastically and handed cocktails in tall glasses.

'The day we signed the contract for the land,' Marnie told them, 'we took our mattress out of the van and laid it right there.' She pointed to the edge of the lounge. 'We slept beneath the stars, and God, we could feel it in our bones. How right this place was.'

'And then eighteen months of building nightmares and near-bankruptcy followed,' Ped added.

Marnie laughed. She interlaced her fingers through his. 'But we did it.'

'Luckily, we had these guys on the inside to help navigate our way,' Ped said, waving over a handsome young Moroccan couple, who he introduced as Driss and Farah.

The woman, Farah, kissed Savannah and Elin on both checks. Her skin smelled of argan oil, and she wore a stylish kaftan that fell to her ankles. 'We only helped so we'd have a place to stay,' she said with a wink.

'Our most esteemed guests,' Marnie said.

'It's incredible,' Driss marvelled, absorbing the view over the terrace as the sun lowered. 'You've turned rubble into gold.' He tipped his glass towards Marnie's and then Ped's. 'To The Surf House.'

They all raised their glasses and drank. Savannah felt the heady sensation of being out in a crowd, alcohol shimmering through her system.

Elin was standing so close at her shoulder that she could feel the nub of her elbow against her bare arm. Savannah took a small step back.

They were joined by a man who was introduced as Aiden,

an Irish surfer with shaggy dark hair who arrived with an eight pack of beer. He clapped hands with Ped, then hugged Marnie with his free arm.

'Won't be long till we're toasting Offshore,' Driss said.

'Dunno about that. We've still not got electrics.'

Marnie explained, 'Offshore is the hostel next door.'

Savannah had seen the bright-yellow building, its name painted on a surfboard and hung above the door.

'When are you hoping to open?' Savannah asked.

'Yesterday,' Aiden said with a smile. He slung an arm around Ped's shoulders. 'These guys are showing me up.'

'We found Mallah together,' Ped explained. 'Bought a plot of land and split it down the middle.'

Aiden talked about how the three of them had been travelling through Europe together, then came to Morocco, found this place, and decided to stay.

Savannah listened, entranced. Here was a group of friends building something beautiful that had purpose and meaning. 'I love it here,' she said, feeling the draw of this place.

Marnie smiled. 'If it gets too cramped in the RV, or you need a proper shower, you know where we are.'

'We're happy in the RV,' Elin said immediately. Her gaze swung to Savannah, an inquiry in her expression. 'Aren't we?'

21

When Bea arrives at Tazi Shisha that evening, Elin is sitting cross-legged on a floor cushion, wearing a pair of dungarees. Her blue hair is piled into a scrunchie, and she waves Bea over.

'You have exceedingly long legs,' Elin remarks as Bea folds her legs beneath her to sit opposite.

'I do,' Bea agrees.

'You smoked shisha before?'

Bea shakes her head. She looks around the space, which is lit by low lanterns, and sees travellers and local surfers sitting around ornate silver pots that have long blue hoses attached.

'It's like breathing a rainbow,' Elin says. She signals to the owner and places her order in French. To Bea, she adds, 'I've ordered us coffee. Moroccan tea rots your teeth.'

The shisha arrives on a circular wooden tray that is set on the low table between them. Elin explains that flavoured tobacco is heated over coals and then filtered through water. She demonstrates by sucking on the pipe, and Bea hears the water bubble lightly.

Elin passes her the second hose, and Bea takes a sip of flavoured air. Her mouth fills with cherry smoke. Her eyes water a little, although it's not unpleasant.

'I Googled you,' Elin says matter-of-factly.

'Okay.'

'Lots of photos of you on the internet.'

'There are,' Bea agrees, thinking this is the reason why she's never agreed to anything that involves nudity, because you don't know who you're going to be sitting cross-legged with in a shisha bar who may have Googled you.

'In one, you're wearing a red ballgown on the back of a horse.'

'Found out I was allergic to horses on that shoot.'

Elin's expression is bright with interest as she asks more questions about Bea's modelling, the countries she's travelled to, what it's like to stride down a catwalk.

When their coffees arrive, Bea takes a sip, preferring the bitter taste to the shisha. 'How long have you been in Morocco?'

'Just over a year.'

'Always in Mallah?'

'Mostly. When the rains arrive, I head off to the desert or the city. Mallah and rain don't mix. The tracks turn to mud. There's nowhere to eat. The surf drops out.'

Under the endless blue skies Bea's so far witnessed, it seems almost impossible to imagine the rains. She steers the conversation towards Savannah, saying, 'I was talking to Seth earlier – you know, the American guy who's looking for his sister?'

Elin nods, her expression remaining neutral.

'You and Savannah came to Morocco together, right?'

'Yeah, she lived in my RV for a while. You get to know someone pretty well in those close quarters.'

'What she's like?'

'Savannah? Spoiled. Loud. Self-obsessed.'

'So you liked her?'

128

Elin laughs. 'She's all those things – but she's also fun, impulsive. She's like this unstoppable whirlwind of energy.' There's light in Elin's eyes as she says, 'I've never seen Savannah do a single thing because she *should*. She goes after what she *wants*.'

Bea lets that description settle, turning the words *should* and *want* through her thoughts. She knows which she's been obedient to. Maybe she'd like to meet this girl who chases down her desires.

'We had a laugh for a while,' Elin goes on, 'but Savannah was only playin' at van life.'

'How do you mean?'

'She's a spoiled California kid at heart. Soon as The Surf House opened its doors, she was off.' She sighs. 'That lot up at The Surf House – they're the barefoot royalty of Mallah. Savannah got in with them, course. Even went up to Marrakesh a few times to visit Driss and Farah. Cast me off.' Elin does nothing to disguise the bitterness in her tone.

'Did you know the Dutch girls she left for Cape Town with?'

There's the smallest hesitation before Elin answers. 'They blew in for a couple of weeks in an old Bedford van. Savannah liked the idea of going overland to Cape Town – but she won't have made it all the way. Something bright and shiny will have caught her attention – and she'll have been off.' Elin takes another draw on the shisha. 'So big brother's come out here to track her down, has he?'

'Something like that. You don't know where she is, then?'

'No – and even if I did, I wouldn't tell him.'

Bea looks at her closely. 'No?'

'He's an arsehole. Savannah just wanted to be free of her family.'

Bea feels a prickle of unease and asks, 'Why, what did she say about them?'

Elin shrugs.

Bea waits, but Elin doesn't expand. She gets a shadowy sense that Elin knows more about Seth than she's letting on.

Bea changes track. 'When did you last see her?'

A fleeting look of discomfort travels across Elin's face. 'Night before she left with the Dutch girls.'

'There was some big beach party, right?'

'Yeah. Everyone from Mallah went. It was put on by a few guys who run a surf camp. Music, DJs, fire-eaters – that kind of thing. It was a little way up the coast at Jailors. Savannah was there. We all saw her that night.'

Bea notes the emphasis in *We ALL saw her*. 'And then, the day after the beach party, Savannah left with the Dutch girls?'

'I guess,' she says with a shrug.

Again, there is an off note. Before she has time to examine it, Elin is lifting a hand and waving. 'Aiden! Hey!'

Bea turns to see Aiden crossing the bar, one hand in the pocket of his shorts. She feels an instant warm flutter in her belly. When he spots Bea, he hesitates, as if deciding whether to come over or move on.

'Have shisha with us,' Elin calls, patting the floor cushion beside her.

He removes the hand from his pocket and rubs the back of his neck, exposing the gauze on his bicep. 'I'm just about to meet Yaz . . .'

'So hang with us until he's here.'

He glances at Bea, as if seeking her approval.

She nods.

As Aiden lowers himself down at their floor table, she catches the salt-earth scent of him and something sharper. Alcohol, she thinks.

'How's the injury?' Elin asks.

He glances at his arm. 'Getting there.'

Elin says to Bea, 'Heard you saw Aiden and Ped's wipeout?'

'Pretty spectacular.'

'Lessons learned and all that,' Aiden says.

'How long till you're back in the water?' Elin asks.

'About a week, I reckon.'

'Hey, d'you remember Savannah, who shacked up with me in the RV when we first came to Morocco?'

'Yeah.'

'Have you heard her brother's in town looking for her?'

He nods.

'You don't know whether she made it to Cape Town?'

He lifts and drops his shoulders. 'No idea.'

Bea can feel Aiden's discomfort at having to sit beside her, their knees almost touching. She glances at him and notes a glassiness to his gaze and wonders how much he's already drunk tonight.

On the table, Elin's phone begins to ring. 'Gotta get this. Big sister calling.' Elin springs to her feet and leaves the table.

Alone together, Bea and Aiden both speak at the same time. Bea says, 'You don't have to stay,' just as Aiden tells her, 'Thanks for driving me to hospital.'

There's an awkward silence.

Bea says, 'It's fine.'

His voice is low as he says, 'I'm . . . sorry about afterwards.'

She looks at him – the strong angle of his nose, the dark spray of lashes, his wide mouth. 'Sorry for kissing me? Or sorry for walking away?'

He doesn't lower his eyes but continues to look right at her.

The burn of attraction heats the air between them. Neither of them turns from it. Eyes on her, he answers, 'The latter.'

Heat moves through her body. She becomes keenly aware of how close their knees are, just inches between them. The noise and colour of the shisha bar recedes. His gaze lowers to her mouth. She sees him swallow.

Then suddenly, there's a large hand on Aiden's shoulder, startling them both.

A local surfer, Yaz, is pulling Aiden to his feet, embracing him. 'Good to see you, brother!'

Aiden claps him on the back, returning his greeting.

'I gotta steal this boy,' Yaz says to Bea. 'He promised me a date night.'

'Course,' Bea says.

Aiden throws Bea an apologetic smile as he's steered to the other side of the shisha bar.

Bea steps out into the cloudless, cool night, tugging the sleeves of her jumper over her hands.

She wishes she were still inside with Aiden. She can't remember a man ever filling her head the way he does. Maybe it's because he wants so little from her. He's not chasing her down or asking for anything. It's more like Aiden's trying to hold himself at a distance.

She passes a lantern-lit tearoom, where two travellers sit on low stools with a backgammon set between them. As she moves beyond them, she feels eyes following her.

She glances back and finds the travellers engaged in their game. She must have imagined it. Yet as she walks on, she can't shake the feeling that she's being watched. The sensation is like a prickling across the back of her neck. Her elbows pull tighter to her body, tension stiffening her spine.

132

A hot flush of fear washes through her body at the memory of Marrakesh, the footsteps of the men. Her instinct is to hurry on, shrink herself down – but then she remembers Marnie barrelling into that alleyway, yelling.

Bea makes herself stop. Turn.

Standing in the shadows of the tearoom, an older woman is watching her, expression cool. In the darkness, it takes Bea a few moments to recognise her.

Momo's mother.

As their eyes lock, Bea's heart rate flares.

Momo's mother stares for a beat longer, then turns and disappears inside.

In The Surf House, Bea pulls her bedroom door closed and stands with her back against it, pulse racing. She needs to get Momo's $5,000.

She takes a breath. Reminds herself that she already has $1,000 tucked away from Seth's initial cash payment, so now she only needs to be paid for bringing him two more leads on Savannah. Then she'll have the full amount.

This line of thinking calms her a little, and she goes to the window and pushes it open onto the night. The stars glitter over a darkened village. The evening call to prayer drifts from the local mosque, the low chant rhythmic and soothing.

There's a light knock at the connecting door, and Marnie enters. She joins Bea at the window, carrying on her skin the smell of freshly applied moisturiser. 'I've just seen Momo's mother in the village,' Bea confides.

'Did she speak to you?'

She shakes her head. 'She was watching me.'

'Ignore her. This is Momo's business.'

'We've only got eight more days to find the money – and my loan application was rejected this morning.'

Marnie's brow creases. 'Are there other banks you can try? Other loan companies?'

'Yes, but they all do similar eligibility checks. I've applied anyway.'

'Listen, The Surf House bookings are good this month. I could see how the accounts are looking. Try to keep some back. That could put a dent in it. We'll make this, okay? I promise you,' Marnie says, squeezing her hand.

Bea feels the warmth and reassurance in their joined fingers.

'What were you doing in the village?' Marnie asks.

'I went to the shisha bar with Elin.'

'Fun?'

'It was okay. Elin was talking about Savannah. Said she stayed in Elin's RV before moving into The Surf House.'

'That's right. I seem to remember the move being a sore point.'

'How come?'

'Elin can be a little ... possessive. Savannah was her discovery.'

Bea finds that comment interesting. 'Elin didn't have much good to say about Seth.' She pauses, then asks, 'What d'you make of him?'

Marnie thinks for a moment. 'Honestly? I can't get the measure of him. Savannah and I didn't talk about her family a whole lot, but I sensed there were tensions. She gave the impression that Seth could be controlling.'

A crawling heat travels up Bea's spine as she wonders if she's made the wrong decision getting involved with Seth. She hates keeping their agreement from Marnie and feels clammy with disloyalty.

'I've met a few people like him on my travels,' Marnie goes

on. 'Intense. Searching for something that isn't there. Sounds like he's been through a lot with losing his dad. I feel sorry for him, I do, but if Savannah doesn't want to be found, that's her choice.'

'So, you don't think Savannah *is* missing?'

'I don't know what went on, but before Savannah left for Cape Town, she went offline, got rid of her phone. She shed everything – her social media accounts, her contact with friends, her family. Her whole identity.'

Bea pictures the green-eyed girl sparkling in Seth's photo. Did she simply strip back everything that wasn't serving her? Start over afresh? Bea admires that kind of bravery.

'I can't help thinking,' Marnie continues, tone reflective, 'that if you're going to those lengths to leave your life behind, there must be someone in it to give you good reason.'

ONE YEAR EARLIER

SAVANNAH

Savannah was surprised to see Seth's name flash up on her cell.

'What's up?' she said, pressing the phone to her ear.

'Wondered how my little sister is getting on?'

'Having a ball.' She mouthed to Elin that she'd take this call elsewhere, then stepped out of the RV.

'I'm in Morocco,' Savannah told him.

'So I learned from the 'gram.'

Course he knew. He'd be keeping tabs on her social media. Not that he ever commented or liked any of her posts. 'A prowler, not a poster.'

'That's me,' he said. 'Still sleeping in an RV?'

'Sure am. It's the size of your en suite.'

'Lavish.'

Conversations always went like this. Sarcastic little pokes that built into an argument. Might as well cut to the chase. 'Gonna tell me why you're calling?'

'Dad and Courtney have set a date for their wedding. He wants you there.'

'One big happy family.'

Seth didn't respond to that. He went on, 'The wedding will be at Courtney's lake house. Dad's booked out the hotel next door. He's got you a room. It's in six weeks.'

'Christ, she doesn't hang around.' Their dad was marrying a woman from the tennis club who was only eight years older than Savannah. 'I won't be back by then.'

'You said you were travelling for three months. It's already been four.'

'You ticking off the days on your *I-miss-my-sis* calendar?'

Seth sighed. 'Look, I'm the messenger. Dad's getting married. He wants you there to celebrate his wedding day.'

'His *third* wedding day.' He'd been married first to their mother, who'd died when Savannah was ten. Then he'd fallen straight into another marriage with a woman half his age. When that didn't work out, he swore off women. And now there was Courtney. 'If he wants me there so badly, why didn't he call himself?'

'Would you have answered?'

She shrugs as she says, 'He wasn't exactly happy when I left.'

'You quit the business.'

'Wasn't for me.'

'What is? Expelled from school. Scraped through college. Dropped out of your graduate programme. Quit the family business. Then disappeared interrailing – and haven't even stuck at that. Now you're hitching through fucking Morocco?'

'I'm happy in *fucking* Morocco.'

'Come on, Savannah. Get back here. We need to show a united front.'

'So this is about you and Dad wanting the shareholders to see us being a smiling, stable family?'

Seth's voice hardened. 'Is it so bad that *I* care about our business?'

And there it was. The crux of everything. The business came first.

'Can I tell him you'll be there?'

'I'm travelling, having a good time out here—'

'Which Dad is bankrolling.'

'It's *my* trust fund!' As she said this, she glanced up and saw that Ped was passing. It was clear from his smirk that he'd overheard that little stamp of her foot. She knew how she must look – a Californian trust fund kid playing at travelling.

The irony was, she didn't even want her dad's money. She had only ever wanted his time.

'What shall I tell Dad?'

She thought for a moment. 'To have a great wedding.'

22

Bea sits astride her board, hands sculling through the cool blue water. She needs this – an afternoon in the waves to clear her head. It's like her thoughts are hundreds of busy footprints criss-crossing on the shore and the sea has the calming power to wash them clean.

She glances across to the rocks, where Aiden sits with Elin, face shaded beneath a trucker's cap. Since his injury, he's often out here helping with Elin's camerawork or instructing his surf school students from the beach. She feels his gaze on her often, like he is always aware of her – and she of him.

Marnie paddles past on her longboard, throwing Bea a shaka. Bea grins, then watches as Marnie picks off the next wave, popping to her feet and cross-stepping gracefully up and down the length of her longboard. There is a beautiful fluidity to the lines she cuts, riding the wave in long, sweeping arcs, travelling and travelling, as if it is a carpet stretched out just for her to dance across. Other surfers turn to watch. There are whoops as she glides by, face to the sun, radiating strength and grace.

Bea watches till the end of the wave, thinking: *One day, I want to do that.*

When she's had her fill of waves and her arms ache, she

paddles in, heart lighter. Aiden and Elin have packed up, so Bea heads back to The Surf House, rinsing off at the outdoor shower. After hanging her wetsuit out to dry, she wraps a towel around her middle and crosses the terrace.

Farah is reading by the pool, hair immaculate, lipstick neat.

'You're back!' Bea says, happy to see her.

Farah sets down her book and stands to kiss Bea on both cheeks. 'I dream of this place.'

'Where's Driss?'

'Taking a call in our room. You know what it's like. Business never sleeps.' She touches the backs of her fingers to Bea's face. 'Look at you, fresh from the sea. So tanned now – and muscles, girl!'

Bea glances at her arms, pleased by the new ridges of muscle from her daily surfs. To keep her figure willowy while modelling, she ate a calorie-deficient diet and had no spare energy for exercising. She had to tune out of her body's demands – whereas now she's learning to listen. She eats when she's hungry, feeding her body with healthy fats and proteins, and her energy is soaring.

Farah's gaze flicks to the studio. 'What's the story with the American guy in there? He caught me the moment I arrived. Was asking questions about Savannah. His sister, right?'

Bea nods. 'Apparently, no one's heard from her since she left here with a couple of Dutch girls. You knew her, didn't you?'

'Savannah stayed for a while when The Surf House first opened. Same room as you.'

Bea is surprised to feel the fine hairs on the backs of her arms standing on end. She pictures the green-eyed girl from Seth's photo and feels a strange synergy flowing between them. They are the same age. They both washed up in Mallah. They know the same people. Slept in the same room. And now Savannah has disappeared . . .

'What is she like?' Bea asks.

Farah thinks for a moment, considering her response. Then she smiles. 'Savannah has an infectious energy. Like she wants to be doing three things at once. She visited us in Marrakesh. Loved the city.'

'Good houseguest?'

'I barely saw her. I was mid-research on my thesis, so weekends were head down. Driss took her out though. Introduced her to some friends. I think she came up a couple more times and hung out with them.'

Bea asks, 'And then she left for Cape Town with the Dutch girls?'

'That's right. I remember how excited she was.'

'Did you meet them?'

'Once. I was passing their van, and they had a map spread out. Savannah pulled me over to see the route she was taking. Hugging the west coast for a time, then cutting inland. It looked incredible. Ambitious, though.' A flicker of tension tightens Farah's brow.

'What is it?' Bea asks.

'Three girls driving across the continent?' She pauses. 'There are risks.'

Bea nods slowly. 'You don't know how to contact them, d'you?'

Farah shakes her head. 'Seth asked. I can't even remember their names.' She turns then, and Bea follows her gaze to see Driss exiting The Surf House. He looks preoccupied as he returns his phone to his pocket, tension furrowing his brow.

When he spots Bea and Farah, he smiles, an ease returning to his face. 'Good to see you!' he says to Bea, kissing her on both cheeks, his fingertips lightly brushing her waist. Then he goes to Farah's side, linking his hand with hers.

Farah says to him, 'You're brilliant with names. Do you recall those Dutch travellers who Savannah was headed to Cape Town with?'

'In the old green van?'

'That's right. Two blonde girls. What were their names?'

Driss thinks for a moment. 'Lise, I think. One of the girls was called Lise.'

Bea has a name. It's not much – but it's a start.

She sits on her bedroom floor, phone propped on her knees, scrolling through Savannah's Instagram feed.

There's an energy about Savannah's posts that shines. She shares colourful details of her travels, her captions dusted with typos, and there's a genuine sense that this is her, in the moment, sharing her adventure.

Bea scrolls through the photos: a picture of Savannah's bare toes dug into the black sand; pouring mint tea from an ornate teapot; a blue corridor of painted doorways, the caption reading: *Monday blues.*

The next photo halts Bea. It is a picture of this room.

Hairs rise on the back of her neck as Bea pushes to her feet and takes three steps forward, so she is standing exactly as Savannah must have been when she took the photo, facing the open window. She glances from the screen to the view. In both, the curtains are lifting in the breeze.

Studying the photo, she sees Savannah's side profile caught in the reflection of the freestanding mirror. Bea adjusts her position, taking a half step until she's in the exact same spot as Savannah. She yanks off the cotton throw that's covering the mirror, then glances sideways at herself.

Savannah's presence suddenly feels so strong, it's almost as if Bea expects to see Savannah's face staring back at her.

She feels a gossamer thread shimmering between them. She and Savannah are the same age. They have slept in the same room. Stood at the same window.

And now Savannah is gone. She's cut herself off from everyone and everything she knows – and disappeared.

Bea feels the echo of that.

The difference is, Savannah has someone who cares enough to fly out to Morocco and search for her. *If I went missing, who would look for me?*

With a jerk, Bea turns her back to the mirror.

She fixes her attention on Savannah's Instagram feed, reading the comments below her image.

moonchi33 *What a place!*
thegirlsurf *Loving seeing your adventures.*
rachel_yak *Surf's up. Mwah.*

She continues looking through the remainder of Savannah's Morocco photos, until they stop on 26th October – the day Savannah emailed her friend Rachel to say she was going offline.

Her last post is a picture of the sunrise over the mountains, captioned: *Got a new adventure up my sleeve.*

There are a handful of comments.

leaderxcheer *Peach of a sunrise.*
bettiewonder *Go slay!*
jake9jordan *Room for another?*
lisew_a1 *More beautiful views to come.*

Bea's gaze stays pinned to that final comment. She looks again at the handle: **lisew_a1**.

Her heart picks up its pace.

One of the Dutch girls?

She clicks on the picture of her. **lisew_a1**'s profile reads: *Overland traveller. 22 countries. Currently in South Africa. From Amsterdam.*

It's her! It's got to be!

The account isn't private, so Bea clicks on the message icon. She pauses for a moment, thinking. Then types:

Hi. I need to speak to you about an American girl you met in Mallah called Savannah. Is there a number I could call you on? It's important. Thanks. Bea.

She presses *Send,* and then she waits.

23

Bea glances over her shoulder, then knocks once on the studio door.

'Yes?' Seth calls.

When she walks in, Seth is sitting on the edge of his bed in a rumpled shirt, shoes off. His hair is dishevelled, and he looks exhausted, mauve shadows beneath his eyes.

'How was your meeting?' she asks.

'Waste of time. The consulate won't do anything because I can't confirm that Savannah disappeared in this country – so, legally, they don't need to help.'

'Want some news to cheer you up?'

He glances up, eyes sharpening.

'I found one of the Dutch girls. She's currently in Cape Town.'

He's on his feet. 'You found her? How?'

'Driss remembered the name of one of them – Lise. Then, when I was trawling Savannah's social media, I saw that someone called Lise had posted a comment. I messaged to say I wanted to talk to her about Savannah. She replied straight away.'

She takes out her phone and shows Seth the message.

I'm working today, but you can call tomorrow any time after 6 p.m. My number's below. Lise

Seth reads the message twice. He hands back the phone, then runs a hand over his face as if he can't quite take it in.

'We've got a lead,' Bea says.

Seth's face breaks into a wide, spontaneous smile as he moves towards her. 'We've got a fucking lead!'

For a moment, it looks as if he's going to hug her, but at the last moment, he puts out his hand, and they shake. It feels a little transactional and businesslike, leaving them both standing awkwardly.

Seth pushes his hands into his pockets and asks, 'Do you think Savannah is still with Lise?'

From everything Bea's learned about Savannah – that she is flighty, changeable, impulsive – she doesn't think it's likely that she made it all the way to Cape Town, but at least this is a start. 'I guess we'll find out tomorrow.'

Seth thanks Bea for her help. Before she goes, he takes out $2,000 from the safe. He holds out the bundle of notes. 'This is for you. You got your first lead.'

Bea stares at the crisp block of dollars in his hand. The money will take her one step closer to paying off Momo. 'You sure?'

'A deal is a deal.'

As she tucks the notes into her pocket, sticky guilt crawls over her skin. She pictures Savannah, bright-eyed and smiling, roaming free on a beach in Morocco, and wonders, *Do you want to be found?*

24

The following evening, after a day of chores and surfing, Bea returns to Seth's studio. Her body hums with anticipation. If they make this call and Lise tells them where Savannah is, then Seth will have his answer – and Bea can clear her debt to Momo.

Seth paces the room, hands jangling loose change in his pockets.

'You ready?' she asks.

Seth nods.

They both stand close to the table where Bea has placed her mobile. She presses *Call* and hits speakerphone. Their eyes are pinned to the screen as they listen to it ring.

A few moments later, it connects, and Bea and Seth glance at each other, their anticipation mirrored.

'*Hallo?*'

'Hi, this is Bea. I messaged you yesterday about Savannah.'

'Yeah. Listen, I'm in a bar, so I need to keep it quick.'

There is a lot of background noise – music, voices, the scraping of chairs – and Bea hopes Lise can hear her as she explains that she is looking for Savannah.

'I met her in Mallah,' Lise replies, her English crisp.

There's a crash of noise in the background, followed by a peal of laughter.

Bea says, 'Savannah planned to travel to Cape Town with you and your friend. Is that right?'

'Yes. But—'

There's another burst of laughter in the background, and what Lise says next is lost.

Bea glances at Seth and can see that his jaw is clenched, gaze pinned to the phone.

'Sorry, I didn't catch that.'

'I said that was Savannah's plan – only she didn't turn up.'

'Wait. What?'

This from Seth. He is leaning forward now, hands planted on either side of the phone.

'Who is that?' Lise asks, wrong-footed.

'I'm Savannah's brother, Seth. I'm trying to find my sister.'

Lise sounds wary as she says, 'What is this about?'

'I was told Savannah left Mallah with you and another girl. That you were headed to Cape Town.' He pauses. 'You're there – but where is my sister?'

There is a defensive note to her voice now. 'How would I know? I've not seen her since we left Mallah.'

Seth's brow ridges with confusion.

Lise goes on. 'Her plan was to come with us. But she changed her mind.'

'She changed her mind?' Seth repeats, alarmed.

'One of her friends came to tell us.'

'Who?' Bea asks.

'I can't remember her name. She was staying in Mallah. Living out of her RV. A New Zealander, I think. Blue hair.'

Seth and Bea both look up, meeting each other's gaze.

ONE YEAR EARLIER

SAVANNAH

Elin pointed to the sopping bikini that was hanging from the RV's wing mirror. 'Salt water rusts the bodywork.'

Savannah, who was lying on the bed, writing her travel journal, rolled her eyes.

'Hang it on the rack.'

Savannah sighed as she pushed her journal aside. With visible effort, she took out the drying rack from beneath one of the seats and set it up. *Jesus, this RV is getting small,* she thought.

Elin went to the fridge. Savannah knew she'd be looking for the orange juice. She always had a glass post-surf – and Savannah had finished it.

'Where's the juice?'

'I've decided to stay at The Surf House for a bit.'

Elin's head shot up. 'What?'

Savannah hadn't planned to say it. The words just came out. She rarely knew what she was going to say until she was saying it.

'When did you decide that?' Elin asked, clearly hurt.

'Been thinking about it for a while.' And she had. That calm space, the interesting crowd, the privacy of a room to herself. 'I've loved travelling with you. But you've got to admit, it's cramped with two of us.'

149

'I like it,' Elin said, a slight flare to her nostrils.

'You like me hanging my bikini on your wing mirror? Finishing your juice? Leaving my damp towels on the driver's seat?'

'You make it more fun.' Elin said this in a small voice, and Savannah felt a tinge of guilt.

They'd had fun, it was true. Dancing late at night in the tiny space of the van. Driving with their music pumped loud. Getting lost in the souks and finding themselves drinking tea with an old lady with no teeth. 'I've loved it, too. But I . . . I'm just not cut out for van life.'

That wasn't strictly true. Savannah loved the freedom of pulling up each day in a different spot. What she meant was: she wasn't cut out for van life with Elin.

Elin looked down at her feet. 'Is this about the other night?'

'Course not,' Savannah said, with a smile that she hoped looked easy.

They'd got stoned lying out on a blanket beneath the stars, heads together, talking. Savannah had squealed when she saw a dazzling shooting star exploding above them. She'd reached for Elin's hand and clasped it to her chest, giddy on freedom and beauty and Moroccan-grade weed.

Elin had rolled towards Savannah, pushed up onto an elbow, and kissed her. She'd tasted of smoke and noodles, and Savannah had laughed and said, 'Jesus, you're more wasted than I thought.'

Elin laughed. Then apologised. Then got to her feet and announced she was taking a piss.

The kiss had taken her by surprise, sure, but it wasn't a big deal. It wasn't the first time she'd been kissed by someone she wasn't attracted to. But after that, the atmosphere between them had shifted. It was subtle, more of a lost easiness. Elin kept picking Savannah up on small things – complaining if she left her toothbrush on the edge of the sink or pointedly plucking long blonde hairs from the sofa cushions.

'The Surf House is only up the road. We can still hang out.'

'Can you afford a room there?'

She knew Elin lived off next to nothing. In New Zealand, she had worked three jobs for a year to save up for the van. Savannah had always made sure she paid her way, contributing for food and fuel, but she'd never let on the type of budget she had to play with. 'Marnie mentioned there was a smaller room available. Maybe she'll do a discount,' she answered vaguely.

'Thought we were in this together? You said you wanted to travel on. Explore the Atlas Mountains.'

'We can still do all that,' Savannah said. Again, words coming out her mouth that she didn't even mean. 'I'm just switching it up at The Surf House for a while. We can have our adventures when the surf season is done.'

Elin looked mildly appeased, although her tone still held a sulky note as she said, 'You promise?'

'Sure,' Savannah replied, but her attention had already drifted through the open doors of the RV to where The Surf House stood on the cliff, bathed in warm evening light.

25

Seth paces the studio. His skin holds a waxy, grey sheen. Bea wants to tell him to sit, have a glass of water – but it's as if he's physically unable to be still.

'Why would Elin tell the Dutch girls that Savannah wasn't coming?' he demands.

Lise had very little else to share. She and her friend, Anke, were due to leave at seven o'clock on the morning of 27th October – the night after the Jailors beach party. Savannah would have simply needed to pack her things and make the five-minute walk from The Surf House through the village to where the vans park on a dirt track.

Except, for whatever reason, she didn't.

According to Lise, Elin told her that Savannah had changed her mind about the South Africa road trip. Elin said Savannah was heading to Marrakesh for a few nights instead. As Savannah had already gone offline and ditched her phone, the Dutch friends wouldn't have been able to contact her to check.

Bea pauses on the Marrakesh detail for a moment. What if Elin was telling the truth? What if Savannah was planning to visit Driss and Farah in Marrakesh? But then, why wouldn't Farah or Driss have mentioned it?

Bea says to Seth, 'Changing her plans like this, suddenly heading off to Marrakesh – from what you've said, it's the kind of thing your sister might do, right?'

Seth pauses his pacing. He plants his hands on the back of the chair he vacated. His shoulders are raised to his ears. 'Yes,' he says, finally. 'But if Savannah went to Marrakesh instead of going with the Dutch girls, what about the bank withdrawal in Ezril? And why didn't Elin tell you this?' His gaze bores into her, making Bea feel as if she's dropped a ball. Was she not asking the right questions, or did Elin have reason to lie? It's possible that Elin was protecting Savannah's tracks from Seth.

She glances sideways at him – the rigid tension in his brow, the tight cast of his shoulders – and wonders, *Was Savannah scared of you?*

Bea's thoughts swirl. Eventually she says, 'We need to speak to Elin.'

Sunset has faded into dusk as Bea walks through the village. She persuaded Seth that it'd be better for her to go alone. If Elin is hiding something, Seth's bullish intensity isn't going to help. She's promised to meet him afterwards for the debrief.

The final surfers are exiting the water, boards under their arms, padding wet-footed and exhilarated back to hostels and vans.

The wheels of a skateboard roll past on the one smooth section of tarmac in Mallah. A girl with long, dark hair ollies a makeshift ramp, then slides out the tail, to cheers from two watching skaters.

This is the same route Savannah should have taken on the morning she left The Surf House and walked to the Dutch girls' van. Bea wonders who else was awake at the early morning hour.

She passes the harbour, where the smell of freshly barbecued fish fills the air, then along the main track, where the street hawkers are still out, wares illuminated with lanterns. She takes a left, heading towards the line of vans parked up – a dozen or so of them, nose to bumper on a stretch of flat ground. Wetsuits hang off wing mirrors and slide doors are open wide to the view. Passing an orange van, Bea smells noodles cooking, a curl of steam escaping from an open window.

There's something romantic about these homes on wheels, she thinks. Maybe it's having everything you need in one place, paring back your belongings to the bare minimum. Knowing you can move on whenever you like.

A couple have set their camping chairs arm to arm and are drinking beers, watching the final shift of light as dusk is swallowed by night. They don't speak, just keep their gazes on the water, enjoying the moment of quiet together.

An unexpected pang of loneliness hits hard between Bea's ribs. It surprises her. Does she want someone to watch the sun go down with? She has never chased after relationships. Being single is simpler, less emotional territory to navigate. And yet, she finds her thoughts drawing towards Aiden. She thinks of the intensity with which he listens when she talks and that hard-won smile that chases out the darkness in his eyes. This feeling of wanting more from him catches her off-guard.

Drawing her gaze away from the couple, Bea sees that she's reached Elin's blocky RV. It has none of the style of the smaller campers and is coated by a thin layer of dust, rust beginning to show above the wheel arches. The lights are on inside, and the door is open.

Bea calls, 'Hello?'

'Yeah?'

She steps inside and finds Elin lying on the bed, watching something on her phone, which is propped on her stomach.

'Got a minute?' Bea asks.

'Sure,' Elin says, turning off the phone and sitting up. 'Want a beer?'

'Thanks.'

Elin opens a small solar-powered fridge and rummages at the back for two bottles of beer. She snaps off the caps using a bottle-opener attached to a cupboard door, then places the beers on the small rectangular table and sits down.

'What's up?' Elin asks, as Bea sits down opposite her.

'The other day, we were talking about Savannah, and you mentioned she'd left Mallah with a couple of Dutch girls. Went travelling to South Africa.'

'That's right,' Elin says, picking up her beer. There's a faint narrowing of her eyes.

'D'you remember what day this was?'

'Yeah. After the beach party – 27th October.'

'And you're certain Savannah was leaving with them?'

Elin shrugs. 'That's what she said she was doing. She was telling everyone about it at the party.'

'It's just . . . Seth managed to track down one of the Dutch girls. Lise.'

Elin's discomfort is immediately visible. Her gaze flicks to the door as if she's thinking about exiting through it.

'Lise said Savannah never got in their van.'

A flush of red blooms across Elin's throat.

Bea goes on, pulse flickering. 'She told Seth that you'd been to see them. Said Savannah no longer wanted to make the trip. That they should go on without her.'

Elin stands, knocking the table with her knee, causing the

beer bottles to judder. Elin rescues hers and moves to the open doorway, keeping her back to Bea.

There's a long silence.

'Is that true?' Bea eventually asks.

Elin presses the cool glass bottle against her neck. Says nothing.

'I'm just trying to understand,' Bea says, wary now that Elin blocks the exit.

'I was angry,' she says, swinging around, her voice tight, defensive. 'She'd told everyone she was leaving – going on this big adventure to Cape Town – but she hadn't told me! We had plans. Were meant to be headed to the Atlas Mountains. That's what she'd said!'

'And you found out at the beach party?'

Elin nods, jaw tight. 'I was the one who brought her to Morocco. It was my adventure – but I let her in on the ride. And then when we get to Mallah, she meets the rest of them – Marnie, Ped, Driss, Farah, Aiden – the *cool* people,' she says, and there's a note of bitterness there. 'Ditched me for The Surf House.' She pauses. 'Then the next thing I hear, she's signed up to spend the next six months living out of someone else's van.'

There's a tremor in Elin's voice, her anger cut through with hurt.

'We argued, and I left the beach party. Got back here and saw the Dutch girls. They were packing up their gear ready for the early start. So I told them that Savannah wasn't coming. Said she'd met someone and was heading to Marrakesh instead.' She drops her gaze. 'It was petty. A stupid lie. I . . . I just wanted Savannah to know what it was like to be ditched – to be left on the side of the road – because that's what she does to people.'

Bea asks, 'So they went without her?'

Slowly, Elin nods. 'I heard the Dutch girls leave. It was early, probably around six a.m. Savannah wasn't with them.'

'Did she turn up looking for them?'

'I didn't stick around. I got my board and headed in for a dawnie. When I got back to the van, it was mid-morning. Still no sign of her. I figured she'd be at The Surf House working out her plan, but she wasn't. She had packed up. Gone.'

Bea looks at her. 'Where?'

Elin shakes her head. This time, she meets Bea's eye. 'I've no idea.'

26

The waiter pours the Moroccan tea from an ornate silver pot held at a great height – first Bea's cup, then Seth's. He makes a theatrical finishing flourish, then gives a beaming smile as he departs with a backwards step.

The mint tea is too sweet for Bea's taste, but she sips at it anyway, her throat dry.

She and Seth are sitting in a tiny café, lit only by flickering lanterns. They chose it because it's off the main street and visited by few people.

Beneath the table, Seth's leg bounces up and down as he asks, 'If Savannah didn't leave with the Dutch girls, what now?'

Earlier, it felt like they were so incredibly close, but now everything is once again out of reach. Which means the money Bea was hoping to be paid is also out of reach.

'Here's what we know,' she says, trying to keep a cool head. 'Savannah was at the Jailors beach party on 26th October. She and Elin had an argument, and Elin left. Elin tells the Dutch girls that Savannah is bailing on their adventure – so the next morning, they leave without her. At some point, Savannah packs up her belongings – and . . . what? Does she turn up to find the Dutch girls gone?'

Seth is watching her closely.

'If so, she's got everything on her back, she's already said her goodbyes. She's ready for her next adventure. So, what would she do?'

Seth's eyes lift as if he's conjuring the image of his sister. As if he's trying to picture her next move, rucksack on her shoulders. 'Savannah met Elin by hitchhiking.'

'So, she'd do the same again?'

Seth nods.

They let that image sit there, with all the possibility and uncertainty that it holds.

'But,' Bea muses, 'we know she withdrew all her money in Ezril – that desert town you mentioned – on 27th October. So, she must have got there. How far is it from Mallah?'

Seth takes out his phone and opens Google Maps. After a moment he says, 'Seven hours' drive.'

'And what time was the bank transaction?'

'Six o'clock in the evening,' Seth says.

'So, she was on the road for most of the day. She must have left Mallah by eleven a.m. at the latest. Then arrived in Ezril by evening.'

Seth is quiet.

'What is it?'

'*If* she arrived.'

'But her bank statement shows that she used—'

'—her bank statement shows that her *card* was used. But not who used it.'

'Wouldn't you need to show ID to get out that much cash?'

'I don't know. But I think we need to find out.'

Seth pays for their Moroccan tea, leaving a generous tip for the proprietor, and then they step out into the night.

Bea says goodnight to Seth outside the studio, her head buzzing with the events of the day.

When she enters The Surf House, the lights are on, and she finds Marnie and Ped playing cards with Driss and Farah in the lounge. Marnie, dressed in a dusky green jumpsuit, sits close to Ped, their thighs touching as he stretches forward to pick a card from the deck. There is music playing, easy talk, laughter.

'Bea!' Marnie says, spotting her. 'I knocked for you. Poker night. In for the next round?'

'Sure,' Bea says, lowering herself down beside Marnie. This is where she wants to be, she realises, not sitting in Elin's RV probing for answers or analysing conversations with Seth.

'Where've you been?' Marnie asks.

Guilt heats her cheeks at the thought of the arrangement she's made with Seth. She hates not being honest with Marnie. Their friendship was forged by what happened in Marrakesh. Marnie has her back in a way that no one else ever has. Truth is fundamental. She doesn't want this role as Seth's insider, but she needs to get Momo's money, and locating Savannah is her best chance.

'I went to the teahouse,' Bea answers, not offering up who she was with.

There's a light, easy atmosphere as Driss pours another round of drinks. She accepts a glass of wine and watches as Ped raises the stakes, pushing a pile of dirhams across the table. His expression is confident but closed, giving nothing away.

Marnie is the first to fold, seemingly caring little about the outcome and settling back with her glass of wine.

When Driss reaches for a card and peers at it, his expressions are theatrical, the pursed lips and narrowed eyes.

On Farah's turn, she matches the pot, but her expression

holds a hint of uncertainty. Bea suspects she'll be the next to fold. Yet Farah raises the stakes further. Ped and Driss both watch her carefully.

Farah returns their scrutiny with a confident, easy smile – and both men promptly fold.

As Farah is scooping the money towards herself, Ped asks, 'What did you have?'

She fans out her cards, revealing one pair of sevens.

Marnie bursts out laughing.

'Queen of the bluff,' Driss says proudly, a hand sliding briefly over her thigh.

Bea watches Farah for a moment longer, surprised by how elegantly she orchestrated the game in her favour.

'Evening.'

They all turn to find Seth standing at the edge of the room, looking every bit the outsider in a pale-pink shirt and chinos.

They greet him, but no one invites Seth to join them.

Bea is torn between wanting to make space for him but also wishing he'd leave. Right now. Go back to his studio and not compromise the ease of this moment.

'I thought you'd all want to know,' he says, failing to read the room as he steps forward, standing at the head of the two sofas like he's in a board meeting, 'that I had an interesting lead on Savannah's whereabouts.'

Bea doesn't need to look at the others' expressions to know this is not the time for it. Evenings in The Surf House are for unwinding, letting go of the day.

'I located one of the Dutch girls,' he continues. 'I spoke with Lise this evening, and apparently Savannah never left Mallah with them.'

Ped keeps his gaze on his cards.

'Elin told the Dutch girls that Savannah had changed her mind about the trip, so they left without her.'

Marnie's face is stretched with surprise. 'Wait. *Elin* said that? Why?'

Seth explains about Elin and Savannah's fight at the beach party and Elin's petty vengeance. 'Elin saw the Dutch girls leave early. Savannah wasn't with them.'

'Strange,' Driss says.

Seth asks Marnie, 'When you checked Savannah's room in the morning, was it empty?'

'Yeah. All her stuff was gone.'

Seth nods. 'If Savannah packed up and left but didn't go off with the Dutch girls and didn't come back here, where did she go?'

No one answers.

'Did anyone see Savannah in The Surf House the morning she went missing? Did she have breakfast?'

The four of them exchange glances.

Driss says, 'I had to leave first thing as I had a meeting back in Marrakesh.'

Bea watches Driss carefully and feels Seth doing the same.

'Did you see her on the roads as you drove out?' Seth asks.

Farah's eyes are on Driss as he shakes his head.

'Or did you see any other vehicles?'

'It was almost a year ago. I don't remember what vehicles I passed,' Driss says easily. 'But the road out of Mallah is usually empty. Particularly at that time. You get the odd villager coming in for work, Momo dropping his mother into town, that kind of thing – but I don't remember who I saw that day.'

Momo. His name sends a chill through Bea's body. She thinks of the basket of bread left on the doorstep each morning by his mother. Momo drops his mother in Mallah and then leaves to go to work. He could have been driving back with an empty vehicle. Had he seen Savannah walking alone?

'Did you see Momo's car that morning?' Seth pushes.

'Can't remember.' Driss shrugs. 'But I'm sure he'd have loved to have bumped into Savannah.'

Seth blinks. 'What does that mean?'

Farah shoots Driss a warning look.

Driss says, 'He was a little besotted with her, that's all.'

ONE YEAR EARLIER

SAVANNAH

Savannah shook the sand from her beach blanket, letting it billow in the breeze. She'd bought it at a market last weekend and hadn't even haggled as she'd loved it so much. It was the colours that sold it – sunset oranges and golden yellows, with a vintage print of sunbeams streaming across the fabric.

'Smile.'

She looked up to see Driss pointing his phone camera at her. She beamed as she lifted the blanket higher, letting it fill with wind.

He clicked the shoot button. She wanted the warmth of this moment captured – the beach, sunshine, friends nearby. God, she'd been so happy since she'd moved into The Surf House. She was staying in a small room next door to Marnie and Ped, which wouldn't have been her first choice, but Farah and Driss had the main room, and the others were still being finished.

'Everyone now,' Driss said, gathering the rest of the group, who were flaked out on the sand, lounging on blankets and board bags.

They drew together, bare, tanned arms thrown around one another. She could smell sunscreen, salt, the neoprene tang of wetsuits.

Aiden was the first to break away. 'I'm heading back in,' he said, grabbing his board and jogging to the waterline.

The others watched him paddle into a head-high wave, then spring to his feet and make a sharp cutback. Elin whooped.

Ped grabbed his board after that, and the others were quick to follow.

Savannah didn't mind being left alone again. She had her book. She had the sunshine. She had a whole blissful afternoon ahead, with nothing needed of her. She was perfectly happy right here on her new beach blanket.

'What are you reading?'

She glanced up, surprised to see Momo sitting at the edge of the rocks. He was the local cop who sometimes hung out in Mallah and seemed to know a few of the surfers. '*We Were Liars*,' she answered, holding up the cover.

He nodded, then looked out over the water, watching the others for a time. 'You don't surf?'

'Prefer to keep my feet on land. You?'

'I tried. But this happened.' He pointed to the long scar that ran down the left side of his forehead, still pink at its edges. 'I hit the reef at low tide. Now I am frightened to get back in the sea.'

She looked at Momo. He could only be a year or two older than herself. She thought of her father and Seth and couldn't imagine either of them admitting they were afraid. His openness was refreshing. 'Maybe, with time, you'll change your mind.'

'Perhaps.' His fingertips felt the scar. 'Do you think it is ugly?'

She considered his face. He had a strong, straight nose and even, tanned skin. The scar, curving near to his hairline, only gave texture to his face. 'Before, you were handsome. Now, you are handsome and interesting. That's better.' She smiled.

He did, too.

27

Seth sits alone at breakfast in his usual spot, notebook out. Bea delivers him a plate filled with hot, crispy msemen and silky scrambled egg dusted with cayenne pepper.

'I'm going to Ezril today,' he tells her, glancing over his shoulder to check no one is listening. 'I don't think I'll be back until tomorrow. I want to visit the bank and see if I can access their CCTV footage. I need to know if it was Savannah who withdrew the money.'

Bea understands the darkness in Seth's expression. If he finds evidence that someone else made the withdrawal, then this becomes a very different story.

'Can you see me before I go?' Seth asks.

She gives a quick nod, then returns to the kitchen.

Marnie is rinsing a chopping board, singing lightly to the radio. 'He's not bothering you, is he?'

'Who?'

'Seth,' Marnie says.

'No.'

'If he becomes a problem, tell me, and we'll get him out.'

Bea nods. She's surprised by Marnie's hardness towards Seth – yet also, beneath that, she feels a burst of gratitude for her protection.

*

When the breakfast service is over, Bea visits Seth in the studio.

She finds him writing in his black leather notebook. He puts down the pen and pushes the notebook into his packed case. 'While I'm away, can you look into a couple of things?'

She nods, feeling the rise of reluctance in her chest. She still hasn't got the measure of Seth and keeps circling back to the thought: *Does Savannah want to be found?*

'I'm interested in that window of time after Savannah left The Surf House. Who did she see? Who picked her up?' Seth wraps his hands around the back of the chair. 'We know Driss was on the road that morning. He was alone. He could easily have seen Savannah. Offered her a lift.' He sets his gaze on Bea. 'What do you know about him?'

Bea thinks for a moment. 'The facts? He's known Marnie and Ped for two or three years. He's engaged to Farah. They live and work in Marrakesh. Savannah visited him and Farah a couple of times there. Was introduced to some of their friends.'

Seth nods as he takes in these details. 'What sort of feeling does he give you?'

Bea hasn't spent much time with Driss. Does she like him? She recalls the way his gaze travelled over her body when they first met. Yet she's also seen the tender way he behaves with Farah. 'I haven't got much to go on, but I'm not sure there are any real red flags. I think he's a man used to getting what he wants.'

'What's his business?'

'Farah refers to him as an entrepreneur. Fingers in pies, I think.'

'Will you find out more? I'm interested in those deposits into Savannah's account.'

She nods.

Seth pushes away from the chair and crosses the room, looking out through the balcony door. 'The other person on my mind is Momo.'

Her skin cools at the mention of his name. Driss hinted last night that he was infatuated with Savannah. He could have passed her in his police car on the morning she left The Surf House. If he'd offered her a ride, would she have climbed in with him?

Seth is looking at Bea quizzically. 'What is it?'

She hesitates, unsure what to say.

'Bea?' he prompts.

'I don't trust him.'

'Based on?'

'A dealing with him at a checkpoint.'

'So, he's a bent cop?'

Slowly, she nods.

'You think he could have picked up Savannah?'

'It's possible.'

'Can you speak with him?'

She shakes her head. Her mouth turns dry. 'I can't.'

He looks at her, surprise lifting his brow.

'There was a . . . situation. Sorry . . . I can't talk about it.'

Seth considers her. 'How much trouble are you in, Bea?'

She meets his eye. 'A lot.'

'Does this have anything to do with the loan you were after?'

She hesitates.

Seth holds her gaze, waiting.

Eventually, she nods.

'How much do you owe him?'

'$10,000,' she admits. 'I've paid half already, plus I've got the money you've paid me.'

'So you're $2,000 short?'

She nods.

Seth crosses the room and moves to his wardrobe. He crouches down, and Bea realises he's opening the safe. He removes a stack of notes and counts out $2,000.

Holding out the money, he says, 'Upfront payment for the next lead you'll bring me.'

She stares at the money. 'Really?'

'Really.'

She takes the money, feeling the weight of the notes in her hand. 'I don't know what to say.'

'It's an advance. When I come back from the desert, have something else for me, okay?'

28

Bea finds Marnie pulling her longboard from the rack, two streaks of zinc pasted to her cheeks.

She turns, smiling when she spots Bea. 'Coming in?'

'Soon,' Bea says, gaze flicking to the bay, where peeling lines are gliding alluringly towards shore. She steps closer to Marnie. Her voice is lowered, but she cannot keep her excitement from it as she says, 'I've got the money!'

'What?' Marnie's eyes widen. 'All of it?'

'All of it.'

Relief bursts from Marnie's features, mouth breaking into a wide smile. 'How?'

Bea cannot tell her about Seth's payment, so she says that one of the new loans she applied for came good.

'This is incredible!' Marnie leans her longboard against the rack so she has both arms free to hug Bea.

Bea breathes in the scent of her suncream and perfume oil, feeling relief and warmth wash through her.

When Marnie steps back, she keeps hold of Bea's shoulders, their foreheads almost kissing. 'I knew this would come good if we kept cool heads. I just knew it.'

Bea asks, 'When shall we deliver the money?'

Marnie thinks. 'Maybe we should wait until his deadline?'

Bea nods. 'That's what I was thinking. If we take the money to Momo early, it looks like it came too easily.'

Five more days until the knife and bloodied scarf will be returned. For the first time in weeks, she feels light, buoyant.

Farah emerges from the terrace, zipped into her wetsuit, a white shortboard under her arm. 'Look at you gorgeous women,' she says, beaming. 'Shall we go get some waves?'

Board under her arm, Bea stands on the shoreline. The sky is cloudless, the heat pure and sharp. Shoulder-high waves roll across the bay, glassy blue faces glittering beneath a high sun. Her senses feel sharpened as she breathes in the fizz and energy of the sea.

'Perfection,' Marnie says beside her, awe in her tone.

Farah attaches her leash, and then the three women wade into the glimmering shallows.

Bea slides onto her board and strokes through the water, finding an easy, confident rhythm. Today is a good day. A day for riding waves beneath a blue sky with friends.

Once they reach the lineup, Bea sits astride her board, face tipped to the sun, catching her breath.

Marnie, hardwired to never let a wave go unridden, paddles for the first of the set. She springs lightning-fast to her feet on the drop, and Bea cannot take her eyes off the smooth line she draws across the wave face. She rides with her chin lifted, face lit by the sun, otter-dark hair gleaming. She dances towards the nose of her longboard, her movements playful and unhurried, riding high on the face, curling her bare feet over the nose for a glorious beat – and then she is sliding her way towards the tail, digging the fins in as she makes a gorgeous, deep turn, which draws her back to the most powerful section. She picks up speed, maintaining her graceful stance as she is propelled to the wave's end.

'Goddess!' Farah says, grinning.

Bea sweeps her hands through the water, absorbing the beauty of being out here.

From the water, Mallah looks like a postcard. The stark, red cliff line is populated by clusters of flat-roofed white and blue buildings – and beyond them is nothing but open sky and the dusty promise of the mountains.

She lifts a hand, blocking the sun as she searches out The Surf House. It is the dominant structure, standing forward on the cliff edge. The glass balcony of the studio juts out, like a diver ready to launch. She's relieved that Seth's away until tomorrow. Although she's committed to helping him, his intensity is exhausting, and it feels good to have space to just enjoy the day.

As she looks towards the studio, she catches a movement at the tall window. It looks like a figure crossing the room. Odd. Seth won't be back from Ezril until late tomorrow, and she knows that Marnie is right here. Ped doesn't do any housekeeping, but he's the only person who would have a key.

She narrows her eyes, peering harder.

The sun is reflecting off the window, and she can't see clearly – but it seems like there is someone standing in front of the glass door. She stares for a moment longer – and then the shadow is gone.

Farah paddles over.

'Is Driss surfing today?' Bea asks.

'He's following on. Had a couple of emails to do.'

She thinks of Seth's request to look more closely into Driss's connection with Savannah. Her eyes flick to The Surf House; the place is empty except for Driss and Ped. It would be easy enough for a guest to go into the office, slip a spare key from the hook, and let themselves into a room.

But what would either Ped or Driss want with the studio?

She turns to Farah, asking, 'How did you and Driss meet?'

'At a mutual friend's wedding. And I can promise you, it wasn't Driss's dancing that I fell for.'

Bea laughs. 'So, what was it?'

'Driss has this energy about him. Hardworking, ambitious, focused. He struck me as someone who wouldn't give up. I admire that in people.'

'He's an entrepreneur, right? What kind of things does he do?'

'Import and export, mostly. Property, too. To be honest, I tune out when it's work talk.'

'Does he employ people?'

'Why? You're not thinking of leaving The Surf House, are you?'

'God, no!' She isn't sure how much to say. 'Seth was talking to me about Savannah earlier. He said there were deposits made in Savannah's account in Marrakesh. He couldn't work out where the money came from. I wondered if she'd started working for someone.'

'Not that I heard.' Farah smiles easily.

But Bea is reminded of something Driss said. *Queen of the bluff.*

ONE YEAR EARLIER

SAVANNAH

The dunes were like no landscape Savannah had ever seen. It felt almost lunar as she followed the others barefoot through warm, shifting sand. The air was dry and tasted faintly of chalk. Already, she was thinking about reaching for her water bottle.

'Who's up first?' Marnie called when they reached the highest dune.

They were on a golden ridge of sand that had been sculpted by the wind. From up here, you could see the sea shimmering in the distance.

'Me,' called Aiden, who was holding a beaten-up surfboard with no fins. He tossed the board over the ridge, then ran and jumped on it. Within seconds, he was bucked off and went rolling down the dune in a spray of sand.

Elin was standing at the bottom with her camera and took Aiden's photo as he surfaced, laughing, shaking sand from his long hair.

'Let's see what you've got,' Marnie called to Savannah.

Savannah jumped on without hesitation, instinctively crouching low – and found herself screaming with the adrenalin rush. Rocket-speed, hair flying behind her, she somehow kept her footing – and at the bottom, the board slowed gradually, enabling her to step off to a round of applause.

'You are a wild woman,' Elin declared, camera pointed at Savannah.

Savannah raised her fists to the sky and gave a roar as Elin snapped the photo.

They had good moments like this, when it felt easy and light again – but Elin's mood, Savannah had learned, could switch in an instant.

They all took turns to surf the dunes, everyone's style becoming more flamboyant. Ped and Marnie rode tandem – then crashed in a tangle of limbs and laughter.

'Let's go together,' Driss called to Farah.

'Absolutely not,' Farah replied. 'I like my bones unbroken.'

Driss looked around. Caught her eye. 'Savannah?'

She shrugged. 'Fine.'

Driss leaped on the front of the board, and Savannah clambered on the back. They crouched low, sun on their faces, the spray of sand stinging her shins as they flew. Driss wolf-howled their way down, the sound free and vital.

When the dune levelled, the change in speed sent them flying. They rolled across the sand, and Savannah came to a stop on top of Driss. 'Oh God! Sorry!'

Looking down at Driss through the curtain of her hair, their eyes locked. She could feel the heat of their bodies against one another. Then she blinked and was quickly on her feet, extending her hand to yank Driss up. He grinned at her.

Savannah trudged back up the shifting dunes, her calf muscles protesting. She felt the lens of Elin's camera trained on her back.

Reaching the top, Farah was waiting, a bright smile on her face. She looked between Driss and then Savannah, eyes shaded behind large sunglasses. 'Had fun?'

29

Bea wades to shore with Marnie and Farah. Her eyes sting from salt and sun, and she fizzes with adrenalin. Even though her muscles ache and her ribs feel sore, she still wants more. *The beautiful addiction,* she thinks.

Her gaze travels to the rocks, where Aiden sits with Yaz. He looks up, and when their eyes meet, she feels a burst of warmth move through her body. Her lips lift into a smile.

Farah, noticing, nudges Bea. 'Anything you want to tell us?'

Bea shakes her head, but the smile still raises the corners of her mouth.

'You like him!' Farah beams.

She lifts and drops her shoulders, not knowing what to say.

'Aiden's hot as hell,' Farah says. 'No arguments there.'

Marnie hasn't said a word yet, and Bea wonders if there's a criticism implicit in her silence. She wants her opinion – and her approval. 'What do you think of Aiden?'

Marnie hesitates, like she's choosing her words carefully. 'I adore him, but . . . Aiden's complicated.'

Bea waits.

'I've never known him have a relationship. He's got a reputation for . . . keeping things light.'

'True,' Farah agrees. 'There's no shortage of women moving through his hostel doors. Or his bed.'

Bea feels something delicate inside her shrivel.

Back at The Surf House, she rinses off in the outdoor shower, still thinking about Aiden. *Keeping things light . . .* Is that how he operates? She turns those words over in her mind. But Aiden hasn't chased after her or tried to charm her into bed. It's almost the opposite. When they kissed in his truck, she'd felt his hesitation – as if he wanted her yet wished he didn't.

Inside The Surf House, Ped and a handful of guests are sinking beers in the lounge and talking about tomorrow's forecast. Bea goes to the kitchen and pours herself a tall glass of water, trying to rescue the headache that's forming behind her eyes.

She cuts two slices of crusty white bread and slathers them with butter and homemade apricot compote. She eats standing up, relishing this new, guilt-free experience of eating. Her senses tingle with delight. She rinses her plate, then slips away to her room, wanting to be alone to think more about Aiden.

When Bea opens her bedroom door, she hesitates. The hairs on the backs of her arms stand on end.

There is a smell in the room she cannot place, almost stale, musty.

Something isn't right.

She scans the room, pulse fluttering in her throat.

Then she sees it: a large bag on the centre of her bed.

Bea blinks.

It is a rucksack, navy, the buckles closed.

Hers.

The one that was stolen in Marrakesh.

*

Bea swings around as if expecting to find someone at her shoulder.

But there is no one there.

Blood crashes in her ears.

She remains frozen in the doorway, unwilling to cross the threshold into her room.

She catches the faint drift of voices from downstairs.

There's a deep gnawing at her gut. In Marrakesh, she was attacked by two men – she killed one, and the other took her rucksack and ran. Had the surviving man tracked her down? Was he leaving it here as some kind of threat?

The fear is hot-cold, pushing boiling jets of blood through her veins, while her skin feels icy.

'Marnie?' she calls, her voice small.

There's no answer.

She takes a couple of steps along the corridor and pushes open Marnie's door. 'Marnie?'

The room is empty. Their bed is made, a cream throw turned back. A light breeze blows in through the open window.

Bea backs out of the room, then races downstairs. She checks the lounge, office, and kitchen, before finding Marnie in the utility room, soaking a stained tea towel.

She turns, smiling, hair still wet from the surf. Seeing Bea's expression, her smile vanishes. 'What is it?'

Bea shakes her head. 'You need to see this.'

Marnie follows Bea upstairs.

Bea pushes open her bedroom door and points. 'My rucksack. The one that was stolen in Marrakesh.'

Marnie's eyes widen. 'Are you sure?'

'Yes.'

'How did it get here?'

'I've no idea.'

'Have you looked inside?'

Bea shakes her head.

Marnie draws in a breath as if gathering herself. 'We need to.'

The rucksack looks exactly as it did when Bea was last wearing it, but there is a faint smell of mildew, as if it's been stored somewhere dank.

Bea's hands tremble as she unclips the front buckles and then unzips the main section. She begins to remove items of clothing. A black vest, a pair of jeans, underwear, a jumper from Anthropologie that she used to love – relics of her old life. Everything is creased and bunched, her toiletries mixed in with the clothes, as if everything has been pulled out and repacked in a hurry.

She lays each of the items on the bed, feeling like she wants to wash her hands, as if everything has been contaminated. From the front pocket, she removes her purse. Unzips it. 'Everything is here except for the cash.'

Marnie considers her belongings. 'Anything else missing?'

She does a mental tally of the items. Her Kindle is here, along with her phone charger, and her EarPods. Then there are her clothes and wash things. 'My passport,' she says, with a lurch.

Marnie nods slowly.

'Who put my rucksack here?' Bea asks, unable to mask the fear in her voice.

Marnie's brow is furrowed, her teeth pressing into her bottom lip. Her head shakes from side to side.

Then she looks up, right at Bea. Her face has paled. 'Momo,' she whispers. 'Momo said he had a cousin who worked for the Marrakesh police, didn't he? He could have got hold of it.'

'Why would Momo leave it in my room like this?'

Marnie looks rattled. 'Maybe he wants us to know that

179

he can come into this building. Come into your private space whenever he wants.' They both look around, gazes snapping to the doorway, as if he could still be lurking there.

'It's another threat?'

'A reminder that he holds all the cards,' Marnie says darkly.

'What do we do?'

Marnie chews on her lower lip as she thinks. 'We stick to the plan. In five days, we deliver the money.'

'You think he'll give us what we need?'

'That was the deal,' Marnie says.

Bea eyes the rucksack and its spilled contents. 'But now there is this.'

30

Bea feels bleary-eyed and edgy the following morning as she fetches the basket of fresh bread from the doorstep. In the kitchen, she removes the clean tea towel and is greeted by the sweet, yeasty smell of oven-warm rolls. Then she blinks.

Slipped between the fresh bread, there is a note.

Marnie, who's spooning apricot compote into a white bowl, pauses. 'What is it?'

Bea doesn't take her eyes off the note. Just points. 'It's from Momo,' she says with dead certainty.

Marnie sets down the bowl, wipes her hands on her apron, and takes out the sheet of paper that contains several lines written in French. As she reads, her jaw tightens. 'No, no, no . . .'

'What is it?' Bea asks, heart hammering.

Marnie looks at her, face pale. 'Momo wants more money.' She shakes her head. 'But we had an agreement . . .'

'He's asking for an extra $5,000,' Marnie says, reading from the note.

'He can't do this,' Bea whispers.

Marnie translates: '*This rucksack came to the attention of a police officer in Marrakesh . . .*' Marnie glances at Bea and says, 'Must be Momo's cousin.' She continues reading: '*If the owner*

181

would like to be reunited with the passport that was found inside, an additional $5,000 will be required.'

'On top of the $5,000 we were about to pay?'

Marnie nods.

'When?'

Reading from the note, she answers, 'Six days.'

'Fuck!'

'Can you get more money? Is there any spare from your bank loan?'

It takes Bea a moment to understand Marnie's question. 'No,' she says. 'None.'

Marnie's face falls.

They stand in the kitchen together, silent.

'What now?' Bea asks.

Anxiety shadows Bea throughout the day. She has no appetite, is too preoccupied to surf, and is barely able to raise a smile for Salty when he lingers at the backdoor of the kitchen. Needing to put her attention somewhere, she decides to spend her afternoon researching Driss, having promised Seth some progress.

She's scrolling through a slim article about his rags to riches success, when Seth walks into the lounge. His shoes are dusty, cheeks shining with sunburn. 'You're back already,' she says. 'How was Ezril?'

He just shakes his head. 'Would you bring me a carafe of water? Headache.'

'Sure.' Bea goes to the kitchen and takes a fresh bottle of filter water from the fridge. She sets it on a tray with a clean glass and follows Seth out to the studio. He slumps on the edge of his bed and removes his shoes.

She pours him a glass, and he drinks thirstily.

'You okay?' Bea asks.

When he sets down the empty glass, there's a slight tremor in his hand. 'Fine.'

'Did you visit the bank?'

'No one remembers Savannah. I showed her photo around and not a single person could recall seeing her.'

'What about CCTV?'

'It's all stored on some cloud or other. There are permission issues, but they've agreed to trawl back through – for a price, of course.'

'You think they'll find the transaction?'

'I'm going to call every day until they do.'

Bea nods, pleased by his determination.

'What's been happening here?'

She thinks of her returned rucksack and Momo's latest threat. Instead of sharing this, she focuses on what Seth wants to know: whether she's made progress with locating Savannah.

'I've been doing some digging into Driss. I've found two businesses he's involved with. They both appear to be above board.'

Seth listens without expression.

'The thing I keep returning to is that Driss was alone in his vehicle on the morning Savannah left The Surf House. He said he'd been driving back for an early meeting – do you remember?'

Seth nods.

'So, I tracked down the contact details for his PA. She confirmed that Driss was at the meeting he claimed to be at.'

'How did you get that information?'

'I pretended I was on the staff of the company he met with and needed to check a detail for the fire safety log.'

He nods, impressed. 'So, what's your feeling on Driss now?'

'Just because he was at the meeting, it doesn't mean he didn't see Savannah on the way to it.'

'That's true. Anyone could have driven past her. Talking of which, I've arranged to see Momo later.'

Bea's stomach instantly tightens. She pictures him slipping quietly into her room, depositing the rucksack on her bed. Did he look around? Touch her things? Press his fingers to her pillow?

It's right that Seth is putting his focus on Momo. She knows firsthand that he's capable of deception and bribery, and Driss hinted at his infatuation with Savannah.

Seth says, 'I've framed it that I'd like his help tracking Savannah's movements. But really, I want time with him to see if he lets anything slip.'

'Where are you meeting?'

'Right here.'

Momo arrives later that afternoon. Bea, who is baking in the kitchen, feels her entire body stiffen as she listens to the clip of his polished shoes crossing the lounge.

His presence feels like a physical threat – she wants to crouch, hide, but she knows that intimidation is his game. Instead, she draws a deep breath into her abdomen. Then she fills a glass jug with ice, fresh lemon, and filtered water and delivers it to the studio.

Seth opens the door, and she enters. She keeps her head held high, shoulders back. She feels Momo's gaze on her as she sets down the tray. The air smells masculine, the spiced scent of aftershave and a hint of sweat.

It is strangely empowering to be in the same room as Momo and not cower or run. 'Let me know if you need anything else,' Bea says to Seth, before leaving the studio.

In the kitchen, she continues baking, thankful for the distraction of sifting flour and rubbing in butter. Her gaze regularly flicks to the studio, and it's only fifteen minutes before she sees Momo exiting.

Once Seth has seen him off the premises, he returns to speak to Bea.

'So?' she asks from the kitchen doorway.

'Momo was very interested to hear about Savannah's disappearance. Asked lots of questions. Wrote things down. Said he remembers her well.'

'What did you make of him?'

'Hard to read.'

'Did you ask him whether he was on the road that morning?'

'Yes – and he said he was. That he wishes he'd spotted her. He sounded emphatic on that point.'

'Did he say anything else?'

'No. But he did *do* something that surprised me.'

Bea waits.

'A work call came in for me, so I stepped out onto the balcony to answer. I'd left my notebook on the table.'

'Momo saw it?'

Seth nods. 'It was open on a photo of Savannah. Momo just stood there, staring. Then he . . .' Seth hesitates. He shifts his weight, looking uncomfortable. 'He reached out and ran a finger over her face.'

ONE YEAR EARLIER

SAVANNAH

Savannah held up her palms to the heat of the beach fire. It was Marnie's birthday, and a big group of them had come down to the bay at sunset to celebrate. A local woman Marnie knew had cooked up a huge tagine, and they'd eaten in the traditional way, all sitting around together, scooping up steaming vegetables and tender chicken with their warm, charred flatbreads.

Savannah's phone began to ring, cutting through the night, interrupting the sounds of the waves, the crackle of fire, laughter. Glancing at the screen, she saw Seth's name – and silenced the call.

'You're not going to get that?' It was Driss. He lowered himself down at her side. He smelled of fresh aftershave.

'My brother.'

She lifted the phone, revealing the screen, which read: *14 missed calls.*

'He's keen to get hold of you.'

'He's keen for me to come back home.'

'And you don't want to?'

She looked around her – at the beach, at her friends, at The Surf House. 'I'm happy here.'

'You weren't happy in California?'

186

'My father and brother think there is only one way to live life – like they do.' She shook her head. 'Plus, I feel like I've only just scratched the surface here.'

'It is true. Farah and I still need to show you our city.'

'Exactly. How can I leave Morocco without going to Marrakesh?' She smiled, her mood improving a little.

Her cell rang again.

Driss looked from the phone to her. 'Maybe it is time to tell your brother.'

Savannah walked to the shoreline with the phone pressed to her ear.

'I've been trying to get hold of you. Jesus, answer your phone, would you?' Seth snapped.

She sighed, looking out over the dark water.

'I'm trying to sort the travel details for Dad's wedding. I've put a flight on hold for you from Marrakesh. I'll pick you up at LAX, and we'll drive straight to the lake house.'

'I told you, I'm not coming back.'

There was a long silence. Savannah heard laughter behind her and saw Farah and Driss with their heads bent together.

'Of course you are. It's Dad's wedding.'

'He's not called. Not sent me an invite.'

'You know what Dad's like.'

'Yeah. I do.'

There was a long silence. She and Seth had been so close, once. When they were kids and their mother had still been alive, their favourite thing had been driving out to the Andrew Molera State Park to walk in the hills. Savannah would stalk the paths, hoping to catch sight of a mountain lion, Seth sticking close at her side with a stick in case she needed protection.

187

'Seth,' she said, trying to appeal to him, 'I don't want to leave here. I'm happy.'

Seth sighed, like her happiness was of little relevance. 'Then Dad's going to cut off your trust fund.'

'What?'

'That's what he said.'

'He can't do that.'

'There's a clause that means he can still access it until you're twenty-five.'

'The asshole!'

'He's stopping your money because he wants you to come home. He loves you.'

'There's a difference between love and control.'

When Seth spoke again, there was a weariness in his tone, as if she were a child testing his patience. 'Look, Savannah. Just come home. Go to the wedding. See Dad. Get things right. You can always disappear off on your travels again later.'

The way he said it – like what she was doing out here meant nothing – made her blood boil. 'Tell him he can keep the money. I don't want it. I've never wanted it.' *I wanted love.* 'I'm not coming back for the wedding, Seth.'

'He's not going to like it—'

'I'm not coming back at all.'

31

Bea walks into the village, Salty at her side. The surf is blown out today – too much wind on the water – and there are no surfers in the bay. With her eyes on the sea, she doesn't notice Aiden coming in the other direction until she almost collides with him.

From beneath his sun-faded cap, he is smiling at her. 'Hey. What are you up to?'

She runs her fingertips over Salty's velvet ears. Her mood's been agitated all day, thoughts wrapped tight to the extra money she needs to find to pay off Momo. She came into the village to get some air and stretch her legs. 'Just walking,' she tells him.

'I'm headed over the dunes.' He hesitates. 'D'you and Salty wanna come?'

She looks at the dog, who tips his head to one side as he stares back at her. 'We'd like that.'

As they leave behind the village, dry, cracked pavements give way to thick mounds of shifting, golden sand. The dunes have been landscaped by the wind, and theirs are the first footprints on the contoured sand. The late afternoon light is golden and dusky, and gulls wheel overhead, their winged shadows dancing.

Away from the village, the wind strengthens, a gust blasting in from the sea and whipping up the sand, which stings against

189

her bare calves and makes Salty clamp his tail. After a few more minutes of trotting with his ears flattened, Salty has had enough and turns and lopes back to the village.

'Looks like it's just us,' Aiden says.

Bea holds onto that word like he's handed her a precious shell: *us*.

This stretch of coast takes the full force of the prevailing wind. Without the shelter of the bay and the harbour, huge, unrideable waves barrel straight into the rocky coastline, sending flumes of water into the sky.

She follows Aiden's path as he picks his way over the dunes. His skin looks deeply tanned in the golden light.

'How's your arm?' Bea asks.

'It's good. I'm hoping to be back in the water in a couple more days.'

'Yeah? That's great.'

'Been enjoying seeing you out on the twin fin.'

She's riding a smaller board now – a six-foot twin fin that Marnie's lending her. It's harder to paddle as it's less buoyant, but it has an amazing, skateboard-like manoeuvrability on the waves.

'The way you get low into your turns is cool to see. You're picking it up so quickly. A natural surfer.'

Bea feels the compliment land with a warmth that suffuses her whole body. She rolls the word *surfer* on her tongue. Maybe she *is* a surfer. It's happened by degrees – her daily paddle outs, the regular checking of the forecast, planning her time around the swell.

Surfing has been a quiet revelation. Being out amongst the waves makes her feel like she's reconnecting with part of herself that was numbed. She's learning how to listen to her body, to ride the board intuitively. There is no lens trained on her, no prize at the end of it. All she's searching for is a moment's grace gliding on a wave.

'Come on,' Aiden says, as the dunes give way to a shelf of rock. 'I want to show you something.'

She follows him as they clamber over dark boulders, moving towards the water's edge. Looking at the darkening ocean, ravaged with waves, she asks, 'Do you miss the surf back home in Ireland?'

'Not the winter sea temperature. But I miss the adventure of it. Chasing down a forecast, the emptiness of the waves, warming up after in a pub with a blazing fire.' Aiden smiles, his expression light with the memory.

'Has your family been out to Mallah to see Offshore?'

'Nah. Not their kind of thing.'

'They must be proud hearing about the life you're making here.'

A swift darkness descends over his features. He takes a few steps ahead of her, bending to pick up a loose stone, which he turns through his fingers. He launches it towards the water. 'Nothing to be proud of,' he says in a voice so quiet she almost misses it.

Bea wonders what happened back home in Ireland that caused Aiden to leave. She senses the darkness coiled tight and wonders if that's what draws him out to the waves at night.

She steps forward so that she's at his shoulder. 'Aiden . . . please don't say that, about there being nothing to be proud of.'

His eyes are on hers, dark and skittish.

'I see the way you are with your students,' she goes on, 'and I hear the good things people say about Offshore.'

He looks right at her, studying her intently with the same

focus with which he absorbs the surf, as if he's trying to work out something. There's such intensity in his gaze that she can barely catch her breath.

A loud rumbling noise fills her ears.

Aiden turns towards the water. 'Here we go.'

Bea follows his gaze to see a surging wave bowling towards the rocks. There's a rushing sound that comes from almost beneath them and then, seconds later, a huge jet of whitewater explodes from the centre of the rocks, roaring high into the air, like a whale's spout.

She screams with shock and delight. 'A blowhole!'

The spray catches in the breeze and mists their faces. As the wave recedes, drawing the water back out, she can see the deep hole in the rock that leads to the sea.

'The blowhole only works on a high tide and with a big swell,' Aiden tells her. 'I love coming to see it.'

She wonders whether he comes alone or if this is a place he brings other women. Marnie and Farah's comments play on her mind.

Bea feels rather than sees the next wave rumbling beneath them. The soles of her feet vibrate with the energy. With a deafening boom, the wave cracks against the rock and surges into the narrow cave, then is forced upwards in an explosion of water.

Aiden grabs her hand and pulls her back. Salt water rains down, and Bea tips her face up, laughing into the downpour. She thinks of the water fountain on her photoshoot – how she put her face to the jet, trying to feel something other than the deadening numbness.

Now, she feels the cling of wet fabric against her skin, the roar of the sea beyond them, the graze of sun-warmed rock beneath her feet. And her hand – still held by Aiden.

Her fingers entwine with his, palms wet and hot. She turns into him.

'Bea . . .' He says her name with thirst – as if his lips are dry and her name is water.

She leans forward and kisses him. There is salt on their lips and heat in their mouths.

His body responds to hers with urgency, a low moan of desire rising from his throat. His hand slips from hers and moves across her body, fingers sliding over the bare, wet skin of her arms.

She feels the contours of his chest through his sodden T-shirt, slides her hands beneath the damp fabric.

Another wave breaks against the rocks, but they do not pause to watch it surge from the blowhole – they just feel its briny mist entwine with their breath as they continue to kiss.

Eventually, eventually, they slow. They stand and breathe together. She looks right at him and can see the darkness returning to his eyes, as if some part of him is already pulling back.

He shakes his head. 'I'm sorry . . .'

'Whatever this is, Aiden, I want it.'

'I'm not in a good place to start anything right now.'

She says, 'I'm not asking you to.'

Relationships aren't for her. She has tried. There have been other men – but as soon as things became physical, any attraction that was initially there just . . . shut down. It was like there was a valve in her body that switched off, dial turned to *we're done here!* It was humiliating and impossible to explain, so it was easier to hold herself at a distance.

Yet with Aiden, she feels . . . different. Maybe it's because other men chased after her, wanting to show her off because they were dating a *model*. But with Aiden, there is no parading. Their places are outside – the cliff at night, the sea, this blowhole.

Maybe because he wants nothing, she is able to give something.

His eyes hold her. 'What are you asking for?'

She looks right at him. 'Only this,' she says before she presses her mouth to his.

It is after dark when Bea returns to The Surf House. In her room, she flops onto her bed and replays the brush of Aiden's stubble against her cheek, the warm musk scent of his neck, the taste of salt on his skin.

They'd stayed at the blowhole until the sun went down and Bea began to shiver in her damp clothes. Then they wandered back through the village, him peeling off when he reached Offshore. Already, she wonders when she'll see him again. There are no plans laid, no dates set, no numbers swapped. The unpredictability of what happens next is intoxicating.

There's a shout from next door, and Bea sits up.

Through the paper-thin wall, she hears Ped's booming voice. The frequency of his and Marnie's arguments has been increasing, and she hates living on top of them, having to bear witness to the cracks in their relationship.

The wall muffles some of Ped's words, but his tone and volume shred at her nerves.

There is a pause. She waits, wondering if Marnie is now speaking, but she cannot make out her voice.

Then Ped speaks again. Not loud this time, but urgent, rushed, hissing through clenched teeth. Bea holds her breath, listening.

Marnie's response sounds panicked, quick. There's the rush of footsteps across the room – and then a sharp cry.

Something smashes into the joining wall, hard enough to rattle the window frame.

Silence.

Bea waits, stomach clenched.

Eventually, she hears Ped say something in a low, urgent voice, followed by the faint sound of crying.

Then comes a dull thud, the sound of something – someone? – being hit.

Without pause, Bea is on her feet, bursting through the connecting door.

She finds Marnie sitting on the floor, her back to the wall, head in her hands. There's a smashed lamp at the foot of their bed, the ceramic base splintered into dusty pieces.

Ped is standing by the desk, his face a mask of fury, eyes glittering with rage. He looks possessed. All that controlled energy exploded.

He glances from Bea to Marnie, and then stalks out, slamming the door behind him.

Bea goes to Marnie, gathering her in her arms. 'It's okay . . .' she whispers. She kisses Marnie's face, which is wet with tears.

'He didn't mean it,' Marnie says.

Bea helps Marnie to her feet. She leads her to a wicker chair in the corner of the room. Marnie sits, drawing up her bare feet and locking her arms around her knees. She digs her nails into her calf muscles, raking at her skin.

Bea places a blanket around Marnie's shoulders, then crouches at her side. 'Marnie, did he hit—'

'God! No!' Her face creases with disgust at the suggestion. 'Ped would never do that.'

'Sorry. It just sounded—'

'Ped is stressed, okay? We've got shit going on.' She gets to her feet, the blanket falling from her shoulders, and paces to the window.

Bea wants to tell her to watch out for the smashed lamp, but Marnie is already on the other side of the room. She forces the window wide and then leans her upper body right out.

'Careful—' Bea warns, stepping forward.

Marnie ignores her, taking a deep lungful of salt air, head tipped to the stars. She stays there, hanging half in the room, half out, breathing in the night.

Bea wills her to come back into the safety of the room.

After a few more breaths, Marnie lowers herself from the window and turns to face Bea. She looks calm again, all traces of fragility vanished. 'I'm sorry we disturbed you tonight. It's not fair. We'll do better.' Her gaze flicks back to the darkened sea, voice fixed as she says, 'We have to do better.'

32

The day after Marnie and Ped's argument, they are careful with one another. Marnie slips from the kitchen as Ped enters; Ped takes his coffee to the office to drink; Bea's asked to pass a message between them about a forthcoming booking.

A prickling tension tightens the atmosphere inside The Surf House and makes knots of Bea's stomach. That's why she's surprised when Marnie rallies the guests, telling them they're partying at Rooftops tonight.

So now Bea is standing at the base of a ladder that is propped against a disused building.

'Come on up!' Marnie calls.

Music streams into the night, a wild electronic beat that vibrates through her body. Bea begins to climb, hand over hand, sandals slipping on the wooden rungs. Best not to look down, she decides, instead focusing on Marnie, who waits, grinning.

When she's on the top rung, Marnie stretches out a hand, pulling her onto a flat roof festooned with lights.

Rooftops is the remains of a hostel that folded during construction, so it is only a shell of a building. There are sheer drops on all four sides of the roof, which are only partially blocked by some low pallet seating and clusters of planters housing cactuses.

'What d'you think?' Marnie asks, opening her arms to Rooftops.

Rafiq, a DJ from Marrakesh who has wooden beads plaited into his goatee, has set up his decks on a makeshift table. Beers are sold from a huge cool box, and no one asks questions about how they were sourced.

After a day of clean swell, the vibe is one of celebration. Surfers, still with telltale streaks of zinc on their cheeks, fill the space, wearing large tees and narrow shorts. Bea recognises most of the crowd – travellers who park up in their vans, surfers staying at Offshore and other hostels, the seasonal staff and local surf instructors and cooks.

She scans Rooftops for Aiden and is disappointed not to find him.

'Here,' Marnie says, passing Bea a drink. 'Rum and coke.'

They clink plastic glasses, and Bea takes a sip. It tastes like there's almost no mixer, and she coughs and laughs at the same time. 'You trying to get me drunk?'

'Would you like me to?' Marnie says, holding Bea's gaze with a challenge.

Marnie's wearing a thin cotton playsuit that reveals her slender, tanned thighs. Her gold earrings are jagged and dazzling, and her throat is bare. There is something about her tonight that feels loose, untethered.

When Seth's head emerges warily above the step ladder to Rooftops, Marnie calls, 'Up here!'

'You invited him?' Bea asks, surprised. 'I didn't think you liked him . . .'

'Maybe I've been too quick to pass judgement. He's just lost his dad, and Savannah's cut ties. I think he's lost. Needs to be made to feel welcome.'

Surprised by Marnie's U-turn, Bea greets him, and the three of them settle on low pallets softened by cushions.

Seth leans forward, elbows on his knees, glancing around. 'This is different,' he says, eyeing the cross-legged group on a floor rug who are taking turns to draw from a huge shisha pipe. He assesses the drop at the roof's edge.

'A health and safety issue, right?' Marnie says with a grin.

He smiles.

'I'm going to fetch us more drinks,' Marnie announces, springing to her feet.

The night is airless and humid – rare for it to feel that way on the coast. Bea feels her lower back slick with sweat.

Seth leans into Bea. Voice lowered, he says, 'I've got something.'

'A lead?'

He nods.

'On Momo?'

He shakes his head. 'Ped.'

She blinks. 'Ped?'

Seth looks enlivened, thrumming with whatever it is he has found out.

'Have you noticed that he's rarely in the same room with me? Always goes out of his way to avoid me?'

Ped has been closed, almost aggressively so, in his answers to Seth's questions. Bea has put it down to Ped's reticent manner – and yet, with the other guests, on occasion, he can be expansive.

She glances across the bar, which is filling with travellers in sandals and cross-body bags. Ped stands at the edge with a couple of surfers she recognises from the lineup. Marnie is further along, ordering drinks. They don't acknowledge one another. She thinks of last night's raised voices and rough words, the crash of the lamp splintering against the wall, Marnie hunched on the ground.

Bea turns back to Seth. 'So Ped avoids you.'

'He won't be able to tomorrow.' There's a feverish look in his expression. 'I've booked a surf lesson.' The corners of Seth's mouth lift into a triumphant smile.

'You? Surfing?'

'Don't judge me on the shirts. I grew up in California. It's practically part of the curriculum. I may not be a natural – or have surfed for a decade,' he adds, 'but hey, that's what an instructor's for, right?'

'What's the lead?'

Seth clocks Marnie returning with Driss, Farah, and Elin, who are carrying glasses and jugs of cocktails, and the conversation halts.

They squeeze up, making room for the others, while Marnie pours generous measures of the cocktail and passes them around. Bea sips the sweet, strong liquid, unable to place the ingredients. It's cloying, and she can feel the vapours in her mouth.

Marnie tips her glass towards Seth's, then drinks hers down in one. He mirrors her action, then proffers his empty glass for a refill.

'What do you think of Morocco?' Driss asks Seth.

Seth glances across Rooftops, taking in the makeshift bar. 'It's like nowhere I've ever been.' It is a careful statement – neither a compliment nor a slight.

'Savannah loved Mallah,' Elin says defensively.

Bea's noticed that Elin hasn't yet met her eye, awkwardness still lingering from their last conversation.

Seth nods at this, then addresses Driss and Farah. 'I heard Savannah came to stay with you in Marrakesh?'

'Yes,' Farah answers, eyes bright. 'The city isn't for everyone, but Savannah thrived on the chaos and colour of the place. It's what we love, too. But you need a balance – that's why we come here.'

Driss and Farah share stories of their earlier travels to Mallah, the sandstorms that blew in off the desert, the wild evenings on the beach. Marnie finishes her drink and refills it. Bea places her hand over the rim of her glass as Marnie tries to top it up, already feeling light-headed, but Seth keeps pace. There is something intense in the way Marnie and Seth lift each drink to their mouths, almost in time, eyes on one another.

Marnie glances across the room at Ped. He meets her eye, but there is no smile or warmth.

'Ped's not going to join us?' Bea asks Marnie.

'No.'

'I don't think Ped likes me very much,' Seth says, the edges of his words now loosened by alcohol.

Marnie takes a slow sip of her drink, then presses her lips together. 'Ped doesn't like many people.'

'Did he like Savannah?'

It's Driss who answers, laughter in his voice, 'He wasn't her greatest fan after that Rooftops night. Do you remember?'

'The after-party!' Farah says, eyes twinkling.

'Oh God,' Marnie says. 'Ped's board! I slept through the whole thing – but he was livid for days.'

Driss explains, 'We'd all been here, at Rooftops. Savannah didn't want the night to end, so she invited a crowd back to The Surf House to party. A group of travellers were messing around in the pool on Ped's board. Put a ding in the nose.'

Marnie winces at the memory. 'Didn't go down well.'

One of the local surf instructors approaches their table, clapping hands with Driss, then kissing Farah.

Elin turns to Seth, her voice low. 'You've had to pull Savannah out from parties before, I hear?' Her loaded tone cuts through the easy atmosphere.

'Excuse me?' Seth says.

Elin keeps her voice quiet, but Bea, who sits on the other side of Seth, hears clearly. 'She told me how you dragged her out.' There's a pause. 'By her hair.'

Seth looks like he's been slapped. 'That's what she told you?'

'Did you?'

'Jesus.' He pinches the bridge of his nose. Shakes his head. 'I know the night she's talking about. Did she mention that she was so high she'd stolen our dad's car? She drove it to a party completely off her face. Dad wanted to call the cops – but I said I'd fetch her. When I found her, she was totally out of it. I helped her back to my car, but she was staggering everywhere, and her hair got caught in the zip of my jacket. She started yelling, freaking out, screaming at me to get off her. Everyone was watching.' He shakes his head, expression raw with emotion. 'D'you know how that feels? Your sister shouting that you're hurting her, when you're only trying to keep her safe?'

Finished, Seth gets up from the table and heads for the bar.

Elin holds up her palms, like, *what did I do?*

Bea is about to follow and check he's okay, when Marnie stands, saying, 'I'll go.' She takes one of the cocktail jugs with her and, when she catches up with Seth, she refills his glass. The tension in his face begins to ebb as they talk and drink.

Bea threads through the thickening crowd, feeling the heat of other bodies. The music is loud, and the alcohol is making it hard to think clearly. Aiden is still absent, and she's beginning to wish she'd not come either.

202

She grabs a mineral water from the cooler and presses it against her cheek, deciding if she's going to call it a night.

'Marnie could use one of those.'

She looks up to find Ped at her shoulder.

Bea glances back through the crowd towards Marnie. She's pulling Seth through the group of dancers, and there's something loose in her movements as she swings her hips.

She glimpses someone different in Seth to the buttoned-up, focused brother who came out here searching for his sister. He's hurting, vulnerable, but also a man who likes to take risks.

Marnie begins to dance, her movements fluid and sensual. Seth's gaze is pinned to her body as she sinks low to the ground. Her muscles flex, tanned skin stretching tight over beautifully sculpted legs and arms.

Bea glances at Ped. There is a flicker of tension at the edge of his mouth.

Eyes still on Marnie, he says, 'Look out for her tonight.'

ONE YEAR EARLIER

SAVANNAH

Savannah danced with her arms raised, fingers weaving through the night, hips slinking low to the earth. She could feel the backs of her knees slick with sweat.

Rooftops was crammed with people partying and dancing and drinking. She swayed closer to the edge, peering down at the long drop to the ground below.

There was a hand on her arm. 'Careful, there.' Driss was at her shoulder, dark eyes warm. He guided her away from the edge.

'Looking out for me,' Savannah said, and she laughed and kept on spinning, feeling the night against her bare midriff.

Nights like these, she thought. Here she was, dancing beneath the stars, no one to keep tabs on her. She loved Morocco for its souks and sunshine and incredible flavours – and for its distance from California.

When the night at Rooftops started to wind down, Savannah wasn't ready. 'After-party at The Surf House!' she announced, gathering a crowd. She looped an arm around Elin's waist and called to Aiden to 'Keep up!'

A trail of people followed her to The Surf House. She flicked on the pool lights, and the water glowed turquoise, alluring and cool in the warm night. Lanterns twinkled; music spilled across the terrace. Driss and Farah lounged back on sofas, smoking, their legs entwined.

A group of German surfers, who were staying in another hostel, grabbed a board from the rack and skimmed it across the pool, seeing who could stay on their feet from one side to the other.

Elin, beer in hand, glanced around the terrace with a smirk. 'Sure Ped and Marnie will want you partying here?'

'They're cool. They'll probably join us.'

Elin raised an eyebrow.

Savannah weaved to the speaker and turned it up. She hopped up onto the wall, dancing along the edge of it to cheers. She could feel her hair swaying at her back.

Out beyond the cliff top, she could see a figure standing in the dark, watching. She didn't stop moving but let her gaze wander across the person, taking in their shape and silhouette.

Momo.

He always stayed on the edge of things. He was a young man, drawn to this world of partying and surfing, but he was also a police officer, so he couldn't be where people were drinking and casting off the order of things. Savannah wanted him to come play. Loosen up. She slowed her dancing, rocking lower and lower, sensuous.

Suddenly, a booming voice cut across the party. 'What the fuck?'

Ped was standing on the poolside, feet planted wide, shoulders back. He was only wearing a pair of shorts and looked like he'd been roused from sleep.

Someone else who needed loosening up.

'Is that my board?'

The German surfers clambered apologetically from the pool, water sluicing across the terrace as they sheepishly returned the board to the rack, then disappeared back to whichever hostel they came from.

Someone turned down the music, and the atmosphere drained away. Elin exited, lifting a hand in salute to Savannah as she disappeared over the cliff path.

The party didn't need to stop, Savannah decided. Ped just needed to relax. He was as bad as Seth. She wasn't going to let a little tantrum ruin things.

'Everyone out,' he said to the final stragglers, casting a thick arm towards the exit.

Driss clapped a hand on Ped's shoulder as he moved inside The Surf House, apologising for the disturbance, but Ped's expression didn't mellow.

Savannah made no move to leave.

Ped spun around, eyes shining. 'This was you, wasn't it? Bringing everyone back here.'

She could guess what he was thinking from the disparaging way he looked at her: *Spoiled trust funder.*

Well, she wasn't anymore. She was making her own way.

'Go to bed, Savannah,' he said, as if she were a child.

She smiled at Ped, her lips peeling over her teeth. She felt the alcohol warming her veins, shimmering through her skin. She walked towards the shallow end of the pool and paused there.

A ripple moved across the surface as she dipped in her first foot. She took another step and another, the water sliding over her bare legs, soaking into her shorts, making her top stick slickly to her skin.

She dived forward, kicking down to the bottom of the pool. She hung there, eyes open to the water blur, hair fanning around her, that shimmer burning deep in her lungs.

Down here, Ped's anger was only a shadow on the surface.

33

Leaving Rooftops behind, Bea wanders along the cliff top. The deep reggae bass softens, pulsing into the starlit night. Sweat cools pleasingly against her skin as she moves further away from the crush of the crowd.

As she nears Salty's nook, she looks to see if Aiden is there – but finds it empty. She'd love to sit out here with Aiden tonight, watch the waves, talk, feel the warmth of his body beside hers. She knows what their deal is. Light. Casual. Nothing deeper. Yet she finds herself storing moments of her day ready to share with him.

As she crosses the terrace towards The Surf House, she hears a strange gasping sound in the darkness. Her senses spring alert.

There is a low moan, then a breathless sound.

Creeping forward, she makes out two figures in the darkness, pressed against the studio wall.

It takes a moment for the scene to come clearly into view. It is Marnie, her back against the wall, jumpsuit around her ankles. Seth holds her hips.

Bea must make a sound of surprise, because Marnie and Seth freeze.

When Marnie looks up and sees her, Marnie winks.

Bea's cheeks flame as she backs away.

She hurries into The Surf House, taking the stairs two at a time.

At the top, she sees that Marnie and Ped's door is open a crack. The light is on. Is Ped back already?

Look out for Marnie tonight.

Her stomach lurches.

Bea slips into the bathroom. Closes the door. She peels off her clothes, steps into the shower, and lets the hot water scald her.

Her thoughts spin wildly. Marnie doesn't even want Seth. Bea knows that. Yet there was a strange, destructive energy about Marnie this evening. She needs her to be the strong, fierce, determined woman she believed her to be – not someone who cheats on her partner against a wall.

Bea hears the click of the latch. The shower steam swells as Marnie lets herself into the bathroom. 'Jesus, Marnie! You could knock!'

Marnie begins peeling off her jumpsuit, wriggling free of it until she is standing in just her underwear.

'What are you doing?'

'I need to shower,' she says, alcohol slurring the edges of her words. She tugs down her underwear and Bea sees hand marks around her breasts and hips; her neck is flushed. She steps into the stream of hot water, and Bea moves back, the cold tiles pressing against her shoulder blades.

Marnie leans her head forward, letting water pour over her scalp. A channel of water cascades down her spine and into the grooves at the tops of her buttocks.

She reaches for the soap and hands it to Bea. 'Wash me,' she whispers.

The soap is in Bea's hands. She looks at it for a moment, then finds her hands moving to Marnie's wet shoulders, her skin hot and glistening beneath her touch. She slides her hands down her arms. Marnie stands there, naked, her darkened nipples hard and erect.

She's no idea what this is. What game Marnie is playing.

'Wash yourself,' Bea says sharply, pushing the soap at her. Then she moves past Marnie and grabs a towel, wrapping it around herself and leaving the bathroom.

Marnie doesn't even look at her as she leaves.

In her room, Bea pulls a T-shirt over her still-damp skin and dives into bed.

She hears the bathroom light turn off, the extractor fan go quiet. Hears the tread of bare feet across the corridor, the squeak of the door opening then shutting. She catches the low timbre of Ped's voice. He must be back.

She realises she is braced, waiting for the explosion. But tonight, there are no raised voices. Nothing thrown. No bedsprings creaking. Just the quiet movement of Ped's feet as he leaves the room, descends the stairs, and exits the building. A minute later, she thinks she catches the distant sound of the van door opening.

Marnie must be listening, too, because then Bea hears the depression of the bedsprings, followed by the light exhale of breath as Marnie begins to cry.

Later, there is a gentle knock on the connecting door.

Marnie steals into Bea's room in the darkness and switches on the lamp. She stands in a T-shirt and pair of boxer shorts, hair damp, bare feet pressed together.

Bea sits up, blinking into the light.

Marnie perches on the end of her bed, hands in her lap. 'I'm

209

sorry,' she says, head lowered. There's something vulnerable in the rounding of her shoulders that Bea's not seen before. 'I've messed up.'

Silence wraps around them both.

'Seth,' Bea says eventually. 'Why?' Even as she asks the question, Bea knows the answer. Marnie uses her body, her sexuality, to draw people to her. It's a currency. She wonders what love she was denied growing up that made her learn to act like that.

Marnie shrugs. 'Guess I wanted to prove something.'

Bea doesn't follow. 'To who?'

Marnie's gaze remains on her lap. A single tear falls from the corner of her eye onto her hand. 'Ped . . .'

Bea shakes her head. 'I don't understand.'

Marnie's next words are so quiet that Bea isn't sure she catches them fully. 'I think Ped is cheating.'

Bea blinks. It takes a moment for this to land. 'Are you sure?'

'Those long trips chasing swell? There's a woman.'

'Have you talked to him?'

More tears leak from the corners of Marnie's eyes. She shakes her head. 'What if he . . . loves her? What if he leaves me?'

Bea is at her side now, taking Marnie's small hands in her own. 'He loves you.'

She turns her face towards Bea. Her eyes are large and round with distress. 'Then why is he cheating?'

'People make bad decisions.'

'Like fucking Seth?'

'Like that.' Bea smiles sadly. 'Does Ped know?'

'About Seth? God, no, I don't think so.'

'I thought . . . I heard him leave. He's gone to the van.'

She nods. 'He sleeps there some nights,' she says with a small shrug of her shoulders. 'This room – it's Ped's.'

Bea doesn't follow.

'We've been having problems for a while. So . . . sometimes he sleeps in here.'

Which is why Ped came in on the first night he returned to The Surf House, Bea realises.

Marnie squeezes Bea's fingers. 'I love you,' she says. 'You are my family. I'm sorry for tonight. I'm sorry this is messy. I'm going to do better.' Marnie wraps her arms around Bea, hugging her tightly.

'Tomorrow's a fresh start,' Bea says, mirroring Marnie's motto.

She feels Marnie's head nod against her. Then she pulls back and places a kiss on Bea's forehead like all the other evenings. 'G'night, Bea.'

34

Bea is relieved when Marnie doesn't come down to help prepare breakfast. She's not got the headspace to navigate her emotions.

She opens the kitchen door to say good morning to Salty, who lies in a patch of sun on the doormat. She strokes the soft fur on his tummy, and he submits easily to the pleasure, flopping fully onto his side. Dogs are so much simpler than people, she thinks.

As she continues to circle her hand across his belly, she sets her gaze on the bay. The morning is hazy, the desert wind kicking up enough dust to raise it to the sun. The swell is solid, but it's ruffled by the strong breeze. Still, good enough to surf. She'll get in after breakfast, clear her head.

She notices Ped out on the terrace, feet planted, breathing deep into his abdomen. Her teeth press together as she thinks about what Marnie confided last night. All those long trips away, not surfing but cheating.

Ped's gaze is focused and still as he watches Seth emerge from the studio. His skin is dour, eyes puffy, and his short blond hair is rumpled at the back of his head. He fumbles in his pocket for his sunglasses and pulls them on.

Ped's attention remains lasered to Seth, the muscles in his back tense, his shoulders stiff.

Does he know?

Seth hasn't noticed Ped and seats himself at his usual table, alone in the shade. He slumps back in his chair, rubbing at his brow. He exhales hard, dropping his head.

Ped remains where he is for a moment – and then Bea watches him draw back his shoulders, roll his head a little as if loosening his neck. He moves towards Seth's table with powerful, easy strides. As he passes, he claps Seth on the shoulder, startling him. 'See you in the water in half an hour, mate!'

Seth's mouth opens and closes.

'Surf lesson.'

'Great . . .' Seth says, nodding. He gives a quick, awkward smile.

When Ped has moved on, Seth slumps back in his chair.

Bea sets about making Seth's coffee with little care, then delivers it to his table. She sets it down, the coffee slopping over the edge of the mug.

He looks up uncertainly, trying for a smile.

'Good night?' she asks pointedly.

His smile fades. 'Bit too much to drink. Struggling a bit this morning.' He rubs his head; there's a blotch of colour rising on his neck. 'I don't normally drink. Doesn't really suit me. Sorry if I was . . . not myself.'

She feels herself thaw a little. She knows how persuasive Marnie can be – Seth was in the beam of her attention, and it burns so brightly that it can be dazzling.

He glances at his watch. 'God, I don't feel like a surf lesson.'

'Sure you want to go ahead?'

He looks at her for a moment, then seems to set his resolve. 'I need to.'

She remembers their hurried conversation at Rooftops last night, Seth leaning close to tell her that he had a lead.

'Just . . .' she begins, thinking of Ped's hawk-like gaze, '. . . be careful.'

Bea takes her board from the rack and jogs down to the water. Salty trots at her side, and she is pleased to have his easy company.

She passes Elin, who watches her warily from her perch on the rocks, where she's setting up her camera.

Driss and Farah are down by the shore, attaching leashes. They both look a little jaded, too. 'Hope you're feeling better than us after last night?' Farah says.

'Is Rooftops always like that?' Bea asks.

'It is when Marnie has that glint in her eye.'

It was more than a glint, Bea thinks, remembering how hard she'd been drinking and how she went after Seth with intent. She wonders at what point Marnie decided: *Him. I'm going to fuck him.*

Maybe she admires her for that, though. It was reactive, sure, but she still had the confidence to go after what she wanted.

As Driss and Farah paddle out together, Bea hangs back. She wants to be out there on her own this morning.

She takes her time wading in. The water is surprisingly cool, even on the hottest of days. She calls goodbye to Salty, who barks forlornly from the shallows, and then she is paddling out, the motion fluid and easy, her shoulders strong and toned from weeks of surfing.

When she glances back, Salty is lying on his belly in the wet sand, muzzle on his paws, waiting for her.

She makes her way out to the lineup, then sits astride her board, legs dangling into the water. She spots Seth and Ped some distance away and narrows her eyes as she watches them, wondering what Seth's lead is.

214

She turns away, setting her gaze on the horizon. She comes out here for her head – to let her thoughts settle and quieten. She takes a breath and allows herself to be lulled by the rise and fall of the swell. When a set rolls in that she wants, she paddles into position. Her pop-up is sharp and smooth. She can feel it all, the fizz of the ocean in her ears, the glitter of the sun against the wave face, water droplets in the atmosphere making a rainbow haze at the wave's back. She feels the power of the swell beneath her as if it's travelling up through the balls of her feet.

She rides the wave till its end, then dives off and allows herself to float, absorbing the beauty of the moment.

'Hey!'

She looks around and sees Aiden paddling towards her on a longboard. He is grinning, water caught in his dark lashes.

'You're back in the surf!'

'Sure am.'

A wave breaks, and they duck dive beneath it, letting it surge over them. They emerge, hair slicked to their heads, blinking water from their eyes.

'Bet it feels good.'

He looks at her. 'Feels very good.' And there's that smile again.

When the next wave comes, they both paddle into position. It's a clean, shoulder-high wave, and Aiden calls, 'Let's get this one!'

They begin to paddle, Aiden out in front, Bea nearest the peak. They take off together and, surfing at Aiden's side, Bea can see the beauty of the line he carves, cross-stepping to the nose of the board. Then he is hanging ten, right in front of her, toes on the nose, back arched, hands clasped with insouciance at his back. As the wave slows, he cross-steps back and digs his heels in over the fins, turning the board.

Bea feels a powerful sense of belonging, that this is where she is meant to be.

She comes off the wave a little earlier than Aiden, beaming with the pleasure of it all. Last night is washed away, and there is only this moment, laughing beneath a hazy sky.

She looks around for Aiden and sees a board floating – not his but a blue foamie.

Then she spots a dark shape nearby. A surfer, spread-eagled, facedown.

Immediately, she is paddling hard.

The surfer doesn't move or lift their head for air.

Even before she's reached them, she feels it somewhere deep inside. A knowledge settling.

She screams for help.

Grabbing the surfer by his shoulders, she tries to turn him – but he is a deadweight, and she cannot flip him onto his back.

Farah has spotted her and is paddling over, fast. She slips off her board and, together, they manage to turn the surfer.

'Oh God,' Bea whispers.

Seth floats on his back, eyes unmoving.

'We need to get him onto the beach!' Bea yells. She hooks her arm around his neck and begins to swim him to shore. 'Undo his leash!'

Farah does as she says, releasing the drag of the board from him.

The whitewater from a broken wave rolls towards them, pushing them the final distance to shore. Other surfers have spotted them now. Aiden, ditching his board, comes sprinting along the shoreline.

'On his back!' he yells, as they lower Seth onto the sand.

Then Aiden is kneeling at Seth's shoulder, white-faced as he checks his breathing.

'Ambulance!' Bea yells to someone, who begins to run.

Aiden starts to administer chest compressions. He counts to thirty, then lowers his mouth to Seth's and breathes into it.

Bea waits for the moment where Seth's eyes open and he coughs up seawater, but it doesn't come.

Seth's eyes remain closed.

Aiden performs another round of chest compressions.

Salty slinks over, ears flattened, wheedling around Aiden's ankles.

'Away!' Bea calls.

Salty scuttles to the side, tail between his legs, and Bea notices Ped standing there. His arms hang loose at his sides, watching.

Bea looks past him, up towards the cliff, desperate to see a medic, an ambulance – anyone who can help. But she knows the nearest hospital is over an hour's drive. Marnie is descending the steps with her board and, seeing the commotion, she suddenly begins to run.

'Keep going!' Bea begs Aiden.

He repeats another set of chest compressions, counting aloud as he pumps Seth's chest, his own face red with the exertion.

Aiden completes six rounds, then staggers back, hands on his knees, salt water dripping from his hair.

He looks at Bea, then shakes his head.

Seth is dead.

35

They must move Seth's body because of the incoming tide. Bea hangs back with Salty, trembling fingers twined in his fur.

Driss, Ped, Aiden, and Farah lift Seth's body on the count of three. There is no way to do it gracefully. They hold Seth by his arms and ankles, but his head lolls, the back of his skull dusting the beach.

Driss looks waxy-skinned as he staggers through a deep patch of sand and, for a moment, Bea thinks he's going to let go. Farah says something to him, and Driss regains his footing and keeps his gaze on the ground.

The group reach the cliff, readjusting their positions so that they can carry him up the narrow, steep steps.

There's a hand at Bea's back. 'Y'okay?'

She turns and finds Marnie, her wetsuit peeled down to her hips. The skin at her chest is flushed and blotchy.

'I . . .' Bea begins, her throat dry. She can barely swallow. 'He . . .' She cannot seem to find the words she's searching for. Isn't even sure what she's trying to say. All she knows is that this morning, she made Seth coffee. Talked with him. Watched him walk from The Surf House towards the beach. He was alive.

And now he isn't.

She pulls her gaze to the water. The tide is coming in; the rocks will soon be hidden. 'What happened? Could he have hit the reef?'

Marnie lifts and drops her shoulders. 'I didn't see any marks.'

Neither did she.

Drowned, then, Bea thinks. *But how? How?*

He was with Ped. That's what she knows.

Her heart is racing. All she keeps thinking is, *Seth had a lead on Ped.*

And now he's dead.

Salty noses her leg, reminding her that he's there. She lowers her face to him, breathing in the biscuity smell of his coat.

'You're shaking,' Marnie says. 'We need to get you out of your wetsuit.'

Bea looks up towards the cliff edge. The group carrying Seth's body are silhouetted by the sun, four dark figures delivering a body to The Surf House.

It was once a place of sanctuary.

And now?

It is a couple of hours before the police and ambulance arrive. Bea hears the rap at the door. She moves slowly, distantly, like she is behind a thick pane of glass and everything else is on the other side of it – muted, distant, unreachable. She knows this feeling. The numbness, the safety of it.

Officer Karim enters first. She recognises him immediately by his neat moustache and the dark, hooded eyes that once swept over Marnie's van at the checkpoint. He is followed by Momo, who looks at Marnie, then at Bea.

She finds her gaze narrowing as she stares at Momo, thinking of him drifting into her bedroom, planting her stolen rucksack on the bed, leaving his bribery note demanding more money. Her throat turns slick with saliva as the pressure twists at her stomach.

Marrakesh . . . the bribes . . . Seth's death . . . It's too much.

Marnie begins leading the officers through The Surf House, their dark uniforms and guns incongruous in the light space. Bea knows she needs to join them. The police will want a statement. Her legs are trembling, but she takes a low, steady breath and follows.

'He's out here,' Marnie is saying, leading them along the poolside to the small, shaded terrace that backs onto the kitchen. 'The tide swallows the beach, so we had to move him.'

Seth's body is laid in the shade of a lemon tree. A beach towel has been draped over him, but it's too short to cover him entirely. His feet poke out, bare and white and exposed.

Officer Karim pulls back the beach towel.

Bea forces herself to keep looking, not to flinch from the sight of death. Already, Seth's skin has a strange waxy sheen. A blue thread from the towel hangs limply across his cheek, and she wants to brush it off.

'Who is this man?' asks Officer Karim.

'Seth Hart. He was one of our guests,' Marnie answers.

'You are the owner of this place?'

'Yes. I run it with my husband,' Marnie says, although Bea knows she and Ped are not married.

'Where is he?'

'Inside,' Marnie says. 'Bea, would you mind fetching Ped?'

Grateful to have a task, she turns quickly and walks into The Surf House. The place is deserted, no sign of Ped in the kitchen or lounge. She checks the office and his bedroom, but finds them empty, too.

Bea is crossing the terrace when she spots him. He is backing out of Seth's studio, closing the door softly behind him. She watches as Ped slips something into the pocket of his shorts. He pauses for a moment, tips back his head, and takes a long, steady breath.

Then Ped pushes away from the wall, about to move off – when he sees Bea. Their eyes meet. His clear gaze bores into her, a challenge in it.

Her head pounds with questions . . . Seth booked that surf lesson because he needed to talk to Ped. He had a lead on Savannah – was finally getting close. And now, Seth's dead . . .

'What were you doing in Seth's room?'

'Getting his passport. The police will need it for identification.'

She looks at him carefully. 'We have a copy on file.'

Ped says, 'Best to show them the original. It'll have his next of kin details.'

She wants to demand that Ped show her the passport, but he would ask, *Why?* – and what would she answer? *Because I don't trust you. Because maybe you were rooting around for something else. Because it's proof that you're a liar.*

But Bea can say none of these things. Not yet, at least.

'The police are here,' she says eventually. 'They want to see you.'

'Was Seth travelling with anyone?' Officer Karim asks.

'No,' Ped answers. 'He came alone.'

'For a holiday?'

Marnie smiles. 'Yes.'

Bea flinches. Momo knows this is a lie. Seth already spoke to him about his concerns over Savannah. Bea glances towards Momo, but he does not contradict Marnie's statement.

221

Bea understands why Marnie said what she did. She won't want to give the police any reason to turn their focus on The Surf House. She will want them off the property. Bea hasn't got a work permit. Hasn't even got identification if they ask for it. But most importantly, there's Marrakesh.

'Seth was surfing, yes?' Officer Karim asks.

'That's right,' Ped says. 'He booked an hour's lesson with me at ten o'clock. Afterwards, he wanted to stay out to free surf. He'd hired the board for the day, so there was no problem with that.'

'He was well in your lesson?' Officer Karim asks.

'Correct.'

'Then, what do you think happened?'

Bea's gaze is fixed on Ped.

'He must have got unlucky. Had a wipeout. Hit the sea bed, perhaps.'

Ped stands with his feet planted, taking up space. His arms are folded across his chest.

Unlucky? Bea thinks.

'The sea is very dangerous,' Momo says gravely.

'It can be,' Ped agrees.

'Who found Seth?' Momo asks.

Bea finds herself raising her hand.

Momo looks at her fully then, and Bea can feel sweat break out beneath her arms. The tension must show on her face, because Marnie takes a step closer. She places a hand on her own abdomen as a silent reminder for Bea to breathe.

'Explain.'

'I was surfing and . . . I saw someone floating facedown in the water. I swam over, tried to turn him, but I couldn't. Farah – another guest here – came to help me.'

'It took long?' Momo asks, his eyes narrowing.

She pushes her hands into her pockets. 'I don't know how long. Half a minute. Maybe more.'

Marnie steps in, 'That's right. They did a brilliant job. Then Aiden ran over and attempted to resuscitate him. But it was too late.'

When Bea lifts her gaze, she finds Momo watching her. His dark gaze is pinned to hers. Unease spikes across her skin. She can guess what he is thinking: *one body is unfortunate; two can't be coincidence.*

36

'This is the studio,' Bea says, unlocking the door. She pushes it open and then steps to one side, allowing Momo to enter.

Officer Karim finishes up a call, then follows. 'Come, please?' he says to Bea, who has no choice but to enter the studio, too.

The place is sun-bright and gleaming. Officer Karim's gaze sweeps the space with interest. He pulls open the wardrobe door to reveal a selection of shirts hung neatly. He taps a forefinger on his lips, then crouches low to look beneath the bed.

Bea hangs back near the exit, hands linked behind her back, like she's auditioning for the role of head girl.

When Officer Karim straightens, he crosses the bedroom into the en suite. She can see his reflection in the mirror as he opens the bathroom cabinet and peers inside. 'Is this how Seth Hart kept his room?' he asks Bea.

She nods.

Officer Karim looks satisfied. 'Please pack Seth's belongings.'

'Yes.'

She removes Seth's black suitcase from beneath the bed. She begins with the wardrobe, folding pressed shirts carefully. Then she opens drawers, removing underwear, socks, cotton T-shirts, shorts. The smell of laundry detergent and expensive aftershave reaches her.

The clothes he must have changed out of this morning are folded neatly on a chair – waiting for him to step back into on his return.

Who will receive his repatriated body? His parents are deceased, and Savannah is . . . what?

Missing?

Hiding?

Dead?

It doesn't feel right. None of this feels right.

Something on the wall must catch Momo's eye, because he calls out in Arabic to Officer Karim, who joins him. Momo runs a finger down the long crack, following its path. It is partially concealed by a wall hanging, which Momo pushes aside so they can examine the full extent of the crack.

They converse in Arabic for a few moments, and then they step out onto the balcony together.

Bea continues to pack, moving to Seth's desk and carefully slotting his laptop within its case, then removing the charger from the wall. She zips the suitcase, everything stowed, then sweeps the room one final time.

She turns on the spot and looks at all the cleared surfaces. Something's bothering her.

She moves around the room once again, rechecking the desk, the bedside drawers, the wardrobe, even crouching, as Officer Karim did, to look beneath the bed.

There is nowhere left to check. Every surface and drawer has been cleared.

But she has not seen it anywhere.

Seth's notebook is gone.

37

Every detail regarding Savannah's disappearance is contained in that notebook. It includes printed emails, correspondence, notes on leads. It was the map of information that Seth was following to find his sister.

Bea stands in the centre of the studio, heart pounding dangerously. Her hands are clammy. It's gone. Someone has taken it.

When Ped exited the studio earlier, he slipped what he claimed to be Seth's passport into his pocket. Was it? Seth's notebook is A5 size, too large to fit in a pocket – but it's possible Ped could have concealed it beneath a T-shirt or slotted it into the waistband of his shorts.

Then Bea's gaze moves to the balcony, where Momo and Karim are talking. Momo points with his right hand towards the bay. He keeps his left pressed to his side. What if *he* has Seth's notebook? When she unlocked the studio for the police, Momo was the first to step inside – Karim hung back for a few moments, finishing his call. Momo would have had enough time to swipe the notebook from the desk and tuck it out of sight beneath his thick uniform.

Her head swims between Ped and Momo. One of them has the notebook, she's certain.

She knows in her gut that Savannah's disappearance is much more than a traveller choosing to go off-grid. This feels dangerous.

She's told no one that she's been helping Seth with his investigation – and she needs to keep it that way.

Bea is making for the door when she thinks of the one place she hasn't checked for Seth's notebook: the safe.

With a quick glance towards the officers, who are still talking on the balcony, she moves to the wardrobe where the safe is kept.

She knows the safe override code and punches it in.

Please be in here . . .

She casts another glance towards the police – still talking – then turns the dial. The safe unlocks.

Pulse rate accelerating, she pulls open the door.

Her eyes scan the dark rectangular space for the black notebook.

It is not here.

Her heart sinks.

That's it then. The notebook is gone. Seth's gone. Every door they prised open together has been slammed shut.

She is pushing to her feet when her gaze lands on a thick envelope at the back of the safe. With a glance over her shoulder, she reaches in and lifts out the envelope.

It is filled with US dollars. Hundreds of them.

The police officers don't know the money is there.

No one does – except her.

She stares at the money. *My God, there may be enough to pay off Momo's bribe!* She peers over her shoulder and sees that Momo and Karim are finishing up their conversation.

She has only moments.

227

Heart thumping, her fingers circle the cash. She can feel the weight of the money in her hand, but the moment she grips it, she hears the balcony door slide open and the men's footsteps return.

She freezes. She has no pockets. No bag. Nowhere to put it.

She pushes the envelope of notes beneath the neckline of her top, then hastily locks the safe.

'All finished?' Officer Karim asks as Bea stands.

She keeps her back to him, feeling the burn of her cheeks. She takes a moment to settle her expression, then she turns. 'Yes.'

She mustn't look down – but she is acutely aware of the wedge of money pressed against her breastbone as she makes her way to the door.

Reaching it, she places her fingers on the door handle and pushes it open, when she hears—

'Wait.'

It is Officer Karim's voice – and Bea freezes.

She turns. He is looking right at her, dark eyes pinned to hers. 'Is there a safe in the room?'

Bea feels the blood leave her face. She is on the threshold of the exit, and all she wants is to leave. 'Yes,' she answers, mouth dry.

'Show me,' Officer Karim says.

Tiny beads of sweat gather beneath her arms. She doesn't move. He continues watching her and she thinks, *It's all over.*

'Show me the safe,' Officer Karim repeats.

Bea blinks. There's no choice. She steps back into the room. Her face is hot. Slowly, she approaches the wardrobe and opens it to reveal the locked safe. She can feel the dollar bills sticking to the damp skin at her breastbone.

'There is an override code?' Officer Karim asks.

'Yes,' she answers, suddenly latching onto this. 'But I don't know it. I'll go to the office. Fetch the code . . .'

She can feel Momo's eyes on her. Is she imagining it, or have they lowered to her chest where the money is hidden? Her heart pounds against the block of notes. She cannot help it – her gaze drops to her chest. She can see the outline of the bank notes pressed beneath her T-shirt. Instinctively, she lifts a hand to conceal it, pretending to scratch her throat.

Momo is watching.

Officer Karim says curtly, 'Fetch the code, please.'

She nods quickly and hurries from the studio, blood crashing in her ears.

Inside The Surf House, she rushes through the lounge and takes the stairs two at a time. In her room, she locks the door behind her and removes the money from her bra.

She's breathing hard as she flicks through the bills. Almost immediately, she loses count. She starts over, trying to focus as she splits the notes into piles.

She makes the final count as $4,000. She's only $1,000 short of being able to cover Momo's price for the return of her passport.

There's no time to reflect on this because the police are waiting. She shoves the money beneath her pillow, then heads for the door. She descends the stairs, then crosses the terrace towards the studio.

She walks in to find the men waiting, arms folded. 'You have the code?' Officer Karim asks.

'Yes.'

Both officers stand behind her as she crouches at the safe. The air is thick with the masculine scent of sweat and fading aftershave. Her fingers are clammy and trembling as she punches in the numbers, then turns the dial. She reaches for the metal latch and pulls open the safe door to reveal the empty space.

Both officers lean closer.

There is a long moment of silence.

'Nothing,' says Officer Karim finally.

She slowly closes the safe door, then pushes to her feet. Momo is watching her.

With her shoulders drawn back, they are almost the same height. Their eyes meet. She makes her lips turn up into a warm smile. 'If you need any more help, do let me know.'

38

When darkness arrives, Bea pulls on a hoodie and steals out onto the cliff top, alone.

Mallah is lit by stars. She breathes in the salt-dust air as she walks towards the rocky nook where Salty sleeps – but is disappointed to find the cliff empty of both Salty and Aiden. She slumps down, shoulders rounded.

Her fingers pick at a cracked piece of rock. She works at the jagged edges of it, seeing if she can loosen it. Her mood is low, wracked by worries. Thoughts dart anxiously, raking through the past twenty-four hours, then arrowing further back to a childhood memory she's not examined in years.

She must have been only nine years old and remembers she'd just broken up for the Easter holidays. To mark the occasion, she asked her mum if they could have a movie night. Bea chose a film, poured popcorn into a large bowl, and fetched a blanket to wrap around them – but her mum sat at the other end of the sofa, messaging someone on her phone. Bea waited for her to finish – but after forty minutes of hearing her bursts of private laughter, her mum still showed no interest in the film or Bea.

'Please watch with me?' Bea asked, hitting pause on the remote. 'This was meant to be our night.'

Maybe she sounded sulky or demanding, because her mum's face instantly hardened. 'I've been working all day. Can't I have a bit of time to myself? Is that too much to ask?'

Bea doesn't remember the back and forth of the argument, just that it ended with her mum snatching up her bag and saying, 'If you're going to be a brat – I'm leaving.'

The front door slammed, and Bea drew her knees to her chest, tears stinging the corners of her eyes, certain that her mum would walk around the block, cool off, and return. An apology waited on the tip of Bea's tongue, ready to salvage what she could of the ruined night. But an hour passed and then another.

Scared by the darkness and the strange noises in the empty flat, Bea wanted the safety of her bedroom. She counted to three, then sprinted from the lounge to her room, shut the door and barricaded herself inside, piling up books and toys as high as she could. Then she sat huddled in her bed, trying to ignore her full bladder, the duvet wrapped tight around her like a protective cloak. Eventually, she must have fallen asleep, because she woke to daylight and the sound of her mother's key in the lock.

After that, whenever Bea behaved in a way that her mum didn't like, she walked away. Left the room. Left the flat. Left her. Bea learned that if she felt a difficult emotion – fear, anger, anxiety – she must take great pains to not show it in case her mum left. She kept quiet rather than confronting her. She smiled when she wanted to cry. She said *yes* when she meant *no*.

Maybe that's why she made a good model. She could pretend to feel whatever emotion was asked of her – sexy, confident, vivacious – rather than showing the ugly loneliness inside.

Her fingers finally pull free the loose rock. She feels the sharp, hard edges in her palms as she tightens her grip around it.

Lurching to her feet, she moves to the edge of the cliff and makes a fist around the rock.

Rage boils. She feels the heat of it in her bones and teeth, a furnace that cracks something open. She launches the rock out into the night, watching as it hurls downwards towards the sea, hitting the moonlit water. Then she is turning, grabbing more rocks from the earth, filling her hands with them, launching them.

Wild fury overtakes her. She is furious with her mum for leaving her . . . With Momo for threatening her . . . With Ped for lying . . . With the men in Marrakesh for attacking her . . .

Tears stream down her cheeks. Her breath is ragged. The rock she clutches slides from her fingers as she realises that, most of all, she is furious with herself. In that Marrakesh alleyway, she stood there, silent and scared, and she didn't fight or even shout. Neither of those men had a weapon, yet she did nothing. Not until the moment Marnie barrelled in and forced her into action.

Bea has been quiet for too long.

She looks over her shoulder at The Surf House. Seth is dead. Savannah is missing. And she is certain Ped is involved.

This time, she will be heard.

She's still on the cliff top, cheeks stiff with dried tears, when Aiden comes across her.

'Bea?' he asks in a low voice, placing a hand on her upper arm, looking right into her eyes. 'Are you okay?'

'Can we walk?' she asks, needing motion.

'Sure.'

They make their way down the cliff steps and into the dark bay. The tide is out and the wet sand shimmers silver. They walk together, their footsteps falling into rhythm.

It's hard to believe that hours earlier, they were both in this bay, Bea pulling in Seth's body, Aiden administering CPR.

She replays the moment she saw Seth floating facedown. She drills into each of the thoughts and decisions that came next. Did she swim to him fast enough? Did she hesitate in turning him? If she'd been faster, stronger, better – could she have saved him?

She shakes her head. 'I . . . I keep going over it. How when I got to Seth . . . I couldn't turn him. Wasn't quick enough . . .'

'This isn't on you.'

She glances at Aiden, thinking of how hard he fought to save Seth's life, repeating round after round of CPR with an exacting focus.

He tells her, 'We can replay a scenario as much as we like. Create our different endings. But it won't change the one that happened.' She can see the weight he's carrying, the heaviness of trying to revive Seth's breathing with his own.

She finds Aiden's hand and holds it tight to hers. They walk on in the dark, listening to the breaking waves.

There are so many shadows in her thoughts. She thinks of Seth's body laid on the terrace beneath a towel, the officers standing over him. Then of Ped exiting Seth's room, slipping something into his pocket. Then of Momo, watching her as she kneeled before the empty safe.

Her thoughts feel like waves, continually rolling onwards with an energy of their own. Crashing on top of one another, crushing her beneath their weight.

She doesn't want to think about any of it. Her head is spinning. She wants to feel anything else.

She reaches for Aiden. Finds herself pressing her mouth to his. Her kiss is urgent, desperate. For a moment, she thinks he's going to be pull away, leave her – but after a beat, his body responds. Lips and mouths and tongues meet.

His hands find her waist, pulling her close. She lifts his T-shirt, feeling the heat of skin, the ripple of muscle. It's as if she is melting, turning liquid against him. This. She needs this.

Aiden kisses her with possession, matching her urgency. It's as if, all this time, they have been waiting for someone to fire the start gun.

She sinks her teeth into his shoulder. Tastes salt on his skin. Feels his hands lower to her hips.

She presses herself to him, skin against skin. Her fingers undo his shorts. He yanks down her underwear. Her wanting is deep and overwhelming.

He lowers her to the ground, the damp sand cool against her shoulder blades and the backs of her thighs. Aiden's mouth finds her left nipple, and she feels the low vibration of his lips as he moans.

Desire is sheer and red and consuming. She angles his hips against her own. She cannot wait, will not slow. She gasps at the bloom of pleasure as she draws him inside her.

Their bodies move together, wild, rhythmic.

Her fingers press into his back.

'Bea . . .' he says, his mouth against her ear.

They slow. Look at one another. There is wanting in his gaze.

With delicious slowness, a new rhythm builds like a wave drawing in and out. His hands grip her by the hips as they rock. She lets out a low, deep moan.

The beach disappears. Thought vanishes.

Desire is molten.

There is no performance, no awareness of how she must behave or be. She is flesh and skin and sinew and pulse.

She tips back her head, thoughts obliterated as they lose themselves in each other, while the stars spin above.

39

All day, she thinks of Aiden. The heat of his touch. The way her body responded to his with an intuitiveness that felt primal. Her skin seems to thrum with desire.

And yet beneath the pleasure, anxiety roams, flashing its teeth. Seth's death stalks through her thoughts, leaving her wired and edgy. She cannot settle to anything.

In the late afternoon, she bakes a cake, needing to put her attention somewhere good. She hopes that filling The Surf House with the comforting smell of cardamom and sugar will chase out the dark tensions – but she still finds herself standing in the kitchen, gaze locked on the window as she watches Ped moving around the poolside, cleaning the filter, fixing a loose slat on a sunlounger.

It's almost dusk when she realises what she needs to do. She places a hunk of cake into a plastic container, then leaves The Surf House, pulling on sunglasses against the lowering sun.

She finds Salty waiting for her and slips half a carrot from her pocket. 'Here,' she says, pleased with the gentle manner he takes it from her cupped palm. He chews for a moment, then lets the carrot drop from his mouth as he sniffs at the plastic container. He looks at her, all eyes, as if to say, *Whadabout the cake, lady?*

'No chance,' she tells him as she descends the cliff steps. 'This cake is currency.'

Reaching the sand, early evening light washes the bay gold. It should be beautiful, yet it is tainted with the raw memories of Seth.

She drags in a breath, then forces herself to walk on and cross the exact stretch of beach where he was pulled in.

There are only a few surfers still in the water. She scans the edge of the bay, searching for Elin – and finds her perched on a large red rock with her camera balanced on a tripod in front of her.

As Bea approaches, without looking up from the camera, Elin says, 'Give me a minute.'

Bea waits.

'Paddle, paddle!' Elin shouts to whomever she is filming, despite them being out of earshot. She trains the camera on them, following their wave. After a few more seconds, she says, 'Got it!'

Then Elin sits back and turns her full attention to Bea, who is holding up the plastic container.

'Is that cake?' Elin asks; there's a smile in her voice now, catching Bea off-guard.

'Yep.'

Salty sits on his haunches, looking dejected at the transaction.

Elin brings the container towards her, removes the lid, and breathes in. 'That smells insane. What we got?'

'Cardamon and pistachio carrot cake.'

Elin takes a bite, then groans with delight. 'Moist, deeply flavoured, spiced, with a crunch of pistachio.' She licks her fingers.

So she's caught Elin in a good mood.

Using the opportunity, she says, 'You were out filming yesterday, right?'

'Yep. And I know your next question. Did I get any footage of Seth?'

Bea nods.

''Fraid not. I've done a quick check. Wanted to spot the wave it happened on – y'know, in case the cops wanted to see. But I didn't get it. I was mostly filming take offs by the harbour wall. People are saying they saw him surfing in the centre of the bay.' She shrugs. 'Take a look yourself. Footage is all saved.'

'Thanks.'

Elin glances at her sideways. 'You liked Seth, didn't you?'

She wonders, *Did I?* They weren't friends, exactly. 'I'm not sure how well I knew him. But I respected him for coming out here, searching for Savannah.'

'I've been meanin' to say,' Elin begins, tugging at her earlobe, 'sorry I wasn't straight with you about Savannah. I dunno. Guess I felt bad about how I treated her.' She pauses. 'Did Seth get anywhere with tracking her down?'

Bea considers Elin, still uncertain whether she can trust her fully. 'There was one lead. Seth mentioned it yesterday before he . . . died. He'd found something out about Ped. Needed to speak to him.'

Elin's looking at her as if she's waiting for more.

'That's all he said,' Bea clarifies.

Elin shrugs as if that's the end of it. She doesn't look curious at the mention of Ped's name. Doesn't lean close and offer up any thoughts on Ped. Just says, 'Come see the footage, if you like.'

Back at the RV, Elin takes two beers from the fridge and shakes some salted cashews into a plastic bowl. They sit together in front of her laptop, waiting for the footage to load.

'Here we go,' Elin says, once the video is ready. 'It's a full morning session. Three hours' worth.'

Bea scrolls through the timestamps. She knows Seth had a lesson with Ped from 10.00 a.m. to 11.00 a.m. Bea dragged Seth from the water at 12.05 p.m., so he could have drowned any time between the end of the lesson and when Bea found him.

She starts the footage a little way into Seth's lesson and scans the lineup. She sees Ped demonstrating a take off, Seth sitting astride his board, watching.

There's a knock on the side of the RV. A young guy, wearing a visor over sandy blond hair, says, 'Hey, Elin. I've got those fins if you wanna take a look?'

'Sure.' She turns to Bea. 'You okay in here?'

'Course.'

Elin grabs her beer and a handful of cashews, then exits the RV.

Bea leans on an elbow, continuing to watch. Around five minutes before the end of the lesson, she sees Ped stroking off to catch a wave of his own, carving too close to Seth and sending spray into his face. Seth looks pissed off, pointing hard at Ped. Ped seems to be shouting something back at him as he paddles nearer.

She zooms in. The quality is grainy, but she can see the men's faces and gestures well enough to tell they are not shooting the breeze. Seth's words are punctuated with sharp, jabbing hand gestures. Then Ped slams his fist into the water. Shakes his head. Paddles away.

What were you arguing about? she wonders, leaning closer.

Seth stays on his board for half a minute, then he turns and paddles in the opposite direction, out of shot.

Bea fast-forwards through the next few minutes of footage, the camera trained tight to the harbour wall. There are no more sightings of Seth, but she does see Ped paddling out alone, taking off on a set wave, and then disappearing out of shot again.

About fifteen minutes later, she spots Ped again. But this time, he is on land. He is talking to another man. They are standing at the edge of the frame, out of focus. All she can see is that they have their heads bent close together. Is that Momo? The camera angle shifts again as Elin zooms in on her surfer, and the two men are lost.

Bea keeps her eyes peeled for Seth – but there is no sight of him. She sees Driss sitting on his board in the middle of the bay, looking towards The Surf House.

Then she blinks. Ped has come back into shot. But this time, he is swimming. He passes Driss – and seems to pause for a moment. There is no board with him.

'Odd,' Bea says, looking at the screen.

She watches as Ped swims to shore and then, once again, he's cut from the frame.

She plays the remaining footage all the way through. At the end, the camera turns, and Bea sees herself in the shot with Farah as they drag Seth's body to shore. Then she sees Aiden dropping his board, running towards them. Bea catches Elin's recorded voice behind the camera, saying, 'Oh shit!' – and the video ends.

Bea sits back. She stares at the black screen, her head abuzz with questions. What were Ped and Seth arguing about? Why was Momo hovering on the shoreline, speaking to Ped? And why, later, did Ped swim to the middle of the bay without his board?

Out of all the questions, it's that last one she returns to. Ped, swimming, no board.

Why?

An image rises into her thoughts: Ped standing on the bottom of the pool, keeping entirely still, breath-hold training.

What was it Marnie had told her?

Ped can stay underwater for several minutes before he needs air.

Bea remains sitting there for some time, her thoughts turning over questions about Ped. As she stares ahead, thinking, Savannah appears in front of her.

Bea blinks, confused.

She rubs a hand across her eyes, then looks again.

Savannah is smiling at her from the screen of Elin's laptop.

It takes Bea a moment to understand that the laptop must have fallen into screensaver mode, and she is now looking at a photo of Savannah. In the picture, she is grinning, blonde hair loose at her shoulders. Bea can see the fine splattering of freckles across the bridge of her nose and the reflection of Elin's camera caught in her pupils. She looks beautiful, vital, so full of life.

Then the photo switches. Another of Savannah. Elin must have linked her screensaver to a specific folder on her laptop. This time Savannah is lying on the beach, writing in a pink journal, her eyes on the page, not on the camera. There's something about the angle of the photo that makes Bea wonder if Savannah knew it was being taken.

In ten seconds, the image changes again. A third picture of Savannah. In this one, she is in the dunes, walking up a steep bank of sand, carrying an old surfboard. Driss is a few paces ahead of her, his hair a little longer than it is now. At the top of

241

the dune, Bea sees Farah sitting on a high ridge of sand. She is peering down, her face unsmiling as she looks at Savannah.

The pictures continue to change but the one commonality is that Savannah is the subject of every photo. Each is beautifully composed, and Bea can see that Elin is a skilled photographer, passionate about her subject. She's captured the bright energy of Savannah, as though she is a flame that Elin is drawn to.

Did Elin get burned?

Bea is startled when Elin strides back into the RV, carrying two yellow fins. 'Found anything interesting?' she asks, stowing the fins in a hideaway beneath one of the seats.

Bea slides her finger across a key to reawaken the screen, and Savannah's image vanishes. 'Nothing.'

40

Bea walks through Mallah, feeling the dark pressing close to her skin. She shivers. The nights in Morocco are cool, and she's still wearing shorts and a thin cotton top. She wraps her arms around herself and picks up her pace.

She came without her phone and wishes she had a torch to light the dark tracks. There are no streetlights in the village, just the glow of other hostels and homes. Her pulse flutters in her throat, anxiety sweeping in now that she's alone in the night.

Her head is still bursting with the images of Savannah. She feels visceral to Bea, like she knows her. Maybe it's the strange echo of staying in the same room, knowing the same people, walking the same routes – and yet never meeting. It is like Savannah is both in touching distance and unreachable.

Her thoughts move to Seth's missing notebook. If Seth discovered something, a lead, there would be evidence of it in the notebook. But now it's gone.

That can't be a coincidence.

If Seth's death wasn't an accident, then someone is willing to go to devastating lengths to shut down the search for Savannah.

At the street's end, she turns, following the next pathway down a darkened alleyway. It is the part of the walk through the village she likes least – narrow, enclosed, no clear exit – but it is the only way back to The Surf House. Hands balled into fists, she hurries on, hearing her own footsteps. The scent of woodsmoke thickens the breeze, and as she leaves the narrow path, she looks up to see a firepit glowing further along the cliff.

Ped is sitting close to the fire with a glass in his hand. He's talking to a second person, who has their back to Bea. A bottle rests against Ped's chair leg, and he reaches down and refills his glass. He doesn't offer the bottle to the second person, who is now rising to their feet.

As they turn, firelight catches their profile.

Driss.

Bea is rooted to the spot as she watches Driss lean close to Ped's ear, as if he's saying something in a quiet voice that he doesn't want overheard. Then he turns and walks away.

Once Driss is out of sight, Bea reroutes her path towards the fire.

Bea has met a lot of people with big egos on shoots. People who are used to speaking rather than listening. People who don't react well to their authority being questioned. People whose singular drive can run others down. Ped, she thinks, is one of those people.

When she first arrived in Mallah, there was a peaceful atmosphere in The Surf House. Marnie was different, too – playful, full of spark and confidence – but when Ped returned, it was like a little of her light dimmed.

Ped turns and sees Bea through the haze of smoke. He nods, not deigning her with a verbal greeting. She makes sure to offer him a cheery, 'Evening,' in return. 'Enjoying your fire?'

He picks up his drink and takes a slug. She sees the glossy amber liquid slosh towards his lips. He wipes the back of his hand across his mouth. 'Yeah.' Ped has a knack for answering questions with the fewest possible words, as if it's a private game and he's keeping score.

Silence hangs between them. Bea stares into the belly of the fire, thoughts burning. She should go to bed, leave this well alone, but how can she when she's the only one left asking questions? She will not abandon Savannah.

'I've just seen Elin's footage from yesterday's surf.' That's all she says.

She watches Ped closely. Notices the way his thumb stops circling the glass, although his face remains relaxed. He doesn't respond to her prompt.

'Looked like you and Seth were arguing in the water.'

Still, he says nothing.

'What was it about?'

He shrugs. 'He's not a guy who likes to take instruction, that's all.'

'It looked more than that.'

'Yeah?'

Her pulse flickers at her throat, and she wants to turn, leave. Yet beneath that feeling, a stronger drive pushes through: her need for the truth. She plants her feet. 'Seth said he wanted to talk to you about Savannah.'

Ped keeps his gaze on the fire. 'Is that right?'

She waits, feeling her face heat in the flames while the skin at her back remains icy. 'In the footage, it looked like you were out in the bay, swimming without your board.'

Ped slowly tops up his glass. 'I was.'

'Why?'

'I was giving a sea-swimming lesson.'

'To who?'

A pause. 'Momo.'

She almost laughs at the audacity of the lie.

Ped takes a purposeful drink, then looks at Bea. 'Seems you've got a lot of questions. But I've got some, too.' He leans forward, an elbow on his knee as he looks at her. 'Why are you really here?'

She blinks, staring back at him. In the firelight, shadows shift over his face.

'You blow in. A hotshot model. I looked you up, Bea Williams. You don't need to work for your keep. You could afford to be a guest on what people like you get paid.'

'I don't model anymore.'

'Why the sea-change? Why here? Why Marnie?'

'You know what happened. I got robbed. Marnie helped me out, brought me here.'

He nods. 'At Rooftops, I asked you to look out for her.'

She meets Ped's eye, both remembering the moment at the bar: Marnie dancing with Seth, her head tipped back, eyes glittering.

'Marnie is her own person. I'm not going to babysit her.'

He reaches down and takes a log from a pile of dry wood. He stares into the flames as he says, 'I'm not sure this is the right place for you.'

The comment hangs there.

'What does that mean?'

Ped tosses the log to the flames. 'You should be thinking about moving on.'

The words are delivered quietly, but they carry a clear threat. Her skin cools. She's pushed too hard. Not played this right.

As she turns to leave, her gaze lands on something black nestled between the red-hot embers. She is already several steps away before she processes what she's seen – the black rectangular shape, the smooth cover. Seth's notebook.

Ped is burning it! Setting Seth's evidence ablaze. The final lead Seth uncovered will be set down in those pages. She wills herself to keep walking for several more paces.

Then she turns and rushes back, calling, 'Ped! Someone's trying to get into your van!'

Ped is on his feet, racing beyond The Surf House and out onto the street.

Bea knows she only has moments. She sprints back to the fire.

She can see the notebook at the bottom of the firepit, the spine flaming.

Bea grabs a couple of sticks from the pile on the ground and uses them as pincers to drag the notebook from the flames. She flings it free, and it lands in the dust, still smouldering.

She kicks sandy dirt over the notebook, smothering the flames.

She becomes still, suddenly aware of a prickling sensation at the back of her neck. Slowly, she turns her head, looking towards The Surf House. She expects to see Ped's shadow in the doorway – but there's nobody there.

Quickly, she runs her fingers through sand and stones until they meet the notebook, and she pulls it out, ash floating to the ground from the burned pages.

She kicks fresh sand over the area that she's disturbed, and then she hurries back towards The Surf House, the notebook pushed under her top.

Ped comes the other way, and the two of them face one another.

Bea can feel the press of the charred book against her skin. 'Is the van okay?'

He eyes her. 'There was no one there.'

'I saw two people rattling at the doors. Could've just been kids. Maybe I scared them off.'

Ped looks at her for a long moment.

She shrugs her shoulders. Then she walks purposefully past him and up the stairs of The Surf House, feeling the ashy warmth of Seth's notebook against her stomach.

41

Sitting cross-legged on the floor, Bea slips the charred remains of the notebook from beneath her top, leaving black smears on her skin.

The cover is warped and blackened, bubbled with glue. Bea opens it carefully and finds an undamaged photo of Savannah that she has seen before. In it, Savannah stands in the bay, holding up a billowing sunbeam-print blanket in retro oranges and golden yellows. Sunkissed and relaxed, she grins at whoever is taking her picture, whoever made her smile like this.

She wonders how Seth felt as he gathered photos and printed emails and wrote down scraps of information that may or may not lead anywhere. Did he need the physicality of it? Something tangible to keep Savannah close?

She glances towards her bed, where the money from Seth's safe is still hidden beneath her pillow. That money would have been part of her payment *if* she'd found Savannah.

Seth's death hits her afresh, like a blow to the stomach. He came to Morocco searching for his sister – and now he's dead. Wherever Savannah is right now, she doesn't know this fact. Doesn't know that Seth loved her enough to travel here hoping to find her.

She turns to the next page – the early section of the notebook mostly survived the flames – and sees print-outs of emails between Savannah and the family friend in California that Seth mentioned, Rachel. Parts of them are browned and curling, but she can read enough to get the sense that Savannah loved to share stories from her travels. She reads about nights out, markets she shopped at, places she swam. She sees names mentioned – Aiden, Driss, Farah, Marnie, Ped, Elin – and it feels both strange and comforting to see them feature in Savannah's commentary.

She scans each page closely, eyes tiring, but there is nothing more revealing than descriptions of hot days spent at the water's edge, and evenings partying around fires.

Bea's head lifts at the sound of footsteps next door. Marnie's. There is a single knock.

Bea shoves the notebook beneath the bed and gets to her feet just as the connecting door opens.

'Hey,' Marnie says. She looks sleepy, eyes dull and shadowed. 'You okay in here?' She glances around the room. Sniffs. 'Smells of wood-smoke.'

'Does it? Ped and Driss were having a fire.' She wants to confide in Marnie about finding the notebook in the flames – but it's too risky. Marnie's allegiance is to Ped. She'd believe whatever excuse Ped tripped off. It would come back on Bea, and she can't risk that. She needs to tread carefully.

Marnie links her fingers around Bea's. 'You haven't mentioned anything to Ped about me and Seth?'

'Course not.'

'I was half out of my mind. If Ped found out, he'd leave me. I know he would.'

'He's not going to find out – or leave you,' she reassures.

'I know we fight, but we do love each other.'

There's an energy between Marnie and Ped that pulsates, like it is a living, breathing thing. Bea wonders if the volatility is all part of the fabric of their relationship, that push and pull, the turbulence of it. 'I know you do.'

Marnie's features are softened by this acknowledgement. She smiles at Bea, then leans forward and presses a kiss to her forehead. 'G'night.'

Bea listens for the creak of springs as Marnie climbs into bed and the click of the lamp turning off. Then Bea reaches for Seth's charred notebook.

Sitting on the floor, she reopens it at the page she left off – a print-out of the last email Savannah sent Rachel. Seth has highlighted the following sentence: *I'm going offline, babe. I need to decompress, forget about my family, concentrate on the bigger world out here, you know?*

She turns to the next page and sees Savannah's credit card statement, with the final transaction circled in Ezril, the desert town Seth visited. Beside it, Seth has written: *What if it wasn't Savannah who withdrew the money? Is there CCTV footage? Ring EVERY DAY!*

There. That's something practical Bea can do. She can take over this small task and ring daily until the footage is located. She taps the bank's number into her phone. They'll be closed at this hour, but she'll call tomorrow.

She continues to turn the pages, but frustratingly, the back half of the notebook has been badly damaged by the flames. She searches for the last entry, thinking of the lead Seth wanted to discuss with Ped – but there is nothing here but blackened paper. A piece comes away in her fingers, delicate and charred at the corners. She sees Momo's name, followed by the words, *Infatuated? Dangerous?* Then another smoke-damaged line reading, *Police corruption? What was Savannah involved in?*

She pauses on this, thinking of the conversation Momo and Ped were having on the shoreline just minutes before Seth drowned. What were they talking about? She thinks of Ped's odd lie that he went into the water later without his board to give Momo a sea-swimming lesson.

So many thoughts are whirring in Bea's mind that she's struggling to order them. She fetches a blank piece of paper and a pen, then lies on her stomach on the floor and begins to write a list of details about the week leading up to Savannah's disappearance.

- *Savannah meets the Dutch girls, Lise and Anke, and shortly afterwards agrees to travel overland to Cape Town with them.*
- *Savannah emails her friend, Rachel, saying she's going offline.*
- *On 26th October, Savannah goes to the Jailors beach party, where she is seen by Marnie, Ped, Aiden, Driss, Farah, and Elin. That night, she argues with Elin.*
- *After Elin leaves the party, she tells the Dutch girls that Savannah has changed her mind.*
- *After the beach party, Savannah returns to The Surf House and packs her things. This is the last recorded detail of Savannah in Mallah.*
- *On 27th October, Savannah is due to meet the Dutch girls at 7 a.m., but thinking she has changed her mind, they leave without her around 6 a.m.*
- *Later that same day, Savannah withdraws all her money from a bank in a desert town called Ezril. After that, there is no further trace.*

There have been no sightings of Savannah since. No use of social media or contact with friends. Her bank account hasn't been used. Savannah vanished.

Bea studies the timeline, waiting for something to jump out at her. But it doesn't. Seth's notebook hasn't given her anything new.

As she closes the cover, she thinks, maybe the interesting thing isn't necessarily what's inside these pages. It's that Ped specifically went into Seth's studio to locate the notebook – and burn it.

It confirms that Seth found out something that Ped cannot risk anyone discovering.

ONE YEAR EARLIER

SAVANNAH

Savannah followed Driss up a narrow stairway. She caught the deep, spiced notes of his aftershave in the close space. The noise and chaos of the medina fell away as the terracotta stairs drew them higher.

'Oh,' she exclaimed, as they arrived on a rooftop terrace high above the city.

Driss moved to her side. 'My favourite place to watch the sun go down.'

Up here, out of the thrust and heat of the souks, it was like peeling back a new layer to Marrakesh, seeing it from a fresh angle and revealing the beauty at a distance. Music drifted across the terrace, mingling with laughter and the sound of drinks being enjoyed. The sun was already beginning to set, the heat of the day softening into an orange glow. In the distance, Savannah could make out the silhouette of the Atlas Mountains.

Driss led her to a low wooden table, framed by two wide, cushioned seats. Lanterns were strung above them in ornate patterns.

They ordered cocktails, two pomegranate margaritas that were served with dried orange decorating the lip of the glass and fresh jewels of pomegranate floating in deep red liquid.

'To your health,' Driss said, raising his glass to hers.

'I'm sorry Farah couldn't be here,' Savannah said. She'd agreed to spend the weekend in Marrakesh on Farah's insistence that she must experience the heartbeat of the country. But now Farah was bogged down in pressing research for her thesis, so had offered up Driss as her tour guide.

'I am very happy to be showing you Marrakesh,' Driss said. 'Later, I will take you for the best tagine in Morocco and introduce you to my friends. Plus, you will need to return for another weekend so you can do it all again with Farah.'

'Good, because I can tell one weekend in Marrakesh isn't going to be enough.'

Driss looked out over his city, eyes filled with pride. 'There is nowhere like Marrakesh. When I am here, I can feel the city in my veins – a vibrancy. It's like I'm humming.'

'And Mallah? Where does that fit in?'

'Farah needs the coast. Sometimes, the city gets on top of her. The noise. The heat. The dirt. Mallah is her balance.' He paused, then added, 'I enjoy the ocean, but when I am away from the city for too long, I begin to crave it.'

She looked at him, intrigued.

'The chaos. The edge to this place. The hustling. The insatiable appetite for more.'

'More what?'

Driss's eyes burned. 'More of whatever your heart desires.'

Savannah ran her fingers back through her hair, turning to look at the setting sun as it dipped behind the mountains. Soon, the stars would be out, and she imagined it would be a spectacular evening.

Driss leaned back, crossing an ankle over his thigh. 'Tell me. What do you desire?'

'Freedom.'

A smile played across his lips. 'Spoken by the American from the land of the free.'

She grinned.

He continued to study her. 'Freedom from what?'

She thought for a moment. 'From family. From expectations of how I should live.'

'How are you expected to live?'

'To pursue money.'

'And you don't think that's a good pursuit?'

'It's not the only goal.'

'When you have nothing, it seems like the only one.'

From talking to Farah, she knew that Driss came from an impoverished background. As a kid, he used to sell sunglasses to tourists in the medina, then later handbags, shoes, leather belts. Now, he was involved with various bigger-scale businesses. *Smart to have lots of irons in the fire,* her father would counsel. Farah hadn't shared all the details, and Savannah had wondered if she chose not to know them.

'I just need to earn enough to continue to travel. To not be answerable,' Savannah said.

'You want to earn money? Here?'

'Yes.'

'What are you prepared to do for it?' he asked, holding her eye.

She placed her chin on her hand, drawing her face nearer to his. 'What do you have in mind?'

42

Bea stands in the studio, absorbing the emptiness of the space. She's been asked to prepare it for a guest arriving later today. Odd to think that in a few hours, someone else will be using this room, all traces of Seth gone.

Bea sets her cleaning basket on the table, then steps onto the balcony. Before she gets to work, there are two things she needs to do. Firstly, she takes out her phone and emails Rachel, Savannah and Seth's family friend. She explains that she is the surfer who pulled in Seth's body. She asks to be updated when there's a coroner's report on his death. She keeps the email brief, making no noises about possible foul play.

Next, she scrolls to the number for the bank in Ezril. She places the call, and the phone is answered in Arabic.

'Do you speak English?' Bea asks.

'Yes,' the clerk responds.

'I'm calling about some CCTV footage that a friend of mine was trying to get hold of. It's in relation to a missing person.'

'Is this about the transaction made by Savannah Hart?'

'That's right,' Bea says, surprised. 'You remember?'

'Of course. Your friend spoke to me only this morning.'

This morning?

'I had to tell him – like I will tell you – that the footage is only stored for six months. I apologise if one of the other staff members gave the wrong information.'

'You don't have the footage?'

'No.'

Bea feels a lurch of disappointment. 'You said my friend rang this morning? What was the name?'

'I wrote it down. Just a moment.'

Bea waits, phone held close to her cheek.

There is the rustling of paper. Then the clerk returns to the line. 'Ped Hampson.'

Ped.

Bea thanks the clerk and ends the call. She stands very still, her heart pounding. Why would Ped be interested in knowing who withdrew Savannah's money? Or was it that he already knew the person's identity – and needed to ensure no one else found out?

Bea stares out over the sea. Waves, horizon, blue sky. She takes a step closer to the edge and, placing her hands on the glass railing, looks down. Just golden sand and rocks below. She's not afraid of heights, but there's something about the glass balcony that unsettles her.

Behind her, the door to the studio juts open, and she starts as Ped strides in, carrying a toolbox. 'What are you doing in here?' he barks.

'Cleaning before the new guest arrives.'

He looks from the cleaning basket on the table to where Bea now stands on the balcony, with a phone in her hand. 'Cleaning?'

Bea pushes her phone into her pocket, then steps back into the studio and gathers her cloth.

Ped crosses the room and crouches by the bedside table, removing an empty drawer. He turns it over to check the runner.

They both work in silence, and the air in the studio prickles with tension. Bea swaps her cloth for the dustpan and brush and sets to sweeping beneath the bed. Noticing a fine dusting of white powder gathered near the wall, she pulls the bed out a little and exposes a deep crack. 'This doesn't look good.'

Ped stops what he's doing. He approaches the wall, running a hand over the crack. There's a ball of tension working at his jawline. 'It's fine,' he says tightly. 'Natural movement.'

She knows Ped built this studio, and she wonders whose palm he had to grease to get permission to set it right on the edge – and whether he thought an extra room for his guesthouse was worth losing his friendship with Aiden over.

She doesn't voice these questions. Instead, she files them with the rest of the evidence that is building against him . . .

Seth has a lead on Ped. They argue in the surf and, less than thirty minutes later, Seth is dead.

Ped then lets himself into Seth's studio, steals the notebook containing his leads on Savannah's disappearance, and burns it.

After that, Ped rings the bank in Ezril about CCTV footage of Savannah's last transaction.

She glances at him sideways, taking in his squared shoulders, the jut of his jaw, the thick fists she's heard slammed against the bedroom wall.

What is he worried about someone finding out? Is he prepared to kill to protect what he's hiding?

Ped looks up – right at her. Their eyes lock. For a moment, she fears she's spoken the questions aloud. Cold dread inches down her spine as he continues to glare at her.

Then Ped snatches up his toolbox and leaves.

Bea leans back against the cracked wall, letting out the breath she was holding.

43

It's after midnight when Bea pulls on her jumper and walks to the cliff top. Her muscles ache from an afternoon spent in the surf. She needed to burn off the anxiety fizzing in her veins and paddled hard for every wave. Her take offs were fast, her bottom turns improving, her wipeouts heavy.

She's pleased to find Aiden sitting on the rock. His shoulders are rounded, eyes on the water.

'You're here,' she says.

He moves over, making space for her. 'Seems to be our place.'

That *our*.

Salty raises his head for a quick rub between the ears. He yawns, tongue lolling, then sinks his muzzle to his paws.

'Any update from the police on what happened to Seth?' Aiden asks.

She shakes her head. Neither Momo nor Officer Karim have been back to The Surf House – and to be honest, it's a relief. 'Don't think they're interested. There's no family here putting pressure on them or asking questions.'

She rubs her hands across her eyes. Her head feels so full. It's not just Seth's death and Savannah's disappearance, but also the extra money she still needs to find for Momo.

She must have sighed, because Aiden is turning to look at her. 'You okay?'

She wants to tell him she's fine. She wants to sit out here enjoying the evening and his company. She wants to choose where she puts her attention and live in that moment, but she can't seem to access it.

Instead, all the mistakes she's made are coiling tighter. She thinks back to the photoshoot in Marrakesh. If she'd just finished the shoot, she'd have flown back to the UK, got on with her life. There would never have been a body left in a Marrakesh alleyway. Never have been a police checkpoint and a bribe. She would never have met Seth or learned about Savannah.

But, she thinks, glancing at the sea, if she'd finished that shoot, continued that career, there would also have been no Surf House, no Marnie, no Aiden. Despite how messed up things are right now, there is also a baseline note of happiness – like she can glimpse the life she wants, even if she's not quite living it.

Aiden is watching her closely, waiting for her answer. She wonders what to tell him. There is so much he can't know.

'Bea? What is it?'

'I need money,' she says, the words surprising her. She has two days left to pay Momo. Seth's money covers most of it, but she's still $1,000 down.

Aiden doesn't blink. 'How much?'

'$1,000.'

'Can you tell me why?'

She shakes her head.

He looks at her carefully. 'Are you in trouble, Bea?'

She promised Marnie that they'd never tell anyone about Marrakesh. Marnie's kept it from Ped – and it's right that she does the same. But she needs to give Aiden something. She takes a breath. 'I'm being blackmailed.'

His eyes widen. 'By who?'

'I can't tell you what's going on – other than that I made a mistake. A big one. Someone found out about it, and now there is a price to pay.'

'When do you need the money?'

'Two days.'

'And if you don't get it?'

She shakes her head. 'I can't tell you any more. I'm sorry. I understand if you can't help. I didn't plan to ask you . . .' She trails off, eyes lowering.

Aiden unfolds himself from the rock.

Has she offended him by asking? He's been clear that he wants to keep whatever this is casual, no strings. It was stupid of her to ask. She is about to apologise when Aiden says, 'Let's go get your money.'

When they step inside Offshore, the air holds the neoprene odour of wetsuits and the claggy smell of used cooking oil.

In the main lounge, the lights are on low. A speaker left on charge blinks a blue light. Offshore is quiet at this time of night. As she follows Aiden up the stairs, she catches the faint sound of snoring.

He flicks on a low lamp, and she realises she is in his bedroom. His bed is made, sheets creased but fresh. There is a framed print on the wall of Mallah, golden light angling off a wave, the village in the background. There is a book and a water glass by his bed. Nothing else is on display. He opens a bedside drawer and pulls out a money box, and begins counting out the cash.

Bea watches uncomfortably.

He straightens and brings her the full amount.

'Aiden, I don't know what to say. Thank you so much.' She takes it and tucks it into the pocket of her hoodie. 'I'll pay you back.'

'No rush.'

She nods, unspeakably grateful.

He takes a step closer.

Her breath catches in her throat. 'Bea,' he begins, and her name on his lips makes her stomach swoop. 'I'm not going to ask you any questions about the money. It's your business. But I just need to know one thing.'

She holds his eye, feeling the thump of her heartbeat.

'When you hand over the money, will it be safe? Because if it won't be, please, tell me, and I'll come.'

She doesn't know if it will be safe, but she cannot involve anyone else. She has Marnie. They will do this together.

'It'll be safe,' she whispers.

They stare at one another. Aiden lifts a hand, and she thinks he is going to reach for her. Her body anticipates his touch, but his arm moves past, pushing the bedroom door closed with his palm.

Silence falls around them. Aiden's gaze travels slowly down the length of her body. His desire is visible. She wants him to touch her – but he doesn't. He only looks.

They are standing close and she can almost feel the heat radiating between them.

Her breathing shallows. Her lips turn dry. She licks them.

Aiden swallows.

He lifts his hand and places it lightly against her right hip. She feels his thumb brush her hip bone, lifting the hem of her T-shirt until his fingertips meet the warmth of her skin. She catches her breath.

263

His eyes do not leave hers as he glides his thumb across her smooth midriff. Every one of her nerve endings lights with pleasure.

'I want you,' he whispers.

Her stomach lifts with longing.

He leans towards her and places his lips on the delicate, exposed skin of her throat. An electric current of desire travels through her, and she lets out a low moan.

The hand on her waist draws her close, so that their hips press together, and she feels the hard, muscular heat of him. Then his other hand is sliding into her hair, tilting her towards him, where their mouths finally meet.

His lips are soft and knowing. His tongue dips into her mouth, tasting her, wanting her. She moans, and the sound makes him pull her closer.

Then they are moving, travelling across the room, feeling the give of his bed beneath her.

She peels off his T-shirt and is struck by the exquisiteness of his body. Years of surfing have carved deep ridges of muscle across his chest and back and sculpted a hard, flat abdomen.

Then he is undressing her, and she feels cool air against her bare skin. He swallows as he stares at her body, his pupils wide and dark. She needs him to touch her. Taste her.

Then the space between them is closed as their bodies press together, skin sliding against skin.

She grips his hips, needing all of him.

Her mouth parts with a gasp as he slides inside her. Her body fills with heat. She is melting.

They begin to move, slowly, eyes never leaving each other's. There is a deep intensity in his gaze as he maps her face. The way he is looking at her – this is not a fuck.

'Bea . . .' he moans as their rhythm builds.

Her mouth is on his, tasting her name on his lips.

Wave after wave of pleasure travels through her. She is liquid. She no longer knows where her body ends and his begins. Her desire is as vast as the ocean.

Afterwards, they lie together, the bed warm, sheets tangled around them. Her limbs feel loose, relaxed. There's a faint humming in her skin. *My God*, she thinks, *I've never had sex like it.*

Aiden is staring at the ceiling, arms cushioned behind his head. She never wants to leave this bed. With other men, she would be pulling on clothes, calling an Uber, making an excuse about an early start so she could return to her own room. But right now, she feels a deep sense of contentment, like something that was tight and jangling in her body has settled.

She rolls towards Aiden and smooths her palm over the contours of his abdomen. His ribcage rises and falls softly as he draws in breath. She wonders what it would be like to fall asleep together, his arm wrapped around her waist. She pictures his face in rest, the furrow between his brows faded. She imagines waking him up with fresh coffee and more sex, and how she could happily spend an entire day in this bed.

Aiden pulls back the sheet and climbs out. In the low lamplight, she watches him pull on shorts and a T-shirt. It is the middle of the night. She knows he has nowhere to go. Nothing that needs doing – and yet he is showing her, gently and without words, that it's time for her to leave.

The blow of rejection hits in the chest. Aiden has been straight with her from the start. Told her what this is. And she agreed to it. It was what she wanted, too – once.

But now?

She makes sure to keep her tone easy as she says goodbye. Then she leaves the hostel, stepping out into the dark night alone. As she looks across to The Surf House, the warm humming of her skin fades, cooled now into goosebumps.

44

Bea glances at the kitchen clock. 'When do you think Momo will come?'

'Any time now,' Marnie replies.

Bea nods, jaw tight. The bribe money is tucked in an envelope in the office safe, ready to hand over. Keeping busy, she takes a spatula and folds cocoa powder into the brownie mixture. Her palms are sweating, and she pauses to wipe them on her thighs.

'Can't believe your mum came through for you,' Marnie says.

Bea keeps her eyes on the mixing bowl. She couldn't tell Marnie about taking Seth's money from the safe, or that she asked Aiden for help. 'Me neither.'

Marnie moves to her shoulder and looks at the glossy chocolatey mixture as Bea spoons it into the waiting tin.

'D'you always bake when you're on edge?'

She nods. 'It's my hands. They need something to do.'

Marnie squeezes Bea's arm, saying, 'Remember, we're in this together, every step of the way.'

Hearing a male voice, Bea freezes.

Marnie catches her eye. Shakes her head. It's only a guest passing through the lounge. 'You don't have to be here when Momo comes,' she says.

267

While Bea doesn't want to be anywhere near Momo, she won't let Marnie handle this alone. 'Together.'

Marnie glances out of the kitchen window, watching Ped, who is kneeling at the poolside, cleaning a filter. In a low voice, she says, 'Ped can't know about what's going on. If he comes in when Momo's here, distract him.'

Bea nods. She sprinkles a pinch of smoked sea salt on top of the brownie mixture, then places it into the oven. 'Why do you think Momo wanted to do the transaction here?'

'Power play,' Marnie answers. 'Just like the rucksack. He wants us to know that he can come here and there's nothing we can do about it.'

Bea can feel a tension headache squeezing around her skull. 'D'you think he'll hand over everything like he's said?'

Marnie's jaw sets. 'He has to.'

Momo knocks at 8 p.m.

Bea follows Marnie to the door, shoving her hands into her pockets to disguise their trembling.

Momo is dressed in his uniform. He looks tired, something defeated about his gait. The raised scar near his hairline is pink, as if he's been scratching it. At his side, he carries a brown paper bag with handles. Bea prays the knife, scarf, and her passport are inside.

Momo's lips turn up into a smile as he meets her eye. A bolt of fury, hot and red, grips her. She wants to tear the bag from his hands and press the blade of the knife to his throat.

Marnie places a hand at her shoulder and manages to smile as she invites Momo inside, leading him into the office. She addresses him in French, making pleasantries.

In the office, Momo stands in the doorway, blocking the exit.

Bea's heart pounds erratically as Marnie fetches the envelope of cash from the safe. She needs this done. Needs Momo to be true to his word.

Behind him, she hears the tread of footsteps and can tell from the long, firm strides that it is Ped. Marnie flicks her a look.

Ped appears at Momo's side, an oil stain smeared across his surf tee. He glances at Momo, taking in his uniform. It must look like he's here on official business. 'Everything okay?' Ped asks Marnie.

'Yes. Momo was just passing and delivering something.' Marnie says something to Momo in French.

He holds up the paper bag and says in English, 'Bread.'

'Bea, could you show Ped that repair you mentioned earlier?' Marnie prompts.

'Oh. Yes.' Bea leaves the office, Momo stepping back to allow her to pass.

She can feel Ped's reluctance as he follows. She moves towards the kitchen, Ped behind her, no idea what to show him. Her mind goes blank. All she can think of is putting space between him and Momo.

She steps out onto the terrace, feeling the night breeze on her skin. Behind her, she hears Ped's footsteps stop.

'What's the repair?' He's standing with his arms folded across his chest.

Bea glances around helplessly, searching for inspiration. She sees the Surf Studio and says, 'The crack in the studio wall.'

Ped raises an eyebrow. 'You want to show me a repair that I already know about?'

'I . . . I thought you could take a closer look.'

He is glaring now. 'I built that studio with my bare hands,' he says, raising them. 'I know when it's time to *take a closer look*.'

LUCY CLARKE

Her mouth opens then closes. Bea can think of nothing to say in response.

With a dismissive shake of his head, Ped turns. She watches him cross the terrace and, to her relief, rather than return to The Surf House, he stalks out into the night.

After a moment, Bea hurries back to the office. She finds Marnie sitting alone at her desk.

'Momo's gone?' Bea asks.

'Yes.' Marnie reaches across to the safe and pulls out the paper bag Momo arrived with.

Bea's hands tremble as she takes it. *Please,* she is thinking.

She peers into the bag, and relief bursts in her chest as she sees the wooden-handled knife and her scarf. Then she spots the third item – her passport.

She pulls it out and flips immediately through the pages, checking everything is as it should be. She sees her photo, the stamps in and out of Paris and New York and Singapore . . . pages thick with the last few years of travel.

When she looks up, Marnie is watching her, eyes bright. A deep smile spreads from the corners of her mouth. 'It's over.'

They wait until midnight.

Bea is growing familiar with the middle-of-the-night hours in Mallah, starlit and dazzling, waves still streaming into the bay. It's a far cry from home with the orange glow of streetlamps and steady thrum of traffic. There's a remoteness to this landscape, a feeling that – out here – you're living at the edge of things.

They take the cliff-top path, Marnie holding a torch, Bea with the bloodstained knife and scarf pushed into her bag. Salty finds them and trots ahead, as if he knows exactly where they need to go.

270

They walk mostly in silence, eyes on the darkened track. No sign of Aiden tonight, she notes. Better that way. She doesn't want to have to answer any questions.

She and Marnie pick their way carefully over the dusty, rocky earth, the torch beam illuminating low shrubs and the tramp of dust that rises from their footsteps.

They walk for twenty minutes, until Marnie is happy with the spot they reach. She turns off the torch. 'This is good. It's deep here, and we've got an outgoing tide.'

'What if they wash up?'

'Then someone would find an old, stained scarf and a knife washed free of fingerprints and blood.'

Bea removes the scarf from the bag. It's a remnant from her old life. The cream material has pale lines of gold thread running through it. A rust-brown bloodstain has soaked deep into its fibres.

She remembers the blood pouring from the man's neck in thick spurts of red. The smell of iron mixed with the dry, stale scent of the alleyway. Most of the time, she tries not to think of him. But sometimes, she can't help picking at the scab, opening it up and letting herself imagine what he was like as a boy. What went wrong in his life to make him think it was okay to follow women into narrow alleyways. She thinks of his family, too. Somewhere out there, there'll be a grieving mother or father – and this is her fault, she knows.

'Here,' Marnie says, passing Bea a rock. 'Wrap the scarf around this.'

Bea does as she says, the material stiff with dried blood. 'Do you think about what happened?'

Marnie looks at her. In the moonlight, the planes of her face are beautiful. The gold-leaf nose stud catches the light. Bea

271

recalls what she said that first evening she arrived in Mallah: *We put this behind us. Move forward. It's a fresh start.*

'Sometimes, I do the wishing thing. Y'know, wishing those men had never laid eyes on you. Wishing the guy in the football shirt had turned and run like his friend.' She pauses. Her eyes lower to the ground. Her voice is quieter when she speaks again. 'I also think about his hands on my throat. How there was no air. I . . . I thought I was going to die. It hurt to swallow for days.'

Marnie never said, never complained. But now Bea remembers that first morning at The Surf House, Marnie plating soft foods for breakfast – eggs and mashed avocado – and leaving most of it untouched.

'Sometimes, I wake in the night,' Marnie continues, 'and I've been dreaming that we're back in the alleyway – and his hand is at my throat. I *hate* that,' she says, the words squeezed out like bitter pips. 'I hate that he gets to be in my head, my dreams.'

'I'm sorry.'

'No. It's my own weakness. Bea, if I'd been holding the knife, I would have put it in his neck – and would have been glad to.' She looks directly into Bea's eyes. 'Don't waste a second of your life feeling guilty that that man is dead. Don't.'

Bea allows that swirling shadow of guilt to heat, to fire into something else. What she feels is rage. Rage that he touched her. Rage that his hands went down her body. Rage that he tried to choke the air from Marnie's lungs.

Marnie says, 'You saved my life, Bea. It was me or him, and you chose me. I'll never forget that.'

Bea stares at her. Sees that there are tears in the corners of her eyes.

Then Marnie lifts the knife, saying, 'Ready?'

Bea keeps one hand on Salty. Then she nods.

They throw the items out over the cliff edge.

The edge of the scarf unravels and billows like smoke as it wafts towards the sea. She hears the faint splash as the knife hits the water.

Bea puts her arms around Marnie, and they hug on the dark cliff top, bodies pressed close. Their binding secret disappearing with the tide.

They return along the cliff-top path in the dark. When they reach Salty's rock, Bea tells Marnie, 'I'm going to sit out here for a while.'

'You sure?'

She nods. 'I'm not ready for sleep.'

Marnie's gaze drifts to the water, and Bea's follows. They both make out Aiden in the surf, just a shadow amongst the dark, breaking waves. They watch silently for a time, seeing Aiden stroking through the inky black, then launching to his feet. His form is indistinct in the darkness, a blur of shadow-grey, just the wake left by his board leaving a ghostly glow.

Marnie says, 'You care about him, don't you?'

Bea keeps her eyes on the water as she answers honestly, 'More than I was expecting.'

Marnie allows this response to settle. Then she says quietly, 'I'd like to see Aiden happy.'

Bea nods slowly, thinking how much she'd like that, too. She turns to Marnie and says with meaning, 'Thank you for coming with me tonight.'

Marnie takes Bea's face in her hands and stands on her tiptoes to press a kiss to her forehead. 'G'night, then.'

'Goodnight,' Bea says.

When Marnie has gone, Bea sits on her usual rock and Salty

settles into position at her feet. She places her hand on the soft fur between his ears and lets her heart rate slow.

The sea is ruffled with whitewater from the breaking waves, and the draw and suck of the sea feels peaceful. She watches Aiden, his form rising and falling with the dark swell.

It is done. The knife and scarf gone. Her passport returned. The money paid. Everything is back where it started. If she wanted to, she could leave. She could get a taxi to the airport tonight – and be back in London by tomorrow.

She turns and peers over her shoulder at The Surf House. The lights are off, and she wonders if Ped is somewhere within the darkened building.

She feels the echo of Savannah, wondering if she once sat out here alone, looking up at her room in The Surf House. Did she miss California? Miss Seth? Think about returning home? Or did she feel like she belonged here?

Where are you now? she whispers.

Bea may have her passport back, but she's not going anywhere. She promised Seth she'd find Savannah – and she will keep her word.

ONE YEAR EARLIER

SAVANNAH

The surf café was a bamboo bar on the cliff top, with pallet seating and floor rugs. The two Moroccan surfers who ran it made exceptional coffee and fresh smoothies, and were always keen to talk waves, which guaranteed a good crowd of customers.

Savannah ordered a mango smoothie, watching as fresh bananas and ripe mango were blended with ice, yoghurt and orange juice. She'd just returned from her third trip to Marrakesh and felt strung out and wired. She'd been living off adrenalin, and there was nothing left in the tank. The smoothie would help, she decided as she reached for it, then weaved through the tables looking for one in the shade.

She heard her name called and turned to see Elin waving to her. Savannah didn't have the energy for a one-on-one so was relieved to see she was sitting with Aiden, who always diluted Elin's intensity.

Savannah pulled out a chair, and before she'd even lowered herself into it, Elin was asking, 'You all right? You look knackered.'

'I'm fine. Been in Marrakesh for few days.'

'It's becoming a regular stop. What's the draw?'

'It's a cool city,' Savannah said casually.

'Who are you hanging out with?'

'Friends of Driss's. They're interesting. Fun.' She wasn't sure *fun* was the word to describe the people she was involved with.

Calling them *mates of Driss's* wasn't entirely accurate either. He'd made an intro, stepped back.

Elin's interrogation didn't ease up. Her eyes narrowed. 'Something's up, isn't it?'

God, Elin could be a bloodhound. 'Everything's cool.'

'Is it Seth? Is he on your case again?'

It was easier just to agree. Give Elin something to sink her teeth into. 'Yeah. He's threatening to fly over, drag me back home.'

Elin shook her head. 'That arsehole needs to live his own life.'

Savannah felt a stirring of conscience. Maybe she'd been guilty of dramatizing Seth's behaviour in the past, playing to the idea of being the hunted sister. Seth might be a puppet to their dad, but he loved her; she knew that.

'You heard Elin's going to start shooting film for me?' Aiden said.

'Surf tutorials,' Elin confirmed.

'That's great.'

'Yep,' Elin agreed. 'Means I can see out the season here.' She looked at Savannah and added, 'After that, the Atlas Mountains will be waiting for us. You're still sticking around for that, right?'

They'd talked about travelling through the mountains together, but that was a while back. Savannah didn't fancy being cooped up in an RV with Elin again. She couldn't be bothered with the drama of saying as much, so she kept her commitment vague. 'Depends how long I can make my money stretch.'

Elin nodded seriously. 'You could see if there's any work going at The Surf House?'

Savannah tried to look like she was considering the idea, but she'd already found all the work she needed. She'd taken her first two payments, and now her bank account was back to healthy.

'You guys heard about the beach party next week up at Jailors?' Aiden asked.

She liked Aiden. He was easy-going and quick to crack a joke. Didn't take himself too seriously.

Elin nodded. 'It's big, right? Run by the surf camp guys?'

He nodded. 'Everyone from Mallah will be heading over for it. It's always a good night. Make sure you come.'

'We'll be there,' Savannah said.

Aiden slugged back his coffee, then stood. 'Surf lesson in five. We better go.'

'Have a good one,' Savannah said, waving them both off.

At the table next to her, two blonde girls were examining a paper map. It was spread out and weighted by two empty coffee mugs, a highlighted route riding across the edge of it.

Savannah leaned over. 'Journey planning?'

'Yes. Overlanding across Africa,' answered the girl nearest to her, who wore a red bandana around her neck. She introduced herself as Lise and the other girl as Anke.

'That's a serious adventure,' Savannah said. 'How long do you think it'll take?'

'We've planned to be away for nine months – but we'll see. If we're having fun, we stay longer.'

'When are you leaving Morocco?' Savannah asked.

'Next week. We have a van repair that needs doing. Then we go.'

Savannah peered at the highlighted map. She felt the stir of excitement at the adventure of it – the sheer propulsion of being on a journey of that scale.

'We're looking for a third person to split the fuel costs,' Lise said easily. 'Spread the word if you know anyone who might like to come.'

Savannah nodded slowly as she studied the route snaking across the African continent.

'I'll do that,' Savannah said, a seed of an idea beginning to emerge.

45

Overnight, the rains arrive. The always-blue sky turns violent grey, sheeting with rain. Mallah, once beautiful for its barrenness, is now a river of red mud. Drains overflow. Water pours from corrugated iron roofs.

Bea walks through the village, shoulders hunched against the rain, grocery bags weighing down each arm. Mud is flecked up the back of her legs, and she's cold. Without the heat of the sun to warm her or brighten the landscape, everything looks drab and washed out.

She passes closed beachside eateries and collapsed parasols. A pack of stray dogs huddle together in the shelter of an abandoned building site, and Bea searches them for Salty – but doesn't locate him.

Although she's desperate to get indoors and dry off, the thought of returning to The Surf House makes her stomach churn. She knows Ped will be in there, storming around, his bad temper seeping into the seams of the building. The rains have caused leaks to sprout in two of the rooms, and he's been roaming with buckets and towels all day.

Squinting against the rain, Bea sees the sign for Offshore. She has a sudden urge to go inside, climb into Aiden's bed and not leave until the rain stops. They've never turned up at the other's territory. By some unspoken arrangement, they meet at the cliff top or in the sea, and those feel like their places. She wonders how he'd feel about changing the rules.

She reaches the hostel, and before she can talk herself out of it, she pushes open the main door, which deposits her in the entrance of the lounge. Her hair is pasted to her head, and water drips from the shopping bags she's carrying. A group of surfers who are huddled in the lounge look up. Aiden is at the centre of them, and she immediately sees they are midway through a surf tutorial, Aiden pointing to something on screen.

When he clocks Bea, he stops talking, and his features stretch in surprise. Then he frowns slightly. 'You okay?'

Everyone's eyes are on her. She nods quickly, instantly regretting walking in. 'I was just passing, so thought I'd say hi. But I can see you're busy.'

An Italian surfer she recognises from the water is staring at her, a faint smirk on his lips. Her T-shirt, she realises, is stuck to her skin, and her nipples push against the fabric. She wants to cross her arms over her body, but she has shopping bags in both hands.

'Maybe catch you later,' she says, already backing towards the door.

'Sure,' Aiden says. Is there a lack of conviction in how he says it?

Her skin prickles with humiliation as she steps back out into the rain and splashes her way across the street to The Surf House.

She wipes her sandals thoroughly on the mat, then unpacks the food without any grace. She pulls her phone from the pocket of her wet shorts, towels it off, then slogs upstairs to her room in search of dry clothes.

As soon as she's closed her door, she hears Ped's raised voice through the walls. She catches her name and freezes.

'You never asked me, Marnie. I just get back – and Bea's here, moved in!'

'How many times do we need to go through this? I couldn't ask you – you were in the middle of fucking nowhere, chasing waves!'

'That's what we do, isn't it? That's what this whole thing is about. Surfing. Travel. Freedom. If you want to go off and do something – then do it!'

'This is where I want to be. At The Surf House. With you.'

Ped says nothing.

The pitch changes now, voices quietening. Bea only catches the occasional word.

'Doing my best . . .'

'Toxic . . .'

There's a low thud against the wall, like a fist thrown in frustration.

'She needs to go . . .'

Bea doesn't move a muscle. She waits, listening for more. With all her concentration honed onto the conversation, her phone slips through her fingers, falling with a clack on the wooden floor.

The voices fall quiet. There is an awful pause.

She freezes, breath held.

Then she hears footsteps, fast and light, moving towards the connecting door. A loud rap. Then Marnie's voice. 'Bea?'

Instinctively, Bea crouches behind the bed. Doesn't answer.

'Bea?' she calls again.

'You said she was in the village!' Ped hisses.

'She is.'

Bea knows her door will open, that Marnie will come in. She flattens herself to the ground, then inches beneath the bed, lying on her stomach. She is almost under it when she hears the depression of the handle, and Marnie's voice, so close to her now: 'Bea?'

She holds her breath. The wooden floorboards are cold beneath her. There's a line of dust as far as a hoover has been pushed under. Inches away from her face, a dead cockroach lies on its back, legs curled. Beyond it, she can see Marnie's tanned, bare feet, toe rings on, nail varnish chipped.

'I can't do this anymore,' Ped says, stepping into the room. The scar from the smashed granola jar is visible at his ankle. 'No more whispered conversations and sleeping in the van. I want this room back.'

'We're managing.'

'Are we? We've got nothing, Marnie. If we don't keep guests this autumn and winter, then we're done for. This whole thing falls apart. It's over.'

'Don't say that!' Her voice is high-pitched, a cry almost. 'The Surf House is everything. You are everything.'

'Then Bea goes. Our bookings are tailing off. Our borrowings are out of control. We can't afford to keep her.'

Bea knows her exit isn't only about money. It's because she's been asking too many questions.

'She's my friend,' Marnie says, her voice small.

'You've seen the amount of money we owe. The interest is skyrocketing. Plus, the studio needs repairing – that crack is getting worse. Have you seen it? That whole thing could crumble—'

'Don't!'

Ped is silent.

'Do you love me?' Marnie asks, a challenge in her tone.

281

There's a hesitation. 'Course.'

Her voice lowers, turns husky. 'Show me.'

Bea sees Marnie's step forward, closing the gap between her and Ped.

'Not now, Marnie.'

'Why not?'

'Because we're in Bea's room! Because we're fighting! Because I've got a thousand things that need doing!'

'See,' Marnie says, voice sullen, as if she's proven a point.

'You need to sort your head out,' Ped snaps. Then he turns and strides through the connecting door. Bea hears the heavy tread of his feet as he crosses their room, exits, and thunders downstairs.

She lies very still.

Above her, she hears the depression of the bed as Marnie sits on the edge of it. Then the groan as she draws her legs onto the mattress and lies back.

Bea cannot announce herself. She will have to wait it out. She hears the rearranging of pillows, the squeak of the mattress as Marnie turns onto her side, settling her face onto the pillow.

Marnie inhales deeply as if breathing in Bea.

Once it is safe to come out, Bea wriggles herself from beneath the bed. As she moves, something catches her eye above her. She shuffles a little closer, noticing a pink item wedged between the mattress slats. A book?

The cover is leather, plain, in a bright pop of neon pink. Something about it feels familiar. She tries to tug it free, but it's wedged in tight.

Intrigued, Bea rolls out from beneath the bed, then lifts the mattress and reaches for it.

It's not a novel – it's a journal. From the deep indentations from the slats, she guesses it's been hidden there for a long time. She blows on it, releasing a small billow of dust.

After glancing briefly towards the connecting door, she opens the journal. Looping handwriting fills page after page. From the dates of the entries, she sees they were written over a year ago.

Her heart kicks hard between her ribs as understanding lands.

She knows who this belongs to.

Bea flicks back to the very first page, looking inside the cover. There it is. An inscription.

Savannah Hart's Travel Journal.

46

Bea runs her fingertips across the page, feeling the faint grooves where Savannah's pen once pressed. She turns a page, then another, eyes trailing over the neatly written entries, the stub of a ferry ticket, a drawing on the corner of a receipt.

Caught near the spine of the journal, Bea sees a long golden hair. Gently, she plucks it between thumb and forefinger, lifting it to the light. The blonde shade wavers from honey to deep caramel as the light catches it.

Savannah's presence suddenly feels so visceral it's as if she is standing in the room. A shiver travels between Bea's shoulder blades and tiny hairs rise on the backs of her arms.

Savannah set down her words and thoughts in the pages of this journal – maybe because she had no one else she could tell. Then she hid it beneath the mattress to keep those words safe.

And now Bea has found it.

The deep pull of connection strengthens.

She was meant to find this.

Carefully, Bea replaces the strand of golden hair within the journal.

Bea wonders why, when Savannah packed up and left The Surf House, she didn't take this journal with her. Did she forget?

Was she rushing? Did she leave it here on purpose, wanting it to be found?

Bea remains seated on the bedroom floor, her spine pressed against the bedframe. She turns to the first entry and begins to read.

The opening entries tell Savannah's story of leaving LA, catching a flight to Paris, and setting off on her interrailing adventure.

Bea can hear Savannah's voice as she writes of long train journeys through European cities. Of coffees drunk on pavement tables, hungrily watching people's lives rolling by. Of late-night drinking in hostels, returning to her room alone. Of croissants eaten on train platforms. Of long, dreary waits sitting on her luggage.

She reads a line, then pauses.

She rereads it again, aloud. '*I feel like I am passing through this country, walking its pavements and parks, but that I'm not really in it. I'm drifting. It's as if someone could just pass right through me and I'd realise that I'm not even here.*'

Goosebumps have risen on the backs of her arms. Bea knows that feeling. It's like she's reading her own words.

Her heart rate accelerates as she reads on. Savannah's entries are nothing like her peppy Instagram captions, which were bright and breezy and full of verve. That was a carefully constructed brand, no different to Bea's modelling portfolio. But in these pages, no one is watching.

Bea reads and reads – and then she comes to the first entry with a name she recognises. Savannah sticking out her thumb and seeing an RV pull up with Elin behind the wheel.

There was a long drive, an impromptu night pulled in on a roadside, then a ferry crossing to Morocco. And then later,

Mallah. That first sight as they drove down the winding track towards the village, the bay unfurling like a dream.

She reads of the evening Savannah met Marnie, Ped, Aiden, Driss, and Farah – right here, at the opening night of The Surf House. She writes of the confidence and ease of this group of friends. How warmly they brought her and Elin into the fold, sharing their stories, talking about Mallah like it was in their bones, how it was something to them and their passion felt infectious.

Bea feels the shift in Savannah's writing. It becomes brighter, sharper, as if she's shaken off the lethargy and boredom of the long journeys and hustle of moving through city after city. It was like she was searching for something – and found it here.

Bea looks up, staring through the rain-smeared window, her brow furrowed.

So why did you leave?

Bea inhales entry after entry. It's like she's picked up the most compulsive novel, but with a cast of characters she knows. Now she's travelling towards an ending that she is desperate to discover.

Savannah writes of the growing discomfort of living in Elin's RV, her rules beginning to grate, a mistaken kiss, the decision to move into The Surf House.

Bea's gaze flicks to the doorway, imagining her walking into this room, a pack on her shoulders.

And then the tone of the entries shifts.

One name keeps appearing and reappearing. It's like Savannah's lens is pausing on someone, zooming in.

Bea feels the uncomfortable sensation that she's travelling towards something she doesn't want to see. Something instinctive and unstoppable is happening in these entries, and Bea finds herself leaning closer to the journal, her complete focus given over to its pages as she reads:

The Surf House is empty now. They're all in the sea. I'm sitting on the bed writing this, cheeks flushed, heart hammering.

There's been an energy building between us for days. When we are in the same room, I find his eyes sliding to meet mine. It's like we have a heightened awareness of each other.

Earlier, I heard him next door: bare feet on wood. The drop of a towel. The slide of drawers. Clothes being pulled on. I could feel him, like there was no wall between us.

I knew he was aware of me, too. Moving. Listening. Waiting.

He paused outside the connecting door. Knocked. 'Savannah?'

'Hey,' I said, slipping from the bed. Opening the door.

Ped was standing there, eyes on me. The back of his neck was still wet from the shower, water caught at the edges of his lashes.

He said he had a photo to show me. We both knew I didn't need to see it. But I crossed that threshold into his room.

Their room.

Ped took out his phone.

I stood close at his shoulder.

Our arms were touching, bare flesh against bare flesh. I could smell soap on his skin and the tang of sunscreen beneath it. I knew he was every bit as aware of me as I was him. My fingers rotated, slid beneath the hem of his T-shirt until they met the hard lines of his torso.

He didn't say we shouldn't. He didn't say Marnie's name. He didn't try to stop me as I put my mouth against his.

Bea stares at the entry. Everything she liked about Savannah evaporates.

She drags her gaze away from the page, focus travelling towards the connecting door. Savannah stepped through that doorway into Marnie's bedroom – and betrayed her. Bea feels the blow as a deep, churning disappointment.

There's a bitter taste in her mouth as she reads on, Savannah's entries describing encounter after encounter with Ped, the two of them often stealing away to the van, lying in the dark at night, talking about their dreams and passions.

There's a rap on the door, and Bea starts. The door opens, and Marnie stands on the threshold between rooms. She's dressed for bed in an oversized tee of Ped's. 'What are you doing sitting in the dark?' She walks in and turns on the bedside lamp.

Bea hadn't realised the day had slipped away. She blinks into the bright light.

'What's that?' Marnie asks.

Bea looks down and sees she has the open journal clasped in her fingers. She snaps it shut.

Marnie's head tips to one side, studying her.

'It's . . . my travel journal,' Bea manages at last.

Marnie's curious expression shifts into a small smile. 'I didn't know you kept one. I love that.'

Bea smiles weakly, pushes to her feet and places the journal into a drawer.

Marnie crosses the room and moves to the window, looking out onto the rain-smeared evening. 'Let's hope the rain stops tonight. I think we're running out of buckets.'

Bea can see the shadow of Marnie's earlier argument with Ped. She seems a little diminished, her shoulders rounded, her voice flat. She lingers at the window. In the reflection of the glass,

Bea catches Marnie's expression and senses there's something she came in here to say. Is she going to bring up the argument with Ped – tell Bea that she needs to leave?

Bea prompts, 'Everything okay?'

Marnie turns and looks at her. Her expression is thoughtful, serious.

She recalls Ped's words: *She needs to go.*

Marnie continues to stare at her, gaze softening. Then she shakes her head and says, 'Everything's fine.'

Bea holds her eye. Nods.

'Well, g'night then,' Marnie says, stepping forward and pressing a kiss to her forehead.

'Goodnight,' Bea echoes.

Bea listens to the sounds of Marnie climbing into bed, placing her phone into her bedside drawer, and turning out the light.

Then Bea pulls out Savannah's journal and continues to read.

47

The next entries are all about Ped. Bea's jaw clenches as she reads of clandestine meetings in the van or the dunes beyond the village.

Ped confided in Savannah that The Surf House wasn't what he'd hoped it would be. He felt trapped, all his money and time locked between four walls. He missed the freedom of living out of a van, of dropping everything to follow a forecast. When he heard about the Dutch girls' plans to travel through Africa, he said he admired their bravery and sense of adventure – and that those were the things he'd once loved about Marnie.

Bea feels a sickening sense of disloyalty as she reads on, but she knows she must.

As she nears the end of the journal, she reads with urgency, her gaze skimming over entries in her hurry to understand.

The Dutch girls' van is repaired and ready. We went out for shisha last night, and they told me they're heading out of Morocco in two days, right after the Jailors beach party.

I asked if that ride was still going.

An overland trip to Cape Town. That's a proper adventure, crossing the continent. Months of travel, of seeing different places.

They've saved the seat for me.

I've told Marnie I'm leaving – that I won't be needing the room. I've told Aiden. I've told Driss and Farah. I've rolled it into my decision to go offline, ditch social media. I'm done with the bullshit. Done with Seth checking up on me. Done with Dad having more ammunition.

I've told everyone that I'm ready for change. Ready for an adventure. That I'm going to explore Africa.

That's what I'm telling everyone.

But that's not what is going to happen.

Bea reads the entry twice. She snaps to the next page – but it is blank.

She turns to the next.

Blank.

She flips through the remaining pages of the journal, but each of them is empty.

No . . . That can't be the end!

She turns back through the pages, certain she must have missed something – but there is nothing further.

She rubs a hand across her brow, rereading Savannah's final entry, trying to gauge a clue from those brief lines.

That's what I'm telling everyone.

But that's not what is going to happen.

What was her plan? If she never intended to go with the Dutch girls, where did she plan to go?

Pushing the journal aside, Bea paces the room, her breathing audible above the sound of falling rain.

The final entries were almost solely about Ped. Every moment, every thought circling back to him. He'd shared details about his life that you don't tell someone you're fucking. You share those things with a person you are intoxicated by.

Bea returns to the journal, which is open on the final entry. She picks it up and rereads it.

> I've told Marnie I'm leaving – that I won't be needing the room. I've told Aiden. I've told Driss and Farah.

Ped's name isn't on that list.

Savannah must have already discussed it with him. Maybe he was always part of the plan.

Bea thinks about Ped's long trips away chasing swell.

She thinks about Marnie's suspicion that Ped is having an affair.

She thinks about Savannah taking out her money so that there is no trace of her. So no one will know whether she is in South Africa or, in fact, right here.

In Morocco.

Bea's heart rate speeds up. Is Ped trying to detach himself from The Surf House, storing up money, ready to make a full break?

Bea goes to the rain-smeared window, the journal still in her grip. She pictures Savannah standing right here, making her plan, the journal pressed to her chest.

What if Savannah isn't missing? What if she's hiding some-where, waiting for Ped?

ONE YEAR EARLIER

SAVANNAH

Stars blistered the clean black sky. The air was tinged with wood-smoke and hashish. Laughter and music swirled together, the stirring sea sonorous in the background.

The beach party was at Jailors, a hidden cove only twenty minutes from Mallah. Savannah had piled in the back of Aiden's truck with Farah, Driss, and some others, hands gripped to the sides as they bounced down the rutted track, wind in their hair.

Once they'd parked up, she'd seen the glow of flame torches on the beach below, felt the bass from a speaker booming through her chest.

They'd grabbed beers and blankets, kicked off sandals, and ran down the dark, cool dunes towards the party.

A group of male surfers she recognised from Mallah were dancing, bare-chested, on the sand. Aiden, a cooler of beer propped on his shoulder, was tossing out cold ones. The vibe was loose and buoyant, something celebratory and expectant in the air.

'You look beautiful.'

The words were a low whisper by her ear.

She turned, and there was Ped, tanned and fit in a surf tee, gaze glued to her. Her stomach flipped.

After that night when Savannah had invited a crowd from Rooftops back to The Surf House, the atmosphere between them had changed. She smiled whenever she thought of the moment Ped had stormed onto the terrace and yelled at the lot of them, the party disbanding. He'd tried to order her to bed, too, but she'd walked into the pool, slipping beneath the surface in defiance of him.

When she'd emerged, her clothes clinging to her skin, Ped had been standing at the poolside, watching. She'd swum towards him, placing her forearms on the tiles. 'Join me?'

Ped hadn't. He'd turned and left. But she'd seen the way his gaze had lowered to her mouth, then slid down to her body. After that, there was a charge in the air whenever they passed – and they seemed to make sure they passed often.

Now, it was her turn to whisper low to his ear. 'I want you.'

She could see goosebumps rise on his skin. Knew how much he wanted to fuck her.

'The dunes,' she said. 'Thirty minutes.'

'It's risky.'

She grinned. 'Course.'

Ped stared at her for a beat more, then turned and disappeared through the crowd.

In the other direction, she noticed Marnie and Farah gathered at the edge of a group, watching three girls breakdancing. Spotting her, Farah lifted a hand in greeting, and she and Marnie crossed the beach towards Savannah.

Gold glitter sparkled on Marnie's cheeks, highlighting her elfin features. Marnie was fun and sexy and generous – and had invited Savannah into her home. She felt a flush of guilt.

'You're heading off with the Dutch girls tomorrow, right?' Farah asked.

'Yep. Leaving first thing. All packed.'

'We've loved having you at The Surf House,' Marnie said. 'Come back any time. We'll need to hear all about your adventures.'

'I will,' Savannah lied.

'One last Moroccan night,' Farah said.

'You're leaving?'

Savannah turned and found Elin standing at her shoulder, face pinched. She hadn't told Elin about her plans. Up and go, that was the idea. She'd already gone offline, so Elin wouldn't even be able to send her a ranty message. 'I only decided a couple of days ago. It's pretty last minute.'

'You weren't gonna bother telling me?'

Marnie and Farah looked awkwardly between them and, taking their cue, they slipped away into the crowd.

'Knew I'd see you tonight.'

'So, what, you're shipping out with those Dutch girls?'

She shrugged. 'Looks like it.'

'What about our plans? The Atlas Mountains?' Elin's face was pinched. 'If you'd wanted to travel across Africa, you should have said. I'd have gone with you. We could have done it together.'

Savannah must have had more to drink than she'd realised, as she let slip a small laugh.

Elin's mouth tightened into a narrow line. 'Nice to know I mean so much to you,' she hissed. 'Jesus, you're a selfish bitch.'

She was on the money there. Maybe there'd be a time when Savannah would look back and regret her behaviour – but tonight wasn't it. She was here to party. Ped would soon be waiting for her in the dunes.

'We're young, Elin. The world is out there. I want to live!

I'm done staying in your RV, listening to you whinge about who drank the last of the juice, or having you ogling me through your fucking camera lens.'

Elin looked like she'd been slapped.

'Oh? You thought I hadn't noticed?' Savannah shook her head dismissively and went to step away.

But Elin caught her arm roughly and swung her around.

'What the fuck?' Savannah snapped.

'What about you?' Elin's voice was low and lethal, knuckles white where she gripped Savannah. 'Don't fool yourself that you're on some life-affirming adventure. You're lost, Savannah!' she spat. 'That's all you are. A pathetic lost girl.'

Savannah felt the blow of truth in those words.

'Fuck you, Elin,' she said, snatching back her arm. 'Maybe I want to get lost. Maybe I want to get so fucking lost that no one ever finds me.'

48

Rain bleeds against the windows. Bea lies awake for hours, turning Savannah's journal entries over in her mind and worrying about Marnie.

When she finally falls asleep, her dreams are disturbed, studded with distorted snapshots. She sees Seth walking in leather shoes through shifting sand. She sees a gold dress discarded in a water fountain. She sees Savannah running into the surf, Ped waiting for her in the deeper water.

Hours later, she is ripped from sleep by a deep rumbling sound.

Bea sits bolt upright in the dark, fists gripping the bedsheet. There's a roaring, crashing boom as the earth shudders, then stills.

Earthquake! she thinks immediately.

From somewhere within The Surf House comes a shocked, high scream.

Next door, she hears Ped shouting. A door thwacks open, then bare feet are running along the corridor.

Marnie's voice calls out after him.

Bea reaches for the lamp – but it doesn't turn on. She pushes out of bed and crosses the floor tentatively, as if it might crack apart beneath her. She gropes towards the door and yanks it open.

Downstairs, urgent voices are speaking in a foreign language. One of the Swedish guests, hair rumpled, eyes creased with sleep, is pointing outside.

Bea has no idea what is happening. Was there an earthquake?

A ceramic jug has fallen from the alcove, shattering across the floor. Barefoot, she skirts around it and heads through the open door onto the terrace.

Outside, in the rising light of dawn, she sees a sight so strange that she halts. She stands on the rain-slicked poolside, dressed only in a T-shirt and knickers, staring.

The studio has collapsed. The front half of it has disappeared over the cliff edge, leaving a caved roof and buckled earth. The double bed that Seth once slept in teeters on the edge, a white sheet billowing in the breeze. The surrounding terrace has cracked, paving slabs lifted as a huge section of land has fallen. It looks unreal, like a film set.

'Oh God!' Marnie gasps, hands lifted to her mouth.

Ped's hands are clasped to the back of his skull, elbows wide, as he shakes his head. 'No . . .'

There's the rushing of footsteps, and Bea sees Aiden racing down the side path from Offshore. He slows to a halt beside them. He's wearing only shorts, hair mussed from sleep. He turns up his palms. 'What the—'

'The cliff collapsed . . .' Ped says, voice thinned by disbelief.

Aiden stares. 'The studio . . . it was empty?'

'Yes, thank God.' Marnie lets out a shuddering breath.

Other voices join theirs as locals and visitors gather in clusters, absorbing the devastation.

From what Bea can see, the section of fallen cliff starts

almost directly in front of The Surf House and runs west for another twenty or thirty metres. Thankfully, there are no other properties in that direction, only the narrow pathway that hugs the cliff line.

She scans the area, trying to rearrange what is missing with the map in her head. She realises that the place where she and Aiden often meet on the rocks has crumbled.

There is a beat of relief that they weren't out there before the next thought lands. *Salty . . .*

Her gaze swings around her as she scans the growing crowd, searching for him. Dawn is just breaking, water-grey clouds brushed with pink light.

'Have you seen Salty?' she asks, turning to where Aiden was just standing – but he's vanished.

She moves closer to the edge, looking down. On the beach below, she sees a heap of earth and rock and the grey breeze-blocks of the studio.

The cliff where she's so often sat, Salty curled into the nook beneath her legs, has gone. Now only jagged, exposed rock remains.

'Bea! Come away!' Marnie yells.

She's already turning, skirting the crowd who are emerging dazed from their beds.

Bea hurries down the wet cliff steps, her breath shallow. Reaching the beach, she races barefoot towards the heaped rubble and earth.

As she gets closer, she can see a bedside table protruding from a section of earth. A pillow is speared on a rock, white feathers swirling in the damp breeze.

The high tide licks at the collapsed cliff, drawing mud out into the water so the shallows are turned a swirling, sludgy brown.

'Salty!' she calls, scrambling over the loose, jagged boulders, searching for any sign of life.

Crushed into the earth is a painting that, only minutes ago, hung on the wall of the studio.

'Bea!' Elin is running towards her. 'Is someone in there?'

'No. I'm looking for Salty.'

'There are still loose rocks coming down. There could be more landfall.'

Bea looks up to the cliff above and, as she does, sees the scattering of stones sprinkle.

She staggers back, feet caked in mud. Wearing only a T-shirt, she begins to shiver in the damp morning air.

'Dogs sense things. He will have moved in time. Promise ya.' Elin places a firm hand on her arm. 'Come on, let's go back up.'

They climb the cliff steps together.

At the top, Marnie stands, white-faced and shivering. Ped puts an arm around her, and she folds herself into the space of his body.

Bea eyes Ped, thinking, *How could you?* He's been cheating on Marnie, sloping off to visit Savannah. What is it they're planning? To get his money out of The Surf House and disappear? To make Marnie leave instead?

Ped catches Bea's eye and signals her over. 'The guests are shaken. Can you make them coffee, look after them? I need to get this area cordoned off.'

She can't look at him as she manages a terse, 'Fine.'

She washes the streaks of mud from her legs at the outdoor tap, wipes her wet feet on the doormat, then heads inside. She puts on fresh clothes, cleans her teeth, splashes water over her face.

The power is down, so she makes the coffee on the hob, lighting it with a match.

There's no fresh bread, so she takes some orange cake from the tin and sets it on a wooden board. She zests an orange into a pan, squeezes in its juice, and adds a tablespoon of honey. Once the sauce is warmed through, she drizzles the sweet, citrus liquid over the cake to freshen it.

She carries the coffee and cake through to the lounge, where four Swedish guests are talking in fast, anxious voices. When they see Bea setting down the tray of food, their postures soften a little, and they switch to English to thank her.

As she pours them steaming mugs of coffee, they ask questions that Bea can't answer: *Why did it happen? Was the building unsafe? Is the rest of The Surf House at risk?* She tries to allay their concerns, but she doesn't have the answers, and she's relieved when they let her go.

Returning to the kitchen, she stands for a moment with her hands on the side, letting her head hang. Her heart rate still thunders, and she tries to slow her breathing as she processes the last few hours.

There's a low noise at the edge of the room. A scratching sound. She turns and looks towards the kitchen door, which inches open.

She finds Salty there, looking up at her expectantly.

'Oh!' she cries. She crouches, throwing her arms around him and pressing her face into his fur.

It's late afternoon when the Swedish group announce that they won't be staying on at The Surf House. The hot water is out. The pool can't be used, and they feel unsafe.

When they ask Ped for a refund, he gives them a thunderous look and stalks off. Bea smooths things over, promising she'll be in touch to arrange a refund once the Wi-Fi is back up, although the truth is, she's no idea if there's enough money in The Surf House account.

Bea goes in search of Marnie and finds her alone in the office, head in her hands. She taps on the doorframe.

Marnie starts, wiping her face. She looks ashen.

'Can I make you some food?'

'No, I'm fine—' Marnie begins, but her voice cracks. Her face creases, tears squeezing from the corners of her eyes.

Bea goes to her, placing a hand on Marnie's back, feeling the ridges of her spine.

'This will finish us,' she whispers. 'We've got no money for the repairs. There's no way we can rebuild.'

'The main house is still standing—'

'Who'll want to stay here now?'

'Surely the insurance will cover it.' Even as Bea says this, she wishes she hadn't.

'We don't have insurance. We didn't have the right building regs. We can't even sell this place – we owe more than it's worth.'

It scares Bea to hear the fragility in Marnie's voice. Her whole body is trembling.

'This place – it's everything,' she says, blinking rapidly. 'It's my home. My life. I can't lose it.'

Bea thinks of what she's learned from Savannah's travel journal – and her heart cracks, because Marnie's at risk of losing so much more.

49

Bea slips outside for some air. She and Salty stand back from the crumbled cliff top beneath a grey sky. The cordon tape flickers in the breeze.

The front of the studio has been lost, and the guts of the building spill out – wooden beams, insulation, metal pipes. A chair leg pokes through a pile of bricks; a mirror hangs miraculously from a remaining wall. The terraced ground surrounding the studio has been uprooted, lifting paving slabs at jaunty angles.

Bea's teeth clamp together. Ped knew about the cracks in the studio, knew that building on the cliff edge without regulation came with risk – but he bowled forward anyway. He likes to see how far he can push things, what he can get away with.

She places her palm on Salty's head and tells him to wait. She ducks beneath the cordon and picks her way carefully across the uneven earth and cracked paving slabs. She needs to unhook the mirror before it falls and shatters. Marnie will have chosen it, finding something appealing in the simple copper curve of its frame. Bea cannot bear to see any more unnecessary wreckage.

'Stop!'

The boom of Ped's voice startles her.

He's standing on the other side of the cordon, face tense. 'It's not safe!'

Her skin flames as she ducks back beneath the cordon. 'I just wanted to—'

'No one is to go into that area.' Ped cuts her off. 'The site is unstable. Don't be so fucking cavalier!'

She baulks. 'Y'know what's cavalier? You building a studio on a fucking cliff edge!'

Ped stares at her. She's never spoken to him like this, challenged him, and she can see his register of surprise.

Fury boils up in her veins. Everything that is wrong with this place is standing in front of her. He's ruined it. Fucked it all – when it could have been so beautiful. 'This was Aiden's land,' she says, gesturing to the terrace and crumbled studio. 'You took it from him. Blocked the view from Offshore.'

'You don't know what you're talking about.' There's a dismissive arrogance to his tone.

She glares right at Ped. She pictures the looping handwriting in Savannah's journal. 'I know more than you think.'

He holds her gaze. There is a contraction, almost a flinch at the corner of his right eye.

The words hold there, and she wills him to ask, to push her one more step.

'Bea? Ped?'

It is Marnie. She's walking towards them, barefoot. She looks so small, like she's light enough to be blown from her feet by the wind. She glances to the studio. Then back at them. 'What's going on?'

Ped looks at her, then says, 'I was about to tell Bea that she's going to have to leave.'

Bea's gaze snaps to meet his.

'We've got no guests. No money. We can't afford to keep you on. Not after this,' he says, voice controlled once again. Ped slides his arm around Marnie, drawing her to his side. 'We've loved having you here,' he says, deadpan. 'You've been a great help, but I'm afraid it's over.'

Bea's gaze moves to Marnie's face.

Her eyes are blue pools, dulled, like a pond beneath cloud. She looks past Bea, out beyond the ruined studio. Her voice is flat and lifeless. 'I'm sorry, Bea.'

50

Bea sits on the beach, arms hugged to her knees. The tide is out, wet sand glimmering beneath a dusky sky. She's cold, beginning to shiver, but she won't go back to The Surf House.

She knew Ped wanted her gone. And, deep down, she knew it was only a matter of time before Marnie gave in to him.

Salty is curled at her side, muzzle resting on his paws. Every now and then, he looks up at her, his expression uncertain. She runs a hand across his back, reassuring him that she's okay. But she's far from okay.

Salty's head lifts, and Bea mirrors the turn of his gaze.

Aiden is walking towards her. He looks exhausted. His hair is tangled, and there are shadows beneath his eyes.

He lowers himself down onto the sand beside her. 'Hoped I'd find you here.'

She's on the edge of tears, but she concentrates on the sound of the waves rolling in and out, until she's certain she can hold them at bay. 'I've got to leave,' Bea tells him.

He looks at her. 'The Surf House?'

She nods.

'They can't afford to keep me. Ped wants me out.'

'Bea . . . I'm sorry.' Aiden's head shakes. 'What will you do?'

'There's nothing for me at home,' she admits. 'I've got no work. No apartment. No family. Nothing . . .' The tears that were threatening now gather in the corners of her eyes. 'I have *nothing*.'

Aiden's eyes do not leave hers. 'Then you make something. You get to choose what happens next. Where you want to live. Who you want to spend your time with. What work fulfils you. Bea, you get to choose.'

His gaze is sincere and intent. Maybe he's right. She's let herself be pulled along on life's current, never pausing to ask *what do I choose?*

As she studies Aiden's kind, dark eyes, the way his hair falls around his face, she thinks, *I choose you.*

The enormity of the realisation takes her breath away. She has never felt this way about anyone. Never wanted anything so much in her life as him. *Bea, you get to choose.*

And she has made her choice. 'Aiden, could I stay with you while I work things out?'

Aiden's back stiffens. 'With me?' It's subtle, but it is there: a recoiling.

She knows the rules between them – but they were made before she began to feel this way.

'I . . . I'm sorry, but . . .'

Bea is on her feet. She takes a few steps away, embarrassed, her skin stinging with rejection. She presses her palms together, bringing them to her lips, mortified.

She made her choice – but Aiden said no.

'I can't give you what you want,' he tells her, voice quiet.

'What do I want, Aiden?'

He says nothing.

'Come on,' she says, hurt reshaping into anger. 'Tell me what it is that I want.'

307

He meets her gaze. His eyes are dark and sad. 'Let's not do this.'

'What do I want?' she demands. Maybe she should take a breath, walk away from this, but she is done with parcelling up her emotions into neat little boxes. She needs to hear it. Everything that felt like safety in Mallah – The Surf House, Marnie, Aiden – it's all coming apart. She wants it done, to rip away the final piece.

'Really, Aiden,' she says, and she's shouting now, her voice wild and unchecked. 'What the fuck is it that I want so badly?'

Aiden looks right at her. There is sadness in his expression. 'You want someone to love you.'

His words stop her.

They take the air from her body.

It is like she has been punched firm in the gut. She can feel herself folding, caving.

You want someone to love you.

He is right.

She wants someone to love her – because there is no one.

The truth of this crashes over her. It undoes every lock she's kept so tightly in place. It is why she struggles to look at herself in the mirror, because if no one loves her – not even her own mother – then she must be unlovable. That's what she thinks when she tries to meet her own eye.

She is being swallowed by the terrifying emptiness of being alone. Unreachable. It's like she's being pulled downwards into a place with no light, no air.

Her voice is barely a whisper as she says, 'You're right. I want someone to love me.' Despite the tightness in her throat and the way her chest feels like there is a huge pressure squeezing it, she says, 'And that person isn't you.'

There is no question. No inflection. But she leaves it there as a statement – hoping for Aiden to contradict it.

He stays silent.

Her eyes sting with tears. She cannot stand here a moment longer. She turns.

'Bea, please—' Aiden reaches for her, catching her hand. His face is etched with pain. 'I care about you. I didn't want to. I didn't want to feel anything. But I do, okay? I do!'

He is looking at her with such intensity that she can almost touch the darkness that he holds inside.

She wants him to say something else – words that will change everything. But no words can fix this, because Bea suddenly understands. The very thing they both want stands in bleak opposition. Bea needs to be loved – and Aiden will not let himself be loved.

His gaze leaves hers. 'I'm sorry, Bea.' And this time, he lets go of her hands.

51

Bea walks. It's the only thing she feels able to do. She follows the tideline, wet sand sucking at her bare feet. She walks until the light begins to fade and her tears dry on her face in streaks. Only as the tide rises and the stars come out does she turn.

She's come some distance from the village, but she's pleased about that. She doesn't want to be there. Doesn't want to talk to anyone. As she stands, looking towards Mallah, lights twinkling in the distance, she decides: *I will leave in the morning.*

She'll get a ride to the airport. Take the next flight back to London.

It takes her an hour to return to the main bay. The sea becomes a silver lake holding the light of the moon. She passes the landfall, which looks forlorn and forgotten at the bottom of the cliff, almost eerie now with the ghostly glow of the moon catching broken limbs of furniture.

As she climbs the cliff steps, she wonders where Salty will sleep now that his home in the rocky nook has gone. She hates leaving him behind, knowing he'll be waiting outside the kitchen door in the mornings, lying on his belly, muzzle resting on his paws, with that hopeful, doleful expression. Reaching the top, she calls for him lightly.

There's a scuffling in the distance. Salty?

She calls his name a second time.

The scuffling stops – but Salty doesn't appear. She moves across the darkened poolside towards the terrace and ravaged studio. There are no floodlights on tonight – everywhere is in darkness.

'Salty!' she calls again.

She's answered with a bark – yet he doesn't come running.

Odd.

She follows the sound, which leads her to the cordoned area. She peers into the darkness, trying to make out where he is. She catches sight of him near the edge of the damaged studio.

She ducks beneath the cordon, ignoring Ped's warning.

Where the terraced earth has shifted, the ornate paving stones have lifted and buckled, deep banks of earth revealed. Salty is digging intently, the smell of fresh soil filling her nose.

'Salty,' she says gently. 'Come away.'

But he doesn't budge. His front paws dig furiously, sending a spray of earth between his back legs.

As she moves closer, she realises that he's found something. 'What is it?'

She takes her phone from her pocket, flicking on the torch and directing the white light onto the patch of earth.

He's discovered a bundle of material. At first, she thinks it is the netting that builders lay to stop grasses growing through – but then she notices the colour. The fabric, now streaked with dirt, looks like it was once yellow.

Moving the torchlight across the material, she can see there is a print on the fabric. Somewhere in her consciousness, it registers as familiar. The pattern is faded and earth-stained, but she can make out the image of suns and beams of sunlight.

311

'Away,' she tells Salty.

He ignores her command and continues to dig.

Bea redirects the torch over the fabric, something nagging at her. There's a thought flying low, as if trying to land.

She steps closer, trailing the light across the bunched material.

Yes, she recognises this print. She remembers noticing it somewhere. Was it on a catwalk? Something she saw another model wearing?

Then the thought lands – like plane wheels hitting tarmac – and understanding touches down: she's seen this fabric in a photo. It's a beach blanket. She remembers the way it was held aloft, the material catching the light, floating like butterfly wings in a wash of sun flare.

It was held by Savannah.

Every muscle in Bea's body feels alert, tense.

Dirt continues to fly from Salty's paws as he digs.

Bea steps back. On some primal level, her body knows what she is about to witness before her mind can catch up.

As Salty shuffles his position, Bea sees it.

Knuckles. Fingers. A wrist.

A hand protrudes from the earth. The flesh is almost gone, so all that remains are ghostly white bones.

52

A scream dies in Bea's throat.

She staggers backwards.

Breath heaves through her lungs as she stands in the dark. Salty continues to dig, sending a spatter of soil against her legs.

'Stop!' she cries.

Salty's ears flatten. He seems to shrink.

'Away!'

He looks to her, then lowers his head and slinks past – disappearing into the night.

There is no room in Bea's thoughts to feel bad for him. There is no space at all. Just the awful white noise of horror.

She grips her hair near the roots, gaze pinned to the bones. On the index finger of the hand, she notices a daisy-shaped ring rusted to a coppery gold.

Savannah's ring.

This means . . .

Her mouth turns slick with saliva. A surge of heat rises from her belly.

. . . Savannah is dead.

She hinges forward and retches, heaving nothing but hot liquid onto the earth.

Open-mouthed, she pants. Her breath is ragged and shallow.

Bea wipes the back of her hand across her mouth. She straightens. Drags her gaze back to the bones wrapped in the earth-stained blanket.

Savannah has been buried right here.

Bea must have been walking over her grave this whole time.

Seth slept in the studio, just feet away from where his sister was buried.

Her stomach turns over again with the horror of it.

Who did this?

Her brain scrabbles to picture a murderer, fitting a faceless killer to the horror of these bones. But then the first beat of understanding comes. Savannah's body has been buried in the foundations of the studio – and Bea knows exactly who laid them.

Ped.

Is that why he didn't apply for building regulations, because what if they'd checked his work? Then she thinks of Ped yelling at her earlier for crossing the cordon – not because it was unsafe, but because he knew that Savannah's body lay beneath the cracked earth.

Her gaze holds steady on the edge of the blanket. She makes herself keep on looking. Doesn't turn away. Doesn't close off the feeling or numb it. Bea looks, eyes wide open.

A great wash of sadness swims past the horror as she thinks of Savannah's broad smile in the photos. Bright green eyes that glittered. The verve in her journal entries. She had everything ahead of her.

Now she is dead. Buried in an unmarked grave.

She stares and stares, trying to make sense of it.

She thinks about The Surf House's debts.

The money withdrawn from Savannah's account in Ezril.

Did Ped do this for Savannah's money? Was their romance a ruse?

Bea turns, numbly, then drifts like a shadow towards The Surf House.

Inside, the air smells of damp washing. There are no guests now, and the darkened lounge seems to echo with her footsteps.

She keeps her breath steady as she quietly climbs the stairs. Everything must seem normal.

On the landing, light spills out from beneath Ped and Marnie's bedroom door. She pauses for a moment, listening. She can hear Ped's voice.

Something dark unfurls in her chest. She places her fingers around the handle of their door. Feels the cool, smooth metal beneath her palm. She imagines pushing it open, the surprise on Ped's face as he turns to look at her, registering her expression cracked open with rage.

But her fingers slide away from the handle.

Now she's the one with a plan. She gets to choose what happens next.

She enters her room and goes through her usual routine of getting ready for bed. Once she's settled, she hears a knock at her door like she does every night.

Marnie comes in, face bare of make-up. She looks exhausted. 'Thanks for taking care of things today,' Marnie says. 'Sorry I was a mess. It's been a rough day.'

She looks at Marnie. Right into her eyes. Her blue irises are flecked with gold. Bea thinks, *When Marnie returns to her room, she's going to lie in bed and fall asleep next to . . . a killer?*

'What is it?' Marnie asks, her brow creasing.

315

Bea has been staring for too long. 'Nothing.'

Into the silence, Marnie says, 'Bea, I'm so sorry about earlier – with Ped. I love having you here. You know that. I don't want you to leave. What if I talked to Ped and you stayed on for a bit longer? Maybe found some other work while we don't have guests?'

'Sure,' is all Bea manages.

'We'll find a way.' Marnie leans down and presses a kiss to Bea's forehead. She smells of damp fabric, her neck unwashed. 'G'night.'

The door clicks shut behind Marnie.

Bea hears the low murmur of Ped's voice but doesn't catch what he's saying.

She wonders what his strategy will be. Will he tell Marnie that he's going to sleep in the van? Will he wait until the bedroom lights go out? Ped has got plans tonight.

He has a body to hide.

But Bea also has a plan.

Quietly, she pulls on a jumper and pushes her feet into her sandals. She takes an armful of clothes and stuffs them beneath the duvet.

Then, standing by the bedside table, she turns out the light.

53

Bea's heart rate pulses loud and intrusive in her ears as she creeps through The Surf House. She makes almost no sound as she descends the stairs, then slips through the kitchen door into the night.

There is a coolness in the star-bright sky, and she shivers. The moon is high and almost full – enough to provide the light that she'll need.

She makes her way towards the cordoned area, glances over her shoulder, then ducks beneath the tape.

The earth is loose underfoot as she picks her way to where Savannah's body lies. Her gaze tracks down and settles on the earth-stained blanket and white bones of her hand.

Bea crouches, adjusting her position so there is no moon shadow. She dares not risk the flash, but she takes the pictures holding her camera phone steady: the blanket, the hand, the ring, the cracked earth.

Once she is sure she has the photos, she skirts Savannah's body and continues towards the ruined studio. The front half has been lost to the landslide, but the back section remains, fallen bricks peppering the floor. The door has come off its hinges, and she slips inside, aware of the cliff edge at her back, and the swollen, unstable earth.

She would like to use the torch on her phone but can't risk giving herself away. Instead, she lets her eyes adjust to this new layer of darkness and then begins to move towards the back window, where she will station herself.

Shattered glass crunches underfoot as she sets up her position. She props her phone on the windowsill and frames the body, The Surf House visible in the background. The set-up is almost perfect. She makes a minor adjustment – and then she is ready.

Bea waits.

She is good at waiting. She waits at castings. She waits backstage while her hair is being styled. She waits for feelings to pass. For life to start. Bea knows waiting.

She looks up at The Surf House and wonders if Ped is still inside or whether he's already decamped to the van.

The flash of her phone startles her. She's received an email from Rachel Symmonds. It takes a moment to place the name.

Then she remembers: Savannah and Seth's family friend.

Bea clicks on the message and reads.

Dear Bea,

You asked me to let you know if there was any news on the postmortem results. Yesterday, we heard that Seth died from an epileptic seizure. The report said there were high levels of alcohol in his system, and I guess the stress and exhaustion of searching for Savannah were triggers, too. It's sad. Really, really sad.

Seth's going to be buried here in California next to his parents. I hate that Savannah doesn't know this. If you hear any news on that front, please let me know.

Rachel x

Bea stares at the email. There it is. The truth about Seth's death.

Epileptic seizure.

Her surprise is shot through with anger. Seth should never have gone out surfing without telling someone he was epileptic. She remembers seeing him take medication but didn't know what it was for. If alcohol and exhaustion were triggers for seizures, he should have looked after himself better. It is such a waste.

Her gaze moves to the disturbed earth where Savannah is buried. Brother and sister, both dead. She feels tears stinging the corners of her eyes. She can't give in to them, not yet—

Bea freezes at the sound of an engine starting up.

She glances through the broken window but cannot see any headlights.

There. She catches the steady crunch of earth beneath tyres as if a vehicle is slowly inching forward.

The van, she realises. Ped will need the van to move Savannah's body.

The vehicle stops, the engine cut. She waits, barely breathing, listening.

A door opens – then quietly closes.

Bea hears footsteps. Long, firm strides.

Crouched low, Bea hits record on her phone and watches through the screen.

Ped is dressed in a dark jumper with a black beanie pulled over his head.

He ducks beneath the cordon and goes straight to the body. His back is turned, but she catches the silhouette of a shovel.

She hears the draw of breath and then the clink of metal against earth and stone as he begins to dig.

319

Ped will have a cover story if anyone happens upon him. *I couldn't sleep. Thought I'd make a start on clearing the rubble.*

She watches the rhythm of his digging as he loosens the first paving slabs. She wonders what he is thinking, whether guilt claws at him as he digs deeper and deeper.

After a couple of minutes, he lays down the shovel and bends lower. He uses his bare hands to pull up the first paving stone. Freeing it, he turns to set the stone down behind him.

Bea's breath catches in her throat.

He is facing towards her, moonlight illuminating his face.

It isn't Ped.

She mistook his long strides and broad shoulders, the beanie concealing his hair.

The man digging up Savannah's body is Aiden.

ONE YEAR EARLIER

SAVANNAH

The beach party raged on. A group of locals were sitting around a fire, playing drums and guitars. Two girls had picked up the torch flares and were gladiator-battling with them, the flames dancing lethally.

Aiden came over carrying a couple of beers. 'Want one?'

'Sure.' Savannah took the beer, hands still trembling after her fight with Elin. They snapped back ring-pulls and clinked cans.

She looked at Aiden and thought how handsome he was. That shaggy dark hair, the rich brown eyes, his lovely Irish accent. Wouldn't that have been simpler – to fall for someone single and without complications?

She leaned her head on his shoulder, suddenly exhausted.

'So you're heading off first thing?' he asked.

'Yeah. Why? You gonna miss me?'

'The whole of Mallah will miss you, Savannah.'

She smiled.

'Shame you're gonna miss the grand opening of Offshore next week.'

'Yeah? It's ready?'

'Terrace goes down tomorrow. Doors open Friday.'

'I'll spread the word on my travels. The crowds will flock.'

Aiden smiled. 'Here's hoping.'

Savannah glanced at her watch, realising Ped would be waiting for her in the dunes.

She leaned in and kissed Aiden on the cheek. 'Good luck with Offshore. You'll kill it!'

Savannah found Ped in the dunes. He was lying back on the pillow of his arms, looking up at the stars.

When he saw her, he didn't get up. Just stayed as he was, waited for her to come to him.

And she did. She kneeled astride him, bare knees in the cool sand. His gaze was pinned to her as she peeled off her top, revealing her tanned, braless body.

'You're a fucking goddess.'

Tomorrow, she'd be on the road with the Dutch girls. Seven a.m. they were leaving. But she was only going as far as the border. She'd say she'd changed her mind, leave them with a generous spend for fuel money.

And that's when Ped would follow. He'd been keeping an eye on the forecast, was already laying the tracks that he'd be away for a few days. And he would be – but with her.

They'd have a whole glorious week together. No sneaking around, just the two of them fucking all day long.

God, she wanted that so much.

It was their plan: they'd meet each other all over the world on good surf forecasts. Explore places together. A free-wheeling life. Ped coming to her. The allure, the secretiveness. No boredom. Just raw wanting.

It didn't matter to her whether they'd last. She doubted it mattered to Ped, either. They were in it for the thrill. To see what they could get away with. Ped was too tied into The Surf House to up and leave. And she didn't need him to.

She felt his lips moving lower, towards her navel. Her back began to arch.

'Jesus!' It was Aiden's voice.

Savannah's head snapped around and she saw Aiden standing there, face stung with shock.

'What the fuck is this?'

'Nothing to do with you,' Ped said, getting to his feet and pulling on his T-shirt.

Savannah reached for her top, her back to the men. She shook the sand from the yellow beach blanket that they'd been lying on and wrapped it around her shoulders.

Aiden stared at them both, eyes searching. 'What about Marnie?'

Savannah felt the slap of her name. When she looked at Ped, his face had slackened with guilt. She could see it then: he still loved her.

'What about me?'

They all turned.

Marnie stood on the rise of the dunes, back to the sea. Her face was bleached in the moonlight, gaze pinned to Ped and Savannah.

54

Bea's legs turn boneless. She could dissolve into the earth. It's like she is the one lying in the ground, feeling the cold soil being shovelled onto her, the crushing weight of it against her chest.

She pulls at the neckline of her jumper, searching for air.

Not you, Aiden. Please, not you . . .

It's as if Aiden hears her thoughts. For one moment, he looks up, gaze directed towards where Bea is hidden in the ruins of the studio. She sees his face on her phone screen beneath the red *Record* light. His expression is wretched, mouth set in a grimace, defeat rolling off him.

He seems to shake himself, then turns back to Savannah's body. He lifts the shovel and continues to dig.

Blood roars in her ears.

Aiden knew Savannah was dead.

Knew she was buried here.

Her brain scrabbles to answer the dozens of new questions that are firing to life. *Did Aiden kill Savannah? Why? Does Ped know?*

Nothing makes sense. Her heart drums in her chest, her body hot then cold with fear. Aiden, the man she's fallen in love with, is digging up Savannah's body.

She doesn't want to believe it.

Yet slowly, like a splinter working its way out of the skin, the spiked tip pierces her thoughts . . . She recalls that this strip of land used to belong to Aiden – but he sold it. *Because he knew he'd buried a body on it?*

She thinks of the nights Aiden goes out into the waves so that he doesn't have to be alone with his thoughts. It seemed romantic to her, like he was in commune with the ocean, but it was murkier than that – just an exercise in washing away his guilt.

She thinks of the darkness in his voice when he said his life was nothing to be proud of.

She thinks of Aiden refusing to let her stay with him tonight – because he knew he had a body to hide.

Bea lifts a trembling fingertip to her phone camera. Stops recording.

Aiden continues to dig, breath audible as the mound of earth grows.

Bea feels tiny vibrations of shock travelling through her body, making her skin pucker with goosebumps.

Eventually he sets down the shovel and surveys what's in front of him. There is a pile of paving slabs, a dark heap of fresh soil, and then Savannah's body wrapped within the blanket.

He grips the back of his beanie and stares.

After a long moment, he drops his hands and walks away.

Bea waits, watching.

Is he leaving?

She listens to his receding footsteps, confused. She hugs her arms to her middle, physically holding herself together.

When Aiden returns, he's carrying something large. A surfboard?

She watches as he lays it down beside Savannah's body, and she sees then that it is a board bag. Kneeling, he undoes the zip and opens the bag wide.

Aiden pauses for a moment, looking down. He drags in a breath, then rolls Savannah's body into the board bag. He fastens the zip, then stands, heaving the bag into his arms.

His posture looks almost tender, like he's carrying a sleeping child. But as moonlight catches the planes of his face, she sees his expression is pinched with anguish.

He carries Savannah's body out of sight to where his truck must be parked. She listens closely, hearing the slide of the board bag across the flatbed, then the clunk as he shuts it.

She wonders where Aiden plans to take her. Some other place where she will truly be forgotten?

She will not let that happen. She straightens, her legs stiff, and grabs her phone – and follows. She climbs through the rubble and broken remnants of the studio, ducking beneath the cordon and moving towards the truck.

Closer, she can see Aiden arranging the board bag, then setting two other surfboards on top to conceal it.

While he is occupied, Bea slips through the open truck door, sliding into the passenger seat.

There is no inside light, and she sits in the darkness, breath high in her throat, the sweet coconut smell of surf wax thick in the air.

She hears the slam of the tailgate. Then footsteps as Aiden approaches the cab.

Aiden climbs in, bringing with him the scent of earth. He closes the door, pulls off his beanie, and sits there for a moment, breathing hard.

Bea catches the whiff of alcohol now.

Aiden pushes the key into the ignition – and then he hesitates. She sees the shift in his body as he becomes alert.

Slowly, he turns.

His eyes widen as his gaze meets Bea's.

A streak of earth is smeared at his hairline. There is a wild, captured look in his eyes.

'Bea?'

Even in the darkness, Bea's vision has adjusted enough to make out the fear in Aiden's expression.

'Savannah's body is in the back of your truck,' she says, her voice devoid of emotion.

He rubs his face as if he's locked in a nightmare and is trying to wake himself.

She doesn't want it to be true. She wants him to say that she misunderstood the bones, the blanket, the digging. That it's not Savannah. That there could be some other explanation for this.

It was only weeks ago that she was in this same vehicle, kissing Aiden for the very first time. She remembers the taste of his lips on hers. The tenderness of his hands against her cheek.

He cannot meet her eye. His voice is barely there. 'I'm . . . sorry . . .'

She needs to hear him say it. 'Did you kill her?'

There is silence except for the rapid draw of Aiden's breath.

She waits.

He reaches for the steering wheel, gripping hard. His hands are dirt-stained, knuckles white as he squeezes.

'Aiden, I need to know. Did you kill Savannah?'

Aiden lifts his gaze. His eyes are dark and empty.

He answers with a single word.

327

55

AIDEN

'Yes.'

Aiden feels the burn of that word in his throat, stinging with a searing white heat. 'I killed Savannah.'

He's never said the words aloud. They rise from his throat, searching for air, growing in size. 'I killed her,' he says again, blinking rapidly. 'I killed her . . . and then buried her.'

A sob threatens to shudder through his body – but he chokes it down. He doesn't get to fucking cry.

He glances across at Bea. She sits with her fingers digging into the sleeves of her jumper, those huge eyes pinned to him. Waiting. Waiting for more. For there to be some addendum to explain it away. Because even now, he can see Bea is clinging onto hope, like there's something good in him – something worth saving.

But there isn't.

He sucks his lips between his teeth.

He may never have talked about that night – but he thinks about it. The shame is suffocating. It lives in his head, snaking to the surface after dark when his guard is down and he's edging towards sleep. It comes for him, hissing and sinuous.

Some nights, he gets lucky and drinks enough to sleep. Other times, there's the waves to lose himself in. But now he's in this truck, Savannah's body in the back, and Bea is right here, watching him – there's nowhere to hide.

He grips harder to the wheel. Wants to start the engine, slam the accelerator, drive this truck right off the cliff edge.

'What happened?' Bea asks.

He tries to reach for the words. He swallows, not sure how to do this. 'There was a beach party . . . I'd been drinking hard. I stumbled across Ped and Savannah in the dunes. Together. Marnie saw them, too.'

He remembers how Marnie staggered backwards as if the shock were a physical blow – and then she ran.

Ped called after her, but Marnie wasn't going to stop. She sprinted along the dark beach, sand kicked up by her feet. Aiden followed, because you don't let a woman run off at night alone and upset.

He tells Bea, 'Marnie ran back to my truck. She was a mess – shaking, crying. Begged me to get her out of there.' He didn't think about how much he'd been drinking – just climbed into his truck and fired the engine.

'Ped and Savannah came after us, shouting for us to wait. Marnie yelled at me to drive – so I jammed my foot on the accelerator.' He's blinking quickly as he remembers it all. 'The music was blaring . . . Marnie was sobbing . . . Everything was scrambled. All that noise . . . the dust kicked up by the tyres . . . I just . . . didn't see her . . . didn't see Savannah. And then . . . there she was. Standing there. Right in front of the truck.'

Aiden clutches the back of his head. 'I couldn't stop in time. The sound – Jesus! The sound as the truck hit her! She didn't fly up over the bonnet. I felt her . . . under the wheels.'

He sucks in a breath. 'When I got out, Savannah was lying in the dirt, completely still.' He remembers the eerie red glow of the taillights. 'There were tyre marks on her top. And blood. So much blood coming from her head. Ped was yelling, "What have you done?"'

He remembers the thick, hot rise of nausea, the thunder of adrenalin. He staggered to the bushes. Retched and retched.

Bea is still listening, waiting for him to go on.

'Ped took the keys out of the ignition. The headlights went off. Music stopped. Everything went quiet. I went back to Savannah's side. I wanted so badly for someone to tell me that she was alive.' He shakes his head. 'Marnie looked me in the eye. Said it straight. "She's dead, Aiden."'

He feels it now, the pure blackness that settled over him.

'I just stood there. No one saying anything. Down on the beach, there's still a party going on. Music. Laughter. And we're just . . . standing there with a dead girl at our feet.' He shakes his head. 'I needed to call the police, but Marnie said, "You've been drinking, Aiden. There's a fuck ton of alcohol in your system. You'll go to prison."'

Now Aiden looks through the windscreen onto the black night. He'd pictured it: a dark, hot cell. No hope of ever seeing the ocean again. Left to rot there.

'Because I'm a coward,' he says, 'I never called the police.' He pauses. 'Instead, I buried her.'

56

Bea's hands are gripped to her thighs. The air in the truck feels thick with body heat and souring sweat. She wants to wipe Aiden's words from her head – strip this whole night clean away – because nothing can ever be the same.

'This used to be my land,' Aiden says, his expression wretched. 'I was having a terrace laid – and I buried Savannah here while the ground was all dug up.' Aiden runs a hand over his face, then swallows. 'But there was no way I could use the terrace after that. Didn't want to see hostel guests sitting out there, enjoying a drink as the sun went down – knowing that Savannah was cold in the ground.'

'So you gave the land to Ped and Marnie,' she says.

He nods. 'They risked everything to cover for me.'

'Did you know they'd build on it?'

He shakes his head. 'They said they'd make it into a cliff-top garden – a kinda memorial.' There's no bitterness in his tone. It's like he no longer has the energy for any other emotion.

Silence draws close around them. There's no noise in the truck other than the sound of their breathing, which comes in shallow draws.

There is a loud rap against the window. Bea starts, turning towards the driver's door as it is yanked open.

Ped stands there, shoulders squared, glaring. His narrowed gaze snaps from Aiden to Bea. 'What the fuck is she doing here?'

'Bea saw me moving the body,' Aiden tells him.

A muscle in Ped's jaw clenches.

Marnie stands at Ped's shoulder, huddled in a fleece. Her eyes lock with Bea's. They stare at one another.

You knew, Bea thinks.

Marnie's mouth opens, then closes.

A fresh wave of pain crashes over Bea. She thinks of the dozens of small ways Marnie has lied to her. *All this time, you knew!*

Marnie shakes her head. 'I'm sorry . . . You shouldn't have seen this. I'm so sorry for not telling you about Savannah. I couldn't. I'd promised . . .'

Bea says nothing.

Marnie's voice is low. 'It was an accident. You mustn't blame Aiden. Savannah stepped right in front of his truck. It was crazy. No one could have stopped.'

Bea glances at Ped. There's something tight in his jaw, a twisting at the corner of his mouth. He takes a step away from Marnie. She thinks of Savannah's journal entries, all the passion in her words. Were they in love? Or was it more base: sex and excitement? He's helped cover up her death. Emptied her bank account. Built on the land she was buried beneath.

Ped is looking closely at Aiden. 'You've been drinking, haven't you?'

Aiden hangs his head.

'You can't drive like that,' Ped fires. 'I'll have to.' Then he barks at Marnie, 'You take the van.'

She nods, obedient. Then she turns to Bea, imploring, 'Come with me? Please? We need to talk . . .'

They drive on the empty coast road, the night black. Bea glances in the mirror, but there is no sign of Aiden's truck behind them.

Marnie drives fast, picking sharp lines, wheeling over the central road markings, cutting corners, the van engine straining as she knocks it into the highest gear. In the back, mugs and cutlery rattle.

'Bea,' she says, above the noise of the engine. 'I'm so sorry that I lied to you. Truly.'

'You knew this whole time.'

'We were protecting Aiden.'

'And what about Savannah? Who was protecting her?'

Her thoughts race through the dozens of small lies Marnie must have told her since she's been at The Surf House. Even when Bea asked specific questions about Savannah, there was no tell. Marnie has lied with disarming ease. If it was only about protecting Aiden, why build a brand-new studio on his land, block his view?

'You and Ped profited from Savannah's death by taking Aiden's land and Savannah's money.'

Marnie's face pinches with hurt. She's silent for a moment. Then she exhales. 'The thing you've got to understand about Ped is that he's someone who goes after the things he wants. You've seen his discipline and focus when it comes to surfing. He has this . . . conviction that most of us lack. Once he decided he wanted to build a studio on the land, then that's what he did. I couldn't stop him.'

Bea opens the window onto the night. A sea breeze winds in as they roar onwards.

There's an eerie echo of that first day they met, the long drive from Marrakesh. Then, they were leaving a dead body behind in the city – and now they're taking a dead body to be buried. A dark synchronicity bleeds between them. So much death, so many mistakes. Marnie at the edges of them both – and now Bea, too.

'Shit,' she hears Marnie hiss beneath her breath.

Bea follows her gaze and sees a white police vehicle parked up on the brow of the hill. Her skin goes cold: a police checkpoint.

'Aiden and Ped,' Bea whispers. 'What will they do if they're searched?' She needs to warn them. She reaches into her pocket for her mobile – but it's not there. She feels around the seat, but she doesn't have it. It must have slipped out of her pocket in Aiden's truck. 'I don't have my phone.'

'There's no time,' Marnie says, as she dips the indicator.

57

Blue lights strobe across the roadside. Officer Karim stands in front of the bonnet of his police car, arms folded.

Unease spikes through Bea's chest as Momo steps out from the passenger side of the vehicle. He dusts something from his white shirt, then readjusts his navy cap.

Marnie turns off the van engine as Karim approaches, Momo hanging back at his shoulder.

'Poker faces,' Marnie says. Then she unwinds her window. Smiles. 'Evening officers.'

Officer Karim returns her greeting. 'You are driving late, yes?'

'Yes. I am dropping Bea at the airport.' She turns to Bea. Smiles.

Karim and Momo look to Bea.

She nods quickly, giving a tight smile. 'Flight to catch.'

'Then we must make this quick.' Officer Karim addresses Marnie, 'Are you aware you're driving with only one taillight?'

'No!' Marnie says, her tone high with surprise.

His expression doesn't alter. 'I stopped this vehicle some weeks ago – and I explained a problem with the tyres.'

Marnie doesn't miss a beat. 'You were very helpful, yes. I drove straight home, and my husband pumped the tyres.'

Bea notes the ease of Marnie's lies, the way Ped seamlessly becomes her *husband* to suit Officer Karim's worldview.

'Old vehicle,' Marnie says with warmth.

Officer Karim clasps his hands behind his back. 'Please could you step out of the van? I want to check whether there is anything in this *old vehicle* that needs our attention.'

Marnie doesn't drop her smile, but Bea sees a flicker of tension working at her temple.

Bea clanks open the passenger door and steps out into the cold night. She glances towards the empty road, wondering where Aiden and Ped are. Perhaps, if the police are busy with the van, they'll let them pass.

Officer Karim removes a torch from his pocket, then calls Marnie to his side as he inspects the van.

Bea waits on the roadside, arms hugged to her body.

She hears the clip of shoes on tarmac and looks up to see Momo approaching. A shiver travels down the backs of her arms.

'I will need to see your passport, please,' he says when he reaches her. 'For identification.'

She thinks of that strange discordant smile he gave her in The Surf House when he took the final payment of the bribe, and her body goes cold with dread.

'You've already seen it,' she says, her mouth tight.

Momo's brows draw together. He shifts, planting one hand on the holster at his waist. *Is he carrying a gun?*

What if Momo kept some evidence as insurance – fibres from the scarf or fingerprints from the knife? Or, what if, when she finally does try to leave this country, there is a flag on her passport?

She feels the nightmare reawakening. She wishes Marnie's

lie was true – that she was going to the airport, leaving here. Stepping from a plane onto British soil, into a world she knows, with rules she understands.

Her insides feel like ice, but she tries to adjust her expression to make it appear as though she's in control.

'I will have to tell Officer Karim if you don't have it,' he says eventually. Momo glances at Officer Karim, who is inspecting the nearside tyre. When he looks back at Bea, he asks, 'I want to know . . . are you happy with my mother's bread?'

Bea blinks.

Momo is staring at her, dark eyes on her face.

'Bread?'

He nods once. 'The bread I brought to The Surf House.'

Bea thinks of Momo's visit, the paper bag he gripped at his side containing the knife, scarf, and Bea's passport. When Ped appeared, Marnie had explained that Momo was dropping something off and, on cue, Momo had lifted the bag and said he was delivering bread.

She realises Momo is speaking in code because of Officer Karim. She swallows. 'Yes. I am happy with the bread.'

His mouth lifts into a small smile. And she thinks, *Don't you dare! Don't you fucking dare smile at me!*

She leans towards him. They are the same height and stand eyeball to eyeball. Slowly and clearly, she says, 'There is no more money.'

Momo's smile vanishes. 'No more money?'

'We paid you. And now it's finished.'

His face darkens. 'Finished? Because you are leaving? We have an arrangement with The Surf House.'

'Yes, the arrangement was that you gave me the knife and we paid you. It's over.'

Momo rubs a hand across his jaw. 'Knife?'

Bea is done with his game. 'It's at the bottom of the sea now.'

His brow furrows. 'I do not understand. Knife?'

Her jaw is clenched tight as she hisses, 'The knife from the checkpoint that you hid – and then bribed us thousands of dollars to return.'

Momo's furrowed brow deepens. 'You mistake me.'

'We drove to your house. Marnie handed you the first payment. Your mother was there.'

He nods. 'Money for flour with no gluten. For you. Your diet.' He looks uncomfortable. 'You cannot eat gluten. My mother makes you special bread. I bring it to The Surf House. New bread as you do not like the other, yes? Marnie tells us.'

A strange unfurling sensation sweeps over Bea. She glances at Marnie, who is still on the far side of the vehicle with Officer Karim.

Bea's voice is urgent now. 'Last time, at the checkpoint, what did Marnie say to you?'

'To search the driver's side of the van – and find nothing.' He shrugs his shoulders lightly. 'I do favour for Marnie, yes, as she employs my mother. Maybe she carries alcohol or hashish – but I make sure I do not find it.' He looks serious, concerned.

'But you found the knife and scarf. Took them from the van.'

He holds up his palms. 'I saw a scarf under the seat, yes, but I took nothing from the van.'

The ground feels like it's sliding out from beneath her. Is Momo lying because it's too risky to talk with Officer Karim so nearby? Is this all part of his game?

'What about my rucksack?' she whispers. 'Why did you return it to me if there was no money in it for you?'

He looks confused. 'Rucksack?'

338

'Your cousin in Marrakesh. He works for the police. He got hold of my stolen rucksack. Had it sent to you.'

Momo's expression doesn't clear. His brow remains furrowed. He shakes his head. 'I have two cousins. They are twins – six-year-old girls who live in Essaouira.'

Bea feels like she is falling, with nothing solid to reach for. She never saw Momo with her rucksack. It was simply waiting for her on the bed. Marnie said Momo had put it there.

But Marnie was lying.

58

Bea feels winded. Her chest is tight – breath high and shallow. She swings around, searching for Marnie.

Officer Karim is pointing to something on the van, but Marnie isn't looking in his direction. Her eyes are fixed on Bea. The strobing light of the police car lightens then darkens her face, making her expression shift unnervingly.

Then Marnie lifts the corners of her mouth. Smiles.

Bea forces herself to return the gesture, dragging her lips upwards.

Officer Karim clasps his hands together and announces that they are free to continue their journey. 'Once the fine for the taillight is paid,' he adds.

Marnie sorts out the monies while Bea climbs into the van and sits there, heart thundering. Her head spins with questions, a vertiginous sensation swelling through her thoughts.

Then the driver's door opens, and Marnie is there. Bea keeps her eyes down, grappling with her seat belt and, in her rush, it snags twice.

Marnie is looking at her. 'Y'okay?'

She nods quickly, trying the belt again, but her hands are shaking, and she jams it.

Marnie reaches across her and takes the belt calmly from Bea's fingers. Bea feels the brush of Marnie's thumb against the back of her hand, hears the light jangle of her bracelets, smells the scent of her perfume oil as she slowly draws the belt across Bea's waist, fastening her to the seat.

'Thanks,' Bea manages, her throat dry.

Marnie takes out her phone. 'I'm messaging Ped to tell him to avoid the coast road.' When she's done, she starts the engine, indicates, then carefully pulls out onto the dark, empty road.

Bea sits there, pinned to her seat, thoughts spiked and rapid. Was the bribe fake?

Bea knows that Marnie and Ped are desperate for money – that they could lose The Surf House if they don't pay back their loans. Did Marnie steal from Bea to fund their borrowings?

For weeks, Bea has lived beneath the towering threat of the bribe, believing that if she didn't pay the debt, she'd end up in a prison cell. She was trapped here with no passport and no money. She's begged, lied, stolen. She's become someone she barely recognised to pay off a debt that never existed.

Hurt wrenches through her chest as she thinks of their friendship. Was it all fabricated? The warmth of Marnie's 'G'night' kisses, the waves caught together, all those moments of closeness that felt so large and important to Bea.

Has every moment been a lie?

She drags her fingernails against her thighs, feeling the bite against skin.

Marnie glances at her. 'Hey. It's over now. We're through.' She takes a hand off the wheel. Reaches for Bea's fingers. Squeezes.

Bea feels frozen, every nerve ending exposed.

After a few moments, Marnie replaces her hand on the wheel.

Her voice is casual and light as she asks, 'What did Momo say to you?'

Bea feels the air in the van contract.

She cracks the window wider.

Keeping her focus on the open window, she answers, 'He was just asking what I'll do when I return to England.'

She can feel Marnie watching her.

Bea listens to the tread of tyres against tarmac. Thinking, thinking. If Marnie was behind the bribes, then how did she get Bea's rucksack returned? Does she have a contact in the Marrakesh police? Was it just another reason to up the bribe money?

Marnie is driving fast, the road empty, the conversation falling silent again.

They travel like that for some time, Bea occasionally glancing in the wing mirror to see if Aiden's truck is following.

'Where are we going?' she asks.

'We need to bury Savannah's bones somewhere they won't be disturbed.'

Bea pushes her hands beneath her thighs to stop them shaking. She wants out of this van, out of this whole fucking nightmare.

Marnie glances at her. 'Sure you're okay?'

Bea is deathly silent.

'I'm so sorry you've been dragged into this,' Marnie says. 'But you know what? I'm not sorry you saw it.' Her tone becomes warm and inviting. 'You are family, Bea. I've known that since day one in Marrakesh.'

Something shivery moves down Bea's spine.

'That's why I'm driving out here. Because Aiden is family, too. He made a mistake when his truck hit Savannah – but it was an accident. She stepped in front of him. He couldn't have stopped. His life shouldn't be ruined because of her. He doesn't deserve that. We'd worked so hard, all of us, on The Surf House and Offshore. I wouldn't let her destroy it.'

Bea hears the way Marnie talks. There's no sadness or remorse for Savannah's death. Marnie sees it as an inconvenience, like she can separate fully from the emotion of it.

She suddenly swings the van off the road, onto a dirt track. The wheels spin and slide in the dust.

Bea glances in the mirror again. Still no sign of Ped and Aiden.

Marnie accelerates harder, and Bea hangs onto her seat. The dreamcatcher swings madly. An enamel mug has come loose in the back and is clattering across the floor.

There's a wild, reckless energy about Marnie tonight. Bea needs to keep her head. Get through this.

They hit a pothole, and the van goes flying. It lands with a thud, Bea's head jerking back. The glove compartment flies open.

Marnie pulls up in a cloud of dust. She cuts the engine but leaves the headlights on.

Red dust billows across the full beam. As it settles, all Bea can make out is desert scrub.

'Where are we?' she says, the words leaving her mouth as little more than a whisper.

Marnie turns to look at her. 'Somewhere no one comes.'

A spike of apprehension prickles down her spine.

Then Bea's gaze lowers.

Marnie follows her eyeline to the open glove compartment. She reaches across and flips it shut – but as she does, Bea glimpses it.

A gun.

59

Bea's eyes are locked on the glove compartment.

There was no mistaking it: Marnie has a gun in the van.

Blood thunders in her ears.

'We've got digging to do,' Marnie says, climbing out. She opens the slide door and begins searching for the shovel.

Bea's eyes don't leave the glove compartment. If she opens it, takes out the gun, slips it into her pocket – what then? She's never held a gun. Has no idea how to use one. Yet on a primal level, Bea knows she must be the one who has it – not Marnie.

She hears Marnie in the back of the van. She'll be occupied for only a moment. Bea needs to act now.

She leans towards the glove compartment but is snagged by her seat belt. Her clammy fingers hurry to undo it. Then she's stretching forward, opening it—

'Got it,' Marnie announces.

Bea pushes the glove compartment shut. Withdraws her hands.

Marnie fills the doorway. She looks at Bea's face. Then her gaze lowers to the glove compartment. Her easy expression remains in place. 'You coming?'

Bea nods quickly.

Marnie watches as Bea climbs out, the gun still enclosed in the glove compartment.

Marnie chooses a spot in the beam of the headlights and begins to dig.

The earth looks hard and unforgiving as she works the shovel into the dirt. She strips off her fleece, leaving her in a black tee. The muscles and tendons strain in her bare arms, bracelets jangling.

Bea stands at the edge of the light, watching, arms hugged to her body. Her head is crammed tight with questions. She keeps rolling back through memories of the past few weeks, pausing to examine what was real.

She lingers on the moments they surfed together, Marnie showing her how to position herself on the wave face, cheering when she caught her first green wave, a sunburst of lines fanning from her eyes. *Real.*

Making breakfast together, singing in the kitchen, dancing past one another with the radio on, the smell of cinnamon swirling through the air. *Real.*

She rewinds further to the moment they met. Marrakesh. A back alley. Two men. One taking her rucksack. The other trailing a finger down her body. Then Marnie barrelling in. Waving a knife. Yelling at the men to let her go.

There was no play-acting in that moment.

None.

Nor in the moments that followed . . . the knife smacked from Marnie's grip. The terror in her eyes as she was strangled. Then Bea scrabbling for the knife. Fingers sealing around it. The thrust as she pushed it into the man's neck.

Every dark, gritted moment was real.

They had saved each other.

They were bonded.

That's how it felt.

She pins her gaze to Marnie.

What if the reality was different?

'That day we first met,' Bea says. 'Why were you in Marrakesh?'

Marnie pauses from digging. There's a sheen of sweat on her forehead. 'I told you: I was looking for an art supplier. Got lost. Came across you.'

Bea nods. It's a fine explanation. Perfectly convincing – if you choose to believe it.

'How come?' Marnie asks.

Bea shrugs. 'No reason.'

Marnie stares at her for a long moment. Then she lifts the shovel and hands it to Bea. 'Your turn.'

She wants to tell Marnie *no*, that she's not digging Savannah's grave, that she wants no part in this – but instead she remembers the word Marnie used. *Family.* That's what Bea needs to appear to be.

She takes the shovel, then walks into the full beam of the headlights, positioning herself where Marnie was, and begins digging.

She feels the hard punch of metal against earth as the blade hits the soil, the impact reverberating through her shoulders and back. She's pleased to have something physical to do while she thinks.

When she glances up, Marnie's gone.

She looks over her shoulder – sees her walking towards the van.

Her breath catches. *The gun.*

346

'Where are you going?' Bea calls, not managing to mask her apprehension.

Marnie either doesn't hear or chooses not to answer.

Bea raises a hand to block the beam of the headlights as she squints to keep Marnie in sight. She hears the van door open. The internal light switches on, illuminating Marnie as she climbs into the driver's seat.

She is frozen, watching, waiting for Marnie to reach across to the passenger side. Unlatch the glove compartment. Withdraw the gun.

But Marnie doesn't do that.

Instead, she starts the engine.

What is she doing?

Almost as soon as Bea has this thought, she answers it.

The blood drains from her body. Marnie doesn't need a gun. All she needs is to touch the accelerator, drive off.

If Bea is left out here in the desert without water or shelter, she will die.

The shovel clatters to the earth. Then Bea is hinging forward, running towards the van.

60

As Bea runs, she catches a glimpse of lights in the distance.

Headlights.

Aiden's truck?

She slows to a standstill.

The van engine is still running, but Marnie steps out now. 'They're here,' she says, watching the truck approaching.

'Why have you started the engine?' Bea asks, breathless.

'The battery runs down if you leave on the headlights. We don't want to get left out here in the middle of nowhere.' There's a pause. 'Do we?'

Bea holds her eye. Silence hums between them. She feels Marnie reading her distrust. Bea consciously adjusts her expression, trying to replace her anxiety and suspicion with confidence.

Then they both turn, looking behind them as the truck grows nearer. Looking into the glare of headlights, she can't make out Ped or Aiden.

At her side, Marnie is silent, waiting.

The truck pulls up and the engine is cut. The driver's door opens, and Ped steps out. He looks grim-faced.

'You avoided the checkpoint?' Marnie asks.

'Used the back lanes.'

Bea keeps her gaze on the passenger side, waiting to see Aiden. There's no interior light, and she has a sudden chilling sensation that he isn't in the vehicle.

She watches Ped approach the tailgate, reaching in for a shovel.

'Where's Aiden?' Bea asks him, her voice thin.

Ped doesn't answer. To Marnie, he says, 'We've got a problem.'

The two of them speak in low voices, Marnie glancing at the truck. She nods, then moves towards the passenger door, opening it – and there is Aiden.

'I know this is hard,' Marnie says to him in a soft murmur. 'But we need to get it done.'

After a few moments, Aiden steps out, head hanging low, shoulders rounded. Desperation leaves him in waves.

'There's a shovel waiting for you,' Marnie tells Aiden.

As he lifts his gaze, his eyes meet Bea's. He stares at her, dark eyes searching, as if he's looking for something to hold onto. There is so much regret locked in that gaze.

Then he blinks. Turns away. Begins to walk towards the grave.

61

The grave is deep enough now that both men stand within it to dig. Sprays of soil are sent high into the air.

Bea sits at a distance, arms hooked over her knees, watching. The desert night is cool, a light breeze stirring the scrub. She hears the clink of metal against stone, the crunch of sandy earth beneath the shovels, the slug of fresh dirt landing in a pile.

'Here.'

She looks up to find Marnie holding out a fleece.

'You looked cold.'

Bea stares at Marnie for a moment, experiencing a strange tow of emotions. *I have no idea who you are.* Even now, she wants to believe that their friendship is real. That there is some explanation for the bribes. She wants Marnie to tell her that everything will be okay. *We are family.*

'Thanks,' she manages, taking the fleece and pushing her arms into the sleeves. It holds the warm smell of Marnie's skin.

'You okay?' Marnie asks, lowering herself onto the ground beside her. She sits close, her arm brushing Bea's.

'I need water,' Bea says, getting to her feet. She dusts the dirt from the back of her thighs as she walks to the van.

She climbs into the passenger seat and finds the keys have

been removed from the ignition, so there is no hope of driving away. Glancing through the windscreen, she sees Marnie still sitting by the grave, her concentration on the men.

Taking a breath, Bea reaches for the latch of the glove compartment. She opens it wide and can immediately see that the gun has gone.

Fuck!

Marnie must have removed it when she returned to the van.

No gun.

No van keys.

No phone.

Her breath is tight in her chest. There's no option left but to wait this out. She closes the glove compartment.

She glances towards Aiden's truck. It still seems impossible that Savannah's body lies on the flatbed, concealed within a board bag. All this time, she was dead.

From the moment Seth arrived at The Surf House, asking his questions, Bea sensed that something wasn't right. But she ignored that intuition, batted it away because she didn't want Seth to be right. Her skin begins to prickle hotly as she realises she needed The Surf House to remain untouchable, a beautiful sanctuary. She'd been seduced by the ideals that Marnie lived by – prioritising catching waves, cooking good food, creating a beautiful space for people to share. It was easier to ignore the cracks. Keep on believing that she'd found somewhere she belonged.

Her hands ball into fists, and she suddenly feels very young and stupid. The Surf House wasn't her home. Marnie was never family. What was Bea hoping for, really? Was Marnie some sort of mother replacement? Her best friend? What did Bea even want?

Aiden's words echo in her ears.

You want someone to love you.

351

She feels the punch in her gut . . . Aiden was right. So devastatingly right. Hot-eyed with emotion, she smacks the back of her skull against the van headrest. *Pathetic,* she thinks.

Tears come now, rolling down her face. She tastes the hot salt of them as they reach her lips.

She can't afford to fall apart. She draws a breath. Wipes her face on her sleeve. Focuses.

Ahead, Aiden and Ped have finished the grave and are now walking through the beams of light towards the truck. She hears the clunk of the tailgate as it's lowered, the compression of suspension as one of them climbs onto the flatbed. The slide of the board bag along the truck's floor. And then footsteps again, slower, awkward, as they carry Savannah towards her grave.

When they move in front of the headlights, it's an awful image, backlit and damning. At the graveside, they unzip the board bag and gently nudge the remains of Savannah's body into the earth. Then Aiden just stands there, arms hanging loose at his sides, staring. He looks broken.

Savannah is going to be buried for a second time, and it all feels badly wrong. Bea has a strange, claustrophobic sense of panic, as if it is *her* grave they are digging. As if she will finally be alone, forever, in the cold earth.

If that was her body, who would come looking? Who'd fly out to Morocco and retrace her steps? Her head shakes from side to side. There is no one.

And there is no one left looking for Savannah. Her body will be dumped out here in an arid desert, forgotten. All that remains is her travel journal, pushed under a mattress where she once slept. All other traces extinguished.

Bea thinks, *If I don't stop this, I am part of it.*

And she cannot be part of this.

62

Aiden is standing alone, back to the grave, looking into the night.

Bea studies his face, the heavy dark brows throwing his eyes into shadow, his full mouth that only rarely manages a smile. She wonders if she should despise him for what he did to Savannah . . . and yet, she can't.

In Marrakesh, Bea left a man for dead.

That man would have had family who miss him and grieve for him. Her choices have been no better than Aiden's – and she needs him to know this.

'Aiden.'

He turns towards her.

'That bribe you helped me with . . . the money was to pay off the police because . . .' She stalls. Struggles to find the words. 'I . . . I was attacked in Marrakesh. Marnie found me. She had a knife and . . . it got knocked out of her hand. A man started choking her, so I . . . picked up the knife. Used it. I killed him.' She drags in a breath. 'Then we ran.'

Aiden's gaze holds firm to hers.

'I'm telling you because I understand what it's like to make the wrong choice.'

As she says those words aloud, she realises that's exactly what it was: the wrong choice. 'I should never have run.'

Aiden speaks slowly. 'I . . . I'm sorry.' His head shakes as he says, 'What you did – that was self-defence.' He pauses, gaze flicking to the grave. 'Savannah's dead because I'd been drinking and got behind the wheel of a vehicle.'

There's something that's been nagging at her. 'When Seth was looking into Savannah's disappearance, he discovered that her credit card was last used in Ezril. It was the day after she died.'

Aiden nods. 'It needed to look like Savannah had got in the van with the Dutch girls and disappeared.'

'Who took out the money?' she asks, but she knows the answer before Aiden says it.

'Marnie.'

'And she and Ped kept the money?'

Aiden nods.

Bea lowers her voice. 'Was it Marnie who suggested burying Savannah's body?'

His brow furrows. 'Yes.'

'Would you have called the police otherwise?'

Aiden's expression is clear-eyed as he says, 'Yes.' He stares hard at her as he says, 'But I didn't call them. I chose the easy way out.'

She hears what Aiden is saying. He had a choice – and he made the wrong one. But what Bea is thinking is: *It all comes back to Marnie.*

She steps closer to Aiden, lowering her voice. 'Look, I don't trust—'

'Here you go.'

Bea's skin turns to ice. Marnie is standing at her shoulder. She is bare-armed, skin glowing and vital in the moonlight. She smiles encouragingly at Aiden as she holds out a shovel.

63

The two men stand shoulder to shoulder at the grave.

Ped digs his shovel into the fresh mound of earth, then hovers it above Savannah's remains.

He hesitates. Maybe it feels too much like a funeral service, mourners gathered at a graveside, the closest family members asked to sprinkle the first dustings of earth over the body.

'Let's get this finished,' Marnie says.

Ped swallows, then begins to tip the dry earth over Savannah's remains.

Aiden's arm shoots out and grips Ped's shovel. 'No.'

Marnie and Ped exchange glances.

'We're not doing this.' Aiden rips the shovel from Ped's hands and flings it wide. 'We're not burying her a second time.'

Marnie steps forward. 'I know this is awful, Aiden. *I know.* But we have to do this.'

'Savannah was twenty-three. She had a whole life to live. She wanted to travel the world. She had dreams – and I ended them. And then I fucking hid it from everyone. I lied to the police. Lied to her family.' He looks at Bea. 'Lied to people I care about.'

There is a long silence. The desert hums around them, the stars piercing and bright.

Aiden turns to Ped and Marnie. 'I need to tell the police. I'll leave your names out of it. Say I was alone. Buried her on my land.'

Marnie asks, 'Do you really think going to prison changes anything?'

'I'd be owning up. It'd mean Savannah's body could be returned home. She could be buried with her family. That's something.'

'You think she wanted that?' Marnie asks.

'I dunno what she wanted – but it wasn't this. An unmarked grave in a fucking desert!'

'What does it matter now? She's dead. She died a year ago, Aiden!' Marnie's voice is rising. 'You've got to move on.'

'I can't.' He grips the base of his head. 'I can't fucking live with it. I've tried. I'm not burying her twice!'

'We have to,' Ped says, voice stony.

Aiden swings around. 'You're a fucking piece of shit, Ped! You slept with Savannah – and it ruined everything! You may've helped me bury her – but you got your reward, didn't you? Took my land. Built on her fucking grave.'

Aiden reaches into his pocket for his phone.

'Don't . . .' Marnie whispers.

'I have to do this,' Aiden says. The screen lights up as he begins to dial.

Ped grabs the phone from him and launches it, the illuminated screen twisting through the night. It lands in the scrub with a dull *thunk*.

'What the fuck?' Aiden yells.

Ped faces him, shoulders back, hands loose at his side. Bea knows that face. She's seen it in the lineup, that iron resolve, the commitment. Ped paddles in harder than anyone else, picking off the waves he wants, not minding who's in the way. 'No police.'

But Aiden's the one who's always had the passion, Bea thinks as he launches at Ped, his shoulder socking him in the gut as he wrestles him to the ground. Ped lands hard, the wind knocked out of him.

'I get to choose!' Aiden yells.

Ped swings out a fist, and it connects with Aiden's jaw. He jerks back, like he's been hit by a baseball bat. He lies in the cool earth, still. As Ped staggers to his feet, Aiden kicks out, hooking Ped in the back of the knees and sending him down for a second time.

Aiden scrambles on top of him and brings his fist slamming into Ped's face. Bea flinches as she hears the connection of knuckle against bone.

He raises his fist a second time, but Ped blocks it. The two of them are struggling, rolling across earth and jagged stones.

'Stop!' Bea yells.

She locks eyes with Marnie, who watches, hands in front of her mouth.

Aiden is on top of Ped, holding him by the scruff of the neck. The grave is inches away. Aiden forces Ped's face into the dirt – makes him look. 'She's there, Ped! In the fucking grave.'

Ped is silent.

Aiden's grip at Ped's throat tightens. 'Look! Look at her!'

Bea can see the whites of Ped's eyes as he stares.

'I did that! I killed Savannah!'

Ped's face is creased with anguish, eyes bulging. His voice is choked by Aiden's grip as he splutters, 'You didn't.'

Those two words are thrown into the air like grenades – deadly and urgent – yet when they fall, they don't explode.

Ped heaves in air. 'You didn't kill Savannah.'

Aiden is frozen.

Everyone's gaze is fixed on Ped.

Ped lifts his head off the ground. 'You hit her with your truck, Aiden. But you didn't kill her.'

Aiden doesn't move a muscle.

Ped looks him right in the eye. 'Savannah wasn't dead.'

64

PED

Ped doesn't know how to do this – just that he can't do it lying on the earth beside Savannah's grave. Pushing Aiden from him, he lurches to his feet, dusting dirt from his T-shirt.

He's breathing hard as he eyes Aiden. 'Everything about that night was messed up. You and Marnie finding us. Savannah running after you. Putting herself in front of your truck.' He holds Aiden's gaze. Needs him to understand this next point. 'No one could've stopped. No one.'

Aiden just watches him, says nothing.

'I saw how she went down. Her head – it hit hard, y'know? It was bad. I knew it was bad.' He pauses. 'The music was blaring. No one could think. You staggered away to be sick. Marnie yelled for me to take the key out of the ignition.' He pauses, remembering how the world stilled. 'I glanced up from your truck and, in the wing mirror, I could see Marnie leaning over Savannah. I . . . I thought she was trying to help her.'

Behind him, he can feel Marnie watching him. He's never told her what he saw in that wing mirror. He will not turn and meet her eye. It's Aiden he owes this to.

'Marnie was wearing this jade scarf . . . She'd bunched it into a ball . . .' He swallows. He hates these words that are coming. He fucking hates them! But he's got to say them. 'I saw Marnie press the scarf over Savannah's face.' There's a pause. 'She suffocated her.'

'No . . .' Aiden is shaking his head. 'That's not true . . .'

Ped tried to tell himself it wasn't. Tried to forget the way Savannah's legs had twitched. Tried to cut out those few seconds of memory, like a surgeon removing a tumour. But they stuck. Infected everything.

'You ran over to Savannah. I thought you'd seen, too. But when you reached her, Marnie was getting to her feet, telling you Savannah was dead.'

Ped remembers sprinting over, crouching, knees sliding in the gravel, two fingers against the still-warm skin at her neck. No pulse. No breath. No life. He was too late. He just stared and stared at Savannah. Dead.

Now, Ped turns to face Marnie.

She is frozen in the full beam of the truck's headlights, her eyes wide, fixed on him. He meets her gaze. There's an instant burn of connection. *I loved you, once,* he thinks. This tiny, strong, ferociously determined woman. He'd loved her with all his heart. And then he looked the wrong way – saw something he could never unsee – and that love burned to ashes.

'You killed Savannah.'

Marnie's eyes squeeze shut, like a child who doesn't want to see something scary right in front of them.

Her face contorts into an expression he's never seen before, somewhere between shock and grief and shame and fury, her features arranging and rearranging themselves, unable to settle on an emotion.

Aiden's gaze bores into Marnie. '*You* killed Savannah?'

Marnie starts, swings around to face him, blinking rapidly. 'She . . . she was suffering, Aiden! She would have died from her injuries.'

Ped's head shakes slowly from side to side. 'It was never about suffering. It was about vengeance.'

'*You* were the one who told me not to call the police,' Aiden spits at Marnie. '*You* were the one who said to bury her. *You* were the one who talked me down when I changed my mind.'

'I was protecting you.'

'You were protecting *you!*' he seethes. 'If there'd been a post-mortem, there'd have been fibres of your scarf in her lungs—'

'It wasn't like that. You are family to me, Aiden. You know that. I had to stop you from hurting yourself. You would never have survived prison.'

Aiden turns away as if he cannot stomach more. His eyes lock on Ped. 'Why didn't you say anything?' he asks in a low voice.

Ped feels the shame of his decision like a cold stone in his gut. He's asked himself this question enough times. Why didn't he confront Marnie that night? Why didn't he tell Aiden? And the only answer he can come up with is this: 'I didn't want it to be true.'

His statement hangs there in the desert night. With every fibre of his being, he wishes it weren't true.

Ped's gaze finds Marnie. 'I didn't want to believe you were capable of that.'

Her body heaves forward. She clutches her arms around herself.

That's why he disappears for long spells on a forecast to clear his head or sleeps in the van on the harder nights. He hates their rageful arguments, him always skirting around the one thing he's never admitted: *I saw you kill Savannah.*

'Why didn't you leave me?' Marnie asks, her voice small.

He's thought about it. Course he has. Every fucking day. 'I put everything into The Surf House. My money. My energy. My dreams. If you and I fail, so does The Surf House.'

361

65

MARNIE

Ped, haloed in the moonlight, is looking at her like she is a stranger. Like he no longer knows who she is.

She needs to remind him. Hold him. Wrap her arms around him. She steps forward . . .

He recoils.

Marnie feels the rejection punch through her body. No. She cannot lose him. Ped is *everything*. He's the one who scooped her up when she had nothing, showed her how beautiful life could be. He taught her to surf. To see the wonder in the world. To fall in love with travelling. He is the only home she knows.

But all this time, he's known what she did to Savannah.

Shame and self-loathing wrack her body.

'Why did you kill her?' Ped asks.

'To stop her suffering—'

He cuts across her sharply, his voice a door slamming. 'The truth, Marnie.'

'I . . . I was upset . . .' She thinks of the horror of seeing Ped and Savannah together in the dunes. It was like a knife splitting her open. There had been no warning signs. She and Ped were in love. They were setting down roots, making a life together at

The Surf House. It was the happiest she could ever remember feeling.

And then – there was Savannah in the dunes with Ped. It was like the air had been knocked from her lungs. Shock was still ricocheting through her when Savannah came chasing after them, calling Aiden's name. Marnie yelled, 'Drive!' So Aiden had. But that stupid girl put herself straight in front of his truck. Aiden had no chance.

Savannah had ruined everything – she'd betrayed Marnie, destroyed her relationship with Ped, stolen Aiden's future.

Marnie doesn't remember deciding; she just leant down and pushed her scarf into Savannah's face. There was no fight. Nothing, just a brief twitch of her legs. And it was done. Like it hadn't happened.

Marnie had no idea that Ped had seen.

Later that night, while the men buried her body, Marnie packed up Savannah's belongings and dumped them in the sea on an outgoing tide. The following day, she drove to Ezril. It was a location where the Dutch girls could have feasibly stopped on their way out of Morocco. It was easier than she'd thought to empty Savannah's bank account. She showed Savannah's passport, covered her dark hair in a headscarf, and thanked the cashier in an American accent.

In the weeks afterwards, Ped withdrew from her. She thought it was a mix of guilt over his affair and grief of losing Savannah – so she gave him space. She was pleased when he threw himself into a new project, building a studio on the land Aiden no longer wanted, where Savannah had been buried.

Ped spent hours and hours out there, working on the design, building the structure brick by brick. *A labour of love,* he'd told

Farah – and it made her bristle, wondering exactly what the studio meant to him.

When Seth turned up, his questions dragged everything back to the surface. It felt like Savannah was inhabiting The Surf House again. Ped grew colder and more distant until, one evening, she finally asked, 'Did you love Savannah?'

Ped didn't answer. Just went silent. Like he wanted to hurt her. That was when she picked up the lamp, threw it across their bedroom, and watched it smash inches from Ped's head.

The next night, she fucked Seth. There. One brother for one sister. Done. Account balanced.

Ped knew about Seth. Course he knew.

She wanted to see his fury and jealousy. Watch him go after Seth.

And he did.

When she saw Seth's body in the water, she thought Ped had drowned him – and felt a wild thrill, like it was evidence of how much he cared. Later, she got Ped alone in the office and asked: 'Did you do it?'

And Ped looked at her, aghast. 'Are you insane?'

Now, she looks up and sees the hangdog expression on Aiden's face. All this hurt, all this time wasted, all this destruction because of Savannah.

'Savannah wasn't snow-white,' she hisses, needing to flip the narrative. Reveal the cloud that hung above Savannah's sun-bright image. 'She had a dark little heart.'

Ped's gaze is lasered on Marnie.

'She didn't tell you? You never found out how she got her money, did you?'

Ped says nothing.

'She was involved in identity theft. Part of an operation in

Marrakesh. Driss introduced her to some people. That's how she got by when her precious trust fund was cut off. She was stealing from people.'

'What do you mean?'

'Savannah would get a brief. Someone who needed a new identity. Her job was to search out a similar-looking person and take their passport. She worked with a guy who'd do the stealing. Kept her hands clean.'

'How d'you know this?' Ped demands.

'When I cleared out Savannah's room, I found a burner phone and a list of all her dealings.'

Behind her, there's a sharp inhale of breath.

Marnie turns.

Bea's standing there, eyes wide.

For a moment, Marnie doesn't understand.

The colour has drained from Bea's face.

And then Marnie realises her mistake.

66

Bea feels the sinews in her body tighten as the truth unfurls.

Marrakesh.

Passport theft.

The jade scarf used to smother Savannah.

All the disparate threads pull together.

Her breath hitches in her throat as she stares at Marnie.

'It was you.'

Marnie looks back at her.

'The day of my photoshoot in Marrakesh, I checked out of my hotel – and I passed a woman in a jade headscarf reading in the lobby.' Bea remembers the woman holding a newspaper, eyes flicking up at her.

She stares right at Marnie. 'That woman was you.'

Marnie stays silent.

'My God . . .' Bea whispers as the threads weave into a rope strong enough to hang the truth on. 'You took over Savannah's work, didn't you? You found her burner phone and list of contacts. Used them. You'd already got away with emptying her bank account.' Bea pushes a hand into her hairline as everything clicks into place. 'That's why you were in Marrakesh. Not looking for an art supplier – but looking for a target.'

Marnie's cheeks are burning red. 'We'd got in a mess at The Surf House,' she says, her voice thin. 'Couldn't pay off the loans. It was the only way—'

'You set me up . . .' Bea says, her voice cracking with disbelief.

'No! You're my friend. I love you!' Marnie says desperately.

Bea's head shakes. 'You only ever wanted my passport.'

'Please . . . you've got to understand. It wasn't meant to happen the way it did. I . . . I was told to find a passport for a tall, Western woman in her early twenties. So I chose a hotel and waited in the lobby to see who'd pass through.'

'And there I was,' Bea says. Already broken. An easy target.

Marnie's gaze lowers as she admits, 'It was meant to be simple. It had been before. Sleight of hand theft. Except, the normal contact had brought a friend with him.'

'The guy in the football shirt,' Bea whispers.

Marnie nods. 'It didn't feel right. He had a bad energy. So I said I didn't want to go through with it. Walked away.' Her head begins to shake from side to side. 'But as I was leaving the medina, I noticed them still watching you. I knew they were going to go after you.'

Bea's blood chills.

'So I followed. Kept at a distance. But you started walking further and further out of the medina . . . and I got separated by the crowd . . . couldn't see where you'd turned. I started running, searching. I knew something bad was going to happen.'

Marnie's hands are gripped together, her knuckles white. 'When I found you, they'd backed you into that alleyway. They had your rucksack. Took off your necklace – and then . . .'

Bea's fingers instinctively go to her throat as she remembers.

'I couldn't let it happen. So I came at them.'

Bea thinks of the way the men turned, surprised, but there

was also something else, too. Something dawning as they saw it was Marnie. It was the way the guy in the football shirt held her up against the wall, his hand at her throat. He whispered something into her ear.

'He was going to choke me,' Marnie says.

'But I stopped him.'

Marnie looks at her now, their eyes meeting.

'I killed a man to save you,' Bea says.

67

Bea's ears hum with white noise. She smells sweat rising from her skin. She feels the grit of earth beneath her sandals and presses her heels down harder, reminding herself that the ground is solid. Yet it feels like she is falling . . . like everything firm and rooted has been removed.

It was all a lie.

Right from the start, it had been a scam.

That's all Bea was to Marnie – a naïve traveller she could rinse. But when it went wrong and Marnie didn't get payment from Savannah's contact, Marnie thought of a new way to get money: by faking Momo's bribe.

Bea drops her face to her hands.

'Please, Bea. I didn't know you then. I was just trying to keep us afloat and—'

She breaks off. Marnie's seen Aiden picking up his mobile from the dirt. The screen flares to life, a white-blue rectangle of light that feels dazzling in the desert night.

Marnie's voice is small, desperate as she says, 'Aiden, no . . .'

'Should've called the police a long time ago.'

As he begins to dial, Marnie says, 'I can't let you . . .'

'It's not up to you,' he tells her, lifting the phone to his ear.

Aiden doesn't see Marnie's hand going to her hip.

'Marnie—' Bea cries as she realises what is happening.

'What the fuck?' Ped exclaims.

Aiden looks up. His eyes widen.

Marnie has pulled the gun from her waistband. Her hand is shaking as she points it at Aiden's head.

The black metal looks strange in Marnie's small hand, her gold and leather bracelets fluttering on her wrist. 'Put down the phone.'

Aiden stares, shocked. 'You're pointing a gun at me?'

'Now!' she cries. It's a single word, fired hard.

Aiden tosses the phone to the earth.

Marnie keeps the gun trained on him.

Aiden doesn't lift his palms in a gesture of submission. His gaze thins as he says, 'Do it, Marnie. You've already destroyed everything good.'

'I was protecting you!'

Aiden's voice is calm as he says, 'When we first arrived in Mallah, we dreamed of building something special. That's why we bought that land. To do something good with our lives. We were happy. It was such a pure, easy happiness – just friends, waves, and sunshine.' He shakes his head. 'But it's over. We killed it.'

Marnie's whole body is trembling, the gun shaking as she keeps it directed at Aiden. Her expression is wretched, lips dragged down, eyes bright with pain.

'You need to put down the gun,' Ped says, his voice studiously level. 'We can work this out.'

'Can we?' Marnie cries. She swings around to face Ped, and the gun swerves with her. 'It's for us – everything I've done is for us!'

Ped is rooted to the spot. He makes no movement. Says nothing.

'I've worked so hard to make sure we don't lose The Surf House. That we don't lose each other. I won't let *her*,' she spits, eyes flashing to Savannah's grave, 'destroy that.'

Ped is working hard to control his breathing, keep it slow. He repeats his instruction, 'Put down the gun, and we can talk.'

'The only thing I need to hear is that you love me. I need you to say that, Ped!' Marnie's voice is breaking now, tears spilling down her cheeks. Her hand holding the gun is shaking.

Bea has spent her career learning how to adjust herself to look the way other people need her to. She knows exactly how Ped must arrange his body and face. How very, very important it is that he gets this right.

Marnie blinks rapidly through her tears as she stares at Ped, desperate. 'Say it!'

Ped opens his mouth—

Lie, Bea silently pleads. *Just lie.*

It is a fraction of a second, but it is there. A hesitation. A coldness in his gaze.

'I love you.'

Marnie's eyes widen as she stares at Ped. Then her head begins to shake from side to side.

'Liar!' she screams. Her mouth pulls down in a grotesque mask of agony.

The gun twitches in her hand.

Bea knows what happens next.

She steps forward, fingers outstretched. 'Marnie, please—'

And then it comes, an explosion of sound.

The crack of a gunshot in the desert night.

371

68

Pain bursts into Bea's eardrums.

Her eyes screw shut.

She feels the warm splatter of blood against her cheeks.

There is a voice in the distance.

Then screaming.

It tears right through her.

Rips open her eyes.

She sees blackness.

Stars.

The fresh mound of earth from the grave.

And then Ped, falling forward onto his knees.

Sound wavers in and out as Bea squeezes her palms against her ears.

Gradually, she becomes aware of a low, keening sound nearby. She shifts her gaze, following the sound.

Ped kneels in the earth. Marnie lies on the ground in front of him, a gunshot wound through her right temple.

In the harsh beam of the headlights, fresh blood and shattered bone glitter in the dirt.

'No . . .' Bea moans.

The rest is a blur. A wash of images.

Ped reaching for Marnie's lifeless hands, clutching them against his chest.

Aiden moving to Bea's side, their bodies tilting towards each other, like sails leaning into wind.

A third vehicle parked up, lights off, engine still. Just the flash of torchlight, and leather shoes moving across the desert. Who? Momo?

Then later, later, staggering towards Aiden's truck.

Then nothing. Like drowning, sinking beneath the surface, the air finally gone.

AFTERWARDS

69

The sun dawns. The day rises. The waves roll.

Yet there is no sleep.

Bea stands in the centre of her room, fingertips touching her temple as if she is lost, trying to remember where she is, what has happened.

She looks at the connecting door into Marnie and Ped's room. Blinks. Impossible to believe that Marnie's gone.

When she'd arrived at The Surf House all those weeks ago, she remembers warm, golden light and the wash of waves filling the space. It felt like a refuge.

And now?

She doesn't know what this place is.

She thinks of Ped kneeling beside Marnie's body, folding her hands neatly over her middle. He loved her – and despised her. There is space for both in the human heart, she understands.

Her gaze drifts to Savannah's journal, which rests on the bedside table. She reaches for it, her thumb smoothing the cover. All those words set down, her hopes and dreams and private fears. Her plans for adventures that would never happen.

'I'm sorry,' she whispers to Savannah, her fingers tracing the pages. Bea may have got answers, but they came too late. Far too late. She slides the journal back into its resting place beneath the slats of the bed. Then she turns towards her rucksack, which is propped against the wall, buckled shut, ready for the airport.

She is leaving.

There is no choice.

Momo has told her she must.

He saw it all – everything that happened in the desert.

At the checkpoint, Momo sensed that something wasn't right. Marnie claimed she was driving Bea to the airport, but where was the luggage? Where was Bea's passport? And why was Bea talking about bribes and knives? Momo told Bea that it was her expression that unsettled him the most: 'You looked scared.'

So later, he followed the direction the van had travelled in, curious as to where they were going in the middle of the night. That's when he noticed the blaze of headlights far away from any road. He turned off his own lights – and pulled up at a distance.

He witnessed it all – the freshly dug grave, Aiden's confession, Ped's amendment, and Marnie turning the gun on herself.

As the others stood, shell-shocked and reeling, Momo switched on his torch and stepped forward. He was the one who took control and explained what must happen next.

He told them that he would call in the scene and say that he spotted headlights in the desert and went to investigate. He'd explain to his colleagues that he found Marnie's body *after* she'd turned the gun on herself. He'd share his instinct that the body in the grave was Savannah Hart, a missing US traveller. The wind would have done the work of removing the second set of tyre tracks from Aiden's truck – leaving no trace that Aiden, Bea, or Ped were ever there.

After Momo outlined the plan, he looked at Ped closely and

said something that Bea still doesn't understand. 'I hope this clears my debt.'

Now, Bea lifts her rucksack onto her shoulders. It's time. She feels the weight of those straps, her old life carried on her back.

As she makes to leave, she passes the freestanding mirror, which is still covered by a cotton throw. Her step falters. She reaches out, fingers circling around the corner of the fabric. Then she tugs it free.

The fabric spools at her feet, Bea's full-length image reflected in the mirror.

Bea takes a step closer.

She doesn't adjust her expression to look more pleasing or run a hand through her tangled hair. Instead, she keeps her gaze steady and meets her eye. Holds it there.

What she sees is a bare-faced girl with shadows beneath her eyes and new story lines in the faint brackets around her mouth. She sees a girl who shares the same symmetrical features as her mother – but not the same heart. She sees a girl who is no longer numb but stands with her chin lifted, ready to feel it all.

Downstairs, Bea finds Ped sitting alone in the lounge, head bowed. She wonders what he will do now. There's no money to repair the studio or to repay The Surf House's loans. With Marnie gone, too, Ped's lost half his team.

He looks up when he sees Bea. This great, hulking man – who can hold his breath underwater for long minutes and glide down the face of giant waves with poise – looks shrunken.

He stands and pulls an envelope from his pocket. 'This belongs to you.'

She takes it and finds a stack of dollars inside. It's the bribe money that Marnie stowed away.

'Help you get set up back home.'

Most of this money belonged to Seth, but she hopes he wouldn't mind her having it. 'Thank you,' she says, tucking the envelope into her pocket. 'Can I ask you something?'

He looks at her.

'Why didn't you want me at The Surf House? Right from the start, it was obvious you wished I hadn't come.'

'Marnie put you in the room where Savannah stayed. It was a test. A way for me to prove my loyalty to her. Friendliness was never an option.'

Slowly, she nods, feeling a deep sadness at the complexities and unrest in Marnie's head. Marnie always said that each day was a fresh start, a chance to begin again. Did that give her permission to make mistake after mistake and wipe the slate clean?

She needs to understand one more thing. 'Out in the desert, why did Momo help us? What was the debt he was talking about?'

'A while back, Momo was surfing and he hit the reef. Got knocked out. He almost drowned.'

Bea thinks of the silver scar that runs down Momo's forehead and remembers Marnie telling her about the surfer who Ped pulled in from the reef.

'You saved him?'

Ped nods.

She thinks of the footage of Ped and Momo standing on the shore, talking, on the day of Seth's drowning. She assumed Momo was in uniform – but the dark silhouette could just as easily have been a wetsuit. Ped really had been taking him sea swimming.

She's had it wrong this whole time.

She's about to step away when Ped says quietly, 'I want you to know that Marnie cared about you.'

After everything Marnie did, it feels hard to believe.

'Marnie would have justified the things she did. She'd have believed that she saved you in Marrakesh – not that she put you in danger.' Ped glances out towards the glass doors, where the morning is unveiling itself in brilliant blue. 'Sometimes lying to yourself,' he says, 'is the only way to live with yourself.'

70

Bea has an hour before her taxi arrives. She pulls on her wetsuit and grabs her board. She passes the remains of the destroyed studio as she takes the steps down to the beach.

There, on the shore, just as she'd hoped, sits Aiden. His eyes are on the surf, watching as a head-high set rolls in, glassy and clean. The first wave breaks in an agonisingly perfect blue wall.

Sensing her, Aiden turns. He looks exhausted, as if he's not slept in days, but there's something about his eyes that is different. The way they hold her, clearer now.

'One last surf,' she tells him.

He smiles at that, the first she's seen in a long time. He rises to his feet and steps nearer. 'And after? Are you going back to London?'

Bea is about to answer, *Yes*, but then she remembers the envelope of money. It's enough to take her anywhere she wants. She pictures the grey skies and rain-splattered concrete of London, the horizon swallowed by buildings, and she knows that's not where she wants to be.

'Not London, no,' she says. It's the sea that is calling. She wants wide-open skies and pounding surf and salt on her skin. She wants to paddle hard and feel the rush of springing to her feet on a board. She wants to fall asleep at night to the sound of waves.

'Wherever you go, let me know you're okay?'

She nods.

They're both silent for a beat. She becomes aware of the heat that gathers in the space between their bodies. Somehow, they've travelled closer. There are only inches between them. Bea feels the damp sand beneath her bare feet.

He is looking at her, dark eyes fixed to her face. 'I wish I'd met you before . . .'

He trails off, and she knows the *before* he means. There's so much pain in his expression that all she wants is to reach for him and take it away.

He swallows. 'I've got to find a way to live with what I did.'

Bea begins to say, 'But you didn't kill—'

He shakes his head. 'What Marnie did doesn't change what *I* did. I still buried Savannah. I kept the truth from her family to protect myself.' He looks out over the water. 'The drinking, the night surfing, the hiding from it all – none of those are the answer. I need to be able to look myself in the eye and be okay with the person looking back.'

Bea thinks of her scarf-covered mirrors. Whispers, 'I know.'

Aiden lifts a hand and places it lightly against the side of her chin. His thumb brushes her jawline. A rush of blood pulses through her.

Then the gap between them closes as their mouths lightly find each other. Her body is filled with warmth and desire as their lips brush. It is like swimming through sunlight.

'Bea,' he whispers.

She hears everything in her name. All the words they can-not say.

They stand with their foreheads resting together, their breath warm.

The first tears threaten to leak from the corners of her eyes. She blinks them away and takes a step back. 'Give Salty a rub from me.'

He nods.

They stare at one another.

'You'll be okay?' Aiden asks. He is looking at her like he already knows the answer.

She smiles. 'I will.'

They don't say goodbye. They part as people do who know they'll see each other again, with a deep sense of certainty that this isn't the last time.

Then Bea turns and wades into the sea. She slides onto her board, digs her arms into the silk blue, and begins to paddle.

She can taste the salt and desert on the light breeze. She uses a lull between sets to stroke through this vast mirror, teardrops of water sluicing from her fingertips. Behind her, she imagines Mallah shrinking, The Surf House becoming only a shadow on the cliff line. She doesn't turn.

When she is out beyond the breaking waves, she sits astride her board, eyes on the horizon. Her heart rate settles and grows steady. Her mind clears.

She sees the set coming. Knows already, from the dark lines that begin to rise from the ocean, which wave is hers. She waits for the first to pass beneath her. Then a second.

On the third, she angles her board and begins to paddle. She makes strong, efficient strokes, feels the muscles working in her arms, absorbs the hard planes of the board beneath her.

The moment the wave catches her, there is no hesitation. She sails to her feet, dropping down the face. Everything else melts away as she glides along, fast and low, the breeze in her ears, the roar of her heart thundering in her chest, wet hair blown back, the first blush of the sun's warmth on her face.

She thinks of nothing now, inhabiting her body fully and with feeling. She is connected to the water and the light and the mountains and the swell and the wide-open sky.

This moment is hers alone, as she glides through the pure wash of unwavering blue.

Author's Note

In *The Surf House*, I chose to fictionalise the village of Mallah and the names of the surrounding surf spots. I've also taken the liberty of not distinguishing between the police force and the Royal Gendarmerie.

Acknowledgements

It takes a village.

Firstly, chieftain Judith Murray, thank you for continuing to be the most brilliant literary agent, and making sea swims a mandatory part of our beach-side meetings. Thank you to all at Greene & Heaton, including the lovely Mia Dakin for assisting with such warmth and professionalism, and to Kate Rizzo for continuing to build long-lasting relationships with publishers across the world.

I feel incredibly lucky to have Charlotte Brabbin as my editor. You've helped me unlock the very best version of this book and I'm so grateful for your thoughtful, creative, and smart input. I love working together and diving deeper with every novel.

The wider team at HarperCollins have such a huge role to play in each of my books. Thank you to Susanna Peden, a brilliant publicist, who understands what I'm happy to say Yes to, just as well as when I prefer to say No. Thank you to Maddy Marshall, Emily Merrill, Sarah Shea and Hannah O'Brien for your brilliantly creative marketing ideas that wow me! Thank you to both the international and UK sales teams who work so hard to get my books into the right places – Holly Martin, Harriet Williams, Bethan Moore and Ruth Burrow. Thank you to Claire Ward for your vision with my covers – and threatening to wear a wetsuit to our Teams call! A big thanks to Katie Lumsden who did an incredible copy edit on this manuscript.

Thank you to Gràinne Fox at UTA, my US literary agent. There's no one better to have in my corner on the other side of the pond. Truly.

Thank you to Jane Villiers and the team at Sayle Screen for the incredible TV and film ride. It continues to be wild!

My circle of author friends makes such a difference to this job – thank you for your encouragement, wisdom, and loveliness. I feel very lucky. A special thanks to Mimi Hall for reading two drafts of *The Surf House* and helping me make it so much better. All the gratitude for your friendship and light.

Thank you to Terry Crump for your tales of winters riding waves in Morocco, and to Sigrid Green for sharing your experiences of life as a professional model. Thank you also to Alice Morrison for being my spotter on all things Morocco.

Thank you to my friends and family. You are the people who rearrange my novel in bookstores, who prop up the bar at the book launches, who buy copies for all their friends, and who are there when I need to step away from the desk. Extra thanks to longstanding early readers, Faye Buchan, Laura Crossley and Becki Hunter for being game for a pre-edit read and sharing your thoughts.

A shout out to my brother, Matt, for the fun surfing sessions these past few winters. There's nothing better than paddling out on a sun-bright winter's day and calling it research ;)

Finally, thanks to my husband, James, and our own little groms, Tommy and Darcy, for giving me the space (if not always the quiet!) I need to write. Here's to many more years of riding waves together.